VIRAGO
MODERN CLASSICS
410

Dodie Smith

Born in 1896, Dodie Smith grew up in Manchester. She trained at RADA and began her playwriting career in 1931 when she scored a hit with her play *Autumn Crocus*; *Dear Octopus* in 1938 was her abiding success. In 1939 she went to the USA with her manager, Alec Beesley, whom she married that year. There she wrote for Hollywood, made a close friend of Christopher Isherwood and acquired the first of her beloved Dalmatian dogs. *I Capture the Castle* was published in 1949, selling over a million copies. The Beesleys returned to the UK in 1954 and in 1956 *The Hundred and One Dalmatians* was published. Dodie Smith died in November 1990. Valerie Grove, who introduces this novel, has written her biography, *Dear Dodie* (Chatto and Windus), championed by Fiona MacCarthy in the *Observer* as 'a merry book . . . with a faultless sense of period . . . making a persuasive case for a long neglected talent'.

I CAPTURE THE CASTLE

Dodie Smith

Introduction by Valerie Grove

A *Virago* Book

Published by Virago Press Limited 1996

Reprinted 1996 (twice), 1997 (twice), 1999, 2000, 2001 (twice),
2003 (six times)

First published in Great Britain by William Heinemann Ltd 1949

A CIP catalogue record for this title
is available from the British Library.

Printed and bound in Great Britain by Clays Ltd, St Ives plc

Virago Press
An imprint of
Time Warner Books UK
Brettenham House
Lancaster Place
London WC2E 7EN

www.virago.co.uk

Introduction

Cassandra Mortmain, as one critic said, is a young girl 'poised between childhood and adultery'. Dodie Smith, who had once been such a girl, wrote herself into Cassandra, though she at first doubted whether she could, at the age of forty-nine, recapture the naivety of a seventeen-year-old girl.

I Capture the Castle was written in a fever of nostalgia. Dodie had left England in January 1939 together with her future husband Alec, her Dalmatian Pongo (later to become a literary hero) and their pale grey Rolls-Royce. They went first to New York, and then to California, neither of which suited Dodie at all. She had left England at the pinnacle of her fame, with *Dear Octopus*, the most enduring of her run of six successful plays, being performed to packed houses. Since Alec was a passionate conscientious objector, the outbreak of war made it impossible for them to return, so Dodie settled for an exiled life of Hollywood screenwriting. This was lucrative but deeply unsatisfactory. California seemed a meaningless place, and writing for the movies a prostitution of her skills. America did not inspire her; one play, *Lovers and Friends*, made it to Broadway, but not to London. She lived in a constant state of wretched regret about having left London, where she yearned to be, her ear pressed to the wireless reports, avid for letters from friends with accounts of air raids and wartime experiences, furious at having denied herself the 'good copy' that wartime England would have provided her with for her plays, had she only been there . . .

So, in one of their rented Hollywood houses, Anatole Litvak's splendid house at Malibu, with a large desk looking out over the Pacific and the vast blue sky, she began in February 1945 to write *I Capture the Castle*, the only one of her novels (she was later to write five other works of fiction) with the supreme qualities of imagination and inspired character drawing that have kept it in print, and alive in devoted readers' minds, for nearly fifty years.

She conjured up a family living in penury in the 1930s in a house fashioned from the remnants of a moated medieval castle; Dodie had once glimpsed such a place at Wingfield in Suffolk in 1934. She loved East Anglia, where she had a cottage at picturesque Finchingfield, which she had lent to the impresario Binkie Beaumont when she went away. Of the Mortmains and Godsend Castle she wrote, 'I knew that family; I lived in that castle'. Cassandra/Dodie tries to capture the sense of living there, where the past is 'like a presence, a caress in the air'. She is lyrical about 'the pool of light in the courtyard, the golden windows, the strange long-ago look that one sees in old paintings'. Cassandra is the keeper of a diary (Dodie was an obsessive keeper of diaries) in a sixpenny notebook that begins 'I write this sitting in the kitchen sink', one of the most striking opening lines in twentieth-century fiction. Her older sister, the more beautiful Rose, is twenty-one, yearning for romance with a rich and handsome suitor, but bitterly despairing of ever meeting any marriageable men, 'even hideous, poverty-stricken ones'.

The two girls and their school-boy brother Thomas, live with their difficult, eccentric widower father, a writer who has had a *succès fou* (and *d'estime*) with an experimental novel called *Jacob Wrestling* published just before Joyce's *Ulysses*. Now he has a bad case of writer's block, and prefers (after a period in a prison, following an odd altercation with a neighbour) to live in this isolated castle. He is aloof, secretive, sarcastic, and shutters himself in the castle gatehouse: the iron has entered his soul. His second wife, the glorious Topaz, is a famous artist's model who has been married twice before, to Carlo from the circus, and to Everard, a fashion designer. She wafts about communing with nature, sometimes in a shroud-like nightgown, sometimes naked under her mac.

They are quite penniless ('We have been poor for five years now') so, as with the Fossil sisters in *Ballet Shoes*, every shilling has to be eked out and there is much making do and mending, and leaning on others' kindness. The only income in the family comes from their lodger Stephen, a handsome young hired hand who moons over Cassandra. 'Fair and noble looking,' she notes, 'but his expression is just a fraction daft.' All their fine furniture has gradually been sold, replaced with minimum requirements bought in junk shops: 'all we really have enough of is floor'. They have so few towels that 'on washday we have to shake ourselves'. Lighting is by candle (Dodie's favourite lighting throughout her life, even in her bathroom). Rose, 'a pinkish person who looks particularly fetching by firelight', keeps her candle on a chest of drawers painted to imitate marble 'but looking more like bacon'. Rose ('I could marry the devil himself if he had money') declares that she will go on the streets if necessary; Cassandra retorts that she cannot go on the streets in the depths of Suffolk.

Their fortunes and spirits rise immensely with the arrival of two half-American brothers, Neil and Simon, and their American mother, landlords of Godsend castle and heirs of Scoatney Hall, the nearby manor house where the aroma is of flowers and beeswax. The outcome is predictably romantic after the fashion of a Jane Austen narrative – Rose is instantly determined on marrying the elder brother despite his unprepossessing beard – but there is nothing predictable about the course of events, nor about the original, characterful and amusing personality of Cassandra. As the vicar perceptively says of her, she is 'the insidious type. Jane Eyre with a touch of Becky Sharp. A thoroughly dangerous girl.' She may be fanciful, even whimsical and precious at times (she gathers garlands of wild flowers on Midsummer Day) and while she is possessed of a guileless charm – on first tasting champagne she decides it is 'rather like ginger ale without the ginger' – she is also full of sturdy good sense: 'O joyous night! It is my bathnight. I shall go down and be kind to everyone. Noble deeds and hot baths are the best cure for depression' ... 'I am feeling absurdly happy at the moment. Maybe it is because I have fulfilled my creative urge; or maybe it is the thought of eggs for tea.' She views Rose's ensnaring behaviour towards the men with a younger sister's disapproval: 'There were moments when my deep and loving pity for her merged into a deep desire to kick her fairly hard.' Cassandra has endured years of hearing people say that 'Dear Rose will lead men a dance'.

Rose's engagement duly changes everything. Cassandra's sixpenny notebook is replaced by a two-guinea book, bound in blue and gold leather, a gift with a fountain-pen from Simon, ('But I seemed to get on better with a stump of a pencil') and when Rose goes to London to buy her £1000 trousseau, Cassandra discovers that the fulfilment of one's hopes brings not bliss but 'no kind of feeling': I wonder if there isn't a catch about having plenty of money. Does it eventually take the pleasure out of things? ... It does seem to me that the climate of richness must always be a little dulling to the senses.' It certainly makes Rose a different person on whom Cassandra turns quite spitefully: 'Oh go and sit in your bathroom and count your peach-coloured towels.'

Dodie finished drafting her novel shortly after the war ended, but even the longed-for peace did not rescue her from her anguished involvement in the book; she was so anxious that her first novel should be a success after her long years of frustration and failure with plays. The revisions went on for two years, and tormented her. She rewrote every line, under Alec's critical supervision, hearing every line of dialogue in her head and unable to stop thinking about it even in bed, waking every morning with a visceral dread, her head throbbing with nerves, her mind filled with nagging doubts. She felt she was disintegrating mentally and physically. Her industry was infinite. She drew little sketches of the castle's kitchen and the girls' bedroom in the tower (inspired by Margot Asquith's biographical account of her girlhood with her sister Laura Tennant at their baronial, turreted ancestral home, Glen). Alec made a model of the castle, sharpened her pencils, questioned every detail of topography, and re-read every line dozens of times. She kept a 100,000 word notebook on the progress of the novel, recording how each character changed, and how even the minor characters, down to the Mortmains' dog and the cat, were kept in play. She was still uncertain about the way the story ought to end – it hadn't ended at all in the way she had expected.

The painstaking labour paid off. The book was an instant critical and popular success. Her Boston publisher sold it to the Literary Guild book club which subscribed half a million copies; the London publication in 1949 took *I Capture the Castle* straight to the top of the bestseller lists. Two responses to her novel particularly pleased Dodie. One was that of Christopher Isherwood, one of the three close friends she had made during her years in America, who depended on her for criticism of his own work. She had told him, with a studied insouciance, that it was 'just a little piece for Peg's Paper – written with a care that would not have disgraced Flaubert.' He responded with a treasured letter: 'To say "I couldn't put it down" is hardly original, but true . . . Your tremendous strength is detail. It is like a really good carving; the more you look at it, the more you see . . . I think it is a book that will be very much lived in by many people; because you can live inside it, like Dickens.' He was charmed and moved by the episode in which Cassandra locks her father in the tower to get him to write; he felt that at times he had only just escaped being locked up by Dodie himself.

And at the end of 1949 the postman arrived on his motor scooter delivering the London *Sunday Times* which then, as now, ran a 'Christmas Books of the Year' feature in which celebrities named their favourite reading. There was Ralph Vaughan Williams's nomination: *I Capture the Castle*. To Dodie there could be no greater honour, as she told him; she considered him the greatest living composer; she had been listening to his Mass in G Minor only the night before, and his music personified England for her, and all that she was exiled from and nostalgic for.

However many times she told people in letters that her novel was mere Peg's Paper stuff, she did care desperately about its reception. And she lived to know how long its appeal lingered. Although the play she wrote based on the novel (with Virginia McKenna exquisite as Cassandra, and Roger Moore, Bill Travers and Richard Greene as the three young men) lasted only four weeks at the Aldwych in 1954, the book itself stayed in print, gathering new readers with the decades, often passed on by mothers recommending it to their daughters. By the time Dodie died in 1990 it had become a Red Fox paperback for the teenage market – though of course Dodie had never intended it to be solely a young girls' book.

I discovered when I embarked on Dodie's biography in 1992 that *I Capture the Castle* was regarded by many writers as a seminal work. Antonia Fraser told me that the scene in which Rose is heard singing in her hotel room is one of the most erotic in all literature; Armistead Maupin, who was given it to read as a boy by his English grandmother in the American deep South, paid homage to it by organising his 1993 novel *Maybe the Moon* along Cassandra's 'shilling notebook' lines; and Joanna Trollope told me that when she was about to introduce the dramatist Ian Curteis, her second husband, to her daughters and they asked her what he was like, she said 'Mortmain' and they understood. Everyone I know who reads it – and they range from my own daughters, who all read it at around eleven, to the most unlikely reader, Alan Brien, who read it in his sixties – responds in the same way to the depth and originality of the characters, and the amiability of Cassandra. I have never met a reader who wanted this book to end. It is obviously time to bring *I Capture the Castle* out of the teenage fiction closet and put it where it rightly belongs, as a Virago Modern Classic.

Valerie Grove, London 1995

CONTENTS

I. THE SIXPENNY BOOK

March

Chapter I

I WRITE THIS SITTING IN THE KITCHEN SINK. THAT IS, MY FEET are in it; the rest of me is on the draining-board, which I have padded with our dog's blanket and the tea-cosy. I can't say that I am really comfortable, and there is a depressing smell of carbolic soap, but this is the only part of the kitchen where there is any daylight left. And I have found that sitting in a place where you have never sat before can be inspiring— I wrote my very best poem while sitting on the hen-house. Though even that isn't a very good poem. I have decided my poetry is so bad that I mustn't write any more of it.

Drips from the roof are plopping into the water-butt by the back door. The view through the windows above the sink is excessively drear. Beyond the dank garden in the courtyard are the ruined walls on the edge of the moat. Beyond the moat, the boggy ploughed fields stretch to the leaden sky. I tell myself that all the rain we have had lately is good for nature, and that at any moment spring will surge on us. I try to see leaves on the trees and the courtyard filled with sunlight. Unfortunately, the more my mind's eye sees green and gold, the more drained of all colour does the twilight seem.

It is comforting to look away from the windows and towards the kitchen fire, near which my sister Rose is ironing—though she obviously can't see properly, and it will be a pity if she scorches her only nightgown. (I have two, but one is minus its behind.) Rose looks particularly fetching by firelight because she is a pinkish person; her skin has a pink glow and her hair is pinkish gold, very light and feathery. Although I am rather used to her I know she is a beauty. She is nearly twenty-one and very bitter with life. I am seventeen, look younger, feel older. I am no beauty but have a neatish face.

3

I have just remarked to Rose that our situation is really rather romantic—two girls in this strange and lonely house. She replied that she saw nothing romantic about being shut up in a crumbling ruin surrounded by a sea of mud. I must admit that our home is an unreasonable place to live in. Yet I love it. The house itself was built in the time of Charles II, but it was grafted on to a fourteenth-century castle that had been damaged by Cromwell. The whole of our east wall was part of the castle; there are two round towers in it. The gatehouse is intact and a stretch of the old walls at their full height joins it to the house. And Belmotte Tower, all that remains of an even older castle, still stands on its mound close by. But I won't attempt to describe our peculiar home fully until I can see more time ahead of me than I do now.

I am writing this journal partly to practise my newly acquired speed-writing and partly to teach myself how to write a novel—I intend to capture all our characters and put in conversations. It ought to be good for my style to dash along without much thought, as up to now my stories have been very stiff and self-conscious. The only time father obliged me by reading one of them, he said I combined stateliness with a desperate effort to be funny. He told me to relax and let the words flow out of me.

I wish I knew of a way to make words flow out of father. Years and years ago, he wrote a very unusual book called *Jacob Wrestling*, a mixture of fiction, philosophy and poetry. It had a great success, particularly in America, where he made a lot of money by lecturing on it, and he seemed likely to become a very important writer indeed. But he stopped writing. Mother believed this was due to something that happened when I was about five.

We were living in a small house by the sea at the time. Father had just joined us after his second American lecture tour. One afternoon when we were having tea in the garden, he had the misfortune to lose his temper with mother very noisily just as he was about to cut a piece of cake. He brandished the cake-knife at her so menacingly that an officious neighbour jumped the garden fence to intervene and

4

got himself knocked down. Father explained in court that killing a woman with our silver cake-knife would be a long, weary business entailing sawing her to death; and he was completely exonerated of any intention of slaying mother. The whole case seems to have been quite ludicrous, with everyone but the neighbour being very funny. But father made the mistake of being funnier than the judge and, as there was no doubt whatever that he had seriously damaged the neighbour, he was sent to prison for three months.

When he came out he was as nice a man as ever—nicer, because his temper was so much better. Apart from that, he didn't seem to me to be changed at all. But Rose remembers that he had already begun to get unsociable—it was then that he took a forty years' lease of the castle, which is an admirable place to be unsociable in. Once we were settled here he was supposed to begin a new book. But time went on without anything happening and at last we realized that he had given up even trying to write—for years now, he has refused to discuss the possibility. Most of his life is spent in the gate-house room, which is icy cold in winter as there is no fireplace; he just huddles over an oil-stove. As far as we know, he does nothing but read detective novels from the village library. Miss Marcy, the librarian and schoolmistress, brings them to him. She admires him greatly and says "the iron has entered into his soul."

Personally, I can't see how the iron could get very far into a man's soul during only three months in jail—anyway, not if the man had as much vitality as father had; and he seemed to have plenty of it left when they let him out. But it has gone now; and his unsociability has grown almost into a disease—I often think he would prefer not even to meet his own household. All his natural gaiety has vanished. At times he puts on a false cheerfulness that embarrasses me, but usually he is either morose or irritable—I think I should prefer it if he lost his temper as he used to. Oh, poor father, he really is very pathetic. But he might at least do a little work in the garden. I am aware that this isn't a fair portrait of him. I must capture him later.

5

Mother died eight years ago, from perfectly natural causes. I think she must have been a shadowy person, because I have only the vaguest memory of her and I have an excellent memory for most things. (I can remember the cake-knife incident perfectly—I hit the fallen neighbour with my little wooden spade. Father always said this got him an extra month.)

Three years ago (or is it four? I know father's one spasm of sociability was in 1931) a stepmother was presented to us. We *were* surprised. She is a famous artist's model who claims to have been christened Topaz—even if this is true there is no law to make a woman stick to a name like that. She is very beautiful, with masses of hair so fair that it is almost white, and a quite extraordinary pallor. She uses no make-up, not even powder. There are two paintings of her in the Tate Gallery: one by Macmorris, called "Topaz in Jade," in which she wears a magnificent jade necklace; and one by H. J. Allardy which shows her nude on an old horsehair-covered sofa that she says was very prickly. This is called "Composition"; but as Allardy has painted her even paler than she is, "Decomposition" would suit it better.

Actually, there is nothing unhealthy about Topaz's pallor; it simply makes her look as if she belonged to some new race. She has a very deep voice—that is, she puts one on; it is part of an arty pose, which includes painting and lute-playing. But her kindness is perfectly genuine and so is her cooking. I am very, very fond of her—it is nice to have written that just as she appears on the kitchen stairs. She is wearing her ancient orange tea-gown. Her pale, straight hair is flowing down her back to her waist. She paused on the top step and said: "Ah, girls . . ." with three velvety inflections on each word.

Now she is sitting on the steel trivet, raking the fire. The pink light makes her look more ordinary, but very pretty. She is twenty-nine and had two husbands before father (she will never tell us very much about them), but she still looks extraordinarily young. Perhaps that is because her expression is so blank.

The kitchen looks very beautiful now. The firelight glows

6

steadily through the bars and through the round hole in the top of the range where the lid has been left off. It turns the whitewashed walls rosy; even the dark beams in the roof are a dusky gold. The highest beam is over thirty feet from the ground. Rose and Topaz are two tiny figures in a great glowing cave.

Now Rose is sitting on the fender, waiting for her iron to heat. She is staring at Topaz with a discontented expression. I can often tell what Rose is thinking and I would take a bet that she is envying the orange tea-gown and hating her own skimpy old blouse and skirt. Poor Rose hates most things she has and envies most things she hasn't. I really am just as discontented, but I don't seem to notice it so much. I feel quite unreasonably happy this minute, watching them both; knowing I can go and join them in the warmth, yet staying here in the cold.

Oh, dear, there has just been a slight scene! Rose asked Topaz to go to London and earn some money. Topaz replied that she didn't think it was worth while, because it costs so much to live there. It is true that she can never save more than will buy us a few presents—she is very generous.

"And two of the men I sit for are abroad," she went on, "and I don't like working for Macmorris."

"Why not?" asked Rose. "He pays better than the others, doesn't he?"

"So he ought, considering how rich he is," said Topaz. "But I dislike sitting for him because he only paints my head. Your father says that the men who paint me nude paint my body and think of their job, but that Macmorris paints my head and thinks of my body. And it's perfectly true. I've had more trouble with him than I should care to let your father know."

Rose said: "I should have thought it was worth while to have a little trouble in order to earn some real money."

"Then *you* have the trouble, dear," said Topaz.

This must have been very annoying to Rose, considering that she never has the slightest chance of that sort of trouble. She suddenly flung back her head dramatically and said:

7

"I'm perfectly willing to. It may interest you both to know that for some time now I've been considering selling myself. If necessary, I shall go on the streets."

I told her she couldn't go on the streets in the depths of Suffolk.

"But if Topaz will kindly lend me the fare to London and give me a few hints——"

Topaz said she had never been on the streets and rather regretted it, "because one must sink to the depths in order to rise to the heights," which is the kind of Topazism it requires much affection to tolerate.

"And anyway," she told Rose, "you're the last girl to lead a hard-working, immoral life. If you're really taken with the idea of selling yourself, you'd better choose a wealthy man and marry him respectably."

This idea has, of course, occurred to Rose, but she has always hoped that the man would be handsome, romantic and lovable into the bargain. I suppose it was her sheer despair of ever meeting any marriageable men at all, even hideous, poverty-stricken ones, that made her suddenly burst into tears. As she only cries about once a year I really ought to have gone over and comforted her, but I wanted to set it all down here. I begin to see that writers are liable to become callous.

Anyway, Topaz did the comforting far better than I could have done, as I am never disposed to clasp people to my bosom. She was most maternal, letting Rose weep all over the orange velvet tea-gown, which has suffered many things in its time. Rose will be furious with herself later on, because she has an unkind tendency to despise Topaz; but for the moment they are most amicable. Rose is now putting away her ironing, gulping a little, and Topaz is laying the table for tea while outlining impracticable plans for making money—such as giving a lute concert in the village or buying a pig in instalments.

I joined in while resting my hand, but said nothing of supreme importance.

It is raining again. Stephen is coming across the courtyard.

He has lived with us ever since he was a little boy—his mother used to be our maid, in the days when we could still afford one, and when she died he had nowhere to go. He grows vegetables for us and looks after the hens and does a thousand odd jobs—I can't think how we should get on without him. He is eighteen now, very fair and noble-looking, but his expression is just a fraction daft. He has always been rather devoted to me; father calls him my swain. He is rather how I imagine Silvius in *As You Like It*—but I am nothing like Phebe.

Stephen has come in now. The first thing he did was to light a candle and stick it on the window-ledge beside me, saying:

"You're spoiling your eyes, Miss Cassandra."

Then he dropped a tightly folded bit of paper on this journal. My heart sank, because I knew it would contain a poem; I suppose he has been working on it in the barn. It is written in his careful, rather beautiful script. The heading is, "'To Miss Cassandra' by Stephen Colly." It is a charming poem—by Robert Herrick.

What am I to do about Stephen? Father says the desire for self-expression is pathetic, but I really think Stephen's main desire is just to please me; he knows I set store by poetry. I ought to tell him that I know he merely copies the poems out—he has been doing it all winter, every week or so—but I can't find the heart to hurt him. Perhaps when the spring comes I can take him for a walk and break it to him in some encouraging way. This time I have got out of saying my usual hypocritical words of praise by smiling approval at him across the kitchen. Now he is pumping water up into the cistern, looking very happy.

The well is below the kitchen floor and has been there since the earliest days of the castle; it has been supplying water for six hundred years and is said never to have run dry. Of course, there must have been many pumps. The present one arrived when the Victorian hot-water system (alleged) was put in.

Interruptions keep occurring. Topaz has just filled the kettle, splashing my legs, and my brother Thomas has returned from school in our nearest town, King's Crypt. He is a

9

cumbersome lad of fifteen with hair that grows in tufts, so that parting it is difficult. It is the same mousy colour as mine; but mine is meek.

When Thomas came in, I suddenly remembered myself coming back from school, day after day, up to a few months ago. In one flash I re-lived the ten-mile crawl in the jerky little train and then the five miles on a bicycle from Scoatney station—how I used to hate that in the winter! Yet in some ways I should like to be back at school; for one thing, the daughter of the manager at the cinema went there, and she got me into the pictures free now and then. I miss that greatly. And I rather miss school itself—it was a surprisingly good one for such a quiet little country town. I had a scholarship, just as Thomas has at his school; we are tolerably bright.

The rain is driving hard against the window now. My candle makes it seem quite dark outside. And the far side of the kitchen is dimmer now that the kettle is on the round hole in the top of the range. The girls are sitting on the floor making toast through the bars. There is a bright edge to each head, where the firelight shines through their hair.

Stephen has finished pumping and is stoking the copper—it is a great, old-fashioned brick one which helps to keep the kitchen warm and gives us extra hot-water. With the copper lit as well as the range, the kitchen is much the warmest place in the house; that is why we sit in it so much. But even in summer we have our meals here, because the dining-room furniture was sold over a year ago.

Goodness, Topaz is actually putting on eggs to boil! No one told me the hens had yielded to prayer. Oh, excellent hens! I was only expecting bread and margarine for tea, and I don't get as used to margarine as I could wish. I thank heaven there is no cheaper form of bread than bread.

How odd it is to remember that "tea" once meant afternoon tea to us—little cakes and thin bread-and-butter in the drawing-room. Now it is as solid a meal as we can scrape together, as it has to last us until breakfast. We have it after Thomas gets back from school.

Stephen is lighting the lamp. In a second now, the rosy glow will have gone from the kitchen. But lamplight is beautiful, too.

The lamp is lit. And as Stephen carried it to the table, my father came out on the staircase. His old plaid travelling-rug was wrapped round his shoulders—he had come from the gatehouse along the top of the castle walls. He murmured: "Tea, tea—has Miss Marcy come with the library books yet?" (She hasn't.) Then he said his hands were quite numb; not complainingly, more in a tone of faint surprise—though I find it hard to believe that anyone living at the castle in winter can be surprised at any part of themselves being numb. And as he came downstairs shaking the rain off his hair, I suddenly felt so fond of him. I fear I don't feel that very often.

He is still a splendid-looking man, though his fine features are getting a bit lost in fat and his colouring is fading. It used to be as bright as Rose's.

Now he is chatting to Topaz. I regret to note that he is in his falsely cheerful mood—though I think poor Topaz is grateful for even false cheerfulness from him these days. She adores him, and he seems to take so little interest in her.

I shall have to get off the draining-board—Topaz wants the tea-cosy and our dog, Heloïse, has come in and discovered I have borrowed her blanket. She is a bull-terrier, snowy white except where her fondant-pink skin shows through her short hair. All right, Heloïse darling, you shall have your blanket. She gazes at me with love, reproach, confidence and humour—how can she express so much just with two rather small slanting eyes?

I finish this entry sitting on the stairs. I think it worthy of note that I never felt happier in my life—despite sorrow for father, pity for Rose, embarrassment about Stephen's poetry and no justification for hope as regards our family's general outlook. Perhaps it is because I have satisfied my creative urge; or it may be due to the thought of eggs for tea.

Chapter II

I am reasonably comfortable as I am wearing my school coat and have a hot brick for my feet, but I wish it wasn't my week for the little iron bedstead—Rose and I take it in turns to sleep in the four-poster. She is sitting up in it reading a library book. When Miss Marcy brought it she said it was "a pretty story." Rose says it is awful, but she would rather read it than think about herself. Poor Rose! She is wearing her old blue flannel dressing-gown with the skirt part doubled up round her waist for warmth. She has had that dressing-gown so long that I don't think she sees it any more; if she were to put it away for a month and then look at it, she would get a shock. But who am I to talk—who have not had a dressing-gown at all for two years? The remains of my last one are wrapped round my hot brick.

Our room is spacious and remarkably empty. With the exception of the four-poster, which is in very bad condition, all the good furniture has gradually been sold and replaced by minimum requirements bought in junk-shops. Thus we have a wardrobe without a door and a bamboo dressing-table which I take to be a rare piece. I keep my bedside candlestick on a battered tin trunk that cost one shilling; Rose has hers on a chest of drawers painted to imitate marble, but looking more like bacon. The enamel jug and basin on a metal tripod is my own personal property, the landlady of "The Keys" having given it to me after I found it doing no good in a stable. It saves congestion in the bathroom. One rather nice thing is the carved wooden window-seat—I am thankful there is no way of selling that. It is built into the thickness of the castle wall, with a big mullioned window above it. There are windows

12

on the garden side of the room, too; little diamond-paned ones.

One thing I have never grown out of being fascinated by is the round tower which opens into a corner. There is a circular stone staircase inside it by which you can go up to the battlemented top, or down to the drawing-room; though some of the steps have crumbled badly.

Perhaps I ought to have counted Miss Blossom as a piece of furniture. She is a dressmaker's dummy of most opulent figure with a wire skirt round her one leg. We are a bit silly about Miss Blossom—we pretend she is real. We imagine her to be a woman of the world, perhaps a barmaid in her youth. She says things like "Well, dearie, that's what men are like", and "You hold out for your marriage lines."

The Victorian vandals who did so many unnecessary things to this house didn't have the sense to put in passages, so we are always having to go through each other's rooms. Topaz has just wandered through ours—wearing a nightgown made of plain white calico with holes for her neck and arms; she thinks modern underclothes are vulgar. She looked rather like a victim going to an Auto da Fé, but her destination was merely the bathroom.

Topaz and father sleep in the big room that opens on to the kitchen staircase. There is a little room between them and us which we call "Buffer State"; Topaz uses it as a studio. Thomas has the room across the landing, next to the bathroom.

I wonder if Topaz has gone to ask father to come to bed— she is perfectly capable of stalking along the top of the castle walls in her nightgown. I hope she hasn't, because father does so snub her when she bursts into the gatehouse. We were trained as children never to go near him unless invited and he thinks she ought to behave in the same way.

No—she didn't go. She came back a few minutes ago and showed signs of staying here, but we didn't encourage her. Now she is in bed and is playing her lute. I like the idea of a lute, but not the noise it makes; it is seldom in tune and appears to be an instrument that never gets a run at anything.

I feel rather guilty at being so unsociable to Topaz, but we did have such a sociable evening.

Round about eight o'clock, Miss Marcy came with the books. She is about forty, small and rather faded yet somehow very young. She blinks her eyes a lot and is apt to giggle and say: "Well, reely!" She is a Londoner but has been in the village over five years now. I believe she teaches very nicely; her specialities are folk song and wild flowers and country lore. She didn't like it here when first she came (she always says she "missed the bright lights"); but she soon made herself take an interest in country things, and now she tries to make the country people interested in them too.

As librarian, she cheats a bit to give us the newest books; she'd had a delivery to-day and had brought father a detective novel that only came out the year before last—and it was by one of his favourite authors. Topaz said:

"Oh, I must take this to Mortmain at once." She calls father "Mortmain" partly because she fancies our odd surname, and partly to keep up the fiction that he is still a famous writer. He came back with her to thank Miss Marcy and for once he seemed quite genuinely cheerful.

"I'll read any detective novel, good, bad or indifferent," he told her, "but a vintage one's among the rarest pleasures of life."

Then he found out he was getting this one ahead of the Vicar and was so pleased that he blew Miss Marcy a kiss. She said: "Oh, thank you, Mr. Mortmain! That is, I mean—well, reely!" and blushed and blinked. Father then flung his rug round him like a toga and went back to the gatehouse looking quite abnormally good-humoured.

As soon as he was out of earshot, Miss Marcy said: "How *is* he?" in a hushed sort of voice that implied he was at death's door or off his head. Rose said he was perfectly well and perfectly useless, as always. Miss Marcy looked shocked.

"Rose is depressed about our finances," I explained.

"We mustn't bore Miss Marcy with our worries," said Topaz, quickly. She hates anything which casts a reflection on father.

Miss Marcy said that nothing to do with our household could possibly bore her—I know she thinks our life at the castle

14

is wildly romantic. Then she asked, very diffidently, if she could help us with any advice—"Sometimes an outside mind . . ."

I suddenly felt that I should rather like to consult her; she is such a sensible little woman—it was she who thought of getting me the book on speed-writing. Mother trained us never to talk about our affairs in the village, and I do respect Topaz's loyalty to father, but I was sure Miss Marcy must know perfectly well that we are broke.

"If you could suggest some ways of earning money," I said.

"Or of making it go further—I'm sure you're all much too artistic to be really practical. Let's hold a board meeting!"

She said it as if she were enticing children to a game. She was so eager that it would have seemed quite rude to refuse; and I think Rose and Topaz felt desperate enough to try anything.

"Now, paper and pencils," said Miss Marcy, clapping her hands.

Writing paper is scarce in this house, and I had no intention of tearing sheets out of this exercise book, which is a superb sixpenny one the Vicar gave me. In the end, Miss Marcy took the middle pages out of her library record, which gave us a pleasant feeling that we were stealing from the government, and then we sat round the table and elected her chairman. She said she must be secretary, too, so that she could keep the minutes, and wrote down:

ENQUIRY INTO THE FINANCES OF THE MORTMAIN FAMILY

———

Present:
Miss Marcy (chairman)
Mrs. James Mortmain
Miss Rose Mortmain
Miss Cassandra Mortmain
Thomas Mortmain
Stephen Colly

———

15

We began by discussing expenditure.

"First, rent," said Miss Marcy.

The rent is forty pounds a year, which seems little for a commodious castle, but we have only a few acres of land, the country folk think the ruins are a drawback, and there are said to be ghosts—which there are not. (There are some queer things up on the mound, but they never come into the house.) Anyway, we haven't paid any rent for three years. Our landlord, a rich old gentleman who lived at Scoatney Hall, five miles away, always sent us a ham at Christmas whether we paid the rent or not. He died last November and we have sadly missed the ham.

"They say the Hall's going to be re-opened," said Miss Marcy when we had told her the position about the rent. "Two boys from the village have been taken on as extra gardeners. Well, we will just put the rent *down* and mark it 'optional.' Now what about food? Can you do it on fifteen shillings a week per head? Say a pound per head, including candles, lamp-oil and cleaning materials."

The idea of our family ever coming by six pounds a week made us all hoot with laughter.

"If Miss Marcy is really going to advise us," said Topaz, "she'd better be told we have no visible income at all this year."

Miss Marcy flushed and said: "I did know things were difficult. But, dear Mrs. Mortmain, there must be *some* money, surely?"

We gave her the facts. Not one penny has come in during January or February. Last year father got forty pounds from America, where *Jacob Wrestling* still sells. Topaz posed in London for three months, saved eight pounds for us and borrowed fifty; and we sold a tallboy to a King's Crypt dealer for twenty pounds. We have been living on the tallboy since Christmas.

"Last year's income one hundred and eighteen pounds," said Miss Marcy and wrote it down. But we hastened to tell her that it bore no relation to this year's income, for we have no more good furniture to sell, Topaz has run out of rich

16

borrowees, and we think it unlikely that father's royalties will be so large, as they have dwindled every year.

"Should I leave school?" said Thomas. But of course we told him that would be absurd as his schooling costs us nothing owing to his scholarship, and the Vicar has just given him a year's ticket for the train.

Miss Marcy fiddled with her pencil a bit and then said:

"If I'm to be a help, I must be frank. Couldn't you make a saving on Stephen's wages?"

I felt myself go red. Of course we have never paid Stephen anything—never even thought of it. And I suddenly realized that we ought to have done so. (Not that we've had any money to pay him with since he's been old enough to earn.)

"I don't want wages," said Stephen, quietly. "I wouldn't take them. Everything I've ever had has been given to me here."

"You see, Stephen's like a son of the house," I said. Miss Marcy looked as if she wasn't sure that was a very good thing to be, but Stephen's face quite lit up for a second. Then he got embarrassed and said he must see if the hens were all in. After he had gone, Miss Marcy said:

"No—no wages at all? Just his keep?"

"We don't pay ourselves any wages," said Rose—which is true enough; but then we don't work so hard as Stephen or sleep in a dark little room off the kitchen. "And I think it's humiliating discussing our poverty in front of Miss Marcy," Rose went on, angrily. "I thought we were just going to ask her advice about earning."

After that, a lot of time was wasted soothing Rose's pride and Miss Marcy's feelings. Then we got down to our earning capacities.

Topaz said she couldn't earn more than four pounds a week in London and possibly not that, and she would need three pounds to live on, and some clothes, and the fare to come down here at least every other week-end.

"And I don't want to go to London," she added, rather pathetically. "I'm tired of being a model. And I miss Mortmain dreadfully. And he needs me here—I'm the only one who can cook."

"That's hardly very important when we've nothing to cook," said Rose. "Could I earn money as a model?"

"I'm afraid not," said Topaz. "Your figure's too pretty—there isn't enough drawing in your bones. And you'd never have the patience to sit still. I suppose if nothing turns up I'll have to go to London. I could send about ten shillings a week home."

"Well, that's splendid," said Miss Marcy and wrote down: "Mrs. James Mortmain: a potential ten shillings weekly."

"Not all the year round," said Topaz, firmly. "I couldn't stand it and it would leave me no time for my own painting. I might sell some of that, of course."

Miss Marcy said "Of course you might," very politely; then turned to me. I said my speed-writing was getting quite fast, but of course it wasn't quite like real shorthand (or quite like real speed-writing, for that matter); and I couldn't type and the chance of getting anywhere near a typewriter was remote.

"Then I'm afraid, just until you get going with your literary work, we'll have to count you as nil," said Miss Marcy. "Thomas, of course, is bound to be nil for a few years yet. Rose, dear?"

Now if anyone in this family is nil as an earner, it is Rose; for though she plays the piano a bit and sings rather sweetly and is, of course, a lovely person, she has no real talents at all.

"Perhaps I could look after little children," she suggested.

"Oh, *no*," said Miss Marcy, hurriedly, "I mean, dear—well, I don't think it would suit you at all."

"I'll go to Scoatney Hall as a maid," said Rose, looking as if she were already ascending the scaffold.

"Well, they do have to be trained, dear," said Miss Marcy, "and I can't feel your father would like it. Couldn't you do some pretty sewing?"

"What on?" said Rose. "Sacking?"

Anyway, Rose is hopeless at sewing.

Miss Marcy was looking at her list rather depressedly. "I fear we must call dear Rose nil just for the moment," she said. "That only leaves Mr. Mortmain."

Rose said: "If I rank as nil, father ought to be double nil."

Miss Marcy leaned forward and said in a hushed voice: "My dears, you know I'm trying to help you all. What's the real trouble with Mr. Mortmain? Is it—is it—*drink*?"

We laughed so much that Stephen came in to see what the joke was.

"Poor, poor Mortmain," gasped Topaz, "as if he ever laid his hands on enough to buy a bottle of beer! Drink costs money, Miss Marcy."

Miss Marcy said it couldn't be drugs either—and it certainly couldn't; he doesn't even smoke, once his Christmas cigars from the Vicar are gone.

"It's just sheer laziness," said Rose, "laziness and softness. And I don't believe he was ever very good, really. I expect *Jacob Wrestling* was over-estimated."

Topaz looked so angry that I thought for a second she was going to hit Rose. Stephen came to the table and stood between them.

"Oh, no, Miss Rose," he said quietly, "it's a great book—everyone knows that. But things have happened to him so that he can't write any more. You can't write just for the wanting."

I expected Rose to snub him, but before she could say a word he turned to me and went on quickly: "I've been thinking, Miss Cassandra, that I should get work—they'd have me at Four Stones Farm."

"But the garden, Stephen!" I almost wailed—for we just about live on our vegetables.

He said the days would soon draw out and that he'd work for us in the evenings.

"And I'm useful in the garden, aren't I, Stephen?" said Topaz.

"Yes, ma'am, very useful. I couldn't get a job if you went to London, of course—there'd be too much work for Miss Cassandra."

Rose isn't good at things like gardening and housework.

"So you could put me down for twenty-five shillings a week, Miss Marcy," Stephen went on, "because Mr. Stebbins said he'd start me at that. And I'd get my dinner at Four Stones."

I was glad to think that would mean he'd get one square meal a day.

Miss Marcy said it was a splendid idea, though it was a pity it meant striking out Topaz's ten shillings. "Though, of course, it was only potential." While she was putting Stephen's twenty-five shillings on her list, Rose suddenly said:

"Thank you, Stephen."

And because she doesn't bother with him much as a rule, it somehow sounded important. And she smiled so very sweetly. Poor Rose has been so miserable lately that a smile from her is like late afternoon sunshine after a long, wet day. I don't see how anyone could see Rose smile without feeling fond of her. I thought Stephen would be tremendously pleased, but he only nodded and swallowed several times.

Just then, father came out on the staircase and looked down on us all.

"What, a round game?" he said—and I suppose it must have looked like one, with us grouped round the table in the lamplight. Then he came downstairs saying: "This book's first-rate. I'm having a little break, trying to guess the murderer. I should like a biscuit, please."

Whenever father is hungry between meals—and he eats very little at them, less than any of us—he asks for a biscuit. I believe he thinks it is the smallest and cheapest thing he can ask for. Of course, we haven't had any real shop biscuits for ages but Topaz makes oatcake, which is very filling. She put some margarine on a piece for him. I saw a fraction of distaste in his eyes and he asked her if she could sprinkle it with a little sugar.

"It makes a change," he said, apologetically. "Can't we offer Miss Marcy something? Some tea or cocoa, Miss Marcy?"

She thanked him but said she mustn't spoil her appetite for supper.

"Well, don't let me interrupt the game," said father. "What is it?" And before I could think of any way of distracting him, he had leaned over her shoulder to look at the list in front of her. As it then stood, it read:

Earning Capacity for Present Year

Mrs. Mortmain	nil.
Cassandra Mortmain	nil.
Thomas Mortmain	nil.
Rose Mortmain	nil.
Mr. Mortmain	nil.
Stephen Colly	25s. a week.

Father's expression didn't change as he read, he went on smiling; but I could *feel* something happening to him. Rose says I am always crediting people with emotions I should experience myself in their situation, but I am sure I had a real flash of intuition then. And I suddenly saw his face very clearly, not just in the way one usually sees the faces of people one is very used to. I saw how he had changed since I was little and I thought of Ralph Hodgson's line about "tamed and shabby tigers." How long it takes to write the thoughts of a minute! I thought of many more things, complicated, pathetic and very puzzling, just while father read the list.

When he had finished, he said quite lightly: "And is Stephen giving us his wages?"

"I ought to pay for my board and lodging, Mr. Mortmain, sir," said Stephen, "and for—for past favours; all the books you've lent me——"

"I'm sure you'll make a very good head of the family," said father. He took the oatcake with sugar on it from Topaz and moved towards the stairs. She called after him: "Stay by the fire for a little while, Mortmain." But he said he wanted to get back to his book. Then he thanked Miss Marcy again for bringing him such a good one, and said good night to her very courteously. We could hear him humming as he went through the bedrooms on his way to the gatehouse.

Miss Marcy made no remark about the incident, which shows what a tactful person she is; but she looked embarrassed and said she must be getting along. Stephen lit a lantern and said he would go as far as the road with her—she had left her bicycle there because of the awful mud in our lane. I went out to see her off. As we crossed the courtyard, she glanced up at

21

the gatehouse window and asked if I thought father would be offended if she brought him a little tin of biscuits to keep there. I said I didn't think any food could give offence in our house and she said: "Oh, dear!" Then she looked around at the ruins and said how beautiful they were but she supposed I was used to them. I wanted to get back to the fire so I just said yes; but it wasn't true. I am never used to the beauty of the castle. And after she and Stephen had gone I realized it was looking particularly lovely. It was a queer sort of night. The full moon was hidden by clouds but had turned them silver so that the sky was quite light. Belmotte Tower, high on its mound, seemed even taller than usual. Once I really looked at the sky, I wanted to go on looking; it seemed to draw me towards it and make me listen hard, though there was nothing to listen to, not so much as a twig was stirring. When Stephen came back I was still gazing upwards.

"It's too cold for you to be out without a coat, Miss Cassandra," he said. But I had forgotten about feeling cold, so of course I wasn't cold any more.

As we walked back to the house he asked if I thought La Belle Dame sans Merci would have lived in a tower like Belmotte. I said it seemed very likely; though I never really thought of her having a home life.

After that, we all decided to go to bed to save making up the fire, so we got our hot bricks out of the oven and wended our ways. But going to bed early is hard on candles. I reckoned I had two hours of light in mine, but a bit of wick fell in and now it is a melted mass. (I wonder how King Alfred got on with his clock-candles when that happened.) I have called Thomas to see if I can have his, but he is still doing his home-work. I shall have to go to the kitchen—I have a secret cache of ends there. And I will be noble and have a companionable chat with Topaz, on the way down.

. . . I am back. Something rather surprising happened. When I got to the kitchen, Heloïse woke and barked and Stephen came to his door to see what was the matter. I called out that it was only me and he dived back into his room. I found my candle-end and had just knelt down by Heloïse's basket to have a few words with her (she had a particularly nice warm-clean-dog smell after being asleep) when out he came again, wearing his coat over his nightshirt.

"It's all right," I called, "I've got what I wanted."

Just then, the door on the kitchen stairs swung to, so that we were in darkness except for the pale square at the window. I groped my way across the kitchen and bumped into the table. Then Stephen took my arm and guided me to the foot of the stairs.

"I can manage now," I said—we were closer to the window and there was quite a lot of the queer, shrouded moonlight coming in.

He still kept hold of my arm. "I want to ask you something, Miss Cassandra," he said. "I want to know if you're ever hungry—I mean when there's nothing for you to eat."

I would probably have answered "I certainly am," but I noticed how strained and anxious his voice was. So I said:

"Well, there generally is something or other, isn't there? Of course, it would be nicer to have lots of exciting food, but I do get enough. Why did you suddenly want to know?"

He said he had been lying awake thinking about it and that he couldn't bear me to be hungry.

"If ever you are, you tell me," he said, "and I'll manage something."

I thanked him very much and reminded him he was going to help us all with his wages.

"Yes, that'll be something," he said. "But you tell me if you don't get enough. Good night, Miss Cassandra."

As I went upstairs I was glad I hadn't admitted that I was ever uncomfortably hungry, because as he steals Herrick for me, I should think he might steal food. It was rather a dreadful thought but somehow comforting.

Father was just arriving from the gatehouse. He didn't show any signs of having had his feelings hurt. He remarked that he'd kept four chapters of his book to read in bed.

"And great strength of mind it required," he added.

Topaz looked rather depressed.

I found Rose lying in the dark because Thomas had

borrowed her candle to finish his homework by. She said she didn't mind as her book had turned out too pretty to be bearable.

I lit my candle-end and stuck it on the melted mass in the candlestick. I had to crouch low in bed to get enough light to write by. I was just ready to start again, when I saw Rose look round to make sure that I had closed the door of Buffer. Then she said:

"Did you think of anything when Miss Marcy said Scoatney Hall was being re-opened? *I* thought of the beginning of *Pride and Prejudice*—where Mrs. Bennet says 'Netherfield Park is let at last.' And then Mr. Bennet goes over to call on the rich new owner."

"Mr. Bennet didn't owe him any rent," I said.

"Father wouldn't go anyway. How I wish I lived in a Jane Austen novel!"

I said I'd rather be in a Charlotte Brontë.

"Which would be nicest—Jane with a touch of Charlotte, or Charlotte with a touch of Jane?"

This is the kind of discussion I like very much but I wanted to get on with my journal, so I just said: "Fifty per cent each way would be perfect," and started to write determinedly. Now it is nearly midnight. I feel rather like a Brontë myself, writing by the light of a guttering candle with my fingers so numb I can hardly hold the pencil. I wish Stephen hadn't made me think of food, because I have been hungry ever since; which is ridiculous as I had a good egg tea not six hours ago. Oh, dear—I have just thought that if Stephen was worrying about me being hungry, he was probably hungry himself. We *are* a household!

I wonder if I can get a few more minutes' light by making wicks of match sticks stuck into the liquid wax. Sometimes that will work.

It was no good—like trying to write by the light of a glow-worm. But the moon has fought its way through the clouds at last and I can see by that. It is rather exciting to write by moonlight.

Rose is asleep—on her back, with her mouth wide open.

Even like that she looks nice. I hope she is having a beautiful dream about a rich young man proposing to her.

I don't feel in the least sleepy. I shall hold a little mental chat with Miss Blossom. Her noble bust looks larger than ever against the silvery window. I have just asked her if she thinks Rose and I will ever have anything exciting happen to us, and I distinctly heard her say: "Well, I don't know, ducks, but I do know that sister of yours would be a daisy if she ever got the chance!"

I don't think I should ever be a daisy.

I could easily go on writing all night but I can't really see and it's extravagant on paper, so I shall merely think. Contemplation seems to be about the only luxury that costs nothing.

Chapter III

I HAVE JUST READ THIS JOURNAL FROM THE BEGINNING. I FIND I can read the speed-writing quite easily, even the bit I did by moonlight last night. I am surprised to see how much I have written; with stories even a page can take me hours, but the truth seems to flow out as fast as I can get it down. But words are very inadequate—anyway, my words are. Could anyone reading them picture our kitchen by firelight, or Belmotte Tower rising towards the moon-silvered clouds, or Stephen managing to look both noble and humble? (It was most unfair of me to say he looks a fraction daft.) When I read a book, I put in all the imagination I can, so that it is almost like writing the book as well as reading it—or rather, it is like living it. It makes reading so much more exciting, but I don't suppose many people try to do it.

I am writing in the attic this afternoon because Topaz and Rose are so very conversational in the kitchen; they have unearthed a packet of green dye—it dates from when I was an elf in the school play—and are going to dip some old dresses. I don't intend to let myself become the kind of author who can only work in seclusion—after all, Jane Austen wrote in the sitting-room and merely covered up her work when a visitor called (though I bet she thought a thing or two)—but I am not quite Jane Austen yet and there are limits to what I can stand. And I want to tackle the description of the castle in peace. It is extremely cold up here, but I am wearing my coat and my wool gloves, which have gradually become mittens all but one thumb; and Ab, our beautiful pale ginger cat, is keeping my stomach warm—I am leaning over him to write on the top of the cistern. His real name is Abelard, to go with Heloïse (I need hardly say that Topaz christened them), but

26

he seldom gets called by it. He has a reasonably pleasant nature but not a gushing one; this is a rare favour I am receiving from him this afternoon.

To-day I shall start with:

How We Came to the Castle

While father was in jail, we lived in a London boarding-house, mother not having fancied settling down again next to the fence-leaping neighbour. When they let father out, he decided to buy a house in the country. I think we must have been rather well-off in those days as *Jacob Wrestling* had sold wonderfully well for such an unusual book and father's lecturing had earned much more than the sales. And mother had an income of her own.

Father chose Suffolk as a suitable county so we stayed at the King's Crypt hotel and drove out house-hunting every day—we had a car then; father and mother at the front, Rose, Thomas and I at the back. It was all great fun because father was in a splendid mood—goodness knows he didn't seem to have any iron in his soul then. But he certainly had a pre-judice against all neighbours; we saw lots of nice houses in villages, but he wouldn't even consider them.

It was late autumn, very gentle and golden. I loved the quiet-coloured fields of stubble and the hazy water meadows. Rose doesn't like the flat country but I always did—flat country seems to give the sky such a chance. One evening when there was a lovely sunset, we got lost. Mother had the map and kept saying the country was upside down—and when she got it the right way up, the names on the map were upside down. Rose and I laughed a lot about it; we liked being lost. And father was perfectly patient with mother about the map.

All of a sudden we saw a high, round tower in the distance, on a little hill. Father instantly decided that we must explore it, though mother wasn't enthusiastic. It was difficult to find because the little roads twisted and woods and villages kept hiding it from us, but every few minutes we caught a glimpse of it and father and Rose and I got very excited. Mother kept saying that Thomas would be up too late; he was asleep, wobbling about between Rose and me.

At last we came to a neglected signpost with To BELMOTTE AND THE CASTLE ONLY on it, pointing down a narrow, overgrown lane. Father turned in at once and we crawled along with the brambles clawing at the car as if trying to hold it back —I remember thinking of the Prince fighting his way through the wood to the Sleeping Beauty. The hedges were so high and the lane turned so often that we could only see a few yards ahead of us; mother kept saying we ought to back out before we got stuck and that the castle was probably miles away. Then suddenly we drove out into the open and there it was—but not the lonely tower on a hill we had been searching for; what we saw was quite a large castle, built on level ground. Father gave a shout and the next minute we were out of the car and staring in amazement.

How strange and beautiful it looked in the late afternoon light! I can still recapture that first glimpse—see the sheer grey stone walls and towers against the pale yellow sky, the reflected castle stretching towards us on the brimming moat, the floating patches of emerald-green water-weed. No breath of wind ruffled the looking-glass water, no sound of any kind came to us. Our excited voices only made the castle seem more silent.

Father pointed out the gatehouse—it had two round towers joined half-way up by a room with stone-mullioned windows. To the right of the gatehouse nothing remained but crumbling ruins, but on the left a stretch of high, battlemented walls joined it to a round corner tower. A bridge crossed the moat to the great nail-studded oak doors under the windows of the gatehouse room, and a little door cut in one of the big doors stood slightly ajar—the minute father noticed this, he was off towards it. Mother said vague things about trespassing and tried to stop us following him, but in the end she let us go, while she stayed behind with Thomas, who woke and wept a little.

How well I remember that run through the stillness, the smell of wet stone and wet weeds as we crossed the bridge, the moment of excitement before we stepped in at the little door! Once through, we were in the cool dimness of the gatehouse passage. That was where I first *felt* the castle—it is the place where one is most conscious of the great weight of stone above and around one. I was too young to know much of history and the past, for me the castle was one in a fairy tale; and the queer heavy coldness was so spell-like that I clutched Rose hard. Together we ran through to the daylight; then stopped dead.

On our left, instead of the grey walls and towers we had been expecting, was a long house of whitewashed plaster and herring-boned brick, veined by weather-bleached wood. It had all sorts of odd little lattice windows, bright gold from the sunset, and the attic gable looked as if it might fall forward at any minute. This belonged to a different kind of fairy tale— it was just my idea of a "Hansel and Gretel" house and for a second I feared a witch inside had stolen father. Then I saw him trying to get in at the kitchen door. He came running back through the overgrown courtyard garden, calling that there was a small window open near the front door that he could put Rose through to let us in. I was glad he said Rose and not me—I would have been terrified to be alone in the house for a second. Rose was never frightened of anything; she was trying to scramble up to the window even before father got there to lift her. Through she went and we heard her struggling with heavy bolts. Then she flung the door open triumphantly.

The square hall was dark and cold and had a horrid mouldy smell. Every bit of woodwork was a drab ginger colour, painted to imitate the graining of wood.

"Would you believe anyone could do that to fine old panelling?" exploded father. We followed him into a room on the left, which had a dark red wallpaper and a large black-leaded fireplace. There was a nice little window looking on to the garden, but I thought it was a hideous room.

"False ceiling," said father, stretching up to tap it. "Oh, lord, I suppose the Victorians did their worst to the whole place."

We went back to the hall and then into the large room which is now our drawing-room; it stretches the whole depth of the house. Rose and I ran across and knelt on the wide window-seat, and father opened the heavy mullioned windows so that we could look down and see ourselves in the moat. Then he pointed out how thick the wall was and explained about the Stuart house having been built on to the ruins of the castle.

"It must have been beautiful once—and could be again," he said, staring across to the field of stubble. "Think of this view in summer, with a wheat field reaching right up to the edge of the moat."

Then he turned and exclaimed in horror at the wallpaper— he said it looked like giant squashed frogs. It certainly did, and there was a monstrosity of a fireplace surrounded by tobacco-coloured tiles. But the diamond-paned windows overlooking the garden and full of the sunset were beautiful, and I was already in love with the moat.

While Rose and I were waving to our reflections, father went off through the short passage to the kitchen—we suddenly heard him shouting "The swine, the swine!" Just for an instant I thought he had found pigs, but it turned out to be his continued opinion of the people who had spoilt the house. The kitchen was really dreadful. It had been partitioned to make several rooms—hens had been kept in one of them; there was a great sagging false ceiling, the staircase and the cupboards were grained ginger like the hall. What upset me most was a bundle of rags and straw where tramps must have slept. I kept as far away from it as possible and was glad when father led the way upstairs.

The bedrooms were as spoilt as the downstairs rooms—false ceilings, horrid fireplaces, awful wallpapers. But I was very much fetched when I saw the round tower opening into the room which is now Rose's and mine. Father tried to get the door to it open, but it was nailed up so he strode on across the landing.

"That corner tower we saw from outside must be somewhere about here," he said. We followed him into Thomas's little room, hunting for it, and then into the bathroom. It had a huge bath with a wide mahogany surround, and two mahogany-seated lavatories, side by side, with one lid to cover them both. The pottery parts showed views of Windsor Castle and when you pulled the plug the bottom of Windsor Castle fell out. Just above them was a text left by the previous tenants, saying: "Hold thou me up, and I shall be safe." Father sat down on the side of the bath and roared with laughter. He would never have anything in the bathroom changed so even the text is still there.

The corner tower was between the bath and the lavatories. There was no door to it and we started to climb up the circular stone staircase inside, but the steps had crumbled so much that we had to turn back. But we did get high enough to find a way out on to the top of the walls; there was quite a wide walk with a battlemented parapet on each side. From there we could see mother in the car, nursing Thomas.

"Don't attract her attention," said father, "or she'll think we're going to break our necks."

The walls led us to one of the gatehouse towers; and inside it, opening on to the staircase, was the door to the gatehouse room.

"Thank the lord this isn't spoilt," said father as we went in. "How I could work in this room!"

There were stone-mullioned windows looking in to the court-yard, as well as the ones at the front overlooking the lane. Father said they were Tudor; later in period than the gate-house itself, but much earlier than the house.

We went back into the tower and found the steps of the circular stone staircase good enough for us to go up higher—once we were crawling into the darkness I wished they hadn't been; father struck matches but there was a dreadful black moment each time one burnt out. And the cold, rough stone felt so strange to my hands and bare knees. But when at last we came out on the battlemented top of the tower it was worth it all—I had never felt so high in my life. And I was so triumphant at having been brave enough to come up. Not that I had had any choice; Rose had kept butting me from behind.

We stood looking down on the lane and over the fields

stretching far on either side; we were so high that we could see how the hedges cut them up into a patchwork pattern. There were a few little woods and, a mile or so to the left, a tiny village. We moved round the tower to look across the courtyard garden—and then we all shouted: "There it is!" at the same moment. Beyond the ruined walls on the west side of the courtyard was a small hill and on the top of it was the high tower we had driven so long in search of. It puzzles me now why we hadn't seen it when we first came through the gatehouse passage. Perhaps the overgrown garden obstructed the view; or perhaps we were too much astonished at seeing the house to look in the opposite direction.

Father dived for the staircase. I cried "Wait, wait!" and he turned and picked me up, letting Rose go ahead striking the matches. He guessed the bottom of the staircase must come out in the gatehouse passage, but Rose used the last match as we reached the archway on to the walls; so we went back along them to the bathroom and down the nice little front staircase of the house into the hall. Mother was just coming through the front door to look for us, dragging a cross, sleepy Thomas—he never liked to be left alone in the car. Father showed her the tower on the hill—we could see it easily once we knew where to look—and told her to come along; then dashed across the courtyard garden. She said she couldn't manage it with Thomas. I remember feeling I ought to stay with her, but I didn't. I raced after father and Rose.

We climbed over the ruined walls which bounded the garden and crossed the moat by the shaky bridge at the south-west corner; that brought us to the foot of the hill—but father told us it was ancient earthworks and not a natural hill (ever since then we have called it the mound). The turf was short and smooth and there were no more ruins. At the top we had to scramble over some ridges which father said must have been the outer defences. This brought us to a broad, grassy plateau. At the far end was a smaller mound, round in shape and very smooth, and rising from this was the tower, sixty feet tall, black against the last flush of sunset. The entrance was about fifteen feet up, at the top of an outside flight of stone steps—

father did his best to force the door but had no luck; so we didn't see inside the tower that night.

We walked all round the little mound and father told us that it was called a motte and that the wide grassy plateau was a bailey; he said all this part was much older than the moated castle below. The sunset faded and a wind got up and everything began to look frightening, but father went on talking most happily and excitedly. Suddenly Rose said: "It's like the tower in *The Lancashire Witches* where Mother Demdike lived." She had read bits of that book aloud to me until I got so frightened that mother stopped her. Just then we heard mother calling from below; her voice sounded high and strange, almost despairing. I grabbed Rose's hand and said: "Come on, mother's frightened." And I told myself I was running to help mother; but I was really terrified of being near the tower any longer.

Father said we had all better go. We climbed the ridges and then Rose and I took hands and ran down the smooth slope—faster and faster, so that I thought we should fall. All the time we were running I felt extremely frightened, but I enjoyed it. The whole evening was like that.

When we got back to the house, mother was sitting on the front door-step nursing Thomas, who had fallen asleep again.

"Isn't it wonderful?" cried father. "I'll have it if it takes my last penny."

Mother said: "If it's to be my cross, I suppose God will give me the strength to bear it." Father laughed at that and I felt rather shocked. I don't in the least know if she meant to be funny—but then, I realize more and more how vague she has become for me. Even when I remember things she said, I can't recall the sound of her voice. And though I can still see the shape of her that day huddled on the steps, her back view when we were in the car, her brown tweed suit and squashy felt hat, I can't visualize her face at all. When I try to, I just see the photograph I have of her.

Rose and I went back to the car with her, but father wandered round until it was dark. I remember seeing him come out on the castle walls near the gatehouse—and marvelling that I had been up there myself. Even in the dusk I could see his gold hair and splendid profile. He was spare in those days, but broad—always a large person.

He was so excited that he started to drive back to King's Crypt at a terrific pace—Rose, Thomas and I simply bounced about at the back of the car. Mother said it wasn't safe with the roads so narrow and he slowed down to a snail's pace which made Rose and me laugh a lot. Mother said: "There's reason in everything and Thomas ought to be in bed." Thomas suddenly sat up and said: "Dear me, yes, I ought," which made even mother laugh.

The next day, after making enquiries, father went over to Scoatney Hall. When he got back he told us that Mr. Cotton wouldn't sell the castle, but had let him have a forty years' lease on it.

"And I can do anything I like to the house," he added, "because the old gentleman agrees I couldn't possibly make it any worse."

Of course, he made it very much better—whitewashing it, unearthing the drawing-room panelling from beneath eight coats of wallpaper, pulling out the worst fireplaces, the false ceilings, the partitions in the kitchen. There were many more things he meant to do, particularly as regards comfort—I know mother wanted some central heating and a machine to make electric light; but he spent so much on antique furniture even before work at the castle began that she persuaded him to cut things down to a minimum. There was always a vague idea that the useful things were to come later; probably when he wrote his next book.

It was spring when we moved in. I particularly remember the afternoon we first got the drawing-room straight. Everything was so fresh—the flowered chintz curtains, the beautiful shining old furniture, the white panelling—it had had to be painted because it was in such a poor condition. I was fascinated by a great jar of young green beech leaves; I sat on the floor staring at them while Rose played her piece "To a Water Lily" on mother's old grand piano. Suddenly father came in, in a very exulting mood, to tell us that there was a surprise for us outside the window. He flung the mullioned windows open wide and there on the moat were two swans, sailing sedately. We leaned out to feed them with bread and all the time the spring air blew in and stirred the beech leaves. Then I went into the garden, where the lawns had been cut and the flower-beds tidied; there were a lot of early wall-flowers which smelt very sweet. Father was arranging his books up in the gatehouse room. He called down:

"Isn't this a lovely home for you?"

I agreed that it was; and I still think so. But anyone who could enjoy the winter here would find the North Pole stuffy.

How strange memory is! When I close my eyes, I see three different castles—one in the sunset light of that first evening, one all fresh and clean as in our early days here, one as it is now. The last picture is very sad because all our good furniture has gone—the dining-room hasn't so much as a carpet; not that we have missed that room much—it was the first one we saw that night we explored the house and was always too far from the kitchen. The drawing-room has a few chairs still and, thank goodness, no one will ever buy the piano because it is so big and old. But the pretty chintz curtains are faded and everything has a neglected look. When the spring comes we must really try to freshen up our home a little—at least we can still have beech leaves.

We have been poor for five years now; after mother died, I fear we lived on the capital of the money she left. Not that I ever worried about such things at the time because I always felt sure father would make money again sooner or later. Mother brought us up to believe that he was a genius and that geniuses mustn't be hurried.

What *is* the matter with him? And what does he *do* all the time? I wrote yesterday that he does nothing but read detective novels, but that was just a silly generalization, because Miss Marcy can seldom let him have more than two a week (although he will read the same ones again and again after a certain lapse of time, which seems to me amazing). Of course he reads other books, too. All our valuable ones have been sold (and how I have missed them!) but there are a good many

35

of the others left, including an old, incomplete *Encyclopædia Britannica*; I know he reads that—he plays some kind of a game following up cross-references in it. And I am sure he thinks very hard. Several times when he hasn't answered my knock on the gatehouse room door I have gone in and found him staring into space. In the good weather he walks a lot, but he hasn't now for months. He has dropped all his London friends. The only friend he has ever made down here is the Vicar, who is the nicest man imaginable; a bachelor, with an elderly housekeeper. Now I come to think of it, father has dodged seeing even him this winter.

Father's unsociability has made it hard for any of us to get to know people here—and there aren't many to know. The village is tiny: just the church, the vicarage, the little school, the inn, one shop (which is also the post office) and a huddle of cottages; though the Vicar gets quite a congregation from the surrounding hamlets and farms. It is a very pretty village and has the unlikely name of Godsend, a corruption of Godys End, after the Norman knight, Etienne de Godys, who built Belmotte Castle. Our castle—I mean the moated one, on to which our house is built—is called Godsend, too; it was built by a later de Godys.

No one really knows the origin of the name "Belmotte"—the whole mound, as well as the tower on it, is called that. At a guess one would say the "Bel" is from the French, but the Vicar believes in a theory that it is from Bel the sun god, whose worship was introduced by the Phoenicians, and that the mound was raised so that Midsummer Eve votive fires could be lit there; he thinks the Normans simply made use of it. Father doesn't believe in the god Bel theory and says the Phoenicians worshipped the stars, not the sun. Anyway, the mound is a very good place to worship both sun and stars from. I do a little worshipping there myself when I get time.

I meant to copy an essay on castles I wrote for the school History Society into this journal, but I find it is very long and horridly overwritten (how the school must have suffered!), so I shall paraphrase it briefly:

In early Norman times, there seem to have been mounds with ditches and wooden stockades as defences. Inside the defences were wooden buildings, and sometimes there was a high earthen motte to serve as a look-out place. The later Normans began building great square stone towers (called keeps), but it was found possible to mine the corners of these —mining was just digging then, of course, not the use of explosives—so they took to building round towers, of which Belmotte is one. Later, the tower-keeps were surrounded with high walls, called curtain walls. These were often built in quadrangle form with jutting towers at the gatehouse, the corners and in the middle of each side so that the defenders could see any besiegers who were trying to mine or scale the walls, and fight them off. But the besiegers had plenty of other good tricks, notably a weapon called a trébuchet which could sling great rocks—or a dead horse— over your curtain walls, causing much embarrassment. Eventually, someone thought of putting moats round curtain walls. Of course, the moated castles had to be on level ground; Belmotte tower-keep, up on its mound, must have been very much of a back number when Godsend Castle was built. And then all castles gradually became back numbers and Cromwell's Roundheads battered two-and-a-half sides of our curtain walls down.

Long before that, the de Godys name had died out and the two castles had passed to the Cottons of Scoatney, through a daughter. The house built on the ruins was their dowerhouse for a time, then it became just a farmhouse. And now it isn't even that; merely the home of the ruined Mortmains.

Oh, what are we to do for money? Surely there is enough intelligence among us to earn some, or marry some—Rose, that is; for I would approach matrimony as cheerfully as I would the tomb and I cannot feel that I should give satis-faction. But how is Rose to meet anyone? We used to go to London every year to stay with father's aunt, who has a house in Chelsea with a lily-pond and collects artists. Father met

Topaz there—Aunt Millicent never forgave him for marrying her, so now we don't get asked any more; this is bitter because it means we meet no men at all, not even artists. Oh, me! I am feeling low in spirits. While I have been writing I have lived in the past, the light of it has been all around me—first the golden light of autumn, then the silver light of spring and then the strange light, grey but exciting, in which I see the historic past. But now I have come back to earth and rain is beating on the attic window, an icy draught is blowing up the staircase and Ab has gone downstairs and left my stomach cold.

Heavens, how it is coming down! The rain is like a diagonal veil across Belmotte. Rain or shine, Belmotte always looks lovely. I wish it were Midsummer Eve and I were lighting my votive fire on the mound.

There is a bubbling noise in the cistern which means that Stephen is pumping. Oh, joyous thought, to-night is my bath night! And if Stephen is in, it must be tea-time. I shall go down and be very kind to everyone. Noble deeds and hot baths are the best cures for depression.

Chapter IV

LITTLE DID I THINK WHAT THE EVENING WAS TO BRING—
something has actually happened to us! My imagination longs
to dash ahead and plan developments; but I have noticed that
when things happen in one's imaginings, they never happen in
one's life, so I am curbing myself. Instead of indulging in
riotous hopes I shall describe the evening from the beginning,
quietly gloating—for now every moment seems exciting
because of what came later.

I have sought refuge in our barn. As a result of what
happened last night, Rose and Topaz are spring-cleaning the
drawing-room. They are being wonderfully blithe—when I
dwindled away from them Rose was singing "The Isle of
Capri" very high and Topaz was singing "Blow the Man
Down" very low. The morning is blithe too, warmer, with the
sun shining, though the countryside is still half-drowned. The
barn—we rent it to Mr. Stebbins but we owe him so much for
milk and butter that he no longer pays—is piled high with loose
chaff and I have climbed up on it and opened the square door
near the roof so that I can see out. I look across stubble and
ploughed fields and drenched winter wheat to the village,
where the smoke from the chimneys is going straight up in the
still air. Everything is pale gold and washed clean, and
hopeful.

When I came down from the attic yesterday, I found that
Rose and Topaz had dyed everything they could lay hands on,
including the dishcloth and the roller towel. Once I had dipped
my handkerchief into the big tin bath of green dye, I got
fascinated too—it really makes one feel rather godlike to turn
things a different colour. I did both my nightgowns and then
we all did Topaz's sheets, which was such an undertaking that

39

it exhausted our lust. Father came down for tea and was not too pleased that Topaz had dyed his yellow cardigan—it is now the colour of very old moss. And he thought our arms being green up to the elbows was revolting.

We had real butter for tea because Mr. Stebbins gave Stephen some when he went over to fix about working (he started at the farm this morning); and Mrs. Stebbins had sent a comb of honey. Stephen put them down in my place so I felt like a hostess. I shouldn't think even millionaires could eat anything nicer than new bread and real butter and honey for tea.

I have rarely heard such rain as there was during the meal. I am never happy when the elements go to extremes—I don't think I am frightened, but I imagine the poor countryside being battered until I end by feeling battered myself. Rose is just the opposite—it is as if she is egging the weather on, wanting louder claps of thunder and positively encouraging forked lightning. She went to the door while it was raining and reported that the garden was completely flooded.

"The lane'll be like a river," she remarked with satisfaction, not being a girl to remember that Thomas would have to ride his bicycle down it within an hour—he was staying late at school for a lecture. Father said:

"Let me add to your simple pleasure in Nature's violence by reminding you that there will shortly be at least six glorious new leaks in our roof."

There was one in the kitchen already; Stephen put a bucket under it. I told him the two attic leaks had started before I came down but there were buckets under them. He went to see if they were overflowing and returned to say that there were four more leaks. We had run out of buckets so he collected three saucepans and the soup-tureen.

"Maybe I'd best stay up there and empty them as they fill," he said. He took a book and some candle-ends and I thought how gloomy it would be for him reading poetry in the middle of six drips.

We washed the tea-things; then Rose and Topaz went to the wash-house to shake out the dyed sheets. Father stayed by the fire, waiting for the rain to stop before going back to the gatehouse. He sat very still, just staring in front of him. It struck me how completely out of touch with him I am. I went over and sat on the fender and talked about the weather; and then realized that I was making conversation as if to a stranger. It depressed me so much that I couldn't think of anything more to say. After a few minutes' silence, he said:

"So Stephen got work at Four Stones."

I just nodded and he looked at me rather queerly and asked if I liked Stephen. I said that of course I did, though the poems were embarrassing.

"You should tell him you know he copies them," said father. "You'll know how to do it—encourage him to write something of his own, however bad it is. And be very matter of fact with him, my child—even a bit on the brisk side."

"But I don't think he'd like that," I said. "I think he'd take briskness for snubbing. And you know how fond of me he's always been."

"Hence the need for a little briskness," said father. "Unless—— Of course, he's a godlike youth. I'm rather glad he's not devoted to Rose."

I must have been looking very much puzzled. He smiled and went on: "Oh, don't bother your head about it. You've so much common sense you'll probably do the right thing instinctively. It's no use telling Topaz to advise you because she'd think it all very splendid and natural—and for all I know, it might be. God knows what's to become of you girls."

I suddenly knew what he was talking about.

"I understand," I said, "and I'll be brisk—within reason."

But I wonder if I shall ever manage it. And I wonder if it is really necessary—surely Stephen's devotion isn't anything serious or grown-up? But now that the idea has been put into my head, I keep remembering how queer his voice sounded when he asked me about being hungry. It is worrying—but rather exciting . . . I shall stop thinking about it; such things are not in my line at all. They are very much in Rose's line and I know just what father meant when he said he was glad Stephen wasn't devoted to her.

Topaz came from the wash-house and set irons to heat, so father changed the subject by asking me if I'd dyed all my clothes green. I said I had few to dye.

"Any long dresses at all?" he asked.

"Nary a one," I replied—and, indeed, I cannot see the slightest chance of ever acquiring grown-up clothes. "But my school gym-dress has a lot of life in it yet and it's very comfortable."

"I must alter something of mine for her," said Topaz as she went back to the wash-house. I felt my lack of clothes was a reflection on father and, in an effort to talk of something else, said the most tactless thing possible

"How's the work?" I asked.

A closed-up look came over his face and he said shortly: "You're too old to believe in fairy tales."

I knew I had put my foot in it and thought I might as well go a bit further.

"Honestly, father—aren't you trying to write at all?"

"My dear Cassandra," he said in a cutting voice he very seldom uses, "it's time this legend that I'm a writer ceased. You won't get any coming-out dresses from *my* earnings."

He got up without another word and went upstairs. I could have kicked myself for wrecking the first talk we'd had for months.

Thomas came in just then, wet through. I warned him not to use father's bedroom as a passage, as we usually do, and he went up the front way. I took him some dry underclothes— fortunately the week's ironing was done—and then went up to see how Stephen was getting on.

He had stuck the candle-ends on the floor, close to his open book, and was reading lying on his stomach. His face was dazzlingly bright in the great dark attic—I stood a moment watching his lips moving before he heard me. The saucepans were on the point of overflowing. As I helped him to empty them out of the window I saw that the lamp was lit in the gate-house, so father must have gone back there through the rain. It was slackening off at last. The air smelt very fresh. I leaned out over the garden and found it was much warmer than indoors—it always takes our house a while to realize a change in the weather.

"It'll be spring for you soon, Miss Cassandra," said Stephen.

We stood sniffing the air.

"There's quite a bit of softness in it, isn't there?" I said. "I shall think of this as spring rain—or am I cheating? You know I always try to begin the spring too soon."

He leaned out and took a deep sniff.

"It's beginning all right, Miss Cassandra," he said. "Maybe we'll get some setbacks but it's beginning." He suddenly smiled, not at me but looking straight in front of him, and added: "Well, beginnings are good times." Then he closed the window and we put the saucepans back under the drips, which played a little ringing tune now that the saucepans were empty. The candle-ends on the floor cast the strangest shadows and made him seem enormously tall. I remembered what father had said about his being a godlike youth; and then I remembered that I had not remembered to be brisk.

We went back to the kitchen and I got Thomas some food. Topaz was ironing her silk tea-gown, which looked wonderful —it had been a faded blue, but had dyed a queer sea-green colour. I think the sight of it made Rose extra gloomy. She was starting to iron a cotton frock that hadn't dyed any too well.

"Oh, what's the use of messing about with summer clothes, anyway," she said. "I can't imagine it ever being warm again."

"There's quite a bit of spring in the air to-night," I told her. "You go out and smell it."

Rose never gets emotional about the seasons so she took no notice, but Topaz went to the door at once and flung it open. Then she threw her head back, opened her arms wide and took a giant breath.

"It's only a whiff of spring, not whole lungs full," I said, but she was too rapt to listen. I quite expected her to plunge into the night, but after some more deep breathing she went upstairs to try on her tea-gown.

"It beats me," said Rose. "After all this time, I still don't

43

know if she goes on that way because she really feels like it, if she's acting to impress us, or just acting to impress herself."

"All three," I said. "And as it helps her to enjoy life, I don't blame her."

Rose went to close the door and stood there a minute, but the night air didn't cheer her up at all. She slammed the door and said: "If I knew anything desperate to do, I'd do it."

"What's specially the matter with you, Rose?" asked Thomas. "You've been beating your breast for days and it's very boring. We can at least get a laugh out of Topaz, but you're just monotonously grim."

"Don't talk with your mouth full," said Rose. "I *feel* grim. I haven't any clothes, I haven't any prospects. I live in a mouldering ruin and I've nothing to look forward to but old age."

"Well, that's been the outlook for years," said Thomas. "Why has it suddenly got you down?"

"It's the long, cold winter," I suggested.

"It's the long, cold winter of my life," said Rose, at which Thomas laughed so much that he choked.

Rose had the sense to laugh a little herself. She came and sat on the table, looking a bit less glowering.

"Stephen," she said, "you go to church. Do they still believe in the Devil there?"

"Some do," said Stephen, "though I wouldn't say the Vicar did."

"The Devil's out of fashion," I said.

"Then he might be flattered if I believed in him—and work extra hard for me. I'll sell him my soul like Faust did."

"Faust sold his soul to get his youth back," said Thomas.

"Then I'll sell mine to live my youth while I've still got it," said Rose. "Will he hear me if I shout, or do I have to find a Devil's Dyke or Devil's Well or something?"

"You could try wishing on our gargoyle," I suggested. Although she was so desperate, she was—well, more playful than I had seen her for a long time and I wanted to encourage her.

"Get me the ladder, Stephen," she said.

What we call our gargoyle is really just a carved stone head high above the kitchen fireplace. Father thinks the castle chapel was up there, because there are some bits of fluted stonework and a niche that might have been for holy water. The old wall has been whitewashed so often that the outlines are blurred now.

"The ladder wouldn't reach, Miss Rose," said Stephen, "and the Vicar says that's the head of an angel."

"Well, it's got a devilish expression now," said Rose, "and the Devil was a fallen angel."

We all stared up at the head and it did look a bit devilish; its curls had been broken and the bits that were left were like horns.

"Perhaps it would be extra potent if you wished on an angel and thought of the Devil," I suggested, "like witches saying mass backwards."

"We could haul you up on the drying-rack, Rose," said Thomas.

The rack was pulled up high with the dyed sheets on it. Rose told Stephen to let it down, but he looked at me to see if I wanted him to. She frowned and went to the pulley herself. I said:

"If you must fool about with it, let me get the sheets off first." So she lowered them and Stephen helped me to drape them over two clothes-horses. Thomas held the rope while she sat on the middle of the rack and tested its strength.

"The rack'll bear you," said Stephen. "I helped make it and it's very strong. I don't know about the rope and pulleys."

I went and sat beside her, feeling that if the weight of both of us didn't break anything it would be safe for her alone. I knew from the look in her eye and her deep flush that it wasn't any use trying to dissuade her. We bounced about a bit and then she said:

"Good enough. Pull me up."

Stephen went to help Thomas. "But not you, Miss Cassandra," he said, "it's dangerous."

"I suppose you don't mind *me* breaking my neck," said Rose.

45

"Well, I'd rather you didn't," said Stephen, "but I know you wouldn't stop for the asking. Anyway, it's you who want to wish on the angel, not Miss Cassandra."

I'd have been glad to wish on anything, but I wouldn't have gone up there for a pension.

"It's a devil, not an angel, I tell you," said Rose. She sat swinging her legs a minute, then looked round at us all. "Does anyone dare me?"

"No!" we all shouted, which must have been very irritating. She said: "Then I dare myself. Haul me up."

Thomas and Stephen hauled. When she was about ten feet from the floor, I asked them to stop a minute.

"How does it feel, Rose?" I said.

"Peculiar, but a nice change. Go on, boys."

They pulled again. The carved head must be over twenty feet up and as she rose higher and higher I had an awful feeling in my stomach—I don't think I had realized until then how very dangerous it was. When she was within a few feet of the head, Stephen called up: "That's as high as the rack'll go."

She reached up but couldn't touch the head. Then she called down: "There's a foothold here—it looks as if there were steps once."

The next second she had leaned forward, grasped a projecting stone and stepped on to the wall. The lamp on the table didn't throw much light up there, but it looked terribly dangerous to me.

"Hurry up and get it over," I called. The backs of my legs as well as my stomach were most uncomfortable.

She only had to take one step up the wall to reach the head.

"He's no beauty at close quarters," she said. "What shall I say to him, Cassandra?"

"Pat him on the head," I suggested. "It must be hundreds of years since anyone showed him any affection."

Rose patted him. I got the lamp and held it high, but it was still shadowy up there. She looked extraordinary, almost as if she were flying up the wall or had been painted on it. I called out:

46

> "Heavenly devil or devilish saint,
>   Grant our wish, hear our plaint.
>   Godsend Castle a godsend craves——"

and then I got stuck.

"If he's a devil, it can only be a devilsend," said Thomas. Just then a car on the Godsend road hooted loudly and he added: "There's Old Nick come for you."

I saw Rose start. "Get me down!" she cried in a queer voice and flopped on to the rack. For one awful second I feared the boys might not be expecting the strain, but they were ready and lowered her carefully. As soon as her feet were near the ground she jumped off and sat down on the floor.

"The car horn startled me," she said rather shakily, "and I looked down and went giddy."

I asked her to describe her exact feelings up there, but she said she hadn't had any until she turned giddy. That is one great difference between us: I would have had any number of feelings and have wanted to remember them all; she would just be thinking of wishing on the stone head.

"You never did wish, did you?" I asked.

She laughed. "Oh, I said a few private things all right."

Topaz came downstairs just then, in her black oilskins, sou'wester hat and rubber boots, looking as if she were going to man the life-boat. She said her dyed tea-gown had shrunk so much that she couldn't breathe in it and Rose could have it. Then she strode out, leaving the door wide open.

"Don't *swallow* the night, will you?" Thomas called after her.

"Your luck's started already," I told Rose, as she dashed upstairs to try the tea-gown on. Thomas went to do his home-work in his room, so I thought I might as well start my bath and asked Stephen if he minded me having it in the kitchen; I generally do have it there but, as it means he has to keep out of the way for a good long time, I always feel apologetic. He tactfully said he had a job to do in the barn and that he would help me get the bath ready.

"But it's still full of dye," I remembered.

We emptied it and Stephen swilled it out.

"But I'm afraid the dye may still come off on you, Miss Cassandra," he said. "Hadn't you better use the bathroom?"

The bathroom bath is so enormous that there is never enough hot water for more than a few inches, and a draught blows down the tower. I decided I would rather risk the dye. We carried the bath to the fire and Stephen baled hot water from the copper and helped me to make a screen of clothes-horses with the green sheets on—as a rule, I use dust-sheets for this. As our clothes-horses are fully five feet high, I always have a most respectable and private bath, but I do feel more comfortable if I have the whole kitchen to myself.

"What will you have to read to-night, Miss Cassandra?" asked Stephen.

I told him Vol. BIS TO CAL of our old *Encyclopædia*, *Man and Superman* (which I have just re-borrowed from the Vicar—I feel I may have missed some of the finer points when I first read it five years ago) and last week's *Home Chat*, kindly lent by Miss Marcy. I like plenty of choice in my bath. Stephen set them all out for me while I collected my washing things. And then, after he had lit his lantern to go to the barn, he suddenly presented me with a whole twopenny bar of nut-milk chocolate.

"How *did* you come by that?" I gasped.

He explained that he had got it on credit, on the strength of having a job. "I know you like to eat in the bath, Miss Cassandra. What with books and chocolate, there's not much else you could have in it, is there? Except, perhaps, a wireless."

"Well, don't go getting a wireless on credit," I laughed; and then thanked him for the chocolate and offered him some. But he wouldn't take any and went off to the barn.

I was just getting into the bath when Heloïse whined at the back door and had to be let in. Of course she wanted to come to the fire, which was a slight bore as she is no asset to a bath—her loving paws are apt to scrape one painfully. However, she seemed sleepy and we settled down amicably. It was wonderfully cosy inside my tall, draught-proof screen; and the rosy glow from the fire turned the green sheets to a fascinating colour. I had the brainwave of sitting on our largest dinner-dish to avoid the dye; the gravy runnels were a bit uncomfortable, though.

I believe it is customary to get one's washing over first in baths and bask afterwards; personally, I bask first. I have discovered that the first few minutes are the best and not to be wasted—my brain always seethes with ideas and life suddenly looks much better than it did. Father says hot water can be as stimulating as an alcoholic drink and though I never come by one—unless the medicine-bottle of port that the Vicar gives me for my Midsummer rites counts—I can well believe it. So I bask first, wash second and then read as long as the hot water holds out. The last stage of a bath, when the water is cooling and there is nothing to look forward to, can be pretty disillusioning. I expect alcohol works much the same way.

This time I spent my basking in thinking about the family and it is a tribute to hot water that I could think about them and still bask. For surely we are a sorry lot: father mouldering in the gatehouse, Rose raging at life, Thomas—well, he is a cheerful boy but one cannot but know that he is perpetually underfed. Topaz is certainly the happiest for she still thinks it's romantic to be married to father and live in a castle; and her painting, her lute and her wild communing with nature are a great comfort to her. I would have taken a bet that she had nothing whatever on under her oilskins and that she intended to stride up the mound and then fling them off. After being an artists' model for so many years, she has no particular interest in Nudism for its own sake, but she has a passion for getting into closest contact with the elements. This once caused quite a little embarrassment with Four Stones Farm so she undertook only to go nude by night. Of course, winter is closed season for nudity, but she is wonderfully impervious to cold and I felt sure the hint of spring in the air would have fetched her. Though it was warmer, it was still far from warm, and the thought of her up on Belmotte made my bath more comfortable than ever.

I ate half my chocolate and meant to offer the rest to Rose, but Heloïse was lashing her tail so hopefully that I shared with her instead—her gratitude was so intense that I feared she might get in the bath with me. I calmed her, discouraged her from licking the soap and had just started serious washing when there was a thump on the door.

I still can't imagine what made me call out: "Come in." I suppose I said it automatically. I had just covered my face with soap, which always makes one feel rather helpless, and when I rashly opened my eyes, the soap got into them; I was blindly groping for the towel when I heard the door open. Heloïse let forth a volley of barks and hurtled towards it—it was a miracle she didn't knock the clothes-horses over. The next few seconds were pandemonium with Hel barking her hardest and two men trying to soothe her. I didn't call her off because I know she never bites anyone and I hated the idea of explaining I was in the bath—particularly as I hadn't even a towel to wrap around me; I had blinked my eyes open by then and realized I must have left it somewhere in the kitchen. Mercifully, Heloïse quietened down after a minute or so.

"Didn't you hear someone say 'Come in'?" said one of the men, and I realized that he was an American. It was a pleasant voice, like the nice people in American films, not the gangsters. He called out: "Anyone home?" but the other man told him to be quiet, adding: "I want to look at this place first. It's magnificent."

This voice puzzled me. It didn't sound English but it didn't sound American either, yet it certainly had no foreign accent. It was a most unusual voice, very quiet and very interesting.

"Do you realize that wall's part of an old castle?" it said.

This was not a happy moment as I thought he would come to look at the fireplace wall, but just then Thomas came out on the staircase. The men explained that they had turned down our lane by accident and their car was stuck in the mud. They wanted help to get it out.

"Or, if we have to leave it there all night, we felt we'd better warn you," said the American voice, "because it's blocking the lane."

Thomas said he would come and have a look and I heard him getting his boots from the wash-house.

"Wonderful old place you have here," said the unusual voice, and I feared they might ask to look round. But the other man began talking about how stuck the car was and asking if we had horses to pull it out, and in a minute or so Thomas went off with them. I heard the door slam and heaved a sigh of relief.

But I did feel a little flat; it was dull to think I had never even seen the men and never would. I tried to imagine faces to go with the voices—then suddenly realized that the water was cooling and I had barely begun washing. I got to work at last, but scrub as I might, I couldn't make any impression on my green-dyed arms. I am a thorough washer and by the time I had finished, my mind was completely off the men. I hopped out and got another can of hot water from the copper, which is close to the fire, and was just settling down to read when I heard the door open again.

Someone came into the kitchen and I was sure it wasn't any of the family—they would have called out to me or at least made a lot more noise. I could *feel* someone just standing and staring. After a moment I couldn't bear it any longer so I yelled out:

"Whoever you are, I warn you I'm in the bath here."

"Good heavens, I do beg your pardon," said the man with the quiet voice. "Were you there when we came in a few minutes ago?"

I told him I had been, and asked if the car was still stuck.

"They've gone for horses to pull it out," he said, "so I sneaked back to have a look round here. I've never seen anything like this place."

"Just let me get dried and in my right mind and I'll show you round," I said. I had mopped my face and neck on the drying sheets and still hadn't taken the cold walk to find the towel. I asked him if he could see it anywhere but he didn't seem able to, so I knelt in the bath, parted the green sheets and put my head through. He turned towards me. Seldom have I felt more astonished. He had a black beard.

I have never known anyone with a beard except an old man

in the Scoatney almshouses who looks like Santa Claus. This beard wasn't like that; it was trim and pointed—rather Elizabethan. But it was very surprising because his voice had sounded quite young.

"How do you do?" he said, smiling—and I could tell by his tone that he had taken me for a child. He found my towel and started to bring it over; then stopped and said: "There's no need to look so scared. I'll put it down where you can reach it, and go right back to the yard."

"I'm not scared," I said, "but you don't look the way you sound." He laughed, but it struck me that it had been rather a rude thing to say, so I added hastily: "There's no need to go, of course. Won't you sit down? I'm sure I've no desire to appear inhospitable"—and that struck me as the most pompous speech of my life.

I began to put one arm through the sheets for the towel.

"There'll be a catastrophe if you do it that way," he said. "I'll put it round the corner."

As I drew my head in I saw his hand coming round. I grabbed the towel from it and was just going to ask him to bring my clothes, too, when the door opened again.

"I've been looking for you everywhere, Simon," said the American voice. "This is the darnedest place—I've just seen a spook."

"Nonsense," said the bearded man.

"Honest, I have—while I was in the lane. I shone my flashlight up at that tower on the hill and a white figure flitted behind it."

"Probably a horse."

"Horse, nothing—it was walking upright. But—gosh, maybe I *am* going crazy—it didn't seem to have any legs."

I guessed Topaz must have kept her black rubber boots on.

"Stop talking about it, anyway," the bearded man whispered. "There's a child in a bath behind those sheets."

I called out for someone to bring my clothes, and put an arm round for them.

"My God—it's a *green* child!" said the American. "What is this place—the House of Usher?"

52

"I'm not green all over," I explained. "It's just that we've all been dyeing."

"Then maybe it was one of your ghosts I saw," said the American.

The bearded man came over with my clothes. "Don't worry about the ghost," he said. "Of course he didn't see one."

I said: "Well, he easily might, up on the mound, but it was more likely my stepmother communing with nature." I was out of the bath by then, with the towel draped around me respectably, so I put my head round to speak to him. It came out much higher than when I had been kneeling in the bath and he looked most astonished.

"You're a larger child than I realized," he said.

As I took the clothes, I caught sight of the other man. He had just the sort of face to go with his voice, a nice, fresh face. The odd thing was that I felt I knew it. I have since decided this was because there are often young men like him in American pictures—not the hero, but the heroine's brother or men on petrol stations. He caught my eye and said:

"Hello! Tell me some more about your legless stepmother— and the rest of your family. Have you a sister who plays the harp on horseback, or anything?"

Just then Topaz began to play her lute upstairs—she must have slipped in at the front door. The young man began to laugh.

"There she is," he said delightedly.

"That's not a harp, it's a lute," said the bearded man. "Now that really is amazing. A castle, a lute——"

And then Rose came out on to the staircase. She was wearing the dyed-green tea-gown, which is mediæval in shape with long flowing sleeves. She obviously didn't know that there were strangers in the house for she called out:

"Look, Cassandra!"

Both men turned towards her and she stopped dead at the top of the stairs. For once Topaz had her lute in tune. And she was, most appropriately, playing "Green Sleeves."

53

Chapter V

LATER. UP ON THE CHAFF IN THE BARN AGAIN.

I had to leave Rose stranded at the top of the stairs, because Topaz was ringing the lunch bell. She had been too busy to cook, so we had cold Brussels sprouts and cold boiled rice—hardly my favourite food but splendidly filling. We ate in the drawing-room, which has been cleaned within an inch of its life. In spite of a log fire, it was icy in there; I have noticed that rooms which are extra clean feel extra cold.

Rose and Topaz are now out searching the hedges for something to put in the big Devon pitchers. Topaz says that if they don't find anything she will get bare branches and tie something amusing to them—if so, I bet it doesn't amuse me; one would think that a girl who appreciates nudity as Topaz does would let a bare branch stay bare.

None of us is admitting that we expect the Cottons to call very soon, but we are all hoping it like mad. For that is who the two men were, of course : the Cottons of Scoatney, on their way there for the first time. I can't think why I didn't guess it at once, for I did know that the estate had passed to an American. Old Mr. Cotton's youngest son went to the States back in the early nineteen hundreds—after some big family row, I believe —and later became an American citizen. Of course, there didn't seem any likelihood of his inheriting Scoatney then, but two elder brothers were killed in the war and the other, with his only son, died about twelve years ago, in a car smash. After that, the American son tried to make it up with his father, but the old man wouldn't see him unless he undertook to become English again, which he wouldn't. He died about a year ago ; these two young men are his sons. Simon—he is the one with the beard—said last night that he had just persuaded

54

his grandfather to receive him when poor lonely old Mr. Cotton died, which seems very sad indeed.

The younger son's name is Neil, and the reason he sounds so different from his brother is that he was brought up in California, where his father had a ranch, while Simon lived in Boston and New York with the mother. (I gather the parents were divorced. Mrs. Cotton is in London now and is coming down to Scoatney soon.) Father says Simon's accent *is* American and that there are as many different accents in America as there are in England—more, in fact. He says that Simon speaks particularly good English, but of an earlier kind than is now fashionable here. Certainly he has a fascinating voice—though I *think* I like the younger brother best.

It is a pity that Simon is the heir, because Rose thinks the beard is disgusting; but perhaps we can get it off. Am I really admitting that my sister is determined to marry a man she has only seen once and doesn't much like the look of? It is half real and half pretence—and I have an idea that it is a game most girls play when they meet any eligible young men. They just . . . wonder. And if any family ever had need of wondering, it is ours. But only as regards Rose. I have asked myself if I am doing any personal wondering and in my deepest heart I am not. I would rather die than marry either of those quite nice men.

Nonsense! I'd rather marry both of them than die. But it has come to me, sitting here in the barn feeling very full of cold rice, that there is something revolting about the way girls' minds so often jump to marriage long before they jump to love. And most of those minds are shut to what marriage really means. Now I come to think of it, I am judging from books mostly, for I don't know any girls except Rose and Topaz. But some characters in books are very real—Jane Austen's are; and I know those five Bennets at the opening of *Pride and Prejudice*, simply waiting to raven the young men at Netherfield Park, are not giving one thought to the real facts of marriage. I wonder if Rose is? I must certainly try to make her before she gets involved in anything. Fortunately, I am not ignorant in such matters—no stepchild of Topaz's could be. I know all about the facts of life. And I don't think much of them.

It was a wonderful moment when Rose stood there at the top of the stairs. It made me think of Beatrix in *Esmond*—but Beatrix didn't trip over her dress three stairs from the bottom and have to clutch at the banisters with a green-dyed hand. But it all turned out for the best because Rose had gone self-conscious when she saw the Cottons—I could tell that by the way she was sailing down, graceful but affected. When she tripped, Neil Cotton dashed forward to help her and then everyone laughed and started talking at once, so she forgot her self-consciousness.

While I was hurrying into my clothes, behind the sheets, the Cottons explained who they were. They have only been in England a few days. I wondered how it would feel to be Simon —to be arriving by night for the first time, at a great house like Scoatney, knowing it belonged to you. For a second, I seemed to see with his eyes and knew how strange our castle must have looked, suddenly rising from the water-logged English countryside. I imagined him peering in through the window over the sink—as I bet he did before he came back without his brother. I think I got this picture straight from his mind, because just as it came to me, he said:

"I couldn't believe this kitchen was real—it was like looking at a woodcut in some old book of fairy tales."

I hope he thought Rose looked like a fairy-tale princess— she certainly did. And she was so charming, so easy; she kept laughing her pretty laugh. I thought of how different she had been in her black mood not half an hour before, and that made me remember her wishing on the devil-angel. Just then, a queer thing happened. Simon Cotton had seemed about equally fascinated by Rose and the kitchen—he kept turning from one to the other. He had taken out his torch—only he called it a flashlight—to examine the fireplace wall (I was dressed by then) and after he had shone it up at the stone head, he went to the narrow window that looks on to the moat, in the darkest corner of the kitchen. The torch went out and he turned it to see if the bulb had gone. And that second, it came on again. For an instant, the shadow of his head was thrown on the wall and, owing to the pointed beard, it was exactly like the Devil.

Rose saw it just as I did and gave a gasp. He turned to her quickly, but just then Heloïse walked through the green sheets and upset a clothes-horse, which created a diversion. I helped it on by calling, "Hel, Hel," and explaining Heloïse was sometimes called that for short—which went well, though a worn-out joke to the Mortmain family. But I couldn't forget the shadow. It is nonsense, of course—I never saw anyone with kinder eyes. But Rose is very superstitious. I wonder if the younger brother has any money. He was as nice to Rose as Simon Cotton was. And quite a bit nice to me.

There was one dramatic moment when Simon asked me if we owned the castle and I answered: "No—*you* do!"

I hastily added that we had nearly thirty years of our lease to run. I wonder if leases count if you don't pay the rent. I did not, of course, mention the rent. I felt it might be damping.

After we had all been talking for twenty minutes or so, Topaz came down wearing her old tweed coat and skirt. She rarely wears tweeds even in the daytime and never, never in the evening—they make her look dreary, just washed-out instead of excitingly white—so I was most astonished; particularly as the door of her room was slightly open and she must have known who had arrived. I have refrained from asking her why she made the worst of herself. Perhaps she thought the tweeds would give our family a county air.

We introduced the Cottons and she talked a little but seemed very subdued—what *was* the matter with her last night? After a few minutes she began to make cocoa—there was no other drink to offer except water; I had even used the last of the tea for Thomas and very dusty it was.

We never rise to cocoa in the evening unless it is a special occasion—like someone being ill, or to make up a family row—and I hated to think that Thomas and Stephen seemed likely to miss it; they were still away getting horses from Four Stones to pull the car out. I felt, too, that father ought to be

57

in on any form of nourishment that was loose in the house, but I knew it was useless to ask him to come and meet strangers— I was afraid that even if he came down for a biscuit, he would hear voices when he got as far as his bedroom and turn back. Suddenly, the back door burst open and in he came—it had started to rain heavily again and it is quicker to rush across the courtyard than go carefully along the top of the walls. He was freely damning the weather and the fact that his oil-stove had begun to smoke, and as he had his rug over his head, he didn't see the Cottons until he was right in the midst of things. Topaz stopped mixing cocoa and said very distinctly and proudly: "This is my husband, James Mortmain."

And then a wonderful thing happened. Simon Cotton said: "But—oh, this is a miracle! You must be the author of *Jacob Wrestling*."

Father stared at him with a look in his eyes that I can only describe as desperate. At first I thought it was because he had been cornered by strangers. Then he said: "Why, yes . . ." in a curious, tentative way and I suddenly realized that he was terribly pleased, but not quite believing. I can imagine a shipwrecked man, catching sight of a ship, looking like father did then. Simon Cotton came up and shook hands and introduced his brother, saying:

"Neil, you remember *Jacob Wrestling*?"

Neil said: "Yes, of course, he was splendid"—by which I knew that he thought Jacob Wrestling was the name of a character in the book, instead of meaning Jacob wrestling with the angel, as it really does. Simon began to talk of the book as if he had only just put it down, though I gathered gradually that he'd studied it in college, years ago. At first father was nervous and awkward, standing there with his rug clutched round him, but he got easier and easier until he was doing most of the talking, with Simon just getting in a word occasionally. And at last father flung the rug off as if it were hampering him and strode over to the table saying: "Cocoa, cocoa!"—it might have been the most magnificent drink in the world; which, personally, I think it is.

While we drank it conversation became more general.

Father chaffed us about our green hands and Neil Cotton discovered the dinner dish in the bath and thought it very funny that I had been sitting on it. All the time, Rose got nicer and nicer, smiling and gentle. She sat by the fire, nursing Ab, who is nearly the same colour as her hair, and the Cottons kept wandering over to stroke him. I could see they were fascinated by everything—when Heloïse jumped up to sleep on the warm top of the copper, Neil said it was the cutest thing he'd ever seen in his life. I didn't say very much myself —father and the Cottons did most of the talking—but the Cottons seemed to think everything I did say was amusing.

And then, just when everything was going so swimmingly, Simon Cotton asked the one question I had been praying he wouldn't ask. He turned to father and said:

"And when may we expect the successor to *Jacob Wrestling*?"

I knew I ought to create a diversion by upsetting my cocoa, but I did so want it. And while I was struggling with my greed, father answered:

"Never."

He didn't say it angrily or bitterly. He just breathed it. And I don't suppose anyone but me saw that he somehow deflated; the carriage of his head changed and his shoulders sagged. But almost before I had taken this in, Simon Cotton said:

"There couldn't be, of course, when one comes to think of it."

Father shot a look at him and he went on quickly:

"Certain unique books seem to be without forerunners or successors as far as their authors are concerned. Even though they may profoundly influence the work of other writers, for their creator they're complete, not leading anywhere."

Topaz was watching father as anxiously as I was.

"Oh, but surely——" she began protestingly. Father interrupted her.

"Do you mean that the writers of such books are often one-book men?" he asked, very quietly.

"Heaven forbid," said Simon Cotton. "I only mean that I

was wrong to use the word 'successor.' The originators among writers—perhaps, in a sense, the only true creators—dip deep and bring up one perfect work; complete, not a link in a chain. Later, they dip again—for something as unique. God may have created other worlds, but he obviously didn't go on adding to this one."

He said it in a rather stately, literary way but quite sincerely —and yet I didn't feel it was sincere. And I didn't feel it meant very much. I think it was really a kind and clever way of sliding over a difficult moment; though, if so, he must have been very quick to realize how difficult the moment was. The odd thing was that father seemed so impressed. He jerked his head as if some idea had just struck him, but he didn't answer —it was as if he wanted to think for a minute. Then Simon Cotton asked him a question about the third dream in *Jacob Wrestling* and he came to life again—I haven't seen him so alive since the year he married Topaz. And he didn't talk only about himself; after he had answered the question he drew us all in, particularly Rose—he kept saying things which made the Cottons turn to her, which they seemed very glad to do.

Neil Cotton didn't talk as much as his brother. Most of the time he sat on the copper with Heloïse. He winked at me once in a friendly way.

At last Thomas came in to say the horses were waiting. (There was enough cocoa left for him but none for Stephen, who had stayed with the horses. Luckily I had saved half mine and put it by the fire to keep warm.) Father and I sloshed down the lane with the Cottons to see the car hauled out— Rose couldn't come because of her tea-gown and Topaz didn't seem to want to. There was much pleasant confusion, with the Cottons flashing torches and everyone laughing and making the noises horses expect, and then the car was safely on the road again. After that, the good-byes were rather hurried, but both the Cottons said that they would see us again soon and I am sure that they meant it.

Stephen and Thomas took the horses back and father and I trudged home in the rain. The boys took the lantern so it was very dark—I need hardly say that our family hasn't possessed a working torch for years. Father held my arm firmly and seemed wonderfully cheerful. I asked him what he thought of the Cottons and he said: "Well, I shouldn't think they'd dun us for the rent." Then he said he had forgotten how stimulating Americans could be and told me interesting bits about his American lecture tours. And he said Simon Cotton was the Henry James type of American, who falls in love with England —"He'll make an admirable owner for Scoatney." The only Henry James novel I ever tried to read was *What Maisie Knew*, when I was about nine—I expected it to be a book for children. We had a beautiful plum-coloured edition of James's works then, but of course it got sold with the other valuable books.

As soon as we got back to the castle father went up to the gatehouse room and I rushed to join the girls. They were talking excitedly—Topaz had got over her quiet mood. She was sure Rose had made a hit, and started to plan how to alter a dress for her, a real London dress that Rose has always admired. And they decided about cleaning the drawing-room in case the Cottons called very soon. I said wasn't it wonderful that father actually seemed to like them. Through the back windows of the gatehouse, we could see him sitting at his desk. Topaz said:

"It's happened—the miracle! He's going to start work again!"

Stephen and Thomas came back and I made Stephen drink the cocoa I'd saved for him—I had to hold it ready to pour down the sink before he would take it. Then we went to bed. Rose got all her clothes out and draped them over Miss Blossom, to see if any of them were better than she remembered. They were worse. But even that didn't depress her.

We talked and talked. Suddenly I sat up in bed and said:

"Rose, we're working it up too much. We mustn't. Of course it'll be wonderful if we're asked to parties and things but—Rose, you couldn't *marry* that man with a beard?"

"I could marry the Devil himself if he had some money," said Rose.

I am pretty sure she was remembering Simon Cotton's shadow; but as she didn't mention it, I didn't. There is no point in working up a thing like that about a wealthy man.

After we had blown the candles out I made Miss Blossom talk—I can never think of the sort of things she says unless I pretend she is really saying them. When I asked her what she thought about it all, she answered:

"Well, it's a start, girlies, there's no denying that. Now you just make the best of yourselves. Of course all these old clothes you've draped over me won't help you much, but wash your hair and keep your hands nice—that green stuff on them's funny for once but the joke's over. And now you'd better think of your complexions and get some beauty sleep."

Rose certainly took the hint about the dye; this morning she scrubbed and scrubbed her hands until she got it all off. She used our last grains of scouring powder, so my dye will just have to wear off—it has now reached a grey stage which looks like dirt. Oh, I have just had an idea—after tea I shall attack myself with sandpaper.

How quickly life can change! This time yesterday it was a wintry blank—and now not only have we met the Cottons, but there is a real hint of spring. From up here in the barn I can see blackthorn buds on the hedges. . . . I have just discovered that by moving my head I can make the square opening, near the roof, frame different parts of the lane—it is rather a fascinating game——

Oh! Oh, my goodness! They're here—the Cottons—they've just come round the last bend of the lane! Oh, what am I to do? . . .

They have gone past. There was no way I could warn Rose and Topaz—I couldn't have got out of the barn without being seen. At least I know they are back from their walk because I heard Rose playing the piano some time ago. But how will they be dressed? And, heavens, Rose was thinking of washing her hair! Never did we dare to hope the Cottons would come this very day!

I watched them pass, through the hinge of the barn door; then scrambled up on the chaff again and watched until they disappeared into the gatehouse passage. Ought I to go in? I want to, of course—but there is a huge hole in my stocking and my gym-dress is all dusty from the chaff. . . .

It must be half an hour since I wrote that last line. I didn't go in. I have been lying here on the chaff thinking of them in the drawing-room with the log fire burning. It won't really matter if Rose did wash her hair, because it looks very beautiful when it is drying. I feel sure I did right to stay here—for one thing, I talk too much sometimes. I must be desperately careful never to distract attention from Rose. I keep telling myself it is real, it really has happened—we know two men. And they like us—they must, or they wouldn't have come back so soon.

I don't really want to write any more, I just want to lie here and think. But there is something I want to capture. It has to do with the feeling I had when I watched the Cottons coming down the lane, the queer separate feeling. I like seeing people when they can't see me. I have often looked at our family through lighted windows and they seem quite different, a bit the way rooms seen in looking-glasses do. I can't get the feeling into words—it slipped away when I tried to capture it.

Simon Cotton's black beard looks queerer than ever by daylight, especially now I have realized he isn't at all old—I should guess him to be under thirty. He has nice teeth and rather a nice mouth with a lot of shape to it. It has a peculiar naked look in the midst of all that hair. How *can* a young man like to wear a beard? I wonder if he has a scar?

His eyebrows go up at the corners.

Neil Cotton has such a charming face though no particular feature is striking. Very nice hair, fairish, curly. He looks very healthy; Simon is a bit pale. They're both tall; Simon a bit the taller, Neil a bit the broader. They don't look like brothers, any more than they sound it.

Simon is wearing tweeds, very English-looking.

Neil is wearing a coat such as I never saw in my life before: checked back and front, but plain sleeves. Perhaps it was made out of two old coats—though I hope not, as that would show him to be poor and his brother mean. And it looked rather a noisily new coat. I expect it's just American.

They're coming out of the castle! Shall I run to meet them and just shake hands? No, not with these grey hands . . .

Something awful has happened—so awful that I can hardly bear to write it. Oh, how could they, how could they?

As they came towards the barn, I heard them talking. Neil said: "Gosh, Simon, you're lucky to get away with your life."

"Extraordinary, wasn't it?" said Simon. "She didn't give that impression at all last night." Then he turned to look back at the castle and said: "What a wonderful place! But hellish uncomfortable. And they obviously haven't a cent. I suppose one can't blame the poor girl."

"One can blame her for being so darned obvious," said Neil. "And that ridiculous dress—at this time of the day! Funny, I rather liked her in it last night."

"The stepmother seems quite pleasant. She looked about as uncomfortable as I felt. My God, how that girl embarrassed me!"

"We shall have to drop them, Simon. If we don't, she may put you in a very awkward position."

Simon said he supposed so. They were talking quietly, but it was so still that every word came to me clearly. As they passed the barn, Neil said:

"Pity we didn't see the child again. She was a cute kid."

"A bit consciously naïve, don't you think?" said Simon. "I shall feel worst about dropping the old man—I'd rather hoped I could help him. But I don't suppose there's much one can do if he's a hopeless drunk."

Oh, I could kill them! When father doesn't even get enough to eat, let alone any strong drink! They must have heard some lying gossip. How dare people say he drinks! And he isn't an old man—he's not yet fifty.

I didn't hear any more. I wish now that I had rushed out and hit them. That would have shown them if I am consciously naïve!

What on earth did Rose do? I must go in.

Eight o'clock. In the drawing-room.

I have come in here to get away from Rose. She is drying her hair in the kitchen and manicuring her nails with a sharpened match. And she is talking, talking. I don't know how Topaz can stand it, knowing what she does know—for I couldn't keep it to myself, I couldn't bear to. I might have done if I hadn't found her alone when I got in; but I did and she saw that I was upset. I began to tell her in a whisper— ours is a dreadful house for being overheard in—but she said : "Wait," and pulled me out into the garden. We could hear Rose singing upstairs, so we didn't talk until we had crossed the bridge and gone a little way up the mound.

Topaz wasn't as furious as I had expected—but, of course, I didn't tell her the bit about father. She wasn't even surprised. She said Rose had seen the Cottons coming from her bedroom window and nothing would stop her changing into the tea-gown. (As if anyone ever wore a tea-gown for tea!) And she had behaved insanely, making a dead set at Simon Cotton.

"Do you mean she was too nice to him?"

"Not exactly—that mightn't have mattered so much. She was terribly affected, she kept challenging him—if she'd had a fan she'd have tapped him with it and said 'Fie, fie!' And she fluttered her eyelids. It'd all have been very fetching a hundred years ago."

Oh, I could see it! Rose got it out of old books. We've never known any modern women except Topaz, and Rose would never dream of copying her. Oh, poor, poor Rose—she never even saw modern girls on the pictures, as I did.

"They won't come back," said Topaz. "I'd have known that, even if you hadn't overheard what they said."

I said we didn't want them, that they must be hateful people to talk like that. But Topaz said that was nonsense— "Rose asked for it. Men don't really mind your showing you like them when you do, but they run a mile from obvious fascination—that's what it was, of course, all the challenging and head-tossing, and all directed at Simon in the crudest way. If Mortmain had been in he might have chaffed her out of it—anyway, he'd have talked to them himself. Oh, blast!"

65

Father had gone for a walk—the first he has taken for months. Topaz said Simon Cotton had brought him a book by a famous American critic because one of the essays in it dealt with *Jacob Wrestling*.

"I suppose Simon just might come back to talk to Mortmain," she said. But I knew better.

It was beginning to get dark. There was a light down in the kitchen. We saw Rose pass the window.

"Shall we tell her?" I said.

Topaz thought not—unless we ever get asked to Scoatney— "If we do, we might try to kick some sense into her."

We won't get asked.

Topaz put her arm round me and we trudged down the mound—very awkwardly because she takes longer strides than I can. When we got to the bottom she looked back at Belmotte Tower, dark against the twilight sky.

"Beautiful, isn't it?" she said in her most velvety tones.

Now could she really be interested in beauty at such a moment? Incidentally, when she painted the tower she made it look like a black rolling-pin on an overturned green pudding-basin.

My candle is burning out and the drawing-room is getting colder and colder—the fire has been out for hours; but I can't write this in the same room with Rose. When I look at her I feel I am watching a rat in a trap that hopes it will get out when I know it won't. Not that I ever watched a rat in a trap, nor does Rose think she is in one; but this is no moment to be finicky about metaphors.

Heloïse has just pushed the door open and come in and licked me, which is kind but so chilly as I dry. And I can now hear what is going on in the kitchen far more fully than I could wish. Father is there now and is talking excitedly—he says the American critic has discovered things in *Jacob Wrestling* that *he* certainly never put there and that the arrogance of critics is beyond belief. He is obviously enjoying the thought of discussing it all with Simon Cotton. Rose's exuberance has risen higher and higher. I regret to say that she is now whistling.

Stephen has been in and put his coat round me. It smells of horses.

Am I consciously naïve? Perhaps I am, perhaps this journal is. In future I will write it in stark prose. But I won't really write it at all any more, because I have come to the end of this exercise book—I have already used both inside covers and am now crossing my writing, and crossed speed-writing will probably never come uncrossed.

It must be just twenty-four hours since those Cottons walked in on me in my bath.

Topaz has just yelled that she is making cocoa. Oh, comfortable cocoa! Not so good—Topaz has now yelled that it will have to be made with water because the Cottons drank the milk; there was no tea to offer them. Still, any kind of cocoa is good. But it will be agony to know that Rose will think we are having it to celebrate, while Topaz and I know that it is funeral baked meats.

THE END

SLAM THE BOOK SHUT

II. THE SHILLING BOOK

April and May

Chapter VI

I HAVE A NEW EXERCISE BOOK, THE FINEST I EVER SAW. IT cost a whole shilling! Stephen got Miss Marcy to buy it in London last week; she went up on a cheap day-ticket. When he gave it to me, I thought I would write something like *Wuthering Heights* in it—I never dreamt that I should want to go on with this journal. And now life has begun all over again.

I am up on Belmotte. Spring has come with such a bound that catkins are still dangling on the hazels while daisies are rushing out on the mound—I particularly love them in the short, brilliant grass of the motte, where they look like spring in a child's picture-book as well as the real spring. There are daffodils down in the courtyard garden but I can't see them from here because the washing is flapping; Topaz keeps coming out with more and more things to peg up, and they are all part of the exciting happenings. I have been leaning back against the tower quietly gloating, watching the dazzling white clouds move past—there is quite a breeze but a soft, almost summery one.

It is six weeks to-day since Topaz and I stood on Belmotte in the dusk with life at its lowest ebb—though it ebbed a great deal lower afterwards. At first only Topaz and I were miserable; it was a terrible strain not to show it—we used to slip off for long walks together and let our faces fall. Rose's exuberance lasted about ten days; then she began to feel something else ought to happen. I staved her off for another week by suggesting Mrs. Cotton's arrival must have kept her sons busy. Then the blow fell: Miss Marcy told us that the Vicar had gone over to call and been asked to lunch, and that various Scoatney people had been invited there.

"But no one but the Vicar from Godsend?" I said hastily.

But there *is* no one else in Godsend they would ever ask, except us.

"Your turn next, dears," said Miss Marcy. Rose got up and walked straight out of the kitchen.

That night, after we were in bed, she suddenly said:

"Ask Miss Blossom what went wrong, Cassandra."

I was absolutely stuck—I felt I ought to edge in some advice for the future but I couldn't see how, without telling the brutal truth.

"She says she doesn't know," I said at last. I didn't make Miss Blossom say it herself because I think of her as very sincere.

"I expect it's because we're so poor," said Rose, bitterly. Then she sat up in the iron bedstead (it was my week for the four-poster) and said: "I *was* nice to them—really I was."

I saw my chance and said in Miss Blossom's voice:

"Perhaps you were *too* nice, dearie."

"But I wasn't," said Rose. "I was charming but I was—oh, capricious, contradictory. Isn't that what men like?"

"You just be natural, girlie," said Miss Blossom. Then I went on in my own voice: "How much did you really like them, Rose?"

"I don't know—but I know I don't like them now. Oh, I don't want to talk about it."

And that was all she ever did talk about it—that was almost the worst part of the gloom, our not talking naturally. Never have I felt so separate from her. And I regret to say that there were moments when my deep and loving pity for her merged into a desire to kick her fairly hard. For she is a girl who cannot walk her troubles off, or work them off; she is a girl to sit around and glare.

Topaz was wonderfully patient—but I sometimes wonder if it is not only patience, but also a faint resemblance to cows. It is rather like her imperviousness to cold; father once said she had a plush-lined skin and there are times when I think she has plush-lined feelings. But they certainly aren't plush-lined where father himself is concerned. Three weeks ago I found her crying in Buffer State in front of her portrait of him—for which he never sits. (It is mostly orange triangles.) She said his disappointment was far more important than Rose's, that he had so much enjoyed meeting Simon Cotton and was longing to talk about the American essay on *Jacob Wrestling*.

"Particularly now he's changed his mind about it—he now thinks he *did* mean all the things the critic says he did. And I was sure it had started him writing. But I've just sneaked into the gatehouse while he's over at the vicarage, and what do you think he's working on? Crossword puzzles!"

I suggested there might be money in crossword puzzles.

"Not that kind," said Topaz. "They didn't make sense. Cassandra, what *is* the matter with him?"

I had a most dreadful thought. I wondered if father really had been drinking for years, if he had found a secret wine-cellar under the castle, or was making drink out of something— I know there is some stuff called *wood*-alcohol.

"Oh, don't be idiotic," said Topaz. "You can tell if men are drinking. We must be patient—it's just that he's a genius."

She went to bathe her eyes, and then put on her favourite dress, which is cream satin-damask—Italian—just about dropping to pieces; she wears a little ruby-red cap with it. Then she went down to make potato-cakes for tea.

I was in the garden, looking at a daffodil that was almost out, when father came back from the vicarage.

"Any news?" I called, to be friendly.

"Only that it appears to be quite a distinction *not* to be asked to Scoatney. I gather invitations are being broadcast."

He said it in his loftiest manner; then gave me a quick little embarrassed smile and added: "I'm sorry, my child. You know what the trouble is, don't you?"

I stared at him and he went on: "It's the rent—they've looked into that little matter. I know, because the usual application didn't come in on the March quarter-day. Oh, they're kind enough—the best type of American always is; but they don't want to get involved with us."

I knew Topaz hadn't told him the truth; partly because she thought it would upset him and partly because she has a sort

73

ot women-must-stick-together attitude. I wondered if I ought to tell him myself. And then I decided that if he did feel guilty about the rent it would be a good thing—anything, anything to prod him into working. But as he stood there in his thin old coat, with the March wind blowing his fading gold hair, I felt very sorry for him; so I told him there were potato-cakes for tea.

As it turned out, the potato-cakes were spoilt; because while we were eating them, we had one of those family rows which are so funny in books and on the pictures. They aren't funny in real life, particularly when they happen at meals, as they so often do. They always make me shake and feel rather sick. The trouble arose because Thomas asked Rose to pass the salt three times and she took no notice, and when he shouted at her, she leaned forward and boxed his ears. Topaz said: "Blast you, Rose, you know Thomas gets ear-ache." And Rose said: "You would bring that up—I suppose he'll die and I'll be responsible." Father said: "Damnation!" and pushed his chair back on to Heloïse, who yelped. And I said: "I can't stand it, I can't stand it," which was ridiculous. Stephen was the only person who kept calm; he got up quietly to see if Heloïse was badly hurt. She wasn't, and she came off very well because we gave her most of the potato-cakes. Our appetites came back later when there was nothing worth eating.

Food isn't much better, in spite of Stephen's wages coming in regularly, because we have to go slow until the tradesmen's bills are paid off. Stephen keeps back a shilling a week—this exercise book came out of his savings. I have an uneasy feeling he will spend most of them on me; he certainly spends nothing on himself. He hasn't brought me any poems lately, which is a relief.

That evening of the row was our lowest depths; miserable people cannot afford to dislike each other. Cruel blows of fate call for extreme kindness in the family circle.

Had we but known it, our fortunes were already slightly on the mend, for that was the very day father's Aunt Millicent died. How dreadfully callous I sound! But if I could bring her back to life, truly I would; and as I can't, there seems no harm

74

in thanking God for His wondrous ways. For she left Rose and me her personal wardrobe—which means clothes, not a piece of furniture as I thought at first. When the Vicar saw the death announced in *The Times* we entertained a faint hope that she might have left father some money; but she had cut him out of her will and left everything to a hostel for artists' models—I suppose she thought they ought to stick in hostels and not go marrying her relations. ("Just think," said Rose, "if father hadn't married Topaz we might be rolling in wealth by now." And I asked myself if I would rather roll than have Topaz in the family and decided I wouldn't, which was nice to know.)

After the first exuberance had worn off, we remembered that Aunt Millicent was seventy-four and an eccentric dresser. But to be left anything at all gives one a lift.

The lawyers wrote asking us to come to London and pack the clothes ourselves; they said they would pay all expenses. The prospect of a day in London was heaven, but the problem of what to wear was sheer hell, particularly for Rose—my clothes don't bear thinking about, so I just don't think about them. We sponged and pressed our winter coats and tried to believe that they looked better. And then the weather turned fine—those coats were utterly revolting in the brilliant sunshine. I had a sudden idea.

"Let's wear our old white suits," I said.

Aunt Millicent had them made for us just before the row about father marrying Topaz. They are some kind of silky linen, very plain and tailored. Of course they have had very hard wear and mine is too short, though it has been let down to the last quarter-inch; but they are much the nicest things we have and, by a miracle, had been put away clean.

"They'd be all right if it was midsummer," said Rose, when we tried them on. "But in April——!" Still, we decided to wear them if the fine weather held. And when we woke up yesterday it was more like June than April. Oh, it was the most glorious morning! I suppose the best kind of spring morning is the best weather God has to offer. It certainly helps one to believe in Him.

Mr. Stebbins lent Stephen his cart to drive us to the station and even the horse seemed to be enjoying himself.

"Did you ever see the sky so high?" I said. And then I felt ashamed to be so happy, knowing that I couldn't have been if Aunt Millicent had stayed alive—and it probably hurt her to die, poor old lady. We were driving through Godsend and the early sun was striking the moss-grown headstones in the churchyard. I tried to realize that I shall die myself one day; but I couldn't believe it—and then I had a flash that when it really happens I shall remember that moment and see again the high Suffolk sky over the old, old Godsend graves.

Thinking of death—strange, beautiful, terrible and a long way off—made me feel happier than ever. The only depressing thing was seeing Scoatney Hall through the trees—and that only damped me on Rose's account, for what care I for Cottons? (Anyway, what cared I *then*?) I was careful to avoid her eye until we were well past the park, spending two tactful minutes buttoning a one-buttoned shoe.

We got to Scoatney station in good time. Rose thought we should take first-class tickets as the lawyers would pay.

"But suppose they don't pay at once?" I said. We had Stephen's wages to see us through the day, but Topaz was counting on getting them back. In the end, we just took cheap day-tickets.

Stephen kept begging me to be careful of the traffic; he even ran along with the train to remind me again. Then he stood waving, smiling but a bit wistful-looking. It struck me that never in his life has he been to London.

It was queer how different things felt after we changed from our little toy train, at King's Crypt. The feel of the country went—it was as if the London air was trapped in the London train. And our white suits began to look peculiar. They looked much, much more peculiar when we got to London; people really stared at us. Rose noticed it at once.

"It's because they *admire* our suits," I said, hoping to soothe her—and I did think they looked nicer than most of the drab clothes women were wearing.

"We look conspicuous," she said, with deepest shame. Little

76

did she know how much more conspicuous we should look before we got home.

It was three years since we had been in London. We never knew it well, of course; yesterday was the first time I ever walked through the City. It was fascinating, especially the stationers' shops—I could look at stationers' shops for ever and ever. Rose says they are the dullest shops in the world except, perhaps, butchers'. (I don't see how you can call butchers' shops dull; they are too full of horror.) We kept getting lost and having to ask policemen, who were all rather playful and fatherly. One of them kindly held up the traffic for us, and a taxi-driver made kissing noises at Rose.

I had hoped the lawyers' office would be old and dark, with a Dickensy old lawyer; but it was just an ordinary office and we only saw a clerk, who was young, with very sleek hair. He asked us if we could find our way to Chelsea by 'bus.

"No," said Rose, quickly.

He said: "O.K. Take a taxi."

I said we were a little short of change. Rose flushed scarlet. He gave her a quick look, then said: "Wait a sec."—and left us.

He came back with four pounds.

"Mr. Stevenage says you're to have this," he told us. "It'll take care of your fares, taxi to Chelsea, taxi to get the stuff to the station, and a slap-up lunch. And you must nip back here with the key of the house and sign a receipt. See?"

We said we saw, and went. Rose was furious that no one more important than a clerk had bothered to see us.

"It's not respectful to Aunt Millicent," she said, indignantly. "Treating us like small fry!"

I didn't mind what kind of fry I was, with four pounds in hand.

"Let's find our way by 'bus and save the taxi money," I suggested.

But she said she couldn't stand being stared at any more. "We must be the only girls in London wearing white." Just then a 'bus-conductor said: "Hop on, snowdrops." She haughtily hailed a taxi.

The lily-pond was dry in Aunt Millicent's little flagged

77

garden. I hoped the goldfish had found good homes.

We unlocked the front door. I was surprised to find the hall quite bare—I hadn't realized that all the furniture had been taken away.

"It does feel queer," I said when the door was closed and the sunny day shut out.

"It only feels cold," said Rose. "I suppose the clothes'll be in her bedroom. I wonder if she died there."

I thought it a tactless thing to wonder out loud.

On our way up we looked in at the double drawing-room. The two tall windows stared across the Thames; it was dazzlingly light. The last time I had seen that room it had been lit by dozens of candles for a party. That was the night we first met Topaz. Macmorris's portrait of her had just been exhibited and Aunt Millicent asked him to bring her with him. She wore the misty blue dress he painted her in and he had lent her the great jade necklace. I remember being astonished at the long, pale hair hanging down her back. And I remember father talking to her all evening and Aunt Millicent, in her black velvet suit and lace stock, glaring at him.

There was nothing in the big front bedroom, much to my relief; though I can't say it felt as if anyone had died there, merely cold and empty. The clothes were in the little back dressing-room, lying in heaps on the floor, with two old black leather trunks for us to pack them in. There was very little light because the green venetian blind was down. The cord was broken so we couldn't get it up, but we managed to tilt the slats a little.

Aunt Millicent's old black military cloak lay on top of one of the heaps. It used to frighten me when I was little; I suppose it made me think of witches. It was frightening yesterday, too, but in a different way—it seemed somehow to be part of a dead person. All the clothes did. I said:

"Rose, I don't think I can touch them."

"We've got to," she said, and started to rummage through them.

Perhaps if we had ever been fond of poor Aunt Millicent we might have felt a kindness for her clothes. Perhaps if they had been pretty and feminine it wouldn't have been so horrible. But they were mostly heavy, dark coats and skirts and thick woollen underwear. And rows and rows of flat-heeled shoes on wooden trees, which upset me most of all—I kept thinking of them as dead feet.

"There are dozens of linen handkerchiefs, that's something," said Rose. But I hated the handkerchiefs—and the gloves and the stockings; and a dreadful pair of broken-looking corsets.

"People's clothes ought to be buried with them," I said. "They oughtn't to be left behind to be despised."

"I'm not despising them," said Rose. "Some of these suits are made of wonderful cloth."

But she was bundling them into the trunks in a somehow insulting way. I made myself take them out and fold them carefully, and had a mental picture of Aunt Millicent looking relieved.

"She always liked her suits to be well pressed and brushed," I said.

"As if it mattered to her now!" said Rose.

And then we heard someone coming upstairs.

I went icy cold from my heart up to my shoulders. Then the fear got into my throat so that I couldn't speak. I just stared at Rose, in agony.

"It isn't, it isn't!" she gasped. "Oh, Cassandra—it *isn't*!"

But I knew that she thought it was. And I knew, in the way I so often know things about Rose, that she had been frightened ever since we entered the house, that the casual way she handled the clothes had been all bluff. But I didn't know then that she was doubly frightened, that she thought if it wasn't Aunt Millicent coming up the stairs it was a tramp who had been hiding in the basement—that he would kill us both and put our bodies in the trunks.

Oh, wonderful Rose! With both these fears in her mind, she flung open the door and said: "Who's there?"

The lawyers' clerk stood outside.

"How dare you, how dare you?" she cried, furiously. "Sneaking into the house, terrifying my little sister——"

"Don't, Rose!" I said in a weak voice.

79

The poor clerk apologized profusely. "And I only came to do you a good turn," he finished. Then he handed her a letter.

Rose read it. "But we can't pay this!"

I snatched it from her. It was a reminder that money was owing for the cold-storage of some furs.

"You don't have to pay anything, I fixed that by telephone," said the clerk. "We're your aunt's executors so we get her bills, see? That was actually on my desk when you came in this morning but I hadn't got round to reading it. Those are *your* furs now."

"But Aunt Millicent never had any furs," I said. "She thought they were cruel to animals." And I always thought she was right.

"Well, those belonged to her," said the clerk, "and cruel or not, you'd better pop along and get them. Furs are worth money."

I looked at the letter again. It didn't say what the furs were.

"They must be good ones if she paid out all that to store them," said the clerk. "Tell you what, you shove all this stuff in the trunks and I'll take them down to the station—leave them in the Left Luggage Office for you, see? And you cut along for the furs."

We bundled the clothes in hurriedly—I am ashamed to say I forgot about Aunt Millicent's dead feelings. The clerk and his taxi-driver dragged the trunks downstairs; then he got another taxi for us.

"Wish I could come with you and see the fun," he said, "but I'm due in the Courts at three." His hair was oily and his complexion spotty, but his heart was kind. Rose evidently thought so, too, because she leaned out of the taxi and said she was sorry she had been so cross.

"Don't mention it," he said. "I'm sure I'd have given myself a fright if I'd been you." Then the taxi started and he shouted after us: "Here's hoping they're sables."

We hoped so, too.

"They must be fairly new as she didn't have them when we knew her," said Rose. "I expect her principles dwindled as she got older and colder."

"They'll probably be rabbit," I said, feeling I ought to damp our imaginings; but I didn't really believe Aunt Millicent would have worn anything cheap.

The taxi drew up at a wonderful shop—the sort of shop I would never dare to walk through without a reason. We went in by way of the glove and stocking department, but there were things from other departments just dotted about; bottles of scent and a little glass tree with cherries on it and a piece of white branched coral on a sea-green chiffon scarf. Oh, it was an artful place—it must make people who have money want to spend it madly!

The pale grey carpets were as springy as moss and the air was scented; it smelt a bit like bluebells but richer, deeper.

"What *does* it smell of, exactly?" I said. And Rose said: "Heaven."

There was a different scent in the fur department, heavier, and the furs themselves had an exciting smell. There were lots of them lying about on the grey satin sofas; deep brown, golden brown, silvery. And there was a young, fair mannequin walking about in an ermine cape over a pink gauze dress, with a little muff. A woman with blue-white hair came and asked if she could help us and took away our storage bill; and after a while, two men in white coats came in with Aunt Millicent's furs and dumped them on a sofa.

We shook them out and examined them. There were two very long coats, one of them black and shaggy and the other smoothish and brown; a short, black tight-fitting jacket with leg o' mutton sleeves; and a large hairy rug with a green felt border.

"But what ever animals were they?" I gasped.

The white-haired woman inspected them gingerly. She said the brown coat was beaver and the short jacket, which had a rusty look under its black, was sealskin. She couldn't identify the rug at all—it looked like collie dog to me. Rose tried the long shaggy black coat on. It reached to the ground.

"You look like a bear," I said.

"It *is* bear," said the white-haired woman. "Dear me, I think it must have been a coachman's coat."

81

"There's something in the pocket," said Rose.

She drew out a piece of paper. On it was scrawled: *Meet madam's train 1.20. Miss Milly to dancing class at 3. The young ladies to the Grange at 6.*

I worked it out: Aunt Millicent was father's father's youngest sister. These furs must have been her mother's. That made them—"Heavens!" I cried. "These belonged to our great-grandmother."

A sort of manager person came and talked to us. We asked him if there was anything valuable.

"You couldn't get the beaver to-day for love or money," he said, "but I don't know if you can sell it for much. We treat furs so differently now. It weighs a ton."

The shop didn't buy second-hand furs and he couldn't advise us where to take them. We felt that London was the most likely place to sell them in and wanted to leave them until we could get advice from Topaz; but he said that if they stayed any longer they would run into another quarter's storage charges and Aunt Millicent's lawyers probably wouldn't pay any more. So we said we would take them over our arms —it seemed the only way. We signed things and then loaded up. On the way out, we looked through the archway into the department we had come in by. There was a woman buying pale blue suède gloves. She wore the plainest little black suit, but Rose thought she looked wonderful.

"That's how we ought to dress," she said.

We stood there staring at the scent and stockings and things—we saw one woman buy a *dozen* pairs of silk stockings —until I said:

"We're like Ab when he sees birds fly past the window. At any moment we'll let out wistful cat noises."

Rose said she felt just like that.

"Well, let's walk round the whole shop while we're in it," I suggested. But she said she couldn't bear to, loaded up with furs; so I put my head through the archway and took one big sniff of the bluebell scent, and then we went out of the main door, which was close at hand.

Rose wanted to take the furs straight back to the City by

taxi, but there wasn't one to be seen and I was so ravenous that I persuaded her we ought to have something to eat first. We tottered to Oxford Street—those furs certainly did weigh tons—and found a place with nice white tablecloths and great round cruets. It was a bit of a business getting ourselves settled; we tried folding the furs and sitting on them, but then found we could reach neither the floor nor our plates. In the end we had to dump everything down beside us, which was rather unpopular with the waitress. But I did like the restaurant; most of the people eating there were unusually ugly, but the food was splendid. We had roast chicken (wing portion, two shillings), double portions of bread sauce (each), two vegetables, treacle pudding and wonderful milky coffee. We were gloriously bloat. By the time we finished it was getting on for four o'clock.

"We've seen hardly anything of London," I said, as we drove back to the lawyers'. Rose said she wouldn't have wanted to even if we hadn't been burdened with the furs, because it was no fun being in London in the wrong clothes. After that, she was quiet so long that I asked her what she was thinking about.

"I was willing God to give me a little black suit," she said.

Our friend the clerk laughed his head off at the furs, but he said it was a damned shame. He thought the beaver must have been a man's travelling coat—it was too big for *him*, even—and that the beaver was the lining and the Scotch plaid was the right side. He gave us cups of tea and two squashed-fly biscuits each, but we were too full to eat them; so we put them in an envelope for the journey. When we got the old leather trunks from the Left Luggage Office, the man asked if there were any bodies in them. It was then Rose told me how she had feared that there might have been—ours.

We had a compartment to ourselves on the train and, as it turned cold after sunset, I put on the beaver coat, fur side inwards. It felt wonderfully friendly. It was extraordinary, I had the most affectionate feelings for all those furs—no horror of them at all, as I had of Aunt Millicent's clothes, though I knew they must all have been worn by dead people.

I thought about it a lot, getting warmer and warmer in the beaver, and I decided that it was like the difference between the beautiful old Godsend graves and the new ones open to receive coffins (which I never can bear to look at); that time takes the ugliness and horror out of death and turns it into beauty.

A year ago, I would have made a poem out of that idea. I tried to, yesterday, but it wasn't any use. Oh, I could think of lines that rhymed and scanned but that is all they were. I know now that is all my poems ever were, yet I used to feel I could leap over the moon when I had made one up. I miss that rather.

I leaned back and closed my eyes—and instantly the whole day danced before me. I wasn't merely remembering, it seemed to be trapped inside my eyelids; the City, the traffic, the shops were all there, shimmering, merging. Then my brain began to pick out the bits it wanted to think about and I realized how the day made a pattern of clothes—first our white dresses in the early morning, then the consciousness of what people were wearing in London, then Aunt Millicent's poor dead clothes, then all the exquisite things in the shop, then our furs. And I thought how important clothes were to women and always had been. I thought of Norman ladies in Belmotte tower-keep, and Plantagenet ladies living in Godsend Castle, and Stuart ladies when our house was built on the ruins—and hoops and Jane Austen dresses and crinolines and bustles, and Rose longing for a little black suit. I had the most profound, philosophic thoughts about it all, but perhaps I dreamt them for they all seem to have floated away. When Rose woke me I was dreaming of the white branched coral on the sea-green chiffon scarf.

It was time to change trains. I felt frozen when I took the beaver coat off—I thought I had better because it not only looked peculiar, but trailed on the ground. I was thankful when we were in our little branch-line train and I could put it on again. Rose put on the coachman's coat and we each leaned out of a window to smell the sweet country smell—you don't notice it unless you have been away. We still had our squashed-fly biscuits so we ate them leaning out into the night; only I saved one of mine for Stephen who was to meet us with Mr. Stebbins's cart to take the trunks.

And then it happened. As we stopped at Little Lymping, I looked towards the guard's van to make sure our trunks didn't get pulled out by mistake—the stationmaster is a bit daft. And there, looking out of the train, not six yards away from me, was Simon Cotton. His hair and beard looked very black, the sickly light from the platform lamps made him seem very pale, and even in that quick glance I noticed the naked look of his mouth.

I dodged back and yelled to Rose.

I reckoned we had ten minutes to think in—we were five miles from Scoatney and the little train crawls. But, oh, I needed more time! I couldn't make up my mind if I ought to tell Rose what the Cottons had said about her—I was so frightened that if I didn't she might be silly again.

"Let's be distant with them," I said, while I tidied my hair in the glass between photographs of Norwich Cathedral and Yarmouth Beach.

"Distant? Do you think I intend to speak to them? After they've ignored us?"

"But we'll have to say 'Good evening', won't we? We can say it coldly and sweep on with dignity."

She said we couldn't do anything with dignity, dressed as we were and laden with furs like hearthrugs. She wanted us to jump out of the train as it stopped and dash away before the Cottons saw us.

"But we can't dash away without our trunks," I said. Then I had an idea—"We'll get out on the wrong side of the train and walk along the line to the guard's van. By the time we get there, the Cottons will be out of the station."

She thought it would work. We decided to keep the fur coats on, so that we should be invisible in the darkness at the end of the platform if the Cottons looked back while we were getting the trunks. Rose turned up the huge bearskin collar to hide her bright hair.

"Let's hope no train comes on the other line while we're

85

walking along," I said. But I knew it was unlikely at that time of night, and they come very slowly.

"Anyway, we could push these little trains back with one hand," said Rose.

I hoisted the collie-dog rug over my shoulder, Rose took the sealskin jacket. The instant the train stopped we jumped down on to the line.

We hadn't realized how difficult walking would be—the coats were so awkward to hold up and we kept tripping over things. The paraffin lamps on the platform gave a very weak light and there were no lamps at all so far along as the guard's van. We couldn't reach the doors on our side, so we went round the back of the train and climbed up on to the platform. The doors of the van were open that side, but there appeared to be no guard to put the trunks off. The stationmaster usually helps with luggage but he is the ticket collector, too, and I was sure he would be busy seeing the Cottons off.

"We must manage by ourselves," I said.

The van was so dimly lit that at first we couldn't see the trunks; then Rose spotted them at the far end, behind a lot of tall milk cans. As we went over, we passed a big crate. The feeble little gas mantle was just above it and I saw on the label COTTON, *Scoatney, Suffolk*. Rose saw it, too, and gave a gasp. The next second we heard voices and steps coming along the platform.

We rushed to the doorway; then realized it was too late to get out.

"Quick—get behind the trunks," said Rose. If I'd had time to think, I might have reasoned with her—told her we should look such fools if we were discovered. But she bolted to the trunks and I bolted too.

"They'll never see us," she said as we crouched down.

I didn't think they would, either—the trunks were high and the light was so weak and so far away from us. "But crouch lower," I whispered, "your trunk's not as high as mine."

"Oh, we'll manage it between us, sir," said a man's voice—it wasn't the stationmaster's so I guessed it was the guard come back.

"I'll help," said Neil Cotton, jumping into the van. Then he shouted: "My God!" and jumped out again. The next instant the doors crashed together with such violence that the gas mantle broke, leaving us in blackness.

"What is it, what's the matter?" shouted Simon Cotton.

I couldn't hear what Neil answered, but I heard the guard give a roar of laughter and say: "Well, that's a good 'un, that is."

"Oh, Rose, he saw us!" I whispered.

"Rubbish—why would he slam the doors on us?" she whispered back. "No, it's something else. Shut up! Listen!" I raised my head cautiously. I could just see the outline of the window, a little open at the top. I heard Simon Cotton say:

"Neil, you're crazy."

"I tell you I'm certain."

"Oh, come, sir—I've been sitting in that van," said the guard.

"But you left the doors open."

I saw a faint blur moving in the darkness—it was Rose's face coming up from behind her trunk.

"What *is* it?" she whispered desperately.

"*Ssh!*" I said, straining my ears. I think I shall remember that minute as long as I live—the stars in the square of window, the bead of light above the broken mantle, the smell of stale milk and fish. I heard Simon Cotton say he would get a flashlight from the car.

"And tell mother to stay inside with the door shut," Neil called after him.

Rose began to crawl towards the window. There was a hollow clang; she had collided with a milk can.

The guard gave a low whistle. "Sounds like you're right, sir."

"Of course I'm right," said Neil. "Haven't I fed them in Yellowstone Park?"

And then it dawned on me.

"Rose," I said, "you've been mistaken for a bear."

I heard her gasp. "The idiot, the idiot!" Then she clanged into another milk can.

"Well, seven-eighths of you *is* a bear. And the Circus is at King's Crypt—the tents were close to the railway line, the Cottons couldn't have missed seeing them." I began to laugh, but stopped when I heard her struggling with the doors on the far side of the van. She got them open and I saw her black against the stars.

"Come on, quick," she said as she jumped down on to the line.

I got across to the doorway—and every milk can clanged into the one next to it. Above the din I could hear Neil Cotton and the guard running along the platform and shouting to the engine-driver.

"Oh, Rose, don't be a fool," I cried, "we'll have to explain." She grabbed my hands and pulled until I had to jump.

"If you don't come with me, I'll never forgive you," she whispered fiercely. "I'd die rather than explain."

"Then you quite probably *will* die—because lots of people in the country have guns handy——" But it was no use, she had vanished into the darkness at the back of the train. Passengers were shouting and banging doors—there couldn't have been many of them, but they were making a devil of a noise; fortunately they were concentrating on the platform side of the train. It suddenly came to me that if I could make Rose take her coat off, we could join in the pursuit as if we had no connection with the bear; so I struggled out of my own coat, flung it up into the van and started after her. But before I had gone a couple of yards, the beam of a torch shone out. I saw Rose clearly. She had got beyond the end of the platform and was scrambling up the little embankment, and as she was on all fours she really did look exactly like a bear. There was a wild shout from the people on the platform. Rose topped the embankment and disappeared over into the fields.

"Foxearth Farm's over there," shouted a woman. "They've got three little children."

I heard someone running along the platform. The woman yelled:

"Quick, quick—over to Foxearth!"

There was a thump as someone jumped down on to the line, then Stephen crossed the beam of the torch. The light gleamed on metal and I realized that he was carrying a pitchfork—it must have been in Mr. Stebbins's cart.

"Stop, Stephen, stop!" I screamed.

He turned and shouted: "I won't hurt it unless I have to, Miss Cassandra—I'll head it into a barn."

Neil Cotton went past me.

"Here, give me that," he said, grabbing Stephen's pitchfork. Simon came running along, shooting his torch ahead of him. The guard and some of the passengers came pounding after him and somebody crashed into me and knocked me over. The torch began to flicker on and off; Simon thumped it and then it went out altogether.

"Get the station lanterns," shouted the guard, scrambling back on to the platform. The passengers waited for him, but Simon and Stephen went on after Neil into the darkness.

Perhaps I ought to have explained at once—but what with the noise and being knocked down I was a bit dazed. And I knew how ghastly it would be for Rose—not only the Cottons knowing, but all the local people on the train. And I did think she had a good chance to get away.

"Anyway, Neil will see she's not a bear if he gets close to her," I told myself. Then they all came thudding past with the lanterns, and the stationmaster had his great black dog on a chain and a stone in his hand. I knew it wasn't safe to keep quiet any longer. I started to tell them, but the dog was barking so loudly that nobody heard me. And then, high above everything, I heard the most piercing shriek.

I lost my head completely.

"It's my sister," I screamed, "he's killing her!" And I dashed off along the line. They all came after me, shouting, and someone fell over the dog's chain and cursed extensively. We climbed over the embankment into the field and the men held the lanterns high, but we couldn't see Rose or the Cottons or Stephen. Everyone was talking at once, making suggestions. There was a fat woman who wanted the stationmaster to let

89

his dog off its chain, but he was afraid it might bite the Cottons instead of the bear.

"But it'll hug them to death," moaned the fat woman, "they won't have a chance."

I opened my mouth to make them understand that there wasn't any bear—and then I saw something white in the distance. The men with the lanterns saw it too, and ran towards it. And suddenly Neil Cotton walked into the light, carrying Rose, in her white suit. Simon Cotton and Stephen were a few steps behind.

The fat woman hurried forward.

"Stand back, please," said Neil Cotton, firmly. "She's had a dreadful shock."

"Rose, Rose!" I cried, running to her.

"She's all right," said Simon Cotton, quickly, "but we want to get her to our car." He grabbed one of the lanterns, lit the way for Neil, and they walked stolidly on.

"But the bear, sir——" said the guard.

"Dead," said Simon Cotton. "My brother killed it."

"Are you sure, sir?" said the stationmaster.

"We'd better have a look," said the fat woman. "The dog'll soon find it."

"No, it won't," said Neil Cotton, over his shoulder. "It fell in the river and was carried away by the current."

"Poor thing, poor thing, it didn't have a chance," wailed the fat woman. "Killed first and drowned afterwards, and I dare say it was valuable."

"You go with your sister," Simon Cotton told me, and I was only too glad to. He handed the lantern to Stephen and stayed behind urging the people back to the train.

"Well, it's a rum go," said the stationmaster.

It was certainly a rum go as far as I was concerned.

"What happened, Stephen?" I asked, under my breath.

Rose suddenly raised her head and whispered fiercely:

"Shut up. Get the trunks off the train." Then, as Neil was carrying her carefully down the little embankment, I heard her tell them they could get out through the field at the back of the station. He crossed the line with her and went straight into it—they never went back to the station at all. Stephen lit them with the lantern for a minute or two, then joined me in the guard's van. Before I could get a word out, he said: "Please, please, don't ask me any questions yet, Miss Cassandra." I was throwing the beaver coat and the rug and the jacket out on to the platform. "Well, at least you can tell me where the bear coat is," I began, but just then the guard came back. Poor man, he couldn't make out how the bear had got out of the van. I told him Rose had been in there when Neil Cotton slammed the doors and had opened the far-side doors when she heard the bear growling. "It was after her like a streak," I said. That seemed to clear things up nicely.

The stationmaster helped us to get the trunks on to Mr. Stebbins's cart. The Cottons' car was only a few yards away and there was Rose inside it, talking to Mrs. Cotton. Simon Cotton came out of the station and said to me:

"We're driving your sister home—will you come, too?"

But I said I would stay with Stephen; it was partly embarrassment and partly that I was afraid I should say the wrong thing, not having the faintest idea what had really happened. And I couldn't get anything out of Stephen on the way home. All he would say was: "Oh, it was dreadful, dreadful. Miss Rose had better tell you herself. I'm saying nothing."

I had to wait until she and I were in bed last night for anything like the whole story—oh, she gave us all a brief outline as soon as she got home, but I guessed she was holding things back. All she told us then was that Neil Cotton came rushing at her with the pitchfork; she screamed, and then suddenly he got the hang of things and told Simon and Stephen to pretend there really had been a bear.

"Neil and Simon even pretended it to their mother," she said. "Oh, they were marvellous."

I never heard father laugh so much—he said the story would be built up and embroidered on until Rose had been pursued by a herd of stampeding elephants. And he was greatly impressed by the Cottons' quick-mindedness.

They hadn't come in—just left Rose in the courtyard.

"Neil said they'd leave me to tell my story in my own way," she said. "And now I've told it. And you'll all have to pretend there was really a bear, for ever and ever."

She was ablaze with excitement, not in the least upset at having been so conspicuous. It was I who was upset; I don't know why—perhaps I was just overtired. I suddenly began to shiver and wanted to cry. Topaz hurried us to bed and brought us cocoa, and hot bricks for our feet, and I soon felt better. She kissed us in a motherly way that Rose doesn't appreciate, and told us not to talk too long—I think she wanted to stay and talk herself but father yelled for her to come along to bed.

"Let's finish our cocoa in the dark," I said, and blew out the candle. Rose is always more confidential in the dark.

The first thing she said was:

"How much did Stephen tell you on the way home?"

I told her how he had said it was too dreadful to tell.

"I wondered if he'd seen," she said. Then she began to giggle—the first time for months. The giggles became muffled and I guessed she was stifling them in her pillow. At last she came up for air and said:

"I slapped Neil Cotton's face."

"Rose!" I gasped. "Why?"

She said she had looked round and seen him coming, seen the pitchfork against the sky, and let out the scream we heard. "Then I tried to get out of the coat but I couldn't find the buttons, so I went on running. He yelled 'Stop, stop'—he must have seen by then that I wasn't really a bear—then he caught up with me and grabbed me by the arm. I said 'Let go, damn you' and Stephen heard my voice and called out 'It's Miss Rose'. Neil Cotton shouted 'But why are you running away?' and I said 'Because I don't want to meet you —or your brother either. You can both go to hell!' And I hit him across the face."

"Oh, Rose!" I felt all knotted up by the awfulness of it. "What did he say?"

"He said 'Good God!' and then Simon and Stephen came up, and Stephen said all the people on the train were out after me.

'That's your fault,' I said to Neil Cotton, 'you've made me the laughing-stock of the neighbourhood.' And he said 'Wait—be quiet'—and then he told them to pretend there really had been a bear, as I told you."

"Don't you think it was wonderfully kind of him?" I asked.

She said: "Yes, in a way," then stopped, and I knew she was trying to work out something in her mind. At last she went on: "But it's all part of his not taking us seriously—not just *us*, but England generally. He wouldn't have dared to pretend anything so silly in America, I bet. He thinks England's a joke, a funny sort of toy—toy trains, toy country-side. I could tell that by the way he talked coming home in the car."

I knew what she meant—I had felt it a bit that night they first came to the castle; not with Simon, though. And I am sure Neil doesn't mean it unkindly.

I asked what the mother was like.

"Beautiful, and never stops talking. Father'll want to brain her with a brick."

"If he ever meets her."

"He'll meet her all right. We shall be seeing quite a lot of the Cottons now."

Her tone was so confident—almost arrogant—that I was frightened for her.

"Oh, Rose, don't be silly with them this time!"—I had said it before I could stop myself.

She simply pounced on it. "What do you mean—'silly'? Did Topaz say I was?"

I said I was merely guessing, but she wouldn't leave it at that. She battered at me with questions. What with wanting to defend Topaz and being very tired, I wasn't as strong-minded as I ought to have been—and Topaz *had* said it might be best to tell if we got another chance with the Cottons. But I felt perfectly dreadful when I had told—mean, both to the Cottons and Rose. Still, if it does her any good . . . And I was careful to stress about my being consciously naïve. I left out the bit about father.

93

She wanted to know which brother had said the worst things. I sorted the remarks out as best I could.

"Well, at least Simon was sorry for me," she said. "It was Neil who suggested dropping us. Oh, how I'll pay them out!"

"Don't count it against them," I begged. "Look how very kind they were to-night. And if you're sure they want to be friends now——"

"I'm sure all right."

"Did they say anything about seeing us again?"

"Never mind what they said." And then, to my surprise, she started to giggle again—she wouldn't tell me why. When she stopped, she said she was sleepy.

I tried to keep her talking by being Miss Blossom: "Here, Rosie, have you got something up your sleeve, you naughty girl?"

But she wasn't having any. "If I have, it's staying there," she said. "You and Miss Blossom go to sleep."

But I lay awake for ages, going over it all.

Heavens, Godsend church clock has just struck four—I have been writing up here on the mound for six hours! Topaz never rang the lunch bell for me; instead, she brought me out some milk and two big cheese sandwiches, and a message from father that I was to write as long as I liked. It seems selfish when the others are working hard on Aunt Millicent's clothes, but while we were unpacking them this morning I began to shake again, and when Topaz found out what I felt about them she said I had better write it out of my system. I think I have, because I can now look down on them flapping on the line without any horror—though I don't feel fond of them yet, as I do of the furs.

Stephen cycled to Scoatney station before he went to work and brought back the bear coat; it was hidden in a ditch. Father can remember hearing about this coat when he was little. He says most coachmen were lucky if they got a short goatskin cape to wear in the winter; but great-grandmother said that if her husband, who rode inside the carriage, had a beaver-lined coat, the coachman out in the cold ought to be at least as warmly dressed. He was grateful for the bear coat but embarrassed, as little boys used to jeer and ask him to dance. The sealskin jacket was Aunt Millicent's, in the 'nineties, before she turned against furs. Father thinks she kept all these out of family sentiment and perhaps because she was only happy as a child. How queer to think that the old lady in the black military cloak was the Miss Milly who went to the dancing class! It makes me wonder what I shall be like when I am old.

My hand is very tired but I want to go on writing. I keep resting and thinking. All day I have been two people—the me imprisoned in yesterday and the me out here on the mound; and now there is a third me trying to get in—the me in what is going to happen next. Will the Cottons ask us to Scoatney? Topaz thinks they will. She says the oddness of the bear incident will fascinate them, just as they were fascinated by the oddness of the first night they came to the castle—and that Rose running away will have undone the damage she did by being too forthcoming. If only she doesn't forth-come again! Topaz approves of my telling her last night; she had a talk with her herself about it this morning and Rose listened with surprising civility.

"Just be rather quiet and do a lot of listening until you feel at ease," Topaz advised her. "And for pity's sake don't be challenging. Your looks will do the challenging if you give them the chance." I do love Topaz when she is in a down-to-earth mood.

Is it awful to join in this planning? Is it trying to sell one's sister? But surely Rose can manage to fall in love with them— I mean, with whichever one will fall in love with her. I hope it will be Neil, because I really do think Simon is a little frightening—only it is Neil who thinks England is a joke. . . .

I have been resting, just staring down at the castle. I wish I could find words—serious, beautiful words—to describe it in the afternoon sunlight; the more I strive for them, the more they utterly elude me. How can one capture the pool of light in the courtyard, the golden windows, the strange long-ago look, the look that one sees in old paintings? I can only think of "the light of other days," and I didn't make that up. . . .

Oh——! I have just seen the Cottons' car on the Godsend road—near the high cross-roads, where one gets the first glimpse of the castle. They are coming here! Do I watch and wait again? No fear!

I am going down.

Chapter VII

WE ARE ASKED TO SCOATNEY, TO DINNER, A WEEK FROM TO-DAY!
And there is something else I want to write about, something
belonging to me. Oh, I don't know where to begin!

I got down from Belmotte in time to warn the others—
Rose and Topaz were ironing and Rose put on a clean blouse
hot from the iron. Topaz just tidied herself and then set the
tea-tray. I washed and then reckoned I had only enough time
either to warn father or to brush my hair; but I managed to
do both by taking the comb and brush to the gatehouse with
me. Father jumped up so quickly that I feared he was going
to rush out to avoid the Cottons, but he merely grabbed my
hairbrush and brushed his coat with it—neither of us felt it
was a moment for fussiness.

In the end, we had a few minutes to spare because they left
the car at the end of the lane—the mud is dry now but the
ruts are still deep.

"Mrs. Cotton's with them!" I cried, as they came round the
last bend of the lane. Father said he would meet them at the
gatehouse arch—"It's not going to be my fault if anything
goes wrong this time; I've promised Topaz." Then he looked a
bit grim and added: "I'm glad you're still on the young side
to be marketed."

I bolted back to Rose and Topaz. They had lit a wood fire
in the drawing-room and arranged some daffodils. The fire
made the room feel more springlike than ever. We opened the
windows and the swans sailed by, looking mildly interested.
Suddenly I remembered that first spring afternoon in the
drawing-room, with Rose playing her piece. I saw mother leaning out over the moat—I saw her grey dress so clearly, though
I still couldn't see her face. Something inside me said: "Oh,

97

mother, make the right thing happen for Rose!"—and I had a vision of poor mother scurrying from Heaven to do the best she could. The way one's mind can dash about just while one opens a window!

Then father came in with the Cottons.

Rose thought Mrs. Cotton beautiful but that isn't how I would describe her. Topaz is beautiful—largely because of the strangeness of her face: that look she has of belonging to a whiter-than-white race. Rose, with her lovely colouring and her eyes that can light up her whole expression, is beautiful. Mrs. Cotton is handsome—no, that makes her sound too big. She is just wonderfully good-looking, wonderfully *right*-looking. She has exactly the right amount of colour. Her black hair is going grey without looking streaky because it has exactly the right number of grey hairs in exactly the right places—and it has exactly the right amount of wave. Her figure is perfect, and so were her clothes—just country tweeds but so much more exciting than I ever thought tweeds could be; they had clear colours in them, shades of blue which made you notice her eyes. I rather fear that I stared too hard at her —I hope she realized that it was only admiration. As she is Simon Cotton's mother she can't be much less than fifty, which is hard to believe. Yet now I come to think of it, I can't imagine her being any younger; it is just that she is a different kind of fifty from any I have ever seen.

She came in talking solidly, and solidly is a very good word to describe it; it made me think of a wall of talk. Fortunately she speaks beautifully—just as Simon does—and she doesn't in the least mind being interrupted; her sons do it all the time and father soon acquired the technique—it was him she talked to most. After he had introduced Topaz and me and she had shaken hands with us all, and hoped Rose had recovered from her shock, and said: "Will you look at those swans?"—she started on *Jacob Wrestling* and how she had heard father lecture in America. They went on interrupting each other in a perfectly friendly manner, Rose sat on the window-seat and talked to Simon, and Topaz and I slipped out to bring the tea in. Neil kindly came after us saying he would carry things.

We stood round the kitchen fire waiting for the kettle to boil.

"Doesn't your mother really know Rose was the bear?" I asked.

"Gosh, no—that wouldn't do at all," he said, "it isn't her kind of joke. Anyway, it wouldn't be fair to your sister."

I did see that, of course—Mrs. Cotton would have wondered why on earth Rose was running away. (I suppose Neil guesses it was because she felt they had dropped us. Dear me, how embarrassing!)

"But I can't see how anyone could believe that you killed the bear with a pitchfork," I said.

"I didn't. I only wounded it—badly, I think, but not enough to put it out of action. It came blundering towards me, I stepped aside and it crashed head-first into the river— I could hear it threshing about in the darkness. I picked up a big stone—poor brute, I hated to do it but I had to finish it off. It gave just one groan as the stone hit it and then went down. I held the lantern high; I could see the bubbles coming up. And then I saw the dark bulk of it under the water, being carried along by the current."

"But you didn't have a lantern," I said.

"He didn't have a bear," said Topaz.

For a moment I had almost believed him myself—and felt most desperately sorry for the bear. No wonder Mrs. Cotton has been deceived.

"Mother made us go over to compensate the circus owner this morning," he went on, grinning. "It's just a midget of a circus—he didn't have any bears at all, as a matter of fact; but he said he'd be delighted to back our story up—he hoped it might get him a bit of publicity. I tried to buy one of his lions but he wouldn't sell."

"What did you want a lion for?" I asked.

"Oh, they were kind of cute," he said vaguely.

Then the kettle boiled and we took the tea in.

After Neil had helped to hand things round, he went and sat by Rose on the window-seat. And Simon came and talked to Topaz politely. Father and Mrs. Cotton were still interrupting each other happily. It was fascinating to watch them all, but the conversations cancelled each other out so that I couldn't listen to any of them. I was anxious about Rose. I could see she was letting Neil do most of the talking, which was excellent; but she didn't seem to be listening to him, which was not so good. She kept leaning out of the window to feed the swans. Neil looked a bit puzzled. Then I noticed that Simon kept watching her, and after a while she caught his eye and gave him a smile. Neil shot a quick glance at her, then got up and asked Topaz for some more tea (though I noticed he didn't drink it). Simon went over to Rose. She still didn't say much, but she looked as if everything he said was terrifically interesting. I caught a word here and there, he was telling her about Scoatney Hall. I heard her say: "No, I've never seen the inside." He said: "But you must, of course. We were hoping you'd dine with us one night next week." Then he turned to Mrs. Cotton and she invited us. There was an awful moment when I thought I was going to be left out because she said: "Is Cassandra old enough for dinner parties?" but Neil said: "You bet she is!" and it was all right.

Oh, I do like Neil! When they went, I walked up the lane with him; Father was with Mrs. Cotton, and Rose with Simon. Neil asked how we would get over to Scoatney and when I said we should have to think that out, he arranged to send the car for us. He is the kindest person—though as we passed the barn I remembered how very far from kind he was about Rose that day. Perhaps one ought never to count things one overhears. Anyway, it was Simon who said I was consciously naïve—Neil said I was a cute kid; it's not exactly the way I see myself, but it was kindly meant.

As we walked back to the castle father said how nice they all were, then asked if we had dresses for the party. I had been worrying about this myself, but I said:

"Oh, Topaz will manage something."

"Could anything of Aunt Millicent's be altered? If not— damn it, there must be something we can sell——" He gave me a humble, appealing sort of look. I put my arm through his and said quickly: "We'll be all right." He looked tentatively at Rose. She was smiling faintly to herself. I don't think she had heard a word we had said.

When we went in, Topaz was washing up the tea-things.

"Mortmain, you deserve a medal," she said.

"What for?" said father. "Oh, for talking to Mrs. Cotton? I enjoyed it very much."

Topaz simply stared at him.

"I got used to the vitality of American women when I was over there," he explained.

"Do they all talk as much as that?" I asked.

"No, of course not. But she happens to belong to a type I frequently met—it goes to lectures. And entertains afterwards—sometimes they put one up for the night; they're extraordinarily hospitable." He sat on the kitchen table, swinging his legs, looking rather boyish. "Amazing, their energy," he went on. "They're perfectly capable of having three or four children, running a house, keeping abreast of art, literature and music—superficially of course but, good lord, that's something—and holding down a job into the bargain. Some of them get through two or three husbands as well, just to avoid stagnation."

"I shouldn't think any husband could stay the course for more than a few years," said Topaz.

"I felt that myself at first—the barrage of talk left me utterly depleted. But after a time I got used to it. They're rather like punch-balls—you buffet them, they buffet you, and on the whole the result's most stimulating."

"Unless they knock you out altogether," said Topaz, drily.

"They have that effect occasionally," father admitted. "Quite a number of American men are remarkably silent."

"She seemed to know a lot about *Jacob Wrestling*," I said.

"She'd probably read it up before she came—they do that, and very civil of them. Curious how many of them are prematurely grey; most becoming. And I must say it's a pleasure to see a woman so well turned-out."

He began to hum abstractedly and went off to the gatehouse as if he had suddenly forgotten all about us. I could have slapped him for that "well turned-out" remark, because Topaz was looking so particularly far from well turned-out. She was wearing her hand-woven dress which is first cousin to a sack and her lovely hair, being rather in need of a wash, was pushed into a torn old net.

"Perhaps he'd find it stimulating if *I* talked as much as that," she said.

"*We* shouldn't," I told her. Actually, I had thought Mrs. Cotton very stimulating myself, but had no intention of being so tactless as to say so. "Topaz, will there be moths in his evening clothes? He can't have worn them since Aunt Millicent's parties."

But she said she had taken care of them. "We'll have to get him some studs, though, because he sold his good ones. Oh, Cassandra, it's fantastic—a genius, a man American critics write essays on, and he hasn't a decent stud to his name."

I said many geniuses had lacked shirts to put the studs in; then we got talking about our own clothes for the party.

I am all right—my white, school Speech Day frock will pass for anyone as young as I am, Topaz says. And she can fix up one of her old evening dresses for herself. Rose is the problem.

"There's not a thing of your aunt's I can use for her," said Topaz, "and nothing of my own is suitable. She needs something frilly. As we'll never be able to stop her turning on the Early Victorian charm, we ought to accentuate it."

I could hear Rose playing the piano. I closed the kitchen door and said: "What did you think of her manner to-day?"

"At least it was quieter, though she was still making eyes. But, anyway, it doesn't matter now."

I looked at her in astonishment and she went on:

"Simon Cotton's attracted—really attracted—couldn't you see? Once that happens, a girl can be as silly as she likes—the man'll probably think the silliness is fetching."

"Is Neil attracted, too?"

"I doubt it," said Topaz. "I've an idea that Neil sees through her—I saw him give her a very shrewd look. Oh, how are we going to dress her, Cassandra? There's a chance for her with Simon, really there is—I know the signs."

I had a sudden picture of Simon's face, pale above the beard.

"But would you really like her to marry him, Topaz?" I asked.

"I'd like her to get the chance," said Topaz, firmly.

Miss Marcy arrived then with a book for father. She told us the Vicar has been invited for the same night as we have—she'd heard from his housekeeper.

"Most people have only been asked to lunches or teas," she said. "Dinner's ever so much more splendid."

We told her about the problem of Rose's dress.

"It should be pink," she said, "a crinoline effect—there's the very thing here in this week's *Home Chat*."

She dived into her satchel for it.

"Oh, dear, that would be perfect for her," sighed Topaz.

Miss Marcy blushed and blinked her eyes, then said:

"Could you make it, Mrs. Mortmain? If—if dear Rose allowed me to give her the material?"

"*I'll* allow you," said Topaz. "I feel justified."

Miss Marcy shot her a quick glance and Topaz gave her the very faintest nod. I nearly laughed—they were so different, Miss Marcy like a rosy little bird and Topaz tall and pale, like a slightly dead goddess, but just that second they so much resembled each other in their absolute lust to marry Rose off.

"Perhaps we could offer Miss Marcy something of Aunt Millicent's as a small return," I suggested. They went off to the dining-room, where the clothes are spread out, while I stayed to get Stephen his tea—Topaz had decided that those of us who'd had afternoon tea would have supper with cocoa, later.

Stephen was worried to hear I shall be wearing such an old dress at Scoatney. "Couldn't you have a new sash?" he asked. "I've got some money saved."

I thanked him but said my blue Speech Day sash was as good as new.

"Then a ribbon for your hair, Miss Cassandra?"

"Goodness, I haven't worn a hair-ribbon since I was a child," I told him.

"You used to have little bows on the ends of your plaits before you cut your hair," he said. "They were pretty."

Then he asked how I liked the two Cottons, now I knew them better.

"Oh, I don't know Simon at all—he talked to Rose most of the time. But Neil's very nice."

"Would you call him handsome?"

I said I hardly thought so—"Not really handsome—not the way you are, Stephen."

I spoke without thinking—we all of us take his good looks for granted; but he blushed so much that I wished I hadn't said it.

"You see, you have classical features," I explained, in a matter-of-fact voice.

"It seems a waste when I'm not a gentleman." He grinned —a little sarcastic sort of grin.

"Don't talk like that," I said quickly. "Gentlemen are men who behave like gentlemen. And you certainly do."

He shook his head. "You can only be a gentleman if you're born one, Miss Cassandra."

"Stephen, that's old-fashioned nonsense," I said. "Really, it is. And, by the way, will you please stop calling me 'Miss' Cassandra?"

He looked astonished. Then he said: "Yes, I see. It should be 'Miss Mortmain' now you're grown up enough for dinner parties."

"It certainly shouldn't," I said. "I mean you must call me Cassandra, without the 'Miss.' You're one of the family—it's absurd you should ever have called me 'Miss.' Who told you to?"

"My mother—she set a lot of store by it," he said. "I remember the first day we came here. You and Miss Rose were throwing a ball in the garden and I ran to the kitchen door thinking I'd play, too. Mother called me back and told me how you were young ladies, and I was never to play with you unless I was invited. And to call you 'Miss,' and never to presume. She had a hard job explaining what 'presume' meant."

"Oh, Stephen, how awful! And you'd be—how old?"

"Seven, I think. You'd be six and Miss Rose nine. Thomas was only four, but she told me to call him 'Master Thomas.' Only he asked me not to, years ago."

"And *I* ought to have asked you years ago." I'd never given it a thought. His mother had been in service for years before she married. When she was left a widow she had to go back to it and board Stephen out. I know she was very grateful when mother let her bring him here, so perhaps that made her extra humble. "Well, anyway, I've asked you now," I went on, "so will you please remember?"

"Would I call Miss Rose just 'Rose'?" he asked.

I wasn't sure how Rose would feel about it so I said: "Oh, why worry about Rose? This is between you and me."

"I couldn't call her 'Miss' and not you," he said firmly. "It'd be setting her above you."

I said I would talk to Rose about it, then asked him to pass his cup for more tea—I was getting a bit embarrassed by the subject. He stirred his second cup for a long time, then said:

"Did you mean that about gentlemen being men who behave like gentlemen?"

"Of course I did, Stephen. I swear I did—really."

I was so anxious to make him believe me that I leaned towards him, across the table. He looked at me, right into my eyes. That queer, veiled expression in his—that I fear I used to call his daft look—was suddenly not there; there seemed to be a light in them and yet I have never seen them look so dark. And they were so direct that it was more like being touched than being looked at. It only lasted a second, but for that second he was quite a different person—much more interesting, even a little bit exciting.

Then Thomas came in and I jumped up from the table.

"Why are you so red in the face, my girl?" he said maddeningly—I do understand why Rose sometimes wants to hit him. Fortunately he didn't wait for an answer, but went on to say there was a bit in the King's Crypt paper about the bear being washed up twenty miles away. I laughed and put an egg on to boil for him. Stephen went out into the garden.

All the time I was giving Thomas his tea I was worrying—because I suddenly knew I couldn't go on pretending that Stephen is just vaguely devoted to me and it doesn't in the least matter. I hadn't given it a thought for weeks, and I certainly hadn't been brisk with him, as father suggested. I told myself I would start at once; and then I felt I couldn't—not after I had just asked him to stop calling me "Miss." Incidentally, I never felt less brisk in my life, because being looked at like that makes a person feel dizzy.

I went into the garden to think things out. It was that time of evening when pale flowers look paler—the daffodils seemed almost white; they were very still, everything was still, hushed. Father's lamp was lit in the gatehouse, Topaz and Miss Marcy had a candle in the dining-room, Rose was still playing the piano in the drawing-room, without a light. I'd stopped feeling dizzy; I had a strange, excited feeling. I went through the gatehouse passage out into the lane and walked past the barn. Stephen came out. He didn't smile as he usually does when he sees me; he looked at me with a kind of questioning expression. Then he said: "Let's go for a little walk."

I said: "All right." And then: "No, I don't think I will, Stephen. I want to see Miss Marcy again before she goes."

I didn't want to see Miss Marcy in the least. I wanted to go for the walk. But I suddenly knew I mustn't.

Stephen just nodded. Then we went back to the castle together without saying a word to each other.

When Rose and I were going to bed I asked her if she would mind Stephen dropping the "Miss."

"I don't mind one way or the other," she said. "After all, I'm eating the food he pays for."

I started to talk about the Cottons then, but she wouldn't be jolly or excited about them—she seemed to want to think. And I did some quiet thinking myself.

Early this morning I met Stephen letting out the hens and told him Rose would like him to stop saying "Miss." I was splendidly brisk; it's easy to be brisk in the early morning. He just said: "All right," without very much expression. Over breakfast Rose and Topaz were planning to go to King's

Crypt to buy the stuff for Rose's dress. (They are there now, I have had most of the day to myself.) I was at the fire, making toast. Stephen came over to me.

"Please let me ask Mrs. Mortmain to get you something for the party," he said.

I thanked him but said I didn't need a thing.

"You're sure?" Then he added, very softly and as if he were trying out some difficult word: "Cassandra."

We both blushed. I had thought that dropping the "Miss" for Rose as well would make it quite ordinary, but it didn't.

"Goodness, this fire's hot," I said. "No, honestly—I can't think of anything I want."

"Then I'll just go on saving up for—for what I was saving up for," he said, and then went off to work.

It is now four o'clock. Father has gone to call on the Vicar so I have the castle to myself. It's odd how different a house feels when one is alone in it. It makes it easier to think rather private thoughts—I shall think some. . . .

I didn't get very far with my thoughts. It is the still, yellow kind of afternoon when one is apt to get stuck in a dream if one sits very quiet—I have been staring blankly at the bright square of the kitchen window for a good ten minutes. I shall pull myself together and do some honest thinking. . . .

I have thought. And I have discovered the following things:

(1) I do not reciprocate Stephen's feelings.
(2) I wanted to go that walk with him yesterday evening and—having always loathed girls in books who are too, too innocent, I set it on record: I *think* I thought that if I did go, he would kiss me.
(3) This morning, by the hen-house, I did not wish him to kiss me.
(4) This moment, I do not *think* I wish him to kiss me. . . .

I have thought some more—I have been stuck in the *un*-blank kind of dream. I re-lived the minute when Stephen looked at me across the table. Even to remember it made me feel dizzy. I liked feeling dizzy. Then, in my mind, I went for the walk with him that I *didn't* go. We went along the lane, over the Godsend road and into the little larch wood. There are no bluebells there yet, but I put them in. It was nearly dark in the wood and suddenly cool, cold, there was a waiting feeling. I made up things for Stephen to say, I heard his voice saying them. It got darker and darker until there was only the palest gleam of sky through the tops of the trees. And at last he kissed me.

But I couldn't make that up at all—I just couldn't imagine how it would feel. And I suddenly wished I hadn't imagined any of it. I——

I am finishing this in the bedroom because I heard Stephen washing at the garden pump and dashed upstairs. I have just looked down on him from the window and I feel most guilty about taking him for that walk in my mind; guilty and ashamed, with a weak feeling round my ribs. I won't do that sort of imagining again. And I am now quite certain I don't want him to kiss me. He does look extremely handsome there by the pump but the daft look is back again—oh, poor Stephen, I am a beast, it isn't really daft! Though he certainly couldn't have thought of all those things I made him say; some of them were rather good.

I won't think about it any more. My spare time pleasure-thinking shall be about the party at Scoatney, which is really much more interesting—though perhaps more interesting for Rose than for me. I wonder what it would be like to be kissed by either of the Cottons. . . . NO! I am *not* going to imagine that. Really, I'm shocked at myself! And anyway, there isn't time—Rose and Topaz are due back.

I should rather like to tear these last pages out of the book. Shall I? No—a journal ought not to cheat. And I feel sure no one but me can read my speed-writing. But I shall hide the book—I always lock it up in my school attaché case and this time I shall take the case out to Belmotte Tower; I have a special place for hiding things there that not even Rose knows of. I shall go through the front door to avoid meeting Stephen—I really don't know how I can look him in the face after borrowing him as I have done. I *will* be brisk with him in future—I swear I will!

Chapter VIII

I SHALL HAVE TO DO THE EVENING AT SCOATNEY BIT BY BIT, for I know I shall be interrupted—I shall want to be, really, because life is too exciting to sit still for long. On top of the Cottons appearing to like us, we have actually come by twenty pounds, the Vicar having bought the rug that looks like a collie dog. To-morrow we are going shopping in King's Crypt. I am to have a summer dress. Oh, it is wonderful to wake up in the morning with things to look forward to!

Now about Scoatney. All week we were getting ready for the party. Topaz bought yards and yards of pink muslin for Rose's frock and made it most beautifully. (At one time, before she was an artists' model, Topaz worked at a great dress-maker's, but she will never tell us about it—or about any of her pasts, which always surprises me because she is so frank about many things.)

Rose had a real crinoline to wear under the dress; only a small one but it made all the difference. We borrowed it from Mr. Stebbins's grandmother, who is ninety-two. When the dress was finished, he brought her over to see Rose in it and she told us she had worn the crinoline at her wedding in Godsend Church, when she was sixteen. I thought of Waller's "Go, lovely Rose"—

> How small a part of time they share
> That are so wondrous sweet and fair!

—though I refrained from mentioning it; the poor old lady was crying enough without that. But she said she had enjoyed the outing.

It was fun while we were all sewing the frills for the dress; I kept pretending we were in a Victorian novel. Rose was fairly willing to play, but she always shut up if I brought the Cottons into the game. And we had no nice friendly candle-light conversations about them. She wasn't cross or sulky, she just seemed preoccupied—given to lying in bed not even reading, with a faint smirk on her face. Now I come to think of it, I was just as secretive about myself and Stephen, it would have embarrassed me dreadfully to tell her about my feelings; but then I have always been more secretive than she usually is. And I know that she thinks of him as—well, as a boy of a different class from ours. (Do I think it, too? If so, I am ashamed of such snobbishness.) I am thankful to be able to record that I have been brisk—though perhaps it would be truer to say that I haven't been *un*brisk; except for that second last night when I took his hand—— But that is part of the evening at Scoatney Hall.

It was thrilling when we started to get dressed. There was still some daylight left, but we drew the curtains and brought up the lamp and lit candles, because I once read that women of fashion dress *for* candlelight *by* candlelight. Our frocks were laid out on the four-poster, mine had been washed and Topaz had cut the neck down a bit. Miss Blossom was ecstatic about Rose's—she said: "My word, that'll fetch the gentlemen. And I never knew you had such white shoulders—fancy God giving you that hair but no freckles!" Rose laughed, but she was cross because she couldn't see herself full length; our long looking-glass got sold. I held our small one so that she could look at herself in sections, but it was tantalizing for her.

"There's the glass over the drawing-room fireplace," I said. "Perhaps if you stood on the piano——" She went down to try.

Father came from the bathroom and went through to his bedroom. The next second I heard him shout:

"Good God, what have you done to yourself?"

He sounded so horrified that I thought Topaz had had some accident. I dashed into Buffer State but stopped myself outside their bedroom door; I could see her from there. She was wearing a black evening dress that she never has liked herself in, a very conventional dress. Her hair was done up in a bun and she had make-up on—not much, just a little rouge and lipstick. The result was astounding. She looked quite ordinary —just vaguely pretty but not worth a second glance.

Neither of them saw me. I heard her say:

"Oh, Mortmain, this is Rose's night. I want all the attention to be focused on her——"

I tiptoed back to the bedroom. I was bewildered at such unselfishness, particularly as she had spent hours mending her best evening dress. I knew what she meant, of course—at her most striking she can make Rose's beauty look like mere prettiness. Suddenly I remembered that first night the Cottons came here, how she tried to efface herself. Oh, noble Topaz!

I heard father shout:

"To hell with that. God knows I've very little left to be proud of. At least let me be proud of my wife."

There was a throaty gasp from Topaz: "Oh, my darling!" —and then I hastily went downstairs and kept Rose talking in the drawing-room. I felt this was something we oughtn't to be in on. And I felt embarrassed—I always do when I really think of father and Topaz being married.

When they came down Topaz was as white as usual and her silvery hair, which was at its very cleanest, was hanging down her back. She had her best dress on which is Grecian in shape, like a clinging grey cloud, with a great grey scarf which she had draped round her head and shoulders. She looked most beautiful—and just how I imagine the Angel of Death.

The Cottons' car came, with a uniformed chauffeur, and out we sailed. I was harrowed at leaving Stephen and Thomas behind, but Topaz had arranged they should have a supper with consoling sausages.

It was a huge, wonderful car. We none of us talked very much in it—personally, I was too conscious of the chauffeur; he was so rigid and correct and had such outstanding ears. I just sat back watching the darkening fields drift past, feeling rather frail and luxurious. And I thought about us all and wondered how the others were feeling. Father looked very handsome in his evening clothes and he was kind and smiling but I could see he was nervous; at least, I thought I could, but then it struck me how little I know of him, or of Topaz or Rose or anyone in the world, really, except myself. I used to flatter myself that I could get flashes of what people were thinking but if I did, it was only of quick, surface thoughts. All these years and I don't know what has stopped father working! And I don't really know what Rose feels about the Cottons. As for Topaz—but I never did get any flashes of knowing her. Of course I have always realized that she is kind, but I should never have thought her capable of making that noble sacrifice for Rose. And just as I was feeling ashamed of ever having thought her bogus, she said in a voice like plum-cake:

"Look, Mortmain, look! Oh, don't you long to be an old, old man in a lamp-lit inn?"

"Yes, particularly one with rheumatism," said father. "My dear, you're an ass."

We called for the Vicar, which made it rather a squash, what with Rose's crinoline . . . He is the nicest man—about fifty, plump, with curly golden hair; rather like an elderly baby—and most unholy. Father once said to him: "God knows how you came to be a clergyman." And the Vicar said: "Well, it's His business to know."

After he'd had a look at us he said: "Mortmain, your women are spectacular."

"*I'm* not," I said.

"Ah, but you're the insidious type—Jane Eyre with a touch of Becky Sharp. A thoroughly dangerous girl. I like your string of coral."

Then he got us all talking and even made the chauffeur laugh—the odd thing is that he makes people laugh without saying anything very funny. I suppose it is because he is such a comfortable sort of man.

It was dark when we got to Scoatney Hall and all the windows were lit up. There is a right-of-way through the park and I had often cycled there on my way home from school, so I knew what the outside of the house was like—it is sixteenth-century except for the seventeenth-century pavilion in the water-garden; but I was longing to see inside. We went up shallow steps that had been worn into a deep curve, and the front door was opened before we had time to ring the bell. I had never met a butler before and he made me feel self-conscious, but the Vicar knew him and said something normal to him.

We left our wraps in the hall—Topaz had lent us things to save us the shame of wearing our winter coats. There was a wonderful atmosphere of gentle age, a smell of flowers and beeswax, sweet yet faintly sour and musty; a smell that makes you feel very tender towards the past.

We went into quite a little drawing-room, where the Cottons were standing by the fireplace with two other people. Mrs. Cotton was talking up to the moment we were announced; then she turned to us and was absolutely silent for a second— I think she was astonished at how Rose and Topaz looked. I noticed Simon looking at Rose. Then we were all shaking hands and being introduced to the others.

They were a Mr. and Mrs. Fox-Cotton—English relations of the Cottons; rather distant ones, I think. As soon as I heard the husband called "Aubrey" I remembered that he is an architect—I read something about his work in a magazine once. He is middle-aged, with a greyish face and thin, no-coloured hair. There is something very elegant about him and he has a beautiful speaking-voice, though it is a bit affected. I was next to him while we were drinking our cocktails (my first—and it tasted horrid) so I asked him about the architecture of the house. He launched forth at once.

"What makes it so perfect," he said, "is that it's a *miniature* great house. It has everything—great hall, long gallery, central courtyard—but it's on so small a scale that it's manageable, even in these days. I've hankered for it for years. How I wish I could persuade Simon to let me have it on a long lease."

He said it as much for Simon to hear as for me. Simon laughed and said: "Not on your life."

Then Mr. Fox-Cotton said:

"Do tell me—the exquisite lady in grey—surely she's the Topaz of Macmorris's picture in the Tate Gallery?" And after we had talked about Topaz for a minute or two, he drifted over to her. I had time to notice that Simon was admiring Rose's dress and that she was telling him about the crinoline—which seemed to fascinate him, he said he must go and see old Mrs. Stebbins; then the Vicar joined me and obligingly finished my cocktail for me. Soon after that we went in to dinner.

The table was a pool of candlelight—so bright that the rest of the room seemed almost black, with the faces of the family portraits floating in the darkness.

Mrs. Cotton had father on her right and the Vicar on her left. Topaz was on Simon's right, Mrs. Fox-Cotton on his left. Rose was between the Vicar and Mr. Fox-Cotton—I wished she could have been next to Simon, but I suppose married women have to be given precedence. I have an idea that Neil just may have asked for me to be next to him, because he told me I would be, as we went in. It made me feel very warm towards him.

It was a wonderful dinner with real champagne (lovely, rather like very good ginger ale without the ginger). But I wish I could have had that food when I wasn't at a party, because you can't notice food fully when you are being polite. And I was a little bit nervous—the knives and forks were so complicated. I never expected to feel ignorant about such things—we always had several courses for dinner at Aunt Millicent's—but I couldn't even recognize all the dishes. And it was no use trying to copy Neil because his table manners were quite strange to me. I fear he must have seen me staring at him once because he said: "Mother thinks I ought to eat in the English way—she and Simon have gotten into it—but I'm darned if I will."

I asked him to explain the difference. It appears that in America it is polite to cut up each mouthful, lay down the knife on your plate, change your fork from the left to the right hand, load it, eat the fork-full, change the fork back to your left hand, and pick up the knife again—and you must take only one kind of food on the fork at a time; never a nice comfortable wodge of meat and vegetables together.

"But that takes so long," I said.

"No, it doesn't," said Neil. "Anyway, it looks terrible to me the way you all hang on to your knives."

The idea of anything English people do looking terrible quite annoyed me, but I held my peace.

"Tell you another thing that's wrong over here," Neil went on, waving his fork slightly. "Look at the way everything's being handed to your stepmother first. Back home it'd be handed to mother."

"Don't you care to be polite to the guest?" I said. Dear me, what a superior little horror I must have sounded.

"But it *is* polite—it's a lot more considerate, anyway. Because the hostess can always show you what to do with the food—if you turn out soup on your plate or take a whole one of anything—don't you see what I mean?"

I saw very clearly and I did think it a wonderfully good idea.

"Well, perhaps I could even get used to changing my fork from hand to hand," I said, and had a go at it. I found it very difficult.

The Vicar was watching us across the table.

"When this house was built, people used daggers and their fingers," he said. "And it'll probably last until the days when men dine off capsules."

"Fancy asking friends to come over for capsules," I said.

"Oh, the capsules will be taken in private," said father. "By that time, eating will have become unmentionable. Pictures of food will be considered rare and curious, and only collected by rude old gentlemen."

Mrs. Fox-Cotton spoke to Neil then and he turned to talk to her; so I got a chance to look round the table. Both father and the Vicar were listening to Mrs. Cotton; Aubrey Fox-Cotton was monopolizing Topaz. For the moment, no one was talking to either Rose or Simon. I saw him look at her. She gave him a glance through her eyelashes and though I know what Topaz means about it being old-fashioned, it was certainly a most fetching glance—perhaps Rose has got into better practice now. Anyway, I could see that Simon wasn't being put off by it this time. He raised his glass and looked at her across it almost as if he were drinking a toast to her. His eyes looked rather handsome above the glass and I suddenly had a hope that she could really fall in love with him, in spite of the beard. But heavens, *I* couldn't!

She smiled—the faintest flicker of a smile—and then turned and spoke to the Vicar. I thought to myself: "She's learning" —because it would have been very obvious if she had looked at Simon any longer.

I had a queer sort of feeling, watching them all and listening; perhaps it was due to what father had been saying a few minutes before. It suddenly seemed astonishing that people should meet especially to eat together—because food goes into the mouth and talk comes out. And if you watch people eating and talking—really watch them—it is a very peculiar sight: hands so busy, forks going up and down, swallowings, words coming out between mouthfuls, jaws working like mad. The more you look at a dinner party, the odder it seems—all the candlelit faces, hands with dishes coming over·shoulders, the owners of the hands moving round quietly, taking no part in the laughter and conversation. I pulled my mind off the table and stared into the dimness beyond, and then I gradually saw the servants as real people, watching us, whispering instructions to each other, exchanging glances. I noticed a girl from Godsend village and gave her a tiny wink—and wished I hadn't, because she let out a little snort of laughter and then looked in terror at the butler. The next minute my left ear heard something which made my blood run cold (an expression I have always looked down on, but I really did get a cold shiver between my shoulders): Mrs. Cotton was asking father how long it was since he had published anything.

"A good twelve years," he said in the blank voice which our family accepts as the close of a conversation. It had no such effect on Mrs. Cotton.

"You've thought it best to lie fallow," she said. "How few writers have the wisdom to do that." Her tone was most understanding, almost reverent. Then she added briskly: "But it's been long enough, don't you think?"

I saw father's hand grip the table. For an awful second I thought he was going to push his chair back and walk out—

as he so often does at home if any of us annoy him. But he just said, very quietly: "I've given up writing, Mrs. Cotton. And now let's talk of something interesting."

"But *this* is interesting," she said. I sneaked a look at her. She was very upright, all deep blue velvet and pearls—I don't think I ever saw a woman look so noticeably *clean*. "And I warn you I'm quite unsnubbable, Mr. Mortmain. When a writer so potentially great as you keeps silent so long, it's somebody's duty to find out the reason. Automatically, one's first guess is drink, but that's obviously not your trouble. There must be some psychological——"

Just then Neil spoke to me.

"Quiet, a minute," I whispered, but I missed the rest of Mrs. Cotton's speech. Father said:

"Good God, you can't say things like that to me at your own dinner table."

"Oh, I always employ shock tactics with men of genius," said Mrs. Cotton. "And one has to employ them in public or the men of genius bolt."

"I'm perfectly capable of bolting, in public or out," said father—but I could tell he wasn't going to; there was an easy, amused tone in his voice that I hadn't heard for years. He went on banteringly, "Tell me, are you unique or has the American club woman become more menacing since my day?" It seemed to me a terribly rude thing to say, even in fun, but Mrs. Cotton didn't appear to mind in the least. She just said smilingly, "I don't happen to be what *you* mean by a club woman. And anyway, I think we must cure you of this habit of generalizing about America on the strength of two short lecture tours." Serve father right—he has always talked as if he had brought America home in his trouser pocket. Naturally I wanted to go on listening, but I saw Mrs. Cotton notice me; so I turned quickly to Neil.

"All right now," I said.

"What was it?" he asked. "Did you think you'd broken a tooth?".

I laughed and told him what I had been listening to.

"You just wait," he said. "She'll have him turning out

masterpieces eight hours a day—unless, of course, he goes for *her* with a cake-knife."

I stared at him in amazement. He went on: "Oh, she had our attorney send us all the details of the case. Made me laugh a lot. But I guess she was a bit disappointed that it wasn't a real attempt at murder."

"Can you understand how a ridiculous thing like that could put him off his work?" I asked.

"Why, I don't even understand your father's work when he was on it," said Neil. "I'm just not literary."

After that, we talked of other things—I felt it would be polite to ask questions about America. He told me about his father's ranch in California, where he had lived until he joined Mrs. Cotton and Simon. (It is strange to realize how little he has had to do with them.) I said it seemed very sad that the father had died before he could inherit Scoatney Hall.

"He wouldn't have lived in it, anyway," said Neil. "He'd never have settled down anywhere but in America—any more than I shall."

I almost began to say: "But your brother's going to live here, isn't he?" but I stopped myself. Neil had sounded so cross that I felt it might be a sore subject. I asked him if he liked Rose's dress—mostly to change the conversation.

He said: "Not very much, if you want the honest truth—it's too fussy for me. But she looks very pretty in it. Knows it, too, doesn't she?"

There was a twinkle in his eye which took off the rudeness. And I must admit that Rose was knowing it all over the place.

The most wonderful frozen pudding came round then and while Neil helped himself, I let my left ear listen to father and Mrs. Cotton again. They seemed to be getting on splendidly, though it did sound a bit like a shouting match. I saw Topaz look across anxiously, then look relieved: father was chuckling.

"Oh, talk to the Vicar—give me a rest," he said.

"But I shall return to the attack," said Mrs. Cotton. Her eyes were sparkling and she looked about twice as healthy as anyone normally does.

"Well, how are you enjoying your first grown-up dinner party?" father asked me—it was the first word he had spoken to me throughout the meal but I could hardly blame him for that. He was rather flushed and somehow larger than usual—there was a touch of the magnificence I still remember about him from pre-cake-knife days. He had a slight return of it when he married Topaz, but it didn't last. The awful thought came to me that he might be going to fall in love with Mrs. Cotton. She was talking to him again within a couple of minutes. Soon after that the females left the table.

As we went upstairs, Topaz slipped her arm through mine.

"Could you hear?" she whispered. "Is he really enjoying himself? Or was he just putting it on?"

I told her I thought it was genuine.

"It's wonderful to see him like that"—but her voice sounded wistful. It is one of her theories that a woman must never be jealous, never try to hold a man against his will; but I could tell that she hadn't enjoyed seeing someone else bring father to life.

Mrs. Cotton's bedroom was lovely—there were lots of flowers, and new books lying around and a chaise-longue piled with fascinating little cushions; and a wood fire—it must be heaven to have a fire in one's bedroom. The bathroom was unbelievable—the walls were looking-glass! And there was a glass table with at least half-a-dozen bottles of scent and toilet water on it. (Americans say "perfume" instead of "scent"—much more correct, really; I don't know why "perfume" should be considered affected in England.)

"Simon says this bathroom's an outrage on the house," said Mrs. Cotton, "but I've no use for antiquity in bathrooms."

"Isn't it lovely?" I said to Rose.

"Glorious," she said, in an almost tragic voice. I could see she was liking it so much that it really hurt her.

When we had tidied up we went to the Long Gallery—it stretches the full length of the house and as it is narrow it seems even longer than it is. It has three fireplaces and there were fires in all of them, but it wasn't at all too hot. Rose and I strolled along looking at the pictures and statues and interesting things in glass cases, while Mrs. Cotton talked to Topaz. Mrs. Fox-Cotton had disappeared after dinner; I suppose she went off to her own bedroom.

We got to the fireplace at the far end of the gallery and stood looking back at the others; we could hear their voices but not a word of what they were saying, so we felt it was safe to talk.

"What sort of a time did you have at dinner?" I asked.

She said it had been boring—she didn't like Mr. Fox-Cotton and, anyway, he had only been interested in Topaz: "So I concentrated on the wonderful food. What did you and Neil talk about?"

"Amongst other things, he said you looked very pretty," I told her.

"What else?"

"About America, mostly." I remembered as much as I could for her, particularly about the ranch in California; I had liked the sound of it.

"What, cows and things?" she said, disgustedly. "Is he going back there?"

"Oh, it was sold when the father died. But he did say he'd like to have a ranch himself if ever he could afford it."

"But aren't they very rich?"

"Oh, shut up," I whispered, and took a quick look at Mrs. Cotton; but we were really quite safe. "I don't suppose Neil's rich and it probably takes all Simon's money to keep this place up. Come on, we'd better go back."

As we reached the fireplace in the middle of the gallery, Mrs. Fox-Cotton came in. It was the first time I'd had a really good look at her. She is small, not much bigger than I am, with straight black hair done in an enormous knob low on her neck, and a very dark skin. Both skin and hair look greasy to me. Topaz says the modelling of the face is beautiful and I do see that, but I don't think the modelling would be damaged by a real good wash. She was wearing a clinging dark green dress, so shiny that it looked almost slimy—it made me think of sea-weed. Her Christian name, believe it or not, is Leda.

Rose and I walked to meet her but she sat down on a sofa, put her feet up and opened an old calf-bound book she had brought in with her. "Do you mind?" she said. "I want to finish this before we go back to London to-morrow."

"What is it?" I asked, out of politeness.

"Oh, it's no book for little girls," she said. She has the silliest voice, a little tinny bleat; she barely bothers to open her mouth—the words just slide through her teeth. In view of what happened later, I put it on record that it was then I first decided that I didn't like her.

The men came in then—I noticed she was quick enough to stop reading for *them*. Father and Simon seemed to be finishing a literary argument; I hoped they'd had a really good discussion downstairs. It was interesting to notice where the men went: father and the Vicar talked to Mrs. Cotton, Aubrey Fox-Cotton made a dive for Topaz, Simon and Neil came towards Rose and me—but Mrs. Fox-Cotton got off her sofa and intercepted Simon.

"Did you know there's a picture here with a look of you?" she told him, and put her arm through his and marched him along the gallery.

"Oh, I noticed that," I said. Rose and Neil and I walked after them, which I bet didn't please Mrs. F-C. at all.

It was one of the earliest pictures—Elizabethan, I think; there was a small white ruff at the top of the man's high collar. It was just a head and shoulders against a dark background.

"It's probably only the beard that's like," said Simon.

"No, the eyes," said Mrs. Fox-Cotton.

"The eyebrows mostly," I said, "the little twist at the corners. And the hair—the way it grows on the forehead, in a peak."

Rose was staring hard at the picture. Simon asked her what she thought. She turned and looked at him intently; she seemed to be taking in his features one by one. Yet when she finally answered she only said: "Oh, a little like, perhaps," rather vaguely. I had a feeling that she had been thinking about something quite different from the picture, something to do with Simon himself; and had come back from a very long way, to find us all waiting for her answer.

We strolled back to the others. Topaz and Aubrey Fox-

Cotton were looking at pictures too; they were with the eighteenth-century Cottons. "I've got it," he said suddenly to Topaz, "you're really a Blake. Isn't she, Leda?"

Mrs. F-C. seemed to take a mild interest in this. She gave Topaz a long appraising stare and said: "Yes, if she had more flesh on her bones."

"Rose is a Romney," said Simon. "She's quite a bit like Lady Hamilton." It was the first time I had heard him use her Christian name. "And Cassandra's a Reynolds, of course— the little girl with the mousetrap."

"I'm not!" I said indignantly. "I hate that picture. The mouse is terrified, the cat's hungry and the girl's a cruel little beast. I refuse to be her."

"Ah, but you'd let the mouse out of the trap and find a nice dead sardine for the cat," said Simon. I began to like him a little better.

The others were busy thinking of a painter for Mrs. Fox-Cotton. They finally decided on a Surrealist named Dali. "With snakes coming out of her ears," said Mr. Fox-Cotton. I haven't the faintest idea what Surrealism is, but I can easily imagine snakes in Mrs. F-C.'s ears—and I certainly shouldn't blame them for coming out.

After that, it was decided that we should dance. "In the hall," said Neil, "because the Victrola's down there." Mrs. Cotton and father and the Vicar stayed behind talking.

"We shall be one man short," complained Mrs. Fox-Cotton as we went downstairs.

I said I would watch as I don't know modern dances. (Neither does Rose, really, but she did try them once or twice at Aunt Millicent's parties.)

"What kind do you know?" asked Simon, teasingly. "Sarabandes, courantes and pavanes?"

I told him just waltzes and polkas. Mother showed us those when we were little.

"I'll teach you," said Neil. He put a record on the gramo-phone—I had expected a Victrola to be something much more exciting—and then came back to me, but I said I'd rather watch for the first few dances.

"Oh, come on, Cassandra," he said, but Mrs. Fox-Cotton butted in. "Let the child watch if she wants to. Dance this with me." I settled it by running up the stairs.

I sat on the top step looking down on them. Rose danced with Simon, Topaz with Mr. Fox-Cotton. I must say Mrs. Fox-Cotton danced beautifully, though she seemed almost to be lying on Neil's chest. Rose's dress looked lovely but she kept on missing steps. Topaz was holding herself stiff as a poker—she thinks modern dancing is vulgar—but Mr. Fox-Cotton danced so well that she gradually relaxed. It was fascinating watching them all from up there. The hall was very dimly lit, the oak floor looked dark as water by night. I noticed the mysterious old-house smell again but mixed with Mrs. Fox-Cotton's scent—a rich, mysterious scent, not a bit like flowers. I leaned against the carved banisters and listened to the music and felt quite different from any way I have ever felt before—softer, very beautiful and as if a great many men were in love with me and I might very easily be in love with them. I had the most curious feeling in my solar plexus—a vulnerable feeling is the nearest I can get to it; I was investigating it in a pleasant, hazy sort of way, staring down at a big bowl of white tulips against the uncurtained great window, when all of a sudden I went quite cold with shock.

There were two faces floating in the black glass of the window.

The next instant they were gone. I strained my eyes to see them again. The dancers kept passing the window, hiding it from me. Suddenly the faces were back, but grown fainter. They grew clear again—and just then the record finished. The dancers stopped, the faces vanished.

Aubrey Fox-Cotton shouted: "Did you see that, Simon? Two of the villagers staring in again."

"That's the worst of a right-of-way so close to the house," Simon explained to Rose.

"Oh, hell, what does it matter?" said Neil. "Let them watch if they want to."

"But it startled mother badly the other night. I think I'll just ask them not to, if I can catch them."

Simon went to the door and opened it. I ran full tilt down the stairs, and across to him. There was a light above the door which made everything seem pitch black beyond.

"Don't catch them," I whispered.

He smiled down at me in astonishment. "Good heavens, I'm not going to hurt them." He went down the steps and shouted: "Anyone there?"

There was a stifled laugh quite close.

"They're behind the cedar," said Simon and started to walk towards it. I was praying they would bolt but no sound of it came. I grabbed Simon's arm and whispered: "Please come back—please say you couldn't find them. It's Thomas and Stephen."

Simon let out a snort of laughter.

"They must have cycled over," I said. "Please don't be annoyed. It's just that they hankered to see the fun."

He called out: "Thomas, Stephen—where are you? Come in and talk to us."

They didn't answer. We walked towards the cedar. Suddenly they made a dash for it—and Thomas promptly tripped over something and fell full length. I called: "Come on, both of you—it's perfectly all right."

Simon went to help Thomas up—I knew he wasn't hurt because he was laughing so much. My eyes were used to the darkness by then and I could see Stephen some yards away; he had stopped but he wasn't coming towards us. I went over and took him by the hand.

"I'm so dreadfully sorry," he whispered. "I know it was a terrible thing to do."

"Nonsense," I said. "Nobody minds a bit." His hand was quite damp. I was sure he was feeling awful.

The others had heard the shouts and come to the door. Neil came running out to us with a torch.

"What, my old friend Stephen?" he cried. "Are there any bears abroad to-night?"

"I don't want to come in—please!" Stephen whispered to me. But Neil and I took an arm each and made him.

Thomas wasn't minding at all—he kept choking with

laughter. "We had a squint at you at dinner," he said, "and then you all disappeared. We were just about to go home in despair when you came downstairs."

Once I saw Stephen clearly, in the hall, I was sorry I had made him come in—he was scarlet to his forehead and too shy to speak a word. And Rose made things worse by saying affectedly (I think it was due to embarrassment): "I do apologize for them. They ought to be ashamed of themselves."

"Don't mind your Great-Aunt Rose, boys," said Neil, with a grin. "Come on, we'll go and raid the ice-box."

I once saw them do that on the pictures and it looked marvellous. I thought I would go along, too, but Mrs. Fox-Cotton called me back.

"Who's that boy, the tall fair one?" she demanded.

I told her about Stephen.

She said: "I must photograph him."

"What, at this time of night?"

She gave a whinnying little laugh. "Of course not, you silly child. He must come up to London—I'm a professional photographer. Look here, ask him—No, don't bother." She ran upstairs.

Neil and the boys had disappeared by then. I was sorry, because I was quite a bit hungry, in spite of the enormous dinner; I suppose my stomach had got into practice. I feared that if I hung about, Simon might feel he ought to dance with me—he was dancing with Rose again and I wanted him to go on. So I went upstairs.

It was pleasant being by myself in the house—one gets the feel of a house much better alone. I went very slowly, looking at the old prints on the walls of the passages. Everywhere at Scoatney one feels so conscious of the past; it is like a presence, a caress in the air. I don't often get that feeling at the castle; perhaps it has been altered too much, and the oldest parts seem so utterly remote. Probably the beautiful, undisturbed furniture helps at Scoatney.

I expected to hear voices to guide me back to the gallery but everything was quiet. At last I came to a window open on to the courtyard and leaned out and got my bearings—

I could see the gallery windows. I could see the kitchen windows, too, and Neil and Thomas and Stephen eating at the table. It did look fun.

When I went into the gallery, father and Mrs. Cotton were at the far end and the Vicar was lying on the sofa by the middle fireplace reading Mrs. Fox-Cotton's book. I told him about Thomas and Stephen.

"Let's go and talk to them," he said, "unless you want me to dance with you. I dance like an india-rubber ball."

I said I should like to see the kitchens. He got up, closing the book.

"Mrs. Fox-Cotton said that was no book for little girls," I told him.

"It's no book for little vicars," he said, chuckling.

He took me down by the back stairs—he knows the house well, as he was very friendly with old Mr. Cotton. It was interesting to notice the difference once we got into the servants' quarters; the carpets were thin and worn, the lighting was harsh, it felt much colder. The smell was different, too—just as old but with no mellowness in it; a stale, damp, dispiriting smell.

But the kitchens were beautiful when we got to them—all painted white, with a white enamelled stove and the hugest refrigerator. (Aunt Millicent only had an old one which dribbled.) Neil and the boys were still eating. And sitting on the table, talking hard to Stephen, was Mrs. Fox-Cotton.

As I came in, she was handing him a card. I heard her say:

"All you have to do is to give that address to the taxi-driver. I'll pay your fare when you get there—or perhaps I'd better give you some money now." She opened her evening bag.

"Are you really going to be photographed?" I asked him. He shook his head and showed me the card. It had LEDA. ARTIST PHOTOGRAPHER on it, under a beautifully drawn little swan, and an address in St. John's Wood.

"Be a nice child and help me to persuade him," she said. "He can come on a Sunday. I'll pay his fare and give him two guineas. He's exactly what I've been looking for for months."

"No, thank you, ma'am," said Stephen, very politely. "I'd be embarrassed."

"Heavens, what's there to be embarrassed about? I only want to photograph your head. Would you do it for three guineas?"

"What, for just one day?"

She gave him a shrewd little look; then said quickly:

"*Five* guineas if you come next Sunday."

"Don't do it if you don't want to, Stephen," I said.

He swallowed and thought. At last he said: "I'll have to think it over, ma'am. Would it be five guineas if I came a little later?"

"Any Sunday you like—I can always use you. Only write in advance to make sure I shall be free. You write for him," she added, to me.

"He'll write himself if he wants to," I said coldly—she sounded as if she thought he was illiterate.

"Well, don't you go putting him off. Five guineas, Stephen. And I probably won't need you for more than two or three hours."

She grabbed a wing of chicken and sat there gnawing it. Neil offered me some, but my appetite had gone off.

Stephen said it was time he and Thomas rode home. Neil asked them to stay on and dance, but didn't press it when he saw Stephen didn't want to. We all went to see them off— the bicycles were somewhere at the back of the house. On the way, we passed through a store-room where enormous hams were hanging.

"Old Mr. Cotton sent us one of those every Christmas," said Thomas. "Only he was dead last Christmas."

Neil reached up and took the largest ham off its hook.

"There you are, Tommy," he said.

"Oh, Thomas, you can't!" I began—but I didn't want Neil to call me Great-Aunt Cassandra so I finished up: "Well, I suppose you *have*." And I certainly would have fainted with despair if Thomas had refused the ham. In the end, I undertook to bring it home because he couldn't manage it on his bicycle.

"But swear you won't go all ladylike and leave it behind," he whispered. I swore.

After the boys had gone we went back to the hall and found the others still dancing.

"Come on, Cassandra," said Neil, and whirled me off.

Dear me, dancing is peculiar when you really think about it. If a man held your hand and put his arm round your waist without its being dancing, it would be most important; in dancing, you don't even notice it—well, only a little bit. I managed to follow the steps better than I expected, but not easily enough to enjoy myself; I was quite glad when the record ended.

Neil asked Rose to dance then, and I had a glorious waltz with the Vicar; we got so dizzy that we had to flop on a sofa. I don't fancy Rose followed Neil as well as I had done, because as they passed I heard him say: "Don't keep on putting in little fancy steps on your own." I guessed that would annoy her and it did; when the music stopped and he asked her to come out into the garden for some air, she said "No, thanks," almost rudely.

After that, we all went back to the Long Gallery, where father and Mrs. Cotton were talking as hard as ever. Mrs. Cotton broke off politely as we went in and the conversation was general for a while; but Mrs. Fox-Cotton kept yawning and patting her mouth and saying "Excuse me"—which only drew more attention to it—and soon Topaz said we ought to be going. Mrs. Cotton protested courteously, then rang for the car. There was a late feeling about the evening—just as there used to be at children's parties (the few I ever went to) after the first nurse arrived to take a child home.

I picked up the ham as we went through the hall and tactfully kept it under the wrap Topaz had lent me—it was a most peculiar sort of burnous thing but it came in very useful. Simon and Neil went out to the car with us and said they would come over and see us when they got back from London—they were driving up the next day to stay for a fortnight.

And so the party was over.

"Great Heavens, Cassandra, how did you get that?" said father when he saw me nursing the ham.

I told him, and explained that I had been hiding it in case he made me refuse it.

"Refuse it? You must be insane, my child." He took it from me to guess how much it weighed. We all guessed—which was a sheer waste of time as we haven't any scales.

"You're nursing it as if it were your first-born child," said father when it was returned to me eventually.

I said I doubted if anyone's first-born child was ever more welcome. After that we all fell silent—we had suddenly remembered the chauffeur.

Even when we got home we didn't all rush to compare notes. I got the feeling that we all wanted to do a little private thinking. I certainly did.

I began as soon as Rose and I had blown our bedroom candles out. I wasn't a bit sleepy. I went through the whole evening—it was almost nicer than when it was actually happening until I got to the bit in the kitchen, with Mrs. Fox-Cotton asking Stephen to sit for her; I found I was furious about that. I asked myself why—why shouldn't he make five guineas for a few hours' work? Five guineas is a tremendous amount of money. And surely a photographer has every right to engage models? I decided I was being most unreasonable—but I went on feeling furious.

While I was still arguing with myself, Rose got out of the four-poster and opened the window wider; then sat on the window-seat.

"Can't you sleep?" I asked.

She said she hadn't even been trying and I guessed she had been going over the evening just as I had; I wished I could change minds with her for a while and re-live *her* evening.

I got up and joined her on the window-seat. It was such a dark night that I could only see the shape of her. Suddenly she said:

"I wish I knew more about men."

"Why specially?" I asked, in a quietly encouraging voice. She was silent so long that I thought she wasn't going to answer; then the words came rushing out:

"He's attracted—I know he is! But he's probably been

attracted to lots of girls; it doesn't necessarily mean he's going to propose. If only I knew the clever way to behave!"

I said: "Oh, Rose, have you thought what marriage really means?"

"Yes, I thought to-night—when I looked at him to see if he was like that old painting. I suddenly imagined being in bed with him."

"What a moment to choose for it! I saw you were pretty preoccupied. Well, how did it feel?"

"Most peculiar. But I could face it."

"Is it just the money, Rose?"

"I'm not sure," she said, "honestly, I'm not—I don't understand myself. It's terribly exciting feeling men are attracted to you. It's——but you couldn't understand."

"I think perhaps I could." For a second I thought of telling her about Stephen, but before I could start she went on:

"I like him—really I do. He's so courteous—he's the first person who ever made me feel I matter. And he's handsome— in a way, don't you think? His eyes are, anyway. If I could just get used to the beard——"

"Are you sure you wouldn't rather have Neil? He's so very kind and he's got such a nice clean face."

"Oh, Neil——!" Her tone was so scornful that I realized he must have annoyed her even more than I had suspected. "No, you can have Neil."

Honestly, that was the first time the idea had ever occurred to me. Of course I didn't take it seriously—but I felt it deserved a little quiet thinking about.

"If only I could get Simon to shave," Rose went on. Then her voice went hard. "Anyway, what does it matter? I'd marry him even if I hated him. Cassandra, did you ever see anything as beautiful as Mrs. Cotton's bathroom?"

"Yes, lots of things," I said firmly. "And no bathroom on earth will make up for marrying a bearded man you hate."

"But I don't hate him—I tell you I like him. I almost——" She broke off and went back to bed.

"Perhaps you won't be sure of your feelings until you've let him kiss you," I suggested.

"But I can't do that before he proposes—or he mightn't propose," she said decidedly. "That's one thing I do know."

I had a strong suspicion she was being a mite old-fashioned, but I kept my views to myself. "Well, I shall pray you really fall in love with him—and he with you, of course. And I'll do out-of-bed prayers."

"So will I," she said, hopping out again.

We both prayed hard, Rose much the longest—she was still on her knees when I had settled down ready to sleep.

"That'll do, Rose," I told her at last. "It's enough just to mention things, you know. Long prayers are like nagging."

We were restless for ages. I tried to invent something soothing for Miss Blossom to say but I wasn't in the mood. After a while I heard an owl hooting and calmed myself by thinking of it flying over the dark fields—and then I remembered it would be pouncing on mice. I love owls, but I wish God had made them vegetarian. Rose kept flinging herself over in bed.

"Oh, do stop walloping about," I said. "You'll break what few springs the four-poster has left."

But again and again as I was dropping off she did a wallop. Godsend church clock struck two before I heard her breathing quietly. Then I got to sleep at last.

Chapter IX

IT TOOK ME THREE DAYS TO DESCRIBE THE PARTY AT SCOATNEY—
I didn't mark the breaks because I wanted it to seem like one
whole chapter. Now that life has become so much more
exciting I think of this journal as a story I am telling. A new
chapter happened yesterday which I long to dash straight
into, but I shall resist the temptation and bring myself up to
date first.

One temptation I didn't manage to resist was that of letting
my imagination leap ahead a bit. As Rose had said I could
have Neil, I let myself just toy with the idea; I thought about
it when I woke up the day after the party and imagined his
proposing—I made it happen in the water-garden at Scoatney.
I accepted him and Rose and I arranged to have a double
wedding, and bought the most superb trousseaux. Then I
dozed off again and dreamt I really was married to Neil. We
were shut up together in Mrs. Cotton's bathroom in a terribly
embarrassing way and Stephen's face kept floating in the
looking-glass walls. I was very glad to wake up and find it
wasn't true. Of course Neil never will propose to me now that
I have let myself imagine it. Not that I mind.

I suppose he just *might*—in a completely different way, and
not in the water-garden.

Topaz and I had a good gossip about the party while we
made the beds. She was more and more hopeful for Rose, but
depressed about father—he had snubbed her when she asked
him what he and Mrs. Cotton had talked about.

"All I got out of him was 'Don't be a fool, my dear—how
can one repeat the details of a conversation? She's a highly
intelligent woman and she can listen as well as she can talk.'
And then what do you think he said? That he'd placed her

wrongly—her knowledge of literature wasn't at all superficial; she's very widely read. 'It just shows,' he told me, 'that one shouldn't generalize about nations on the strength of a brief acquaintance'—and you'd have thought from his tone that *I'd* been doing the generalizing."

"How very annoying," I said, trying not to laugh—I was so tickled that father had taken to heart Mrs. Cotton's little snub about generalizing.

"Anyway, how is it he can discuss literature with her and not with me? I'm always trying to talk to him about books, but he never lets me."

I blame father for lots of things but not for that—because it really is agony to talk to her about books. When I was longing for a calm discussion of Tolstoy's *War and Peace*, she said: "Ah, it's the overlapping dimensions that are so wonderful. I tried to paint it once, on a circular canvas"—and then she couldn't remember who Natasha was.

I was most sympathetic with her over father, but rather quick about it, because I wanted to write my journal. I only managed an hour before lunch but was able to work all afternoon, up in the attic. Stephen came to me there when he got back from Four Stones. My heart sank as he held out a folded paper—I had been hoping he had outgrown bringing me poems. He stood waiting for me to read it.

After the first line I realized that it was his own work this time—it was about me, sitting on the stairs at Scoatney while the others danced. I was wondering what I could say about it, when he snatched it away and tore it up.

"I know it's dreadful," he said.

I told him it wasn't dreadful at all. "Some of it rhymed splendidly, Stephen. And it's your very own. I like it much better than the ones you copied out." I felt it was an opportunity to stop him copying again.

"I didn't exactly copy them," he said, not looking at me. "I always changed words in them. I didn't mean to be dishonest, Cassandra—it was just that nothing of my own seemed good enough."

I said I understood perfectly but he must always write his

own poems in future. And I advised him not even to imitate other people's poems.

"I know you made up every word of this last one," I told him, "but it was still a bit *like* Herrick—all that part about lilies and roses and violets. You didn't really see them in the hall last night—there were only white tulips."

"I bet Herrick didn't see all the flowers he wrote about," said Stephen, grinning. "And the only rhyme I could find for tulips was 'blue lips'."

I laughed and told him there were more important things than rhymes—"Lots of good poetry doesn't have them at all. The main thing is to write what you really feel."

"Oh, I couldn't do that," he said. "No, that would never do."

"But why not, Stephen? Of course it would do."

"No, it wouldn't," he said, and smiled straight in front of him as if he were thinking of some private joke. It reminded me of that evening months ago when we were putting saucepans under the drips—he had smiled in just the same private way.

"Stephen," I said, "do you remember—why, it was the very night the Cottons first came here! Do you remember looking out of this window and saying: 'Beginnings are good times'?"

He nodded. "But I wasn't expecting any Cottons," he said, glumly. "Did you dance with them last night?"

"I tried once with Neil."

"People look awful dancing—I'd be ashamed. You'd never do it like that one who calls herself Leda, would you?"

"I'd never dance so well," I said. "But I know what you mean. She does rather drape herself over her partners, doesn't she? You aren't going to let her photograph you, are you?"

I said it most casually, not as if I minded at all. To my surprise, he put on his wooden look—which is quite different from his daft look. The daft look is hazy, dreamy; the wooden look is obstinate to the point of sulkiness. It is a look he gives Rose sometimes, but I couldn't remember his ever turning it on me.

"I might," he said. "If people want to throw their money about——"

"But surely you'd hate it, Stephen?"

"It might be worth hating it to earn five guineas. Five guineas would be almost enough——" He broke off and turned away to go downstairs.

"Enough for what?" I called after him.

"Oh, for—for lots of things," he said, without turning round. "Five guineas is more than I can save in a year."

"But you were so sure you wouldn't do it last night."

He looked back as he went round the curve of the little attic staircase, his head just above the level of the floor.

"P'raps I will, p'raps I won't," he said maddeningly and went on down. A voice in my head said : "I'm damned if you're going to sit for Leda Fox-Cotton." Then the bell rang for tea so I followed him down.

Topaz had boiled half the ham. She said it would go further if we didn't cut it until it was quite cold, but Thomas insisted— he has been very possessive about that ham. We all fanned it with newspapers until the last moment. It was wonderful, of course—ham with mustard is a meal of glory.

Miss Marcy came after tea, to hear all about the party. She told me Mrs. Fox-Cotton's photographs are very well known ; they get reproduced in magazines. She particularly remembered one of a girl hiding behind a giant shell with the shadow of a man coming towards her. "And one got the impression that he was wearing—well, nothing, which surprised me rather because one doesn't often see photographs being as artistic as paintings, does one? But there, he probably had a bathing suit on all the time—it would hardly show on a shadow, would it?"

I laughed—I do adore darling Miss Marcy. But I was all the more determined Stephen shouldn't go near the Fox-Cotton woman.

The next morning Topaz, Rose and I went into King's Crypt with the twenty pounds the Vicar gave for the collie dog rug and bought my first grown-up dress—pale green linen; Rose had a pink one. Topaz said she didn't need anything herself—

and anyway, she looks most unnatural in ready-made clothes. I got some white shoes and a pair of practically silk stockings. If anyone asked me to a garden-party I could go.

When we got home we found father hadn't eaten the lunch Topaz had left for him and wasn't anywhere in the castle. He turned up about nine o'clock and said he had bicycled over to Scoatney—apparently Simon had given him the run of the library while they were away. I asked if he had read anything particularly interesting.

"Oh, mostly American magazines—and some critical essays," he said. "I'd forgotten how advanced American criticism is."

Topaz said she would get him a meal, but he told her he'd had luncheon and dinner. "It seems Mrs. Cotton left instructions that I'm to be fed when I go there." He went off to the gatehouse looking rather smug.

I retired to the attic and went on with this journal. When I came down to the kitchen again Stephen was writing on an opened-out sugar bag. He went scarlet when he saw me and crumpled the sugar bag up. Just then Topaz came in from the garden wearing Aunt Millicent's black cloak and no stockings or shoes. I guessed she'd had one of her nude sessions.

"Thank heaven Nature never fails me," she said as she stumped upstairs. When I turned round Stephen was poking the sugar bag down into the fire.

"Was it another poem?" I asked—I feel I ought to encourage him now he is writing his own poems. "Why did you burn it?"

"Because it wouldn't do at all," he said, still very red in the face. He stared at me for a second, then suddenly dashed out into the garden. I waited for him, sitting by the fire with Ab and Hel, but he didn't come back.

When I went upstairs, Rose was sitting up in bed varnishing her nails; the varnish had been her special treat out of the Vicar's money—I had lavender soap.

"You're using that too soon," I said. "The Cottons won't be back for twelve days yet."

Little did I think we should see them again in only four!

Yesterday was the first of May. I love the special days of

the year—St. Valentine's, Hallowe'en; Midsummer Eve most of all. A May Day that feels as it sounds is rare and, when I leaned out of the bedroom window watching the moat ruffled into sparkles by a warm breeze, I was as happy as I have ever been in my life. I knew it was going to be a lucky day.

It certainly made a false start before breakfast.

Father came down in his best dark suit that he hasn't worn for years. Rose and I gaped at him, and Topaz stopped stirring the porridge to say: "Mortmain—what on earth——?"

"I'm going up to London," said father, shortly.

"What for?" we all said together; which made it rather loud.

"Business," said father, even louder, and went out of the kitchen banging the door.

"Don't worry him, don't ask questions," whispered Topaz. Then she turned to me, looking miserable. "Do you think he's going to see *her*—Mrs. Cotton?"

"Surely he couldn't—not without being asked," I said.

"Oh, yes he could," said Rose. "Look at him, going to Scoatney three days running, letting the servants feed him—grubbing about in the books and magazines! I tell you he'll end by putting them off us."

"It wasn't him who put them off us last time," said Topaz, angrily.

I saw there were going to be high words so I went through into the drawing-room. Father was sitting on the window-seat polishing his shoes with the curtain. When he got up he was covered with Heloïse's white hairs from the seat-pad.

"Is there no place a man in a dark suit can sit in this house?" he shouted as he went to the hall for the clothes-brush.

"Not unless we dye Hel black," I said. I brushed him; but what with the brush having lost most of its bristles, his suit having lost most of its nap and Heloïse having lost more hairs than seemed believable, the result was poor. Topaz came to say that breakfast was ready, but he said he would miss his train if he waited for it.

"Don't fuss, don't fuss," he said when she begged him to have just something. Then he pushed past her in the rudest way and grabbed Rose's bicycle because his own had a flat tyre.

"When will you be back?" Topaz called after him.

He yelled over his shoulder that he hadn't the faintest idea.

"What *is* the matter with him?" said Topaz as we walked back across the garden. "I know he's always been moody but not bad-tempered like this. It's been getting worse ever since we went to Scoatney."

"Perhaps it's better than heavy resignation," I suggested, trying to be comforting. "He was shockingly bad-tempered when we were little—when he was writing. You know about mother and the cake-knife."

Topaz looked suddenly hopeful. "He can *massacre* me if it'll really help him," she said. Then the light died out of her eyes. "But I'm no good to him. It's that woman who's started him."

"Gracious, we don't know if *anything's* started him," I said. "We've had so many false alarms. Where did he get the money to go to London?"

She said she had given him five pounds of the Vicar's rug money. "Though I didn't think he'd spend it on seeing *her*." Then she added nobly: "I suppose I oughtn't even to mind that, if she stimulates him."

Rose came out of the kitchen with a slice of bread and jam, and passed us without a word—I gathered she and Topaz had had a very sharp row while I was brushing father. We found that the porridge was burnt—than which there can be few less pleasing forms of food; and what with this and Topaz's mood of gloom, we had a depressing meal. (The boys, of course, had gone off earlier; after a hammy breakfast.)

"I shall go and dig until I find peace," said Topaz, when we had done the washing-up and made the beds.

I felt she would find it better alone and I wanted to write in my journal; I had finished the evening at Scoatney but there were some reflections about life I wanted to record. (I never did record them—and have now forgotten what they were.) As I settled myself down on Belmotte mound, I saw Rose going along the lane with Mrs. Stebbins's crinoline: Stephen had brought word that the old lady was fretting for it. He had refused to take it back for Rose because he said he'd feel embarrassed. Rose had it over her shoulder; she did look peculiar.

I decided to think a little before I began writing, and lay back enjoying the heat of the sun and staring up at the great blue bowl of the sky. It was lovely feeling the warm earth under me and the springing grass against the palms of my hands while my mind was drawn upwards. Unfortunately my thoughts will never stay exalted for very long, and soon I was gloating over my new green dress and wondering if it would suit me to curl my hair. I closed my eyes, as I usually do when I am thinking very hard. Gradually I slid into imagining Rose married to Simon—it doesn't seem to matter when you imagine about other people, it only stops things happening when you do it about yourself. I gave Rose a lovely wedding and got to where she was alone with Simon at a Paris hotel— she was a little frightened of him, but I made her enjoy that. He was looking at her the way he did at dinner when he raised his glass to her. . . .

I opened my eyes. He was there, the real Simon Cotton, looking at me.

I hadn't heard a sound. One second I had seen him in the Paris hotel, brilliantly clear yet somehow tiny and far away, rather as one sees things in a convex mirror; the next instant he was like a giant against the sky. I had been lying with the sun on my eyelids so that for a minute nothing was the right colour. The grass and sky were bleached and his face looked ashen. But his beard was still black.

"Did I startle you?" he asked, smiling. "I had a bet with myself I'd get up the hill without your hearing. Oh—you weren't asleep, were you?"

"Not quite so early in the day," I said, sitting up blinking. He sat down beside me. It was the queerest feeling—changing the man I had imagined to the real man. I had made him so fascinating, and of course he isn't really—though very, very nice; I know that now.

He and Neil had driven down just for the day; Neil had dropped him at the end of our lane and gone on to Scoatney— which sounded as if he weren't very interested in us.

"I'm sorry to have missed your sister," said Simon, "but Mrs. Mortmain hopes she'll be back soon."

I said I was sure she would, though I really thought she would be gone at least an hour, and wondered if I could be interesting enough to keep him talking as long as that. I asked him if they were having a good time in London.

"Oh, yes—I love London. But it seems a waste not to be here in this weather." He leaned back on his elbow, gazing across the fields. "I never knew the English spring could be so dazzling."

I said it astonished one every year.

"Well, after next week we'll be back here for some time— that is, Neil and I will; mother's absorbed in her new apartment —flat, as I keep forgetting to call it. Leda and Aubrey are helping her to choose the furniture. Oh, that reminds me"— he took an envelope from his pocket—"I ought to have left this at the castle. It's for that nice boy Stephen; his fare to London, from Leda."

"I'll give it to him," I said. I wondered if Stephen had written saying he could go, or if she had just sent the money to tempt him.

Simon handed me the envelope. "Tell me about him," he said. "How does he come to speak so differently from the other village boys?"

Of course Stephen speaks just as we do—except that he chooses rather humble words. I explained about him.

"I wonder what he'll make of Leda," said Simon. "She wants to pose him with some casts of Greek sculpture. She'll have him in a tunic if he's not careful—or out of it. He certainly has a marvellous head—perhaps he'll end in Hollywood."

I shut the envelope in my journal so that it wouldn't blow away.

"What's that? Lessons?" asked Simon.

"Heavens, no! I left school long ago."

"I do apologize," he said, laughing. "I still think of you as that little girl in the bath. Is it a story? Read me a bit."

I told him it was my journal and that I had just finished the party at Scoatney.

"Do I come in it? I'll give you a box of candy if you'll let me read a page."

"All right," I said.

He grabbed the exercise book. After a second or two he looked up from it. "You've swindled me. Is it your own private code?"

"More or less—though it did begin as real speed-writing. It changed by degrees. And I got it smaller and smaller, so as not to waste paper."

He turned the pages and guessed a word here and there but I could see I was safe. After a minute or two he said:

"I was reading the journal in *Jacob Wrestling* again yesterday—I happened to pick up a first edition. It's odd to remember how obscure I found that part when I read it at sixteen. By the time I came to do it in college it seemed perfectly intelligible."

"The only part that still puzzles me is the ladder chapter—you know, where it's printed so that it actually looks like a ladder, with a sentence for every rung. Father won't answer questions about that."

"Maybe he can't. I've always believed it's the description of some mystical experience. Of course you know the theory that each rung leads to the next, even though the sentences seem so unconnected?"

"Indeed I don't," I said. "Dear me, it's so extraordinary to hear of people having theories about father's work and studying it in college thousands of miles away. It must be more important than we realize."

"Well, it's one of the forerunners of post-war literature. And your father's a link in the chain of writers who have been obsessed by form. If only he'd carried his methods further!"

"But didn't you say he couldn't? That *Jacob Wrestling* was complete in itself, as far as he was concerned—that it couldn't have a successor?"

He looked at me quickly. "Fancy your remembering that! Do you know, I'm ashamed to say that didn't mean very much —it was an effort to be tactful when I knew I'd put my foot in it."

I told him I'd guessed that, which made him laugh.

"You nasty noticing child! But I don't think your father spotted me. And in one way, what I said's true, you know—he can't exactly develop his *Jacob Wrestling* method, because other writers have gone far ahead of him on rather similar lines; James Joyce, for instance. He'd have to take an enormous jump over intervening work and he hasn't even kept in touch with it. I wonder if that could be what's stopping him writing, that the next rung of the ladder—since we're talking of ladders—has been used by others. How's that for a theory? Or am I just trying to rationalize my phoniness that first evening?"

"Well, it's a nice change from the theory that he can't write because he went to jail," I said.

"That's fantastic, of course—why, the reports of the case read like something in Gilbert and Sullivan. And mother says his description of his life in prison was even funnier."

"You mean he actually told her?" I gasped—never have I heard him mention one word about his life in prison.

"She asked him point-blank—I must say I wouldn't have dared. She says he looked for a second as if he were going to strike her and then launched cheerfully into a half-hour monologue. Oh, I'm sure prison isn't the root of the trouble."

I said I had never believed it myself. "But it is queer that he's never written a thing since he came out."

"It certainly is. Of course he ought to be psycho-analysed."

I suppose no normally intelligent person living in the nineteen-thirties can fail to have some faint inkling of what psychoanalysis is, but there are few things about which I know less. I asked Simon to explain it to me.

"Good Lord, that's a tall order," he said, laughing. "And I've only the haziest layman's idea of it myself. But let's see, now: I think a psycho-analyst would say the trouble lay much further back than those few months in prison—but that prison might have brought it to the surface. He'd certainly explore that period thoroughly—make your father remember every detail of it; in a way, he'd have to be put back in prison."

"You don't mean physically?"

"No, of course not. Though—let me think now—yes, I suppose it's just conceivable that if the trouble did arise in prison, another period of imprisonment might resolve it. But it's very far-fetched—and quite unworkable anyhow, because if he consented to imprisonment, he wouldn't really feel imprisoned; and no psycho-analyst would dare to imprison him without his consent."

"No psycho-analyst would ever get within miles of him. The very mention of psycho-analysis always annoys him—he says it's all rubbish."

"Well, it sometimes is," said Simon, "but not always. The fact that he's prejudiced against it might be symptomatic. By the way, I suppose you're sure he isn't working on something secretly?"

"I don't see how he could be—we can see right into the gate-house, there are windows back and front, and he hardly goes near his desk. He just sits reading his old detective stories. He did raise our hopes a few weeks ago—Topaz saw him writing. But it turned out to be a crossword puzzle."

"He's rather like a detective story himself," said Simon, "'The Case of the Buried Talent.' I wish I could solve it. I'd so much like to write about him."

I hadn't known that he wrote. I asked what sort of things.

"Oh, critical essays, mostly—just spare-time work. I've only had a few things published. Your father'd be a superb subject—if I could find out what monkey-wrench got thrown into his works."

"It would be even better if you could get the monkey-wrench out," I said.

"Well, finding it's the first step." He lay back on the grass with his eyes closed, thinking. I took the opportunity to have a good look at him. It was queer to notice how young his skin looked, contrasted with the beard. I had been liking him better and better all the time we had been talking and I was planning to tell Rose encouraging things about him. I was glad to see that he has nice ears, because she values good ears. People do look different with their eyes closed, their features seem so much more sculptured. Simon's mouth is very sculptured—an interesting mouth. I heard myself telling Rose: "Do you know, I think he might be quite an exciting sort of man?"

Just then he opened his eyes and said: "You don't like it, do you?"

I felt myself blushing. "Like what?" I said.

"My beard," said Simon. "You were wondering how any man could wear one—unless, of course, it has acquired a fascination of horror for you. Which is it?"

"As a matter of fact, I'm getting used to it."

He laughed and said that was the ultimate humiliation—everyone did. "Everyone except me," he added. "I never see myself in a glass without feeling astonished."

"Would it be rude to ask just why you do wear it?"

"It would be natural, anyway. I grew it when I was twenty-two, for a bet, and then kept it out of sheer pig-headedness—it looked so wonderfully unsuitable for a Wall Street office; I was with a cousin of my mother's there and our dislike was mutual. And I think I felt a beard kept me in touch with literature. But it probably has some deep psychological significance—I expect I'm trying to hide an infamous nature from the world."

"Well, it's quite the nicest beard I ever saw," I said. "Do you think you'll ever get rid of it?"

For some reason, that made him laugh. Then he said: "Oh, in ten or twelve years, perhaps—say when I'm forty. It'll be so useful to come down without it one morning, looking twenty years younger. Does your sister hate it?"

I wondered if I said "Yes", whether he would shave it off to please Rose. And I suddenly wasn't sure that I wanted it to go.

"You must ask her yourself," I said, laughing.

He looked at his watch and said he was afraid he couldn't wait any longer for her. "Neil's picking me up at the Godsend inn at a quarter after twelve. Be a nice companionable child and walk to the village with me."

He got up and held out his hand to pull me to my feet. Then he looked up at Belmotte Tower. "I meant to ask you to show me over that," he said, "but there's no time now. It's more impressive than ever, at close quarters."

"Have you got used to it belonging to you yet?" I asked.

"But it doesn't—well, not for a little matter of around thirty years. Anyway, it takes me all my time to realize that Scoatney does."

As we walked down the mound I told him how I had imagined his first glimpse of Scoatney, that night back in March.

"Large as it is, it had shrunk," he said.

"Do you mean you'd seen it before?"

"Oh, yes, when I was seven. Father brought me over with him when he patched up the row with my grandfather—which unfortunately broke out again when father became an American citizen."

"Did you know Scoatney was going to be yours then?"

"Good Lord, no—there were six lives between me and it. And I loved it with a most precocious passion. I remember standing at the top of the staircase looking down on my grandfather, my father and uncles, and a cousin of my own age all at tea in the hall, and thinking: 'If they were all dead, Scoatney would belong to me.' And then rushing screaming to the nursery, appalled at my wickedness. I sometimes think I ill-wished all my relations then."

"It'd be a powerful lot of ill-wishing for a child of seven," I said. I tried to imagine him, very small and dark, on the Scoatney stairs where I sat watching the dancing.

"My grandfather called me 'the little Yankee', which infuriated me. But I thought he was wonderful. I wish I could have seen him again before he died—perhaps I oughtn't to have waited until he agreed to it, but I didn't like to force myself on him."

Then he told me that the position had been particularly difficult because he had never been sure if old Mr. Cotton would leave him enough money to keep Scoatney up—the estate is entailed but the money isn't, and without it Simon would just have had to lease the house and stay in America.

"It must have been very mixing for you," I said, "not

knowing whether to settle down there or fix your mind on England."

"You're dead right it was mixing—sometimes I think I shall never get un-mixed. Oh, I shall strike roots here eventually, I guess. But I wish I could have known when I stood on those stairs."

We had come to the stile leading to the lane. He sat on the top rail for a moment, looking at the barn.

"That's magnificent," he said. "Wonderful old timbers. Oughtn't I to repair the roof? I'd like to be a good landlord."

I said that was our job, as we have the castle on a repairing lease. Then we caught each other's eyes and burst out laughing. "You won't *count* on us doing it this year?" I added.

He helped me over the stile, still laughing. Then he said:

"Listen, Cassandra, there's something I want your father to know and I don't like to tell him myself. Can you make him understand that I don't mind at all about the rent, that I shall never mind, even if he doesn't pay a cent for the rest of his lease? I'd like him to know that I'm honoured to feel he's my tenant."

"I'd call him more of a guest than a tenant," I said, and we both laughed again. Then I thanked him and promised to tell father.

"Do it tactfully, won't you? Don't let me sound gracious and patronizing."

"But I do think you're gracious—the right kind of gracious. There's a right kind of patronage, too, you know. Perhaps father'll dedicate his next book to you as its 'onlie begetter'."

"What a nice child you are," he said quietly.

"Not too consciously naïve?"

I swear that I said it without thinking—it just leapt from my mouth. It was looking at the barn did it—while we talked I had been remembering that day, gloating over the way things had changed.

His head jerked round. "What do you mean?"

"Oh, nothing in particular," I said, lamely. "I dare say some people think I am."

We were passing the barn. And that minute Heloïse put her

146

head out from where I sat listening that day and let forth a volley of barks—she takes naps on the chaff with one ear well open for rats.

"Were you up there?" said Simon.

I nodded. We were both of us very red.

"How much did you hear?"

"Just that, about me."

Heloïse came dashing out of the barn still barking, which I hoped would mean the end of the subject; and stooping to pat her was a good way to avoid his eyes. But she instantly stopped barking, and then he bent down and patted her, too, looking at me across her.

"I'm so terribly ashamed of myself," he said. "I apologize most abjectly."

"Nonsense. It did me a lot of good," I told him.

"That wasn't all that you heard, was it? Did you hear——"

I didn't let him finish. "Come on, we'll be late for your brother," I said. "Just let me get rid of my journal."

I ran off and put it in the barn, taking my time over it; and I talked very determinedly about the weather as I rejoined him.

"It's the loveliest first of May I ever remember," I said, and then made rather a business of calling for Heloïse, who had disappeared. She put her head out of the frothy cow-parsley looking like a bride.

"The country's all dressed in white lace," I said as we walked down the lane.

He was silent so long that I thought he hadn't heard me. Then suddenly he said: "What? Oh, yes—sorry. I was trying to remember what you could have heard me say about Rose."

I tried to think of the most convincing way to reassure him.

"Well, whatever it was, *she* doesn't know it," I said at last.

I am an honest liar when I take my time; he believed me at once.

"You wonderful child not to tell her."

I heard myself explaining to God as I always do about good, kind, useful lies. Simon started to tell me why they "got Rose all wrong." "It's because she's so original," he said.

147

"Original? Rose?"

"Why, of course—even the way she dresses. That frilly pink dress—and borrowing a real crinoline——"

"It was——" I meant to say "It was Topaz who thought of all that," but I stopped in mid-sentence—"pretty, wasn't it?" I finished up.

"Everything about her's pretty." He went on to talk of her for quite a quarter of a mile: how different she was from the average modern girl—and because of that he hadn't understood her, had thought her affected—when what she was, of course, was unique. Everything Rose does is original, apparently, even the way she dances, inventing little steps of her own. And she is so intelligent—he kindly said I was, too, but Rose is a wit (a fact not as yet disclosed to her family). As for looks—she'd have been a toast at any period of history.

I could whole-heartedly agree about the looks. I told him I could imagine her arriving at Bath with all the bells ringing and Beau Nash welcoming her as the reigning beauty; that fetched him considerably.

Rose lasted us until we were passing the larch wood, when he stopped and spoke about the greenness of the larches.

"There'll be bluebells in there before long—you can see the shoots now," I told him.

He stood staring into the wood for a minute, then said: "What *is* it about the English countryside—why is the beauty so much more than visual? Why does it *touch* one so?"

He sounded faintly sad. Perhaps he finds beauty saddening —I do myself sometimes. Once when I was quite little I asked father why this was and he explained that it was due to our knowledge of beauty's evanescence, which reminds us that we ourselves shall die. Then he said I was probably too young to understand him; but I understood perfectly.

As we walked on, I asked Simon questions about American country and he described some of the old New England villages. They did sound nice; very trim and white—much more spacious than our villages, with wide streets lined with shady trees. And he told me about little places on the coast of Maine, where he had spent vacations. He says "vacations" where we would say "holidays". Although I still think his voice is like extra-good English, I now realize that almost every sentence he speaks has some little American twist—"guess" for "suppose", "maybe" where we use "perhaps", "I've gotten" when we would say "I've got"—oh, there are dozens of words. And he is much more American with me than he is with father, and very much younger; with father he chooses his words so correctly that he sounds quite pedantic and middle-aged, but with me he was almost boyish.

"Why, the may's out already," I said, when we came to the cross-roads—the buds on the hedges were tightly closed, but there were dozens of open ones on the tree by the signpost. I set a lot of store by may—I once spent hours trying to describe a single blossom of it, but I only managed "Frank-eyed floweret, kitten-whiskered," which sticks in your throat like fish-bones.

"'The palm and may make country houses gay,'" quoted Simon. "I think it's that poem that makes me feel the Elizabethans lived in perpetual spring."

Then we remembered the rest of the poem between us and by the time we got to

> Young lovers meet, old wives a-sunning sit,
> In every street these tunes our ears do greet—
> Cuckoo, jug-jug, pu-we, to-witta-woo!

we were into the village.

"Can you hear any birds obliging with those noises?" I said.

"Let's listen," said Simon.

We listened. We heard:

> Somebody hammering,
> A hen announcing an egg,
> A cottage wireless saying it was the British
>   Broadcasting Corporation,
> The pump on the village green clanking

—all rather ugly noises, really, but the church clock striking the quarter somehow drew them together into one pleasant country sound floating on the light spring air. Then Heloïse shattered it all by flapping her ears after rolling on the green.

"And how many things can you smell?" I asked Simon.
We counted up:

Wood smoke,
A farm smell coming on puffs of breeze (we subdivided
    this into :
    Straw, hay, horses, clean cows: good.
    Manure, pigs, hens, old cabbages: bad—but not too awful
        if only in little whiffs),
A wonderful pie cooking somewhere,
    The sweet, fresh smell which isn't quite flowers or grass or
        scent of any kind, but just clean country air—one
        forgets to notice this unless one reminds oneself.

"I wonder how many more things Heloïse smells," said
Simon.
"Let's see, what could Chesterton's dog Quoodle smell?
Water and stone and dew and thunder . . ."
"And Sunday morning—he was so right about that having
a smell of its own," said Simon. Oh, it is amicable being with
someone who knows the poems you know! I do hope I get
Simon for a brother-in-law.
We crossed the green and turned down the short lane that
leads to the prettiest bit of Godsend. The church, which is
Norman (and a bit of it may be Saxon), stands on one side of
the lane between the Queen Anne vicarage and Miss Marcy's
little eighteenth-century schoolhouse; "The Keys" inn is
opposite, but because the lane curves just there they all seem
part of one group—Topaz says the "composition" is very
beautiful. "The Keys" is painted cream and has very irregular
gables; beside it is an enormous chestnut tree—not in bloom
yet but its leaves are at their very best, all new and vividly
green, with some of the sticky buds still unopened. There is a
bench with a long table against the front of the inn, partly
shaded by the chestnut—and sitting there, with stone bottles
of ginger beer, were Rose and Neil.
It turned out that she had come across the fields from Four
Stones to get a cake of scented soap from the post-office shop
(Topaz is giving us a shilling a week pocket-money while the

Vicar's twenty pounds hold out), and had found Neil there buying cigarettes.

"And when I said you'd be along soon, she very obligingly waited," he told Simon. Perhaps I imagined it, but I did think he sounded a bit satirical.

We sat down, Simon by Rose. Neil asked me what I would have to drink. I was going to say lemonade and then a wild idea struck me: "Could I have a cherry brandy? I've always wanted to taste it."

"You can't drink liqueurs before lunch," said Rose in a very grown-up way.

"Yes, she can if she wants to," said Neil, going in to the bar. Rose shrugged her shoulders rather histrionically and turned to talk to Simon. He did look pleased to see her. After a few minutes he suggested we should all lunch there and called out to Neil to arrange it.

As a rule, Mrs. Jakes only serves bread-and-cheese but she managed cold sausages as well, and some honey and cake. Neil ate his sausage with honey, which simply fascinated me —but by then almost everything was fascinating me. Cherry brandy is *wonderful*.

But I don't think my haze of content was all due to the cherry brandy—the glasses are so small. (I had lemonade for my thirst.) It was everything together that was so pleasant— the food out-of-doors, the sunshine, the sky through the chestnut tree, Neil being nice to me and Simon being more than nice to Rose; and, of course, the cherry brandy did help.

While Neil was getting me my second glass I took a good look at Rose. She was wearing her very oldest dress, a washed-out blue cotton, but it looked exactly right for sitting outside an inn. One branch of the chestnut came down behind her head and, while I was watching, a strand of her bright hair got caught across a leaf.

"Is that branch worrying you?" Simon asked her. "Would you like to change places? I hope you wouldn't because your hair looks so nice against the leaves."

I was glad he had been noticing.

Rose said the branch wasn't worrying her in the least.

When Neil came back with my second cherry brandy, she said:"Well, now that we've finished lunch, I'll have one, too." I knew very well she had been envying mine. Then she called after him: "No, I won't—I'll have crème de menthe." I was surprised, because we both tasted that at Aunt Millicent's once and hated it heartily; but I saw what she was after when she got it—she kept holding it up so that the green looked beautiful against her hair, though of course it clashed quite dreadfully with the chestnut leaves. I must say she was being more affected than I ever saw her, but Simon appeared to be enchanted. Neil didn't—he winked at me once and said: "Your sister'll be wearing that drink as a hat any minute."

Neil *is* amusing—though it is more the laconic way he says things than what he actually says; sometimes he sounds almost grim and yet you know he is joking. I believe this is called wise-cracking. Rose was right when she said he thinks England is a joke, a comic sort of toy, but I don't believe he despises it, as she feels he does; it is just that he doesn't take it seriously. I am rather surprised that Rose resents this so much, because England isn't one of her special things in the way it is mine—oh, not flags and Kipling and outposts of Empire and such, but the country and London and houses like Scoatney. Eating bread-and-cheese at an inn felt most beautifully English—though the liqueurs made it a bit fancy. Mrs. Jakes has had those two bottles for as long as I can remember, both full to the top.

We sat talking until the church clock struck two and then the nicest thing of all happened: Miss Marcy began a singing class. The windows of the schoolhouse were open and the children's voices came floating out, very high and clear. They were doing rounds; first, "My dame hath a lame, tame crane," then "Now Robin lend to me thy bow," and then "Sumer is icumen in" which is my very favourite tune—when I learnt it at school it was part of a lesson on Chaucer and Langland, and that was one of the few times when I had a flash of being back in the past. While I listened to Miss Marcy's children singing I seemed to capture everything together—mediæval England, myself at ten, the summers of the past and the summer really coming. I can't imagine ever feeling happier than I did for those moments—and while I was telling myself so, Simon said:

"Did anything as beautiful as this ever happen before?"

"Let's take the kids some lemonade," said Neil. So we got two dozen bottles and carried them across. Miss Marcy nearly swooned with delight and introduced Simon to the children as "Squire of Godsend and Scoatney."

"Go on, make a speech—it's expected," I whispered. He took me seriously and gave me an agonized look. Then he told them how much he had enjoyed the singing and that he hoped they would all come to Scoatney one day and sing for his mother. Everyone applauded except one very small child who howled and got under her desk—I think she was scared of his beard.

We left after that and the Cottons said they would drive us home. Neil went to settle with Mrs. Jakes and I routed Heloïse out of the kitchen—she was bloated with sausage. When I came back Simon was leaning against the chestnut staring at the schoolhouse.

"Will you look at that window?" he said.

I looked. It is a tallish window with an arched top. On the sill inside stood a straggly late hyacinth with its white roots growing in water, a jam jar of tadpoles and a hedgehog.

"It'd be nice to paint," I said.

"I was just thinking that. If I were a painter I believe I'd always paint windows."

I looked up at the inn. "There's another for you," I told him. Close to the swinging signboard with its crossed gold keys there was a diamond-paned lattice open, showing dark red curtains and a little sprigged jug and basin, with the brass knob and black rail of an iron bedstead behind. It was wonderfully paintable.

"Everywhere one turns——" He stared all around, as if he were trying to memorize things.

The Vicar's housekeeper drew the blinds down against the sun, so that the vicarage seemed to close its eyes. (Mrs. Jakes had told us the Vicar was out or we would have called on him.)

Miss Marcy's children were very quiet—I suppose they were all guzzling lemonade. There was a moment of great peace and silence. Then the clock struck the half-hour, a white pigeon alighted with a great flutter of wings on the inn roof just above the open window; and Neil started the car.

"Don't you think *this* is beautiful?" Simon asked him, as we went over.

"Yes, pretty as a picture," said Neil, "the kind you get on jig-saw puzzles."

"You're hopeless," I said, laughing. I did know what he meant, of course; but no amount of pretty-pretty pictures can ever really destroy the beauty of villages like Godsend.

Rose went in the back of the car with Simon. Heloïse and I were at the front—part of the time Neil drove with his arm round her. "Gosh, what sex-appeal she has," he said. Then he told her she was a cute pooch, but would she please not wash his ears? Not that it stopped her; Heloïse can never see a human ear at tongue-level without being a mother to it.

When we got back to the castle I felt it was only polite to ask them in, but Neil had made an appointment for Simon with the Scoatney agent. Simon is obviously most anxious to understand everything about the estate, but I don't think the agricultural side comes naturally to him. It does to Neil—which seems a waste when he isn't staying in England.

"Did Simon fix anything about seeing us again?" I asked Rose, as we watched them drive away.

"Don't worry, they'll be round." She spoke quite scornfully; I resented it after the Cottons had been so nice to us.

"Very sure of yourself, aren't you?" I said. Then something struck me. "Oh, Rose—you're not still counting it against them—what I overheard them say about you?"

"I am against Neil. He's my enemy." She flung back her head dramatically.

I told her not to be an idiot.

"But he is—he as good as told me so, before you came this morning. He said he was still hoping Simon would come back to America with him."

"Well, that doesn't make him your enemy," I said. But I

must admit that his manner to her is a bit antagonistic. Of course, owning Scoatney is really what is likely to keep Simon in England, but I suppose marrying an English girl would tend to as well.

"Yes, it does—anyway, I hate him. But he shan't, he shan't interfere." She was flushed and her eyes had a desperate look —a look that somehow made me ashamed for her.

"Oh, Rose, don't bank on things too much," I begged. "Simon may not have the faintest idea of proposing—American men are used to being just friends with girls. And they probably think we're too comic for words—just as Neil thinks the English country is."

"Blast Neil!" she cried furiously. I would rather see her furious than desperate—it made me think of the day she turned on a bull that was chasing us. (It turned out to be a rather oddly shaped cow.) Remembering this made me feel very fond of her, so I told her all the nice things Simon had said about her on our walk to Godsend. And I made her promise never to tell him I had lied to him—even if she marries him. I should hate him to know, even though I did do it to be kind. Oh, I see more and more I ought never to have let her get it out of me—that conversation I overheard! It not only started her off hating Neil, but has made her extra relentless to Simon—she will marry him or burst.

We found Topaz asleep on the drawing-room window-seat— she looked as if she had been crying, but she woke up quite cheerfully and said our lunch was in the oven, between plates (we had it for tea). When we finished telling her about the Cottons, she said:

"How on earth are we to return their hospitality? I've been wondering ever since we went to Scoatney. Dinner's impossible—with no dining-room furniture. Could we manage a picnic lunch?"

"No, we couldn't," said Rose, "we'd only make a mess of it. Leave them alone—let them run after *us*."

She went off upstairs. Topaz said: "Don't blame her too much—the first time girls feel their power it often takes them like that." Then she yawned so much that I left her to finish her nap.

I got my journal from the barn and remembered Leda Fox-Cotton's note to Stephen inside. I told myself it was ridiculous to feel resentful and that I wouldn't even mention the note to him—I would just leave it where he would be sure to find it when he came back from work. I thought he might not want the others to see it—I felt Rose was liable to be scornful—so I took it to his room. I couldn't remember being there since we first explored the castle, when that was the bit of the kitchen where the hen-roosts were; father turned it into two little rooms which Stephen and his mother had—hers is just a store-room now.

When I opened Stephen's door I was quite shocked at the darkness and dankness; the narrow window was almost over-grown with ivy and the whitewash on the walls was dis-coloured and peeling off in flakes. There was a narrow sagging bed, very neatly made, a once-white chest of drawers with screws sticking out where the handles had come off, and three hooks on the wall for clothes. On the chest of drawers his comb was placed exactly midway between a photograph of his mother with him as a baby in her arms, and a snapshot of me—both in aluminium frames much too large for them. By the bed was an old wooden box, with a copy of *Jacob Wrestling* father gave him years ago on it beside a volume of Swinburne. (Oh dear, is Stephen taking to Swinburne?) That was ab-solutely all—no carpet, no chair. The room smelt damp and earthy. It didn't feel like anywhere in the castle as we know it now, but as the kitchen did when we saw it first, at sunset. I wondered if Stephen was haunted by the ghosts of ancient hens.

I looked at the photograph of Mrs. Colly for a long time, remembering how kind she was to us in the years after mother died. And I remembered going to see her in the Cottage Hospital and then helping father to break it to Stephen that she wasn't going to get better. He just said: "That's bad. Thank you, sir. Will that be all now?" and went into his room. After she died, I felt he must be terribly lonely and I got into the habit of reading to him in the kitchen every night—I expect I rather fancied myself reading aloud. It was then that he got fond of poetry. Father married Topaz the year after and in the excitement of it all, my evenings with Stephen ended—I had forgotten all about them until I stood there looking at his mother's photograph. I imagined she was looking at me reproachfully because I hadn't been kinder to her son and I wondered if I could do anything to improve his bedroom. I could make him some curtains, if Topaz could ever spare the money for them; but the window with the ivy creeping through is the nicest thing in the room, so it would be a pity to hide it. And always at the back of my mind I know it *isn't* kind to be kind to Stephen; briskness is kindest. I looked Mrs. Colly in the eye and sent her a message: "I'm doing my best—really I am."

Then I thought that it would be better for Stephen not to know I had been in his room—I don't know why, exactly, except that bedrooms are very personal; and he might not like to think I knew what a poor little place it is. I had one last look round. The afternoon sun was filtering in through the ivy so that everything was bathed in green light. The clothes hanging on the wall had a tired, almost dead look.

If I had left the letter, he would have guessed that I had put it there; so in the end I just gave it to him as soon as he came back from work. I explained how it had come, in a very casual voice, and then ran upstairs. He made no comment at all except to thank me. I still don't know what his plans about London are.

In the evening, while I was working on my journal in the drawing-room, father walked in—I had been so absorbed that I hadn't heard him arrive home.

"Hello, did your business go well?" I enquired politely.

He said: "Business? What business? I've been to the British Museum." Then he made a dive at my journal. I pulled it away from him, staring in astonishment.

"Good heavens, I don't want to pry into your secrets," he said. "I just want to look at your speed-writing. Do me an example, if you prefer it—do 'God Save the King'."

I thought he might as well see the journal—I chose an un-private page in case he was better at guessing than Simon had been. He peered down, then pulled the candle closer and asked me to point out the word-symbols.

"There aren't any," I told him. "It's mostly just abbreviations."

"No good, no good at all," he said impatiently, pushing the exercise book away. Then he marched off to the gatehouse.

I went into the kitchen and found Topaz cutting ham sandwiches for him; she said he hadn't told her one word of what he had been doing all day.

"Well, he wasn't with Mrs. Cotton, anyway," I said, "because he was at the British Museum."

"As if that proves anything," said Topaz, gloomily. "People do nothing *but* use it for assignations—I met him there myself once, in the mummy room."

She went off to the gatehouse with his sandwiches; he had asked her to bring them to him there. When she came back she said:

"Cassandra, he's going out of his mind. He's got a sheet of graph paper pinned to his desk and he told me to ask Thomas to lend him some compasses. And when I told him Thomas was asleep he said: 'Then bring me a goat. Oh, go to bed, go to bed.' Heavens, does he really want a goat?"

"Of course not," I said laughing. "It's just an idiotic association of words—you know, 'Goat and Compasses'; they sometimes call inns that. I've heard him make that sort of joke before and very silly I always think it is."

She looked faintly disappointed—I think she had rather fancied hauling some goat in out of the night.

A few minutes later, father came rampaging into the kitchen saying he must have the compasses even if it meant waking Thomas; but I crept into his room and managed to sneak them out of his school satchel without disturbing him. Father went off with them. It was three o'clock before he finally came in from the gatehouse—I heard Godsend church clock strike just after he wakened Heloïse, who raised the roof. Fancy sitting up until three in the morning playing with graph paper and compasses! I could hit him!

Chapter X

OH, I LONG TO BLURT OUT THE NEWS IN MY FIRST PARAGRAPH
—but I won't! This is a chance to teach myself the art of
suspense.

We didn't hear anything from the Cottons for nearly two
weeks after we lunched in the village, but we hardly expected
to as they were still in London; and while I was describing that
day it was like re-living it, so I was quite contented—and it
took me a long time, as Topaz developed a mania for washing,
mending and cleaning, and she needed my help. I had to do
most of my writing in bed at night, which stopped me from
encouraging Rose to talk much—not that she had shown signs
of wanting to, having taken to going for long walks by herself.
This desire for solitude often overcomes her at house-cleaning
times.

I finished writing of May Day on the second Saturday after
it—and immediately felt it was time something else happened.
I looked across at Rose in the four-poster and asked if she
knew exactly when the Cottons were coming back.

"Oh, they're back now," she said, casually.

She had heard it in Godsend that morning—and kept it to
herself.

"Don't count on seeing them too soon," she added. "Neil
will keep Simon away from me as long as he can."

"Rubbish," I said; though I really had come to believe that
Neil disliked her. I tried to get her to talk some more—I was
ready to enjoy a little exciting anticipation—but she wasn't
forthcoming. And I quite understood; when things mean a
very great deal to you, exciting anticipation just isn't safe.

The next day, Sunday, something happened to put the
Cottons out of my head. When I got down, Topaz told me

Stephen had gone off to London. He hadn't said a word to anyone until she came down to get breakfast and found him ready to start.

"He was very calm and collected," she said. "I asked him if he wasn't afraid of getting lost and he said that if he did, he'd get a taxi; but he hardly thought he would need to, as Miss Marcy had told him exactly which 'buses to take."

I was suddenly furious at his asking Miss Marcy, when he had been so secretive with us.

"I hate that Fox-Cotton woman," I said.

"Well, I warned him to keep his eyes open," said Topaz. "And of course, her interest really may be only professional. Though I must say I doubt it."

"Do you mean she might make love to him?" I gasped—and for the first time really knew just why I minded his going.

"Well, somebody will, sooner or later. But I'd rather it was some nice girl in the village. It's no use looking horrified, Cassandra. You mustn't be a dog in the manger."

I said I shouldn't mind if it was someone good enough for him.

She stared at me curiously. "Doesn't he attract you at all? At your age I couldn't have resisted him for a minute—not looks like that. And it's more than looks, of course."

"Oh, I know he has a splendid character," I said.

"That wasn't what I meant," said Topaz, laughing. "But I've promised your father not to put ideas into your head about Stephen, so let's leave it at that."

I knew perfectly well what she had meant. But if Stephen is physically attractive, why don't *I* get attracted—really attracted? Or do I?

After breakfast, I went to church. The Vicar spotted me from the pulpit and looked most astonished. He came to talk to me afterwards, when I was waking Heloïse from her nap on one of the oldest tombstones.

"Does this delightful surprise mean you have any particular axe to grind with God?" he enquired. It didn't, of course—though I had taken the opportunity to pray for Rose; I don't believe that church prayers are particularly efficacious, but one can't waste all that kneeling on hard hassocks.

"No, I just dropped in," I said lamely.

"Well, come and have a glass of sherry," he suggested, "and see how well the collie dog rug looks on my sofa."

But I told him I had to talk to Miss Marcy, and hurried after her; seeing her was my real reason for coming, of course.

She obligingly dived straight into the subject to which I had meant to lead up.

"Isn't it splendid about Stephen," she said, blinking delightedly. "Five guineas for just one day—nearly six, if he saves the money that was sent for taxis! So thoughtful—how kind Mrs. Fox-Cotton must be!"

I didn't find out anything interesting. Stephen had come to her for a guide to London; there isn't one in the library but she had helped him with advice. When I left her she was still burbling about the wonderful chance for him, and Mrs. Fox-Cotton's kindness. Miss Marcy isn't the woman of the world Topaz and I are.

Stephen didn't come home until late in the evening.

"Well, how did you get on?" asked Topaz—much to my relief because I had made up my mind not to question him. He said he had taken the right 'bus and only been lost for a few minutes, while he was looking for the house. Mrs. Fox-Cotton had driven him back to the station and taken him round London on the way. "She was nice," he added, "she looked quite different—very businesslike, in trousers, like a man. You never saw such a huge great camera as she has."

Topaz asked what he had worn for the photographs.

"A shirt and some corduroy trousers that were there. But she said they looked too new—I'm to wear them for work and then they'll be all right for next time."

"So you're going again." I tried to make it sound very casual.

He said yes, she was going to send for him the next time she had a free Sunday, probably in about a month. Then he told us about the broken bits of statues he had been photographed with and what ages the lighting had taken and how he had lunched with Mr. and Mrs. Fox-Cotton.

"The studio's at the back of their house," he explained. "You wouldn't believe that house. The carpets feel like moss and the hall has a black marble floor. Mr. Fox-Cotton asked to be remembered to you, Mrs. Mortmain, ma'am."

He went to wash while Topaz got him some supper. "It's all right," she said. "I misjudged the woman."

I talked to him when he came back and everything seemed natural and easy again. He told me he had wanted to buy me a present but all the shops were closed, of course. "All I could get was some chocolate from a slot-machine on the station platform, and I don't suppose it's special London chocolate."

He was too tired to eat much. After he had gone to bed, I thought of him falling asleep in that dank little room with pictures of the studio and the Fox-Cottons' rich house dancing in front of his eyes. It was odd to think he had been seeing things I had never seen—it made him seem very separate, somehow, and much more grown-up.

Next morning, I had something else to think about. Two parcels arrived for me! Nobody has sent me a parcel since we quarrelled with Aunt Millicent. (The last one she sent had bed socks in it, most hideous but not to be sneezed at on winter nights. They are finishing their lives as window-wedges.)

I could hardly believe it when I saw my name on labels from two Bond Street shops, and the things inside were much more unbelievable. First I unpacked an enormous round box of chocolates and then a manuscript book bound in pale blue leather, tooled in gold; the pages—two hundred of them, I counted—have dazzling gilt edges and there are blue and gold stars on the end papers. (Topaz said it must have cost at least two guineas.) There was no card in either of the parcels, but of course I remembered Simon had promised me a box of "candy" if I let him look at my journal. And he had sent me a new journal, too!

There was nothing for Rose.

"He can send me presents because he thinks of me as a child," I pointed out. "He's probably afraid you wouldn't accept them."

"Then he's a pessimist," she said, grinning.

"Well, eat all you can, anyway," I told her. "You can pay me back when you're engaged—you'll get dozens of boxes then."

She took one, but I could see that it was the idea of owning them that mattered to her, not the chocolates themselves. She didn't eat half as many as Topaz and I did; Rose never was greedy about food.

We had scarcely recovered from the excitement of the parcels when the Scoatney car arrived. Only the chauffeur was in it. He brought a box of hot-house flowers and a note from Simon asking us all to lunch the next day—even Thomas and Stephen. The flowers weren't addressed to anyone and the note was for Topaz; she said Simon was being very correct, which was a good sign. She gave the chauffeur a note accepting for all of us but Thomas and Stephen, and saying she was uncertain about them—she didn't like to refuse for them without knowing how they felt; which was just as well because Thomas insisted on cutting school and coming. Stephen said he would sooner die.

I ought to have recorded that second visit to Scoatney immediately after it happened, but describing May Day had rather exhausted my lust for writing. Now, when I look back, I mostly see the green of the gardens, where we spent the afternoon—we stayed on for tea. It was a peaceful, relaxed sort of party—I never felt one bit nervous, as I did when we went to dinner. (But the dinner-party was more thrilling; it glows in my memory like a dark picture with a luminous centre—candlelight and shining floors and the night pressing against the black windows.) Mrs. Cotton was still away and Simon was very much the host, rather serious and just a bit stately, talking mainly to father and Topaz. Even with Rose he was surprisingly formal, but he was jolly with me. Neil took a lot of trouble with Thomas, encouraging him to eat a great deal and playing tennis with him—Neil asked Rose and me to play, too, but she didn't want to as she hasn't had any practice since she left school. So she and I wandered around on our own and drifted into the biggest greenhouse. It was lovely moving through the hot, moist, heavily scented air and it felt particularly private—almost as if we were in a separate world from the others. Rose suddenly said:

"Oh, Cassandra, is it going to happen—is it?"

She looked as she used to on Christmas Eve, when we were hanging up our stockings.

"Are you really sure you want it to?" I asked—and then decided it was a wasted question when she was so obviously determined. To my surprise, she considered it a long time, staring out across the lawn to where Simon was talking to father and Topaz. A pink camelia fell with a little dead thud.

"Yes, quite sure," she said, at last, with an edge on her voice. "Up to now, it's been like a tale I've been telling myself. Now it's real. And it's got to happen. It's got to."

"Well, I feel as if it will," I told her—and I really did. But greenhouses always give me a waiting, expectant sort of feeling.

Neil pressed another ham on Thomas and six pots of jam—father raised a protest but it was very mild; he was in a wonderfully good temper. He borrowed a lot of books from Simon and retired to the gatehouse with them as soon as we got home.

The next exciting day was when we went for the picnic—they called for us unexpectedly. Father had gone to London again (without any explanation) and Topaz made an excuse not to come, so only Rose and I went. We drove to the sea. It wasn't like an ordinary English picnic, because Neil cooked steak over the fire—this is called a "barbecue"; I have been wondering what that was ever since I read about Brer Rabbit. The steak was burnt outside and raw inside, but wonderfully romantic. Simon was at his youngest and most American that day. He and Neil kept remembering a picnic they had been on together when they were very little boys, before their parents separated. I suppose they are only gradually getting to know each other again, but I feel sure Neil is already fond of Simon; with Simon one can't tell, he is so much more reserved. They are both equally kind but Neil's nature is much warmer, more open. He was nice even to Rose that day—well, most of the time; not that I see how anyone could have helped being, because she was at her very best. Perhaps the sea and the fun of cooking the steak did it—something changed her into a gloriously real person again. She laughed and romped and even slid down sandhills on her stomach. We didn't bathe because none of us had brought suits—a good job, too, as the sea was icy.

Simon seemed more fascinated than ever by Rose. Late in the afternoon, when she had just been particularly tomboyish, he said to Neil:

"Did you ever see such a change in a girl?"

"No, it's quite an improvement," said Neil. He grinned at Rose and she pulled a little face at him; just for that minute I felt they were really friendly to each other.

"Do *you* think it's an improvement?" she asked Simon.

"I'm wondering. Shall we say it's perfect for the sea and the sunlight—and the other Rose is perfect for candlelight? And perhaps what's most perfect of all is to find there are several Roses?"

He was looking straight at her as he said it and I saw her return the look. But it wasn't like that time at the Scoatney dinner table—her eyes weren't flirtatious; just for an instant they were wide and defenceless, almost appealing. Then she smiled very sweetly and said: "Thank you, Simon."

"Time to pack up," said Neil.

It flashed through my mind that he had felt it was an important moment, just as I had, and didn't want to prolong it. After that, he was as off-hand to Rose as ever and she just ignored him. It was sad, when they had been so friendly all day.

Neil had driven coming out, so Simon drove going home, with Rose at the front beside him. I didn't hear them talking much; Simon is a very careful driver and the winding lanes worry him. It was fun at the back with Neil. He told me lots of interesting things about life in America—they do seem to have a good time there, especially the girls.

"Do Rose and I seem very formal and conventional, compared with American girls?" I asked.

"Well, hardly conventional," he said, laughing, "even madam with her airs isn't that"—he jerked his head towards Rose. "No, I'd never call any of your family conventional, but—oh, I guess there's formality in the air here, even the villagers are formal; even you are, in spite of being so cute."

I asked him just what he meant by "formality." He found difficulty in putting it into words, but I gather it includes reserve and "a sort of tightness."

"Not that it matters, of course," he added, hastily. "English people are swell."

That was so like Neil—he will joke about England, but he is always most anxious not really to hurt English feelings.

After that, we talked about America again and he told me of a three-thousand-mile car-drive he made from California to New York. He described how he would arrive in some little town at sunset, coming in through residential quarters, where there were big trees and green lawns with no fences round them and people sitting on their porches with lighted windows behind them; and then drive through the main street with the shops lit up and the neon signs brilliant against the deep blue sky— I must say I never thought of neon lighting as romantic before but he made it sound so. The hotels must be wonderful, even in quite small towns there is generally one where most of the bedrooms have a private bath; and you get splendid food in places called Coffee Shops. Then he told me about the scenery in the different States he passed through—the orange groves in California, the cactus in the desert, the hugeness of Texas, the old towns in the South where queer grey moss hangs from the trees—I particularly liked the sound of that. He drove from summer weather to winter—from orange blossom in California to a blizzard in New York.

He said a trip like that gives you the whole feel of America marvellously—and even to hear him describe it made America more real for me than anything I have read about it or seen on the pictures. It was still so vivid for him that though each time we drove through a beautiful village he would say "Yes, very pretty," I could tell he was still seeing America. I told him I was trying to see it too; if one can sometimes get flashes of other people's thoughts by telepathy, one ought to be able to see what their minds' eyes are seeing.

"Let's concentrate on it," he said, and took my hand under

the rug. We shut our eyes and concentrated hard. I think the pictures I saw were just my imaginings of what he had described, but I did get the strangest feeling of space and freedom—so that when I opened my eyes, the fields and hedges and even the sky seemed so close that they were almost pressing on me. Neil looked quite startled when I told him; he said that was how he felt most of the time in England.

Even when we stopped concentrating he went on holding my hand, but I don't think it meant anything; I rather fancy it is an American habit. On the whole, it felt just friendly, and comfortable, though it did occasionally give me an odd flutter round the shoulders.

It was dark when we got to the castle. We asked them in, but they were expecting Mrs. Cotton to arrive that evening and had to get back.

Father came home while I was describing our day to Topaz. (Not one word did he say about what he had been doing in London.) He had travelled on the same train as Mrs. Cotton and asked her to dinner on the next Saturday—with Simon and Neil, of course. For once, Topaz really got angry.

"Mortmain, how could you?" she simply shouted at him. "What are we to give them—and what *on*? You know we haven't a stick of dining-room furniture."

"Oh, give them ham and eggs in the kitchen," said father, "they won't mind. And they've certainly provided enough ham."

We stared at him in utter despair. It was a good thing Rose wasn't there because I really think she might have struck him, he looked so maddeningly arrogant. Suddenly he deflated.

"I—just felt I had to——" All the bravado had gone out of his voice. "She invited us to dine at Scoatney again next week and—— My God, I think my brain's going—I actually forgot about the dining-room furniture. Can't you rig something up?"

He looked pleadingly at Topaz. I can't stand it when he goes humble—it is like seeing a lion sitting up begging (not that I ever did see one). Topaz rose to the occasion magnificently.

"Don't worry, we'll manage. It's fun, in a way—a sort of challenge——" She tried to use her most soothing contralto, but it broke a bit. I felt like hugging her.

167

"Let's just *look* at the dining-room," she whispered to me, while father was eating his supper. So we took candles and went along. I can't think what she hoped for, but anyhow we didn't find it—we didn't find anything but space. Even the carpet was sold with the furniture.

We went into the drawing-room.

"The top of the grand piano would be original," said Topaz.

"With father carving on the keys?"

"Could we sit on the floor, on cushions? We certainly haven't enough chairs."

"We haven't enough cushions, either. All we really have enough of is floor."

We laughed until the candle wax ran down on to our hands. After that we felt better.

In the end, Topaz got Stephen to take the hen-house door off its hinges and make some rough trestles to put it on, and we pushed it close to the window-seat, which saved us three chairs. We used the grey brocade curtains from the hall as a table-cloth—they looked magnificent, though the join showed a bit and they got in the way of our feet. All our silver and good china and glass went long ago, but the Vicar lent us his, including his silver candelabra. Of course we asked him to dinner too, and he came early and sat in the kitchen giving his possessions a final polish while we got dressed. (Rose wore Topaz's black dress, we had found it didn't look a bit conventional on Rose—it suited her wonderfully.)

Our dinner menu was:

Clear soup (made from half the second ham-bone)
Boiled chicken and ham
Peaches and cream (the Cottons sent the peaches—
just in time)
Savoury: Devilled ham mousse.

Topaz cooked it all and Ivy Stebbins brought it in; Stephen and Thomas helped her in the kitchen. Nothing unfortunate happened except that Ivy kept staring at Simon's beard. She told me afterwards that it gave her the creeps.

Mrs. Cotton was as talkative as ever but very nice—so easy;

I think it was really she who made us feel the dinner was a success. Americans are wonderfully adaptable—Neil and Simon helped with the washing-up. (They call it "doing the dishes.") I rather wished they hadn't insisted, because the kitchen looked so very un-American. It was wildly untidy and Thomas had put all the plates on the floor for Heloïse and Abelard to lick—very wrong indeed, because chicken-bones are dangerous to animals.

Ivy washed and we all dried. Then Stephen took Ivy home. She is the same age as I am but very big and handsome. She obviously has her eye on Stephen—I hadn't realized that before. I suppose it would be an excellent thing for him if he married her, because she is the Stebbins's only child and will inherit the farm. I wondered if he would kiss her on the way home. I wondered if he had ever kissed any girl. Part of my mind went with him through the dark fields, but most of it stayed with the Cottons in the kitchen. Neil was sitting on the table, stroking Ab into a coma of bliss: Simon was wandering round examining things. Suddenly the memory of that first time they came here flashed back to me. I hoped Rose had forgotten Simon's shadow looking like the Devil—I had almost forgotten it myself. There surely never was a more un-devilish man.

Soon after that we were into the exciting part of the evening.

It began when Simon asked if they might see over the castle: I had guessed he would and made sure that the bedrooms were tidy.

"Light the lantern, Thomas, then we can go up on the walls," I said—I felt the more romantic I could make it, the better for Rose. "We'll start from the hall."

We went through the drawing-room where the others were talking—that is, father and Mrs. Cotton were. Topaz was just listening and the Vicar opened his eyes so wide when we went in that I suspected he had been dozing. He looked as if he rather fancied joining us but I was careful to give him no encouragement. I was hoping to thin our party out, not thicken it up.

"The gatehouse first," said Rose when we got to the hall—

and swept through the front door so fast that I saw she meant to skip the dining-room. Personally, I thought pure emptiness would have been more distinguished than our bedroom furniture. Little did I know how grateful Rose was to be to the humblest piece of it!

As we walked through the courtyard garden, Simon looked up at the mound.

"How tall and black Belmotte Tower is against the starry sky," he said. I could see he was working himself into a splendidly romantic mood. It was a lovely night with a warm, gentle little breeze—oh, a most excellently helpful sort of night.

I never mount to the top of the gatehouse tower without recalling that first climb, the day we discovered the castle, when Rose kept butting into me from behind. Remembering that, remembering us as children, made me feel extra fond of her and extra determined to do my best for her. All the time we were following the lantern and Simon was marvelling that the heavy stone steps could curve so gracefully, I was willing him to be attracted by her.

"This is amazing," he said as he stepped out at the top. I had never before been up there at night, and it really was rather exciting—not that we could see anything except the stars and a few lights twinkling at Godsend and over at Four Stones Farm. It was the *feel* that was exciting—as if the night had drawn closer to us.

Thomas set the lantern high on the battlements so that it shone on Rose's hair and face; the rest of her merged into the darkness because of the black dress. The soft wind blew her little chiffon shoulder cape across Simon's face. "That felt like the wings of night," he said, laughing. It was fascinating watching his head next to hers in the lantern light—his so dark and hers so glowing. I tried and tried to think of some way of leaving them by themselves up there, but there are limits to human invention.

After a few minutes, we went down far enough to get out on the top of the walls. It took quite a while to walk along them because Neil wanted to know all about defending castles—he was particularly taken with the idea of a trébuchet slinging a dead horse over the walls. Rose tripped over her dress almost the first minute and after that Simon kept tight hold of her arm, so the time wasn't wasted; he didn't let go until we stepped into the bathroom tower.

We left Thomas to show the bathroom—I heard Neil roaring with laughter at Windsor Castle. Rose and I ran on to the bedroom and lit the candles.

"Isn't there some way you can leave us alone together?" she whispered.

I told her I had been hoping to, ever since dinner. "But it's very difficult. Can't you just lag somewhere?"

She said she had lagged on the top of the gatehouse tower, but Simon hadn't lagged too. "He just said 'Wait a minute with that lantern, Thomas, or Rose won't be able to see.' And down I had to go."

"Don't worry—I swear I'll manage something," I told her.

We heard them crossing the landing.

"Who sleeps in the four-poster?" asked Simon, as they came in.

"Rose," I said quickly—it happened to be my week for it, but I felt it was more romantic than the iron bedstead for him to picture her in. Then he opened the door to our tower and was very tickled to see Rose's pink evening dress hanging in it —she keeps it there because the frills would get crushed in the wardrobe. "Fancy hanging one's clothes in a six-hundred-year-old tower!" he said.

Neil put his arm around Miss Blossom and said she was just his type of girl, then knelt on the window-seat to look down at the moat. Inspiration came to me.

"How'd you like to bathe?" I asked him.

"Love it," he said instantly.

"What, bathe to-night?"—Thomas simply goggled at me.

"Yes, it'll be fun." Thank goodness, he caught the ghost of a wink I flickered at him, and stopped goggling. "Lend Neil your bathing-shorts—I'm afraid there's only one pair, Simon, but you could have them afterwards. Rose mustn't bathe because she gets chills so easily." (Heaven forgive me! Rose is as strong as a horse—I am the one who gets chills.)

"We'll watch from the window," said Simon.

I unearthed my bathing-suit, then ran after Thomas, who was yelling from his room that he couldn't find the shorts—for an awful moment I feared he had left them at school.

"What's the game?" he whispered. "Don't you know the water'll be icy?"

I did indeed. We never bathe in the moat until July or August—and even then we usually regret it.

"I'll explain later," I told him. "Don't you dare put Neil off." I found the shorts at last—they were helping to stop up Thomas's draughty chimney; luckily they are black.

"You'd better change in the bathroom," I called to Neil, "and go down the tower steps. You show him, Thomas, and then stay and light us with your lantern. I'll meet you at the moat, Neil."

I gave him the shorts, then went to change in Buffer. Simon called: "Have a good bathe," as I ran through the bedroom, then turned back to Rose. They were sitting on the window-seat looking splendidly settled.

It was only while I was changing that I fully realized what I had let myself in for—I who hate cold water so much that even putting on a bathing-suit makes me shiver. I went down the kitchen stairs feeling like an Eskimo going to his frozen hell.

I had no intention of showing myself in the drawing-room—I had outgrown my suit so much that the school motto was stretched right across my chest; so I went to the moat via the ruins beyond the kitchen. Near there, a plank bridge runs across to the wheat field. I sat on it, carefully keeping my feet well above the water. Neil wasn't down—I could see the full length of the moat because the moon was rising. It was casting the most unearthly light across the green wheat—so beautiful that I nearly forgot the horror of having to bathe. How moons do vary! Some are white, some are gold, this was like a dazzling circle of tin—I never saw a moon look so *hard* before.

The water of the moat was black and silver and gold; silver where the moonlight shimmered on it, gold under the candle-lit windows; and while I watched, a gold pool spread around the corner tower as Thomas came out and set the lantern in the doorway. Then Neil came down looking very tall in the black bathing-shorts and stepped from lantern light to moonlight.

"Where are you, Cassandra?" he called.

I called back that I was coming, then put one toe in the water to know the worst. It was a far worse worst than I anticipated, and a brave idea I'd had of getting my going-in agonies over by myself, and swimming towards him, vanished instantly—I felt that a respite of even a few moments was well worth having. So I walked slowly along the edge of the field, with the wheat tickling my legs coldly as I brushed past, sat down on the bank opposite to him, and began a bright conversation. Apart from putting off the horror of plunging in, I felt dawdling was advisable in order to give Rose more time— because I was pretty sure that once we did get into the moat, we should very soon get out again.

I talked about the beauty of the night. I told him the winning anecdote of how I tried to cross the moat in a clothes-basket after I first heard about coracles. Then I started in on the good long subject of America, but he interrupted me and said: "I believe you're stalling about the swim. I'm going in, anyway. Is it deep enough for me to dive?"

I said yes, if he was careful. "Look out for the mud at the bottom," Thomas warned him. He did a cautious dive—and came up looking a very surprised man. "Gosh, that was cold," he shouted. "And after all the sunshine we've been having!"

As if our moat took any notice of sunshine! It is fed by a stream that apparently comes straight from Greenland.

I said: "I wonder if I ought to bathe, really—after such a heavy dinner."

"You don't get away with that," said Neil, "it was you who suggested it. Come on or I'll pull you in—it's really quite bearable."

I said to God: "Please, I'm doing this for my sister—warm it up a bit." But of course I knew He wouldn't. My last thought before I jumped was that I'd almost sooner die.

It was agony—like being skinned with icy knives. I swam madly, telling myself it would be better in a minute and feeling quite sure it wouldn't. Neil swam beside me. I must have looked very grim because he suddenly said: "Say, are you all right?"

"Just," I gasped, pulling myself up on to the plank bridge.

"You come right back and keep on swimming," he said, "or else you must go in and dry yourself. Oh, come on—you'll get used to it."

I slipped into the water again and it didn't feel quite so bad; by the time we had swum back as far as the drawing-room I was beginning to enjoy it. Topaz and the Vicar, framed in the yellow square of the window, were looking down on us. There was no sign of Rose and Simon at the window high above; I hoped they were too engrossed to look out. We swam through a patch of moonlight—it was fun making silver ripples just in front of my eyes—and then to the steps of the corner tower. Thomas had disappeared; I hoped to heaven he hadn't gone back to Rose and Simon.

After we turned the corner to the front of the castle there was no more golden light from the windows or the lantern, nothing but moonlight. We swam on our backs, looking up at the sheer, unbroken walls—never had they seemed to me so high. The water made slapping, chuckling noises against them and they gave out a mysterious smell—as when thunder-rain starts on a hot day, but dank and weedy and very much of a night-time smell too. I asked Neil how he would describe it but he only said: "Oh, I guess it's just wet stone"—I found what he really wanted to think about was boiling oil being poured down on us from the battlements. Everything to do with castle warfare fascinated him; when we reached the gatehouse he asked how drawbridges worked and was disappointed to find that our present bridge isn't one—we only call it "the drawbridge" to distinguish it from the Belmotte bridge. Then he wanted to know what happened to the ruined walls we were swimming past and was most indignant with Cromwell's Puritans for battering them down. "What a darned shame," he said, looking up at the great tumbled stones. I told him it was the first time I'd known him to have a feeling for anything old. "Oh, I don't get a kick out of this place because it's *old*," he said. "It's just that I keep thinking it must have been a hell of a lot of *fun*."

Once we were round on the Belmotte stretch of the moat it was very dark, because the moon wasn't high enough to shine over the house. Suddenly something white loomed ahead of us and there was a hiss and a beating of wings—we had collided with the sleeping swans. Neil enjoyed that, and I laughed myself but I was really quite frightened; swans can be very dangerous. Luckily ours bore no malice—they just got out of our way and flapped into the bulrushes.

Soon after that, we swam under the Belmotte bridge and round into the moonlight again, on the south side of the moat. There are no ruins there, the garden comes right down to the water; the big bed of white stocks smelt heavenly. It occurred to me that never before had I seen flowers growing above my head, so that I saw the stalks first and only the underneath of the flowers—it was quite a nice change.

I was tired by then so I floated and Neil did too; it was lovely just drifting along, staring up at the stars. That was when we first heard the Vicar at the piano, playing "Air from Handel's Water Music," one of his nicest pieces—I guessed he had chosen it to suit our swim, which I took very kindly. It came to us softly but clearly; I wished I could have floated on for hours listening to it, but I soon felt cold and had to swim fast again.

"There, we've made the complete circuit," I told Neil as we reached the plank bridge. "I'll have to rest now."

He helped me out and we climbed over the ruins and sat down with our backs against the kitchen wall; the sun had been shining on it all day and the bricks were still warm. We were in full moonlight. Neil had patches of brilliant green duckweed on his head and one shoulder; he looked wonderful.

I felt that what with the moonlight, the music, the scent of the stocks and having swum round a six-hundred-year-old moat, romance was getting a really splendid leg-up and it seemed an awful waste that we weren't in love with each other —I wondered if I ought to have got Rose and Simon to swim the moat instead of us. But I finally decided that cold water is definitely anti-affection, because when Neil did eventually put his arm round me it wasn't half so exciting as when he held my hand under the warm car-rug after the picnic. It might have improved, I suppose, but the next minute I heard Topaz calling me—I couldn't tell where she was until Thomas signalled with his lantern from the Belmotte bridge. Then father shouted that they were taking Mrs. Cotton and the Vicar over to look at the mound and Belmotte Tower.

"Mind you don't catch a chill," Topaz warned me.

Neil called: "I'll send her in now, Mrs. Mortmain."

"But I'm not cold," I said quickly—I was afraid Rose hadn't had long enough.

"Yes, you are, you're beginning to shiver—so am I." He took his arm from my shoulders. "Come on, where do we find towels?"

Never has such an innocent question so kicked me in the solar plexus. Towels! We have so few that on wash-days we just have to shake ourselves.

"Oh, I'll get you one," I said airily; then picked my way across the ruins very slowly, so as to give myself time to think. I knew we had two pink guest-towels in the bathroom—that is, they were meant as guest-towels; they were really tiny afternoon-tea napkins, kindly lent by Miss Marcy. Could I offer those to a large wet man? I could not. Then an idea came to me.

When we reached the back door I said: "Come in here, will you? It'll be warm by the kitchen fire. I'll bring a towel down."

"But my clothes are in the bathroom——" Neil began.

I ran off calling over my shoulder: "I'll bring those, too."

I had decided to get my own towel or Rose's—whichever proved to be the drier—and fold it like a clean towel; then go back to Neil with it clutched against me and apologize for having made it a bit damp. There would still be no need to disturb Rose's tête-à-tête with Simon, because both towels were on our bedroom tower staircase—I had thrown them out there while tidying the house for the Cottons—and I could reach them through the drawing-room entrance to the tower. I meant to dress like lightning while Neil was dressing and then get back to the kitchen and keep him talking there a good while longer.

I got the drawing-room door to the tower open very quietly and started up. After I turned the bend I was almost in darkness so I went on all fours, feeling my way carefully. There was an awkward moment when I got tied up in Rose's pink dress, but once clear of that I saw the line of light under the door to our bedroom. I knew the towels were only a few steps higher than that, so I stretched up and felt for them.

And then, through the door, I heard Simon say:

"Rose, will you marry me?"

I stood stock still, scarcely daring to move in case they heard me. Of course I expected Rose to say "Yes" instantly, but she didn't. There was an absolute silence for a good ten seconds. Then she said, very quietly but very distinctly:

"Kiss me, please, Simon."

There was another silence; a long one—I had time to think I wouldn't like my first kiss to be from a man with a beard, to wonder if Neil would have kissed me if Topaz hadn't shouted to me, and to notice that a very cold draught was blowing down the tower on me. Then Rose spoke—with that excited little break in her voice that I know so well.

"Yes, please, Simon," she said.

Then they were quiet again. I grabbed a towel—I could only find one—and started my way down. Suddenly I stopped. Might it not be more sensible to walk right in on them, just in case . . . ? I don't quite know what I meant by "just in case" —surely I didn't imagine Simon might change his mind? All I knew was that the sooner the engagement was official the better. I went back.

When I pushed the tower door open they were still standing in each other's arms. Simon jerked his head round quickly, then smiled at me.

I hope I smiled back. I hope I didn't look as flabbergasted as I felt. Just for one second I didn't think it *was* Simon. His beard was gone.

He said: "Is it all right by you if Rose marries me?"

Then we were all talking at once. I hugged Rose and shook hands with Simon.

"My child, you're like ice," he said as he let my hand

go. "Hurry up and change out of that swim-suit."

"I must take Neil a towel first," I said, "and his clothes, too." I started off to the bathroom for them.

"How do you like Simon without his beard?" Rose called after me. I knew I ought to have spoken about it before but I'd had an embarrassed feeling.

"Wonderful!" I shouted. But was it? Of course he looked years and years younger and I was astonished to see how handsome he was. But there was something defenceless about his face, as if strength had gone out of it. Oh, his chin isn't weak—it wasn't anything like that. It was just that he had . . . a lost sort of look.

How on earth did Rose get him to shave, I wondered, as I collected Neil's things. I guessed she had dared him to. I must say I was astonished at him—it seemed so undignified, using father's shaving tackle and my little enamel basin. (But then, the dignified, stately Simon seems to have vanished with the beard—I find it hard to believe now that I was ever even a little bit in awe of him; not that I think the change is merely due to the beard having gone, it is far more due to his being so much in love with Rose.)

When I went into the kitchen, Neil was standing so close to the fire that his bathing-shorts were steaming.

"Why, I thought you'd forgotten me," he said, turning to smile at me.

"Isn't it splendid?" I cried. "Rose and Simon are engaged."

His smile went like an electric light switched off.

I said: "You don't look exactly pleased."

"Pleased!" For a second he just stood glaring; then he grabbed the towel. "Clear out and let me get dressed," he said —in a very rude tone of voice indeed.

I dumped his clothes down and turned to go, then changed my mind. "Neil—please——" I tried to sound very friendly and reasonable. "Why do you hate Rose so? You have from the beginning."

He went on drying his shoulders. "No, I haven't. I liked her a lot at first."

"But not now? Why not, Neil?"

He stopped drying himself and looked me full in the face. "Because she's a gold-digger. And you know it, Cassandra."

"I do not," I said, indignantly. "How dare you say a thing like that?"

"Can you honestly tell me she isn't marrying Simon for his money?"

"Of course I can!" I said it with the utmost conviction—and really believed it for that second. Then I felt my face go scarlet because, well——

"You darned little liar," said Neil. "And I thought you were such a nice honest kid! Did you take me bathing deliberately?"

I was suddenly angry on my own account as well as Rose's.

"Yes, I did," I cried. "And I'm glad I did. Rose told me you'd interfere if you could—just because you want Simon to go back to America with you! You mind your own business, Neil Cotton!"

"Get the hell out of here!" he roared, looking so furious that I thought he was going to hit me. I went up the kitchen stairs like a streak, but paused on the top step and spoke with dignity:

"I'd advise you to pull yourself together before you see Simon." Then I whisked inside and bolted the door—I wouldn't have put it past him to have come after me.

One good thing about feeling so angry was that it had made me much warmer, but I was glad to get out of my wet bathing-suit and dry myself on Topaz's bedspread. I was just finishing dressing in Buffer when I heard the Belmotte party coming across the courtyard. Simon, next door, said: "Let's go and tell them, Rose." So I ran in and we all went down together.

We met the others in the hall. Mrs. Cotton was close to the little lamp on the bracket so I could see her expression clearly. She looked astonished enough when she saw Simon's beard was gone and got as far as "Simon——!" Then he interrupted: "Rose is going to marry me," and her mouth just fell open. I was almost sure she was dismayed as well as surprised—but only for a second; then she seemed perfectly delighted. She kissed Rose and Simon—and thanked her for getting him to shave. She kissed Topaz and me—I thought she was going to kiss father! And she talked——! I once wrote that her talk was like a wall; this time it was more like a battleship with all guns blazing. But she was very, very kind; and the more one knows her, the more one likes her.

In the middle of the congratulations Neil came in—I was glad to see his dress shirt had got pretty crumpled while I lugged it about. No one would have guessed that he had lost his temper only a few minutes before. He said:

"Congratulations, Simon—I see the beard has gone! Rose dear, I'm sure you know all that I'm wishing you."

I must say I thought that was rather neat; but it didn't seem to strike Rose as having any double meaning. She smiled and thanked him very nicely, then went on listening to Mrs. Cotton.

The Vicar said he had some champagne in his cellar and Neil offered to drive to the vicarage for it—and actually had the nerve to ask me to go with him. I refused just as coldly as I could without making it conspicuous.

But later on, when we were all standing talking in the court-yard before the Cottons went out to their car, he walked me away from the others so firmly that I let myself go with him. He took me as far as the big bed of stocks by the moat; then said:

"Make it up?"

I said: "I don't think I'm keen to. You called me a liar."

"Suppose I apologize?"

"You mean you don't think I am one?"

"Won't you settle for a straightforward apology?"

I felt in the circumstances that I would, but didn't see how I could say so without its reflecting on Rose. So I didn't say anything. Neil went on: "Suppose I add that I wouldn't blame you for lying—if you did? And that I admire you for defending Rose. You don't have to say anything at all, but if you forgive me just squeeze my hand."

He slid his hand down from my elbow. I answered his squeeze. He said: "Good"—then, in a more serious voice than I ever heard him use: "Cassandra, it isn't that I want him to come back to America with me, honest it isn't. Of course, I'd like it from a selfish point of view——"

"I oughtn't to have said that," I broke in. "It's my turn to apologize."

"Apology accepted." He squeezed my hand again, then let it go and sighed deeply. "Oh, maybe I've got her all wrong—maybe she really has fallen for him. Why not? Any girl in her senses would, I guess."

I guessed he guessed wrong about that—it seemed to me that lots of girls wouldn't be attracted by Simon, in spite of his niceness; and that most of them would be by Neil. The moonlight was shining on his hair, which was drying curlier than ever. I told him there was still a bit of duck-weed in it, and he laughed and said: "That was a darned good bathe, anyhow." Then Mrs. Cotton called: "Come on, you two."

After we had seen them off, the night suddenly seemed very quiet. I think we were all a little self-conscious. When we were back in the house father said with a false kind of casualness: "Er—happy, Rose dear?"

"Yes, very," said Rose, with the utmost briskness, "but rather tired. I'm going straight to bed."

"Let's all go," said Topaz. "We shall wake Stephen if we wash the glasses to-night."

Stephen had been in quite a while—though I must say he had taken his time seeing Ivy home. I had asked him to come in and drink Rose's health in the Vicar's champagne but he wouldn't. He smiled in the most peculiar way when I told him about the engagement; then said: "Oh, well, I'm not saying anything," and went off to bed. Goodness knows what he meant.

I had a feeling that he *had* kissed Ivy.

I was longing to get Rose to talk, but I knew she wouldn't until the trek to and from the bathroom was finished; and father and Topaz seemed unusually slow about their washing. When they were shut in their room at last, Rose made sure that both our doors were firmly closed; then jumped into bed and blew the candle out.

"Well?" I said, invitingly.

She began to talk fast, just above a whisper, telling me everything. It turned out I had been right in guessing that she dared Simon into shaving.

"At first he thought I was joking," she said. "Then he thought I was trying to make a fool of him and went all dignified. I didn't take any notice—I just had to see him without that beard, Cassandra; I'd worked up a sort of horror about it. I went close to him and looked up and said: 'You've got such a nice mouth—why hide it?' and I traced the outline of his lips with my finger. Then he tried to kiss me but I dodged and said: 'No—not while you've got that beard,' and he said: 'Will you if I shave it?' I said: 'I can't tell till it's off'—and then I ran and got father's shaving things and Topaz's manicure scissors and a jug of hot water from the bathroom. We were laughing all the time but there was a queer, exciting feeling and I had to keep stopping him from kissing me. He had an awful job with the shave and I suddenly went embarrassed and wished I'd never made him start. I could tell he was furious. And heavens, he was a sight after he chopped off the long hair with the scissors! I bet I looked horrified because he shouted: 'Go away—go away! Stop watching me!' I went and sat on the window-seat and prayed —I mean I kept thinking 'Please God, please God——' without getting any further. It seemed ages before Simon dried his face and turned round. He said: 'Now you know the worst,' in a funny, rueful sort of voice; I could see he wasn't angry any more, he looked humble and touching, somehow —and so handsome! Don't you think he's handsome now, Cassandra?"

"Yes, very handsome. What happened next?"

"I said: 'That's wonderful, Simon. I like you a thousand times better. Thank you very, very much for doing it for me.' And then he asked me to marry him."

I didn't tell her I'd heard. I shouldn't like anyone to hear me being proposed to.

She went on: "Then—it was queer, really, because I'm sure I didn't hear you in the tower—I suddenly thought of you. I remembered your saying I wouldn't know how I felt about him until I'd let him kiss me. And you were right—oh, I knew that I liked him and admired him, but I still didn't know if I was in love. And there was my chance to find out—with the proposal safe in advance! So I asked him to kiss me. And it was wonderful—as wonderful as——"

Her voice dwindled away. I guessed she was re-living it and gave her a minute or so. "Well, go on," I urged her at last, "as wonderful as what?"

"Oh, as ever it could be. Heavens, I can't describe it! It was all right, anyway—I'm in love and I'm terribly happy. And I'm going to make things splendid for you, too. You'll come and stay with us and marry someone yourself. Perhaps you'll marry Neil."

"I thought you hated him."

"I don't hate anyone to-night. Oh, the relief—the relief of finding I'm in love with Simon!"

I said: "Supposing you hadn't found it, would you have refused him?"

She was a long time before she answered, then her tone was defiant: "No, I wouldn't. Just before he kissed me I said to myself: 'You'll marry him anyway, my girl.' And do you know what made me say it? Beyond him, on the dressing-table, I could see my towel I'd lent him for the shave—all thin and frayed and awful. Not one spare towel have we in this house——"

"Don't I know it?" I interrupted with feeling.

"I won't live like that. I won't, I won't!"

"Well, you'll be able to have all the towels you want now," said Miss Blossom's voice. "Ever such congratulations, Rosie dear."

"And all the clothes I want," said Rose. "I'm going to think about them until I fall asleep."

"Would you like the four-poster so that you can gloat in style?" I offered.

But she couldn't be bothered to change.

While I was lying awake re-swimming the moat I noticed my enamel jug and basin silhouetted against the window; it was queer to think they had played a part in Simon's shave. I kept seeing him with two faces—with the beard and without. Then it came to me that there was some famous person who shaved because of a woman. I tried and tried to think who it was but I fell asleep without remembering.

In the very early morning I woke up and thought "Samson and Delilah"—it was as if someone had spoken the words in my ear. Of course, it was Samson's hair that got cut, not his beard, so the story didn't quite fit. But I did think Rose would rather fancy herself as Delilah.

I sat up and peered across at her, wondering what she was dreaming. While I watched, it grew light enough to see her bright hair stretched across the pillow and the faint pink flush on her cheeks. She was looking particularly beautiful—though no one could say Aunt Millicent's nightgown was becoming. It's strange how different Rose seems with her eyes closed— much more childish and gentle and serene. I felt so very fond of her. She was sleeping deeply and peacefully, though in a most uncomfortable position with one limp arm hanging out of the iron bedstead—you have to lie on the extreme outside to avoid the worst lumps in the mattress. I thought what a different bed she was certain to come by. I was terribly happy for her.

III. THE TWO-GUINEA BOOK

June to October

Chapter XI

I AM SITTING ON THE RUINS BEYOND THE KITCHEN—WHERE I sat with Neil, three weeks ago all but a day, after swimming the moat. How different it is now, in the hot sunshine! Bees are humming, a dove is cooing, the moat is full of sky. Heloïse has just gone down to take a drink and a swan is giving her a glance of utter disdain. Abelard went into the tall green wheat a few minutes ago, looking rather like a lion entering the jungle.

This is the first time I have used the beautiful manuscript book Simon gave me—and the fountain pen which came from him yesterday. A scarlet pen and a blue and gold leather-bound book—what could be more inspiring? But I seemed to get on better with a stump of pencil and Stephen's fat, shilling exercise book. . . . I keep closing my eyes and basking—that is, my body basks; my mind is restless. I go backwards and forwards, recapturing the past, wondering about the future—and, most unreasonably, I find myself longing for the past more than for the future. I remind myself of how often we were cold and hungry with barely a rag to our backs, and then I count the blessings that have descended on us; but I still seem to fancy the past most. This is ridiculous. And it is ridiculous that I should have this dull, heavy, not exactly unhappy but—well, *no* kind of feeling when I ought to be blissfully happy. Perhaps if I make myself write I shall find out what is wrong with me.

It is just a week since Rose and Topaz went to London. Mrs. Cotton asked me, too—they are staying at her Park Lane flat—but someone had to be here to look after father and Thomas and Stephen; besides, if I had accepted she might have felt she had to buy clothes for me, as well as give Rose her trousseau. She is wonderfully generous—and wonderfully tactful. Instead of pressing money on us to pay our way here, she insisted on buying the beaver-lined coat for two hundred pounds. As for the trousseau, she said to Rose: "My dear, I always longed for a daughter to dress—let me have my share of your happiness."

I was rather surprised that Topaz agreed to go to London, but the night before they left we had an illuminating talk. I came up from the kitchen with some things I had been ironing for her and found her sitting on her bed beside a half-filled suitcase, staring at nothing.

"I'm not going," she said, her voice quite baritone with tragedy.

"Good heavens, why not?" I asked.

"Because my motives are all wrong. I've been telling myself that it'd be good for Mortmain to be here without me for a bit, and that I ought to see some of my friends—renew my artistic interests, make myself more stimulating. But the real truth is that I want to keep an eye on that woman and be sure she doesn't see him when he comes up to London. And that's despicable. Of course, I'm not going."

"Well, I don't see how you can cry off now," I told her. "And you can always put things straight with your conscience by *not* keeping an eye on Mrs. Cotton. Topaz, do you really think that father's in love with her? You haven't a scrap of evidence."

"I've the evidence of my eyes and ears. Have you watched them together? He listens to her as if he liked it, and he not only listens, he talks. He talks more to her in an evening than he's talked to me all this last year."

I pointed out that he doesn't talk much to any of us.

"Then why doesn't he? What's wrong with us? I'd begun to think he was temperamentally morose—that he just couldn't help it—but after seeing him turn on his charm for the Cottons——! Heaven knows I didn't expect an easy life when I married him—I was prepared even for violence. But I do loathe morosity."

It was no moment to tell her there is no such word; anyway, I rather liked it.

"Perhaps Mrs. Cotton will go back to America with Neil," I suggested comfortingly.

"Not she. She's taken the flat for three years. Oh lord, what a fool I am—how can I stop her meeting him, even if I do stay with her? There are thousands of places they can go. He'll probably renew his interest in the British Museum."

I must say it was a bit suspicious—he hadn't been to London once while Mrs. Cotton was at Scoatney.

"In that case, you might as well go," I said. "I mean, it doesn't matter your motive being to spy, if you know very well that you can't."

"That's true." She heaved a sigh that was almost a groan and sounded very histrionic, then began to pack her shroud-like nightgowns. Suddenly she strode to the window and stood looking at father's light in the gatehouse.

"I wonder!" she said sepulchrally.

I obligingly asked her what.

"If I shall ever come back. I've got my cross-roads feeling— I've only had it three or four times in my life. That night in the Café Royal when Everard hit the waiter——" She stopped dead.

"Why did he do that?" I asked with the utmost interest. Everard was her second husband, a fashion artist; her first was called Carlo and had something to do with a circus. Rose and I have always longed to know about them.

It wasn't any good. She turned a faintly outraged stare on me and murmured foggily: "Let the dead bury their dead." As far as I know, Everard is alive and kicking and I never have seen how the dead can go burying anyone.

Nothing of great importance to me happened between the night of the engagement and Rose and Topaz going to London. Of course, we went to Scoatney several times but Neil wasn't there. He went off to see the Derby and other races; it seemed a pity that he had to go to them alone. After thinking about it a lot, I wrote him a little note. I can remember it word for word:

DEAR NEIL,

I am sure you will be glad to know that Rose really is in love with Simon. When I talked to you last, I was afraid she might not be—so you were justified in calling me a liar, but I am not one now. Rose told me herself and she is very truthful. To prove this, I will tell you she admitted most honestly that she would have married him even if she had *not* been in love. I don't think I quite believe that, but anyway, please do not count it against her, as she is a girl who finds poverty very hard to bear and she has been bearing it for years. And as she fell in love with him at the psychological moment, everything has come right.

I hope you are having a nice time in London.

With love from your future sister-in-law

CASSANDRA

I thought it would be all right to put "with love" in a relationlike way—though I am not quite sure if Rose's marriage really will make me his sister-in-law. Perhaps I shall only be Simon's.

I must now go indoors—partly because the sun is too hot and partly so that I can copy in Neil's reply.

Here I am on the bedroom window-seat with a glass of milk and a now-eaten banana.

Neil wrote back:

DEAR CASSANDRA,

It was nice of you to write that letter and what you say is probably right. I guess I was being unreasonable and certainly very rude. I apologize again.

Mother's apartment is so full that I have moved to a hotel, so I have not seen much of them all, but I joined them at a theatre last night and everyone seemed very happy. It was an opening night and the photographers made a rush at Mrs. Mortmain, who looked stunning.

I hope I see you before I go back home. Maybe we can swim the moat again. How are the swans?

I shall be tickled to death to have you for a sister-in-law.

Love from
NEIL

I wish he weren't going back to America. He is hoping to get a partnership in a ranch, Simon told me; somewhere in a California desert. Deserts do not seem to be deserted in America.

This morning I had a letter from Rose which I will now copy in.

DEAR CASSANDRA,

I am sorry not to have written before but we have been very busy. Getting a trousseau is quite hard work. I think you would be surprised at the way we do it. We hardly go to real shops at all but to large beautiful houses. There are drawing-rooms with crystal chandeliers and little gilt chairs all round and you sit there and watch the manniquins (can't spell it) walk past in the clothes. You have a card and a pencil to mark down what you like. The prices are fabulous—quite plain dresses cost around twenty-five pounds. My black suit will be thirty-five—more, really, because everything is in guineas, not pounds. At first I had a frightened sort of feeling at so much being spent but now it seems almost natural. I believe my whole trousseau is to cost up to a thousand pounds—and that will not mean very many things, really, not at the prices we are paying. But things like fur coats and jewellery will come after I am married. I already have my engagement ring, of course, a square emerald. Lovely.

I expect you will wish I would describe everything we have bought but I haven't the time and I also feel embarrassed at having so much when you have so little. But you are to have a most beautiful bridesmaid's frock—you are to come up to be fitted for it—and I think the ready-made clothes I am wearing now can be altered for you, once I get my trousseau. And when I am married we will shop like mad for you.

Here is some news that will interest you specially. We dined with the Fox-Cottons and saw Stephen's photographs and, my dear, he looks like all the Greek gods rolled into one. Leda is sure he could get a job on the pictures, quite seriously. I said it was a scream to think of him acting and she got quite annoyed. You had better look after your property. I'm joking—don't do anything silly. I intend to find someone really exciting for you.

I don't like the Fox-Cottons much. Aubrey makes an awful fuss of Topaz—he has taken her out several times. She *is* a conspicuous person. She knew some of the manaquins at a dress-show—I could have died. And she knew the photographers at a first-night we went to. Macmorris was there—he looks like a very pale monkey. He wants to paint her again. Her clothes seem wildly eccentric now we are with well-dressed people—it's funny to think I used quite to envy them.

I thought of you yesterday. I was out by myself and I went into that shop where the furs were stored—the clothes there look stodgy after the ones I've been seeing but they do have nice gloves and things. I saw the branch of white coral you lost your heart to, and wondered if I could buy it for you but it is only for display. Then I thought I would buy you a bottle of the scent you said smelt like bluebells but the price is ruinous and I hadn't enough with me—the only pocket-money I have is what Topaz doles out and she is being remarkably cautious with the beaver coat money, though strictly speaking it is yours and mine. Mrs. Cotton spends the earth *on* me, of course, but hasn't offered anything for me to spend myself—perhaps she thinks it wouldn't be tactful, but it would.

Oh, darling, do you remember how we stood watching the woman buying a whole dozen pairs of silk stockings and you said we were like cats making longing noises for birds? I think it was that moment I decided I would do anything, anything, to stop being so horribly poor. It was that night we met the Cottons again. Do you believe one can make things happen? I do. I had the same sort of desperate feeling the night I wished on the angel—and look what that did! He is an angel, all right, not a devil. It's so wonderful that I can be in love with Simon as well as everything else.

Darling Cassandra, I promise you shall never make any more longing cat noises once I am a married woman. And there are other things besides clothes that I can help you with, you know. I have been wondering if you would like to go to college (did you know Thomas is to go to Oxford?). Personally,

I think it would be dreary but you might enjoy it as you are so intelligent. My marriage is going to help us *all*, you know—even father. Being away from him has made me more tolerant of him. Both Simon and Mrs. Cotton say he really was a great writer. Anyway, it doesn't matter any more that he can't earn any money. Give him my love—and to Thomas and Stephen. I will send them all postcards. This letter is private to you, of course.

I do wish you were here—I miss you at least a hundred times a day. I felt so sad being in that shop without you. I shall go back and get you that scent when I have extracted more money from Topaz—it's called "Midsummer Eve" and you shall have it in time for your goings-on on Belmotte.

Heavens, I'm using pages and pages of Mrs. Cotton's elegant notepaper, but it feels a bit like talking to you. I meant to tell you all about the theatres but I mustn't start now—it's later than I thought and I have to dress for dinner.

Love and please write often to your

ROSE

P.S. I have a bathroom all to myself and there are clean peach-coloured towels every single day. Whenever I feel lonely, I go and sit in there till I cheer up.

That is the first letter I ever had from her, as we haven't been separated since we were very small, when Rose had scarlet fever. It doesn't sound quite like her, somehow—for one thing, it is much more affectionate; I don't think she has ever called me "darling" before. Perhaps it is because she is missing me. I do call it a sign of a beautiful nature if a girl who is in love and surrounded by all that splendour is lonely for her sister.

Fancy thirty-five guineas for a suit! That is thirty-six pounds fifteen shillings; I do think shops are artful to price things in guineas. I didn't know clothes *could* cost so much—at that rate, Rose is right when she says a thousand pounds won't buy so very many; not when you think of all the hats and shoes and underclothes. I had imagined Rose having dozens and dozens of dresses—you can get such beauties for two or three pounds each; but perhaps it gives you a glorious, valuable feeling to wear little black suits of fabulous price—like wearing real jewellery. Rose and I always felt superb when we wore our little real gold chains with the seed-pearl hearts. We howled like anything when they had to be sold.

A thousand pounds for clothes—when one thinks how long poor people could live on it! When one thinks how long *we* could live on it, for that matter! Oddly, I have never thought of us as poor people—I mean, I have never been terribly sorry for us, as for the unemployed, or beggars; though really we have been rather worse off, being unemployable and with no one to beg from.

I don't believe I could look a beggar in the face if my trousseau had cost a thousand pounds. . . . Oh, come—Mrs. Cotton wouldn't give the thousand pounds to beggars if she didn't spend it on Rose, so Rose might as well have it. And I shall certainly be delighted to accept clothes from Rose. I ought to be ashamed—being glad the riches won't be on my conscience, while only too willing to have them on my back.

I meant to copy in a letter from Topaz but it is pinned up in the kitchen, most of it being instructions for cooking—about which I am more ignorant than I had realized. We used to manage quite well when she was away sitting for artists, because in those days we lived mostly on bread, vegetables and eggs; but now that we can afford some meat or even chickens, I keep coming to grief. I scrubbed some rather dirty-looking chops with soap which proved very lingering, and I did not take certain things out of a chicken that I ought to have done.

Even keeping the house clean is more complicated than I expected—I have always helped with it, of course, but never organized it. I am realizing more and more how hard Topaz worked.

Her letter looks as if it had been written with a stick—she always uses a very thick, orange quill pen. There are six spelling mistakes. After the helpful cooking hints, she mentions the theatre first-night they went to and says the play was not "significant"—a word she has just taken up. Aubrey

Fox-Cotton's architecture is significant, but Leda Fox-Cotton's photographs are not—Topaz doubts their ultimate motivation. Ultimate with two *l*'s. Dear Topaz! *Her* letter is exactly like her—three quarters practical kindness and one quarter spoof. I hope the spoof means she is feeling happier; there has been less and less of it since she has been worrying about father. It must be months since she played her lute or communed with nature.

She finishes by saying she will come home instantly if father shows signs of missing her. Unfortunately, he doesn't; and he is far less irritable than when she was here—though not conversational. We only see each other at meals; the rest of the day he either walks or shuts himself in the gatehouse (when he leaves it, he now locks the door and takes the key). I regret to say that he is re-reading Miss Marcy's entire stock of detective novels. And he has spent one day in London. While he was gone I told myself it was absurd the way we had all been hypnotized by him not to ask questions, so when he came back I said cheerfully: "How was the British Museum?"

"Oh, I haven't been there," he answered, quite pleasantly. "To-day I went to——" He broke off, suddenly staring at me as if I were some dangerous animal he had only just noticed; then he walked out of the room. I longed to call after him: "Father, really! Are you going queer in the head?" But it struck me that if a man is going queer in the head, he is the last person to mention it to.

That sentence has brought me up with a bang. Do I really believe my father is going insane? No, of course not. I even have a faint, glorious hope that he may be working—he has twice asked for ink. But it is slightly peculiar that he took my coloured chalks—what was left of them—and an ancient volume of *Little Folks*; also that he went for a walk carrying an out-of-date Bradshaw railway guide.

His manner is usually normal. And he has been most civil about my cooking—which is certainly a sign of control.

How arrogant I used to be! I remember writing in this journal that I would capture father later—I meant to do a brilliant character sketch. Capture father! Why, I don't know anything about anyone! I shouldn't be surprised to hear that even Thomas is living a double life—though he does seem all homework and appetite. One nice thing is being able to give him enough to eat at last; I crowd food on to his plate.

And Stephen? No, I can't capture Stephen. Life does turn out unexpectedly. I was afraid it might be difficult being alone with him so much—during the long evenings, with father shut in the gatehouse and Thomas busy with his lessons. I couldn't have been more wrong. After tea, he helps me with the washing-up, then we usually garden—but often in quite different parts of the garden and, anyway, he hardly talks at all.

He hasn't been to London any more and I am sure he hasn't seen the photographs of himself—I should have known if they had been sent here.

It is really a very good thing that he seems to have lost interest in me because, feeling like this, I might not have been brisk with him.

Feeling like what, Cassandra Mortmain? Flat? Depressed? Empty? If so, why, pray?

I thought if I made myself write I should find out what is wrong with me, but I haven't, so far. Unless——Could I possibly be jealous of Rose?

I will pause and search my innermost soul. . . .

I have searched it for a solid five minutes. And I swear I am *not* jealous of Rose; more than that, I should hate to change places with her. Naturally, this is mainly because I shouldn't like to marry Simon. But suppose I were in love with him, as Rose is? That's too hard to imagine. Then suppose it were Neil—because since he went away I have wondered if I am not just a little bit in love with him. All right, I'm in love with Neil and I'm marrying him and he is the rich one. A thousand pounds is being spent on my trousseau with furs and jewellery coming later. I am to have a wonderful wedding with everyone saying: "What a brilliant match that quiet little girl has made." We are going to live at Scoatney Hall with everything we can possibly want and, presumably, lots of the handsomest children. It's going to be "happy ever after," just like the fairy tales——

And I still wouldn't like it. Oh, I'd love the clothes and the wedding. I am not so sure I should like the facts of life, but I have got over the bitter disappointment I felt when I first heard about them, and one obviously has to try them sooner or later. What I'd really hate would be the settled feeling, with nothing but happiness to look forward to. Of course no life is perfectly happy—Rose's children will probably get ill, the servants may be difficult, perhaps dear Mrs. Cotton will prove to be the teeniest fly in the ointment. (I should like to know what fly was originally in what ointment.) There are hundreds of worries and even sorrows that may come along, but—— I think what I really mean is that Rose won't be *wanting* things to happen. She will want things to stay just as they are. She will never have the fun of hoping something wonderful and exciting may be just round the corner.

I dare say I am being very silly but there it is! I DO NOT ENVY ROSE. When I imagine changing places with her I get the feeling I do on finishing a novel with a brick-wall happy ending—I mean the kind of ending when you never think any more about the characters. . . .

It seems a long time since I wrote those last words. I have been sitting here staring at Miss Blossom without seeing her, without seeing anything. Now I am seeing things more clearly than usual—that often happens after I have been "stuck". The furniture seems almost alive and leaning towards me, like the chair in Van Gogh's painting. The two beds, my little jug and basin, the bamboo dressing-table—how many years Rose and I have shared them! We used so scrupulously to keep to our own halves of the dressing-table. Now there is nothing of hers on it except a pink china ring-stand for which she never had any rings—well, she has one now.

I suddenly know what has been the matter with me all week. Heavens, I'm not envying Rose, I'm missing her! Not missing her because she is away now—though I *have* been a little bit lonely—but missing the Rose who has gone away for ever. There used to be two of us always on the look-out for life, talking to Miss Blossom at night, wondering, hoping; two Brontë—Jane Austen girls, poor but spirited, two Girls of Godsend Castle. Now there is only one, and nothing will ever be quite such fun again.

Oh, how selfish I am—when Rose is so happy! Of course I wouldn't have things different; even on my own account, I am looking forward to presents—though. . . . I wonder if there isn't a catch about having plenty of money? Does it eventually take the pleasure out of things? When I think of the joy of my green linen dress after I hadn't had a new dress for ages——! Will Rose be able to feel anything like that after a few years?

One thing I do know: I adore my green linen dress even if it did cost only twenty-five shillings. "Only" twenty-five shillings! That seemed like a fortune when we bought the dress.

Ab has just walked in, mewing—it must be tea-time; that cat has a clock in his stomach. Yes—I can hear Stephen talking to Heloïse in the courtyard; and father shouting through the gatehouse window to know if Thomas has brought him a copy of the *Scout*. (Now, what can a grown man want with the *Scout*?)

I wonder if Thomas remembered the kippers. . . .

Yes, he did—I have just yelled down to him. He often brings us fish from King's Crypt now. Well, it's said to be good for the brain—perhaps it will help father. Oh, kippers for tea, two each! *Three*, if anyone wants them.

I feel better.

I must go down and feed my family.

Chapter XII

IT IS MIDSUMMER DAY—AND AS BEAUTIFUL AS ITS NAME.

I am writing in the attic; I chose it because one can see Belmotte from the window. At first I thought I would sit on the mound, but I saw that would be too much—there I should keep re-living it all instead of writing about it. And I must set it down to-day so that I shall have it for ever, intact and lovely, untouched by the sadness that is coming—for of course it *is* coming; my brain tells me that. I thought it would have come by this morning but it hasn't—oh, so much it hasn't that I can't quite believe it ever will!

Is it wrong of me to feel so happy? Perhaps I ought even to feel guilty? No. I didn't make it happen, and it can't hurt anyone but me. Surely I have a right to my joy? For as long as it lasts. . . .

It is like a flowering in the heart, a stirring of wings—oh, if only I could write poetry, as I did when I was a child! I have tried, but the words were as cheap as a sentimental song. So I tore them up. I must set it down simply—everything that happened to me yesterday—with no airs and graces. But I long to be a poet, to pay tribute. . . .

My lovely day began when the sun rose—I often wake then but usually I go to sleep again. Yesterday I instantly remembered that it was Midsummer Eve, my very favourite day, and lay awake looking forward to it and planning my rites on the mound. They seemed all the more valuable because I wondered if it might not be my last year for them—I didn't feel as if it would, but Rose outgrew them when she was about my age. And I agree with her that it would be dreadful to perform them just as an affected pose; they were a bit peculiar last year when Topaz kindly assisted me and went very pagan.

The nicest times of all were when Rose and I were young enough to feel rather frightened.

We first held the rites when I was nine—I got the idea from a book on folklore. Mother thought them unsuitable for Christian little girls (I remember my astonishment at being called a Christian) and she was worried in case our dresses caught alight when we danced round our votive fire. She died the following winter and the next Midsummer Eve we had a much bigger fire; and while we were piling more wood on, I suddenly thought of her and wondered if she could see us. I felt guilty, not only because of the fire, but because I no longer missed her and was enjoying myself. Then it was time for the cake and I was glad that I could have two pieces—she would only have allowed one; but in the end I took only one. Stephen's mother always made us a beautiful Midsummer cake—the whole family got some of it, but Rose and I never let the others join in our rites on the mound; though after the year we saw the Shape, Stephen took to hanging about in the courtyard in case we called for help.

As I lay in bed watching the sun climb out of the wheat field yesterday, I tried to remember all our Midsummer Eves, in their proper order. I got as far as the year it poured and we tried to light a fire under an umbrella. Then I drifted back into sleep again—the most beautiful, hazy, light sleep. I dreamt I was on Belmotte Tower at sunrise and all around me was a great golden lake, stretching as far as I could see. There was nothing of the castle left at all, but I didn't seem to mind in the least.

While I was getting breakfast, Stephen told me that he wouldn't be in to lunch, as he usually is on Saturdays, because he was going to London to sit for Mrs. Fox-Cotton again.

"She wants to start work the very first thing to-morrow," he explained, "so I'm to go up to-day and sleep the night there."

I asked if he had anything to pack his clothes in and he showed me a moth-eaten carpet-bag that had belonged to his mother.

"Gracious, you can't use that," I told him. "I'll lend you my attaché case—if it's big enough."

"It'll be that, all right," he said, grinning. I found he was only taking his nightshirt, his safety-razor, a toothbrush and a comb.

"Couldn't you buy yourself a dressing-gown, Stephen—out of the five guineas you earned last time?"

He said he had other things to do with that.

"Well, out of your wages then. There's no need to hand them over now we have two hundred pounds."

But he said he couldn't make any change without discussing it with Topaz. "Maybe she'll be counting on me. And two hundred pounds won't last for ever. Don't you go feeling rich, it isn't safe."

In the end he agreed to think about getting a dressing-gown, but I knew he was only saying it to please me. No—I expect he just said it to end the argument; he has given up trying specially to please me. And, no doubt, it is a very good thing.

He had barely left the house when father came down, wearing his best suit—he, too, was off to London, and for several days, if you please!

"Where will you stay—with the Cottons?" I ventured—"ventured" being the way I ask him all questions these days.

"What—where? Yes, I dare say I might. That's a very good idea. Any messages for the girls? Don't speak for a minute."

I stared at him in astonishment. He had picked up a plate from the table and was examining it carefully—just a cracked old willow-pattern plate I had found in the hen-house and brought in to relieve the crockery shortage.

"Interesting. Quite a possibility," he said at last—then walked out to the gatehouse, taking the plate with him. After a few minutes he came back without it and started his breakfast.

I could see he was preoccupied, but I did want to know about that plate. I asked if it was valuable.

"Might be, might be," he said, staring in front of him.

"Do you know anyone who would buy it?"

"Buy it? Don't be silly. And don't talk."

I gave it up.

There was the usual scrimmage to get him off in time to catch the train. I wheeled his bicycle out for him and stood waiting in the courtyard.

"Where are your things for the night?" I asked as he came out towards me empty-handed.

He looked faintly startled, then said: "Oh, well—I couldn't manage a suitcase on the bicycle. I'll do without. Hello——" He caught sight of Stephen's carpet-bag—I had thrown it out of the kitchen because it was crawling with moth-grubs. "Now, *that* I could use—I could sling it across the handlebars. Quick, get my things!"

I began to point out the awfulness of the bag but he chivvied me indoors, shouting instructions after me—so that I heard "Pyjamas!" as I went across the kitchen, "Shaving tackle!" on the kitchen stairs and "Toothbrush, handkerchiefs and a clean shirt if I have one!" as I rummaged round his bedroom. By the time I reached the bathroom there came a roar: "That's enough—come back at once or I shall miss my train." But when I rushed down to him he seemed to have forgotten there was any hurry—he was sitting on the back-door step studying the carpet-bag.

"This is most interesting—pseudo-Persian," he began—then sprang up shouting: "Great Heaven, give me those things!" Godsend church striking the half had brought him back to earth.

He shoved everything into the bag, hung it on his bicycle and rode off full-tilt, mangling the corner of a flower-bed. At the gatehouse, he suddenly braked, flung himself off and dashed up the tower stairs, leaving the bicycle so insecurely placed that it slid to the ground. By the time I had run across and picked it up, he was coming down carrying the willow-pattern plate. He pushed it into the carpet-bag, then started off again—pedalling frantically, with the bag thumping against his knees. At the first bend of the lane he turned his head sharply and shouted: "Good-bye"—very nearly falling off the bicycle. Then he was gone. Never have I known him so spasmodic—or have I? Wasn't he rather like that in the days when his temper was violent?

As I walked back to the house, it dawned on me that I was going to be alone for the night—Thomas was spending the weekend with Harry, his friend at school. For a second, I had a dismayed, deserted feeling but I soon convinced myself there was nothing to be frightened of—we hardly ever get tramps down our lane and when we do they are often very nice; anyway, Heloïse is a splendid watch-dog.

Once I got used to the idea of being by myself for so long I positively liked it. I always enjoy the different feeling there is in a house when one is alone in it, and the thought of that feeling stretching ahead for two whole days somehow intensified it wonderfully. The castle seemed to be mine in a way it never had been before; the day seemed specially to belong to me; I even had a feeling that I owned myself more than I usually do. I became very conscious of all my movements—if I raised my arm I looked at it wonderingly, thinking, "That is mine!" And I took pleasure in moving, both in the physical effort and in the touch of the air—it was most queer how the air did seem to touch me, even when it was absolutely still. All day long I had a sense of great ease and spaciousness. And my happiness had a strange, remembered quality as though I had lived it before. Oh, how can I recapture it—that utterly right, homecoming sense of recognition? It seems to me now that the whole day was like an avenue leading to a home I had loved once but forgotten, the memory of which was coming back so dimly, so gradually, as I wandered along, that only when my home at last lay before me did I cry: "Now I know why I have been happy!"

How words weave spells! As I wrote of the avenue, it rose before my eyes—I can see it now, lined with great smooth-trunked trees whose branches meet far above me. The still air is flooded with peace, yet somehow expectant—as it seemed to me once when I was in King's Crypt cathedral at sunset. On and on I wander, beneath the vaulted roof of branch and leaf . . . and all the time, the avenue is yesterday, that long approach to beauty. Images in the mind, how strange they are. . . .

I have been gazing at the sky—I never saw it a brighter

blue. Great featherbed clouds are billowing across the sun, their edges brilliant silver. The whole day is silvery, sparkling, the birds sound shrill. . . . Yesterday was golden, even in the morning the light was softly drowsy, all sounds seemed muted.

By ten o'clock I had finished all my jobs and was wondering what to do with the morning. I strolled round the garden, watched a thrush on the lawn listening for worms and finally came to rest on the grassy bank of the moat. When I dabbled my hand in the shimmering water it was so much warmer than I expected that I decided to bathe. I swam round the castle twice, hearing the Handel "Water Music" in my head.

While I was hanging my bathing-suit out of the bedroom window, I had a sudden longing to lie in the sun with nothing on. I never felt it before—Topaz has always had a monopoly of nudity in our household—but the more I thought of it, the more I fancied it. And I had the brilliant idea of doing my sunbathing on the top of the bedroom tower, where nobody working in the fields or wandering up our lane could possibly see me. It felt most peculiar crawling naked up the cold, rough stone steps—exciting in some mysterious way I couldn't explain to myself. Coming out at the top was glorious, warmth and light fell round me like a great cape. The leads were so hot that they almost burnt the soles of my feet; I was glad I had thought of bringing up a blanket to spread.

It was beautifully private. That tower is the best-preserved of them all; the circle of battlements is complete, though there are a few deep cracks—a marigold had seeded in one of them. Once I lay down flat I couldn't even see the battlements without turning my head. There was nothing left but the sun-filled dome of the cloudless sky.

What a difference there is between wearing even the skimpiest bathing-suit and wearing nothing! After a few minutes I seemed to live in every inch of my body as fully as I usually do in my head and my hands and my heart. I had the fascinating feeling that I could think as easily with my limbs as with my brain—and suddenly the whole of me thought that Topaz's nonsense about communing with nature isn't nonsense at all. The warmth of the sun felt like enormous hands pressing gently on me, the flutter of the air was like delicate fingers. My kind of nature-worship has always had to do with magic and folklore, though sometimes it turned a bit holy. This was nothing like that. I expect it was what Topaz means by "pagan". Anyway, it was thrilling.

But my front got so terribly hot. And when I rolled over on to my stomach I found that the back of me was not so interested in communing with nature. I began to think with my brain only, in the normal way, and it felt rather shut inside itself—probably because having nothing but the roof to stare at was very dull. I started to listen to the silence—never have I known such a silent morning. No dog barked, no hen clucked; strangest of all, no birds sang. I seemed to be in a soundless globe of heat. The thought had just struck me that I might have gone deaf, when I heard a tiny bead of sound, tap, tap—I couldn't imagine what it could be. Plop, plop—I solved it: my bathing-suit dripping into the moat. Then a bee zoomed into the marigold, close to my ear—and then suddenly it was as if all the bees of the summer world were humming high in the sky. I sprang up and saw an aeroplane coming nearer and nearer—so I made for the stairs and sat there with just my head out. The plane flew quite low over the castle, and the ridiculous idea came to me that I was a mediæval de Godys lady seeing a flying man across the centuries—and perhaps hoping he was a lover coming to win her.

After that the mediæval lady groped her way downstairs and put on her shift.

Just as I finished dressing, the postman came through to the courtyard, calling: "Anyone home?" He had a parcel—for me! Rose had gone back and ordered the "Midsummer Eve" scent; I thought she had forgotten. Oh, it was a fascinating present! Inside the outer wrapping was another—white, with coloured flowers on it—and inside that was a blue box that felt velvety, and inside that was a glass bottle engraved with a moon and stars, and inside that was pale green scent. The stopper was fastened down with silver wire and silver seals. At first I thought I would open it at once; then I decided to make the opening a prelude to the rites, something to look forward to all day. So I stood the bottle on the half of the dressing-table that used to be Rose's and sent her waves of thanks—I meant to write to her after my "goings-on on Belmotte," as she called them, and tell her I had worn the scent for them. . . . Oh, why didn't I write at once? What can I say to her now? . . .

I was hungry but I didn't feel like cooking, so I had the most beautiful lunch of cold baked beans—what bliss it is that we can now afford things in tins again! I had bread-and-butter, too, and lettuce and cold rice pudding and two slices of cake (real shop cake) and milk. Hel and Ab sat on the table and were given treats—they had had their own dinners, of course. They both took to baked beans at once—there is precious little they don't take to, Heloïse even accepted salted lettuce. (During our famine period she became practically a vegetarian.) Then, all three of us very full, we had a sleep in the four-poster, Ab curled up at the foot and Hel with her back against my chest, which was rather hot but always gives one a companionable feeling.

We slept for hours—I don't think I ever slept so long in the day-time; I felt terribly guilty when I woke up and found it was nearly four o'clock. Hel thumped her tail as if I had just come back from somewhere and Ab gave us a look as if he had never seen either of us before in his life—after which he jumped off the bed, did a little claw-sharpening on Miss Blossom's solitary leg and then went downstairs. When I looked out across the courtyard a few minutes later he was high on the curtain walls with one leg pointing to heaven, doing some strenuous washing. It gave me the idea of washing my hair.

After that, it was time to gather flowers for the rites.

They have to be wild flowers—I can't remember if that is traditional or if Rose and I made it up: mallow, campion and bluebells for the garland to hang round our necks, foxgloves to carry, and we always wore wild roses in our hair. Even since Rose has given up the rites she has sometimes come out for the garland-gathering—I kept talking to her yesterday and hearing her answer; it made me miss her more than ever, so I talked to Heloïse instead. We had the most peaceful, com-

panionable walk along the lane and through the fields, with
Heloïse carrying the flower-basket for several seconds at a
time, the whole back half of her waggling with pride. I was
glad to find there were still plenty of bluebells in the larch
wood. One of the nicest sights I know is Heloïse smelling a
bluebell with her long, white, naked-looking nose. How can
people say bull-terriers are ugly? Heloïse is *exquisite*—though
she has put on a bit too much weight, these last opulent weeks.

I gave the flowers a long drink—wild ones die so quickly
without water that I never make my garland before seven
o'clock. By then I had collected enough twigs to start the fire
—Stephen always takes the logs up for me—and packed my
basket. When I finished my garland, it was nearly eight and a
pale moon was coming up though the sky was still blue. I
changed into my green linen frock and put on my garland and
wild roses; then, at the very last minute, I opened Rose's scent.

One deep sniff and I was back in the rich shop where the furs
were stored—oh, it was a glorious smell! But the odd thing
was, it no longer reminded me of bluebells. I waved a little
about on a handkerchief and managed to capture them for a
second, but most of the time there was just a mysterious,
elusive sweetness that stood for London and luxury. It killed
the faint wild-flower scents and I knew it would spoil the
lovely smell that comes from Belmotte grass after a hot day;
so I decided not to wear any for the rites. I took one last sniff,
then ran down to the kitchen for the sack of twigs and the
basket and started off. I was glad Heloïse wasn't there to
follow me, because she always wants to eat the ceremonial cake.

There wasn't a breath of wind as I climbed the mound. The
sun was down—usually I begin the rites by watching it sink,
but trying the scent had taken longer than I realized. The sky
beyond Belmotte Tower was a watery yellow with one streak
of green across it—vivid green, most magically beautiful. But
it faded quickly, it was gone by the time I reached the stones
we placed to encircle the fire. I watched until the yellow
faded, too—then turned towards the moon still low over the
wheat field. The blue all around her had deepened so much that
she no longer looked pale, but like masses of luminous snow.

The peace was so great that it seemed like a soft, thick substance wrapped closely round me making it hard to move; but when the church clock struck nine, I stirred at last. I emptied the sack of twigs into the circle of stones and put on the small logs that Stephen had left ready. He had brought some long, slender branches too, so I set them up over the logs like the poles of a wigwam. Then I went to the tower for my needfire.

Real needfire—from which Midsummer fires should be lit— can only be made by rubbing two pieces of wood together; but when first we planned the rites, Rose and I spent an hour at this without raising so much as a spark. So we decided it would be pagan enough if we took matches to the tower and lit a taper. Then Rose carried it out and I followed, waving foxgloves. We were always fascinated that such a tiny flame could make the twilight seem deeper and so much more blue— we thought of that as the beginning of the magic; and it was tremendously important that the taper shouldn't blow out as we came down the tower steps and crossed the mound—on breezy nights we used a lamp glass to protect it. Last night was so still that I scarcely needed to shelter it with my hand.

Once the fire is blazing the countryside fades into the dusk, so I took one last look round the quiet fields, sorry to let them go. Then I lit the twigs. They caught quickly—I love those early minutes of a fire, the crackles and snappings, the delicate flickers, the first sharp whiff of smoke. The logs were slow to catch so I lay with my head near the ground, and blew. Suddenly the flames raced up the wigwam of branches and I saw the snowy moon trapped in a fiery cage. Then smoke swept over her as the logs caught at last. I scrambled up, and sat back watching them blaze high. All my thoughts seemed drawn into the fire—to be burning with it in the brightly lit circle of stones. The whole world seemed filled with hissing and crackling and roaring.

And then, far off in the forgotten dusk, someone called my name.

"Cassandra!" . . . Did it come from the lane—or from the castle? And whose voice was it? Dead still, I waited for it to call again, trying to shut my ears to the fire noises. Had it been a man's voice or a woman's? When I tried to remember it I only heard the fire. After a few seconds I began to think I must have imagined it. Then Heloïse began barking, the way she barks when somebody arrives.

I ran across the mound and peered down. At first my eyes were too full of the flames to see anything clearly, then gradually the pale light of evening spread round me again; but I couldn't see into the lane or the courtyard because a thick mist was rising from the moat. Heloïse sounded so frantic that I decided to go down. Just as I started off, she stopped barking—and then, floating across the mist, came the voice again: "Cas-san-dra!"—a long, drawn-out call. This time I knew it was a man's voice but I still couldn't recognize it. I was sure it wasn't father's or Stephen's or Thomas's. It was a voice that had never called me before.

"Here I am!" I called back. "Who is it?"

Someone was moving through the mist, crossing the bridge. Heloïse came racing ahead, very pleased with herself.

"Why, of course—it'll be Neil!" I thought suddenly, and started to run down to meet him. Then at last I saw clearly. It wasn't Neil. It was Simon.

Oh, strange to remember—I wasn't pleased to see him! I had wanted it to be Neil—if it had to be anyone at all when I was just starting the rites. I wouldn't blame anybody who caught a grown girl at them for thinking her "consciously naïve."

As we shook hands, I made up my mind to take him indoors without referring to the fire. But he looked up at it and said:

"I'd forgotten it was Midsummer Eve—Rose told me about the fun you always have. How pretty your garland is."

Then, somehow, we were walking up the mound together.

He had driven down to see the Scoatney agent; had been working with him all day: "Then I thought I'd come and call on you and your father—is he out? There are no lights in the castle."

I explained about father—and said he might possibly have turned up at the flat.

"Then he'll have to sleep in my room—we're like sardines in that apartment. What a glorious blaze!"

As we sat down I wondered how much Rose had told him about the rites—I hoped he only knew that we lit a fire for them. Then I saw him look at the basket.

"How's Rose?" I asked quickly, to distract him from it.

"Oh, she's fine—she sent you her love, of course. So did Topaz. Is this the Vicar's port that Rose told me about?"

The medicine bottle was sticking right out of the basket.

"Yes, he gives me a little every year," I said, feeling most self-conscious.

"Do we drink it or make a libation?"

"We?"

"Oh, I'm going to celebrate too. I shall represent Rose—even if she does feel too old for it."

Suddenly I stopped feeling self-conscious. It came to me that Simon was one of the few people who would really find Midsummer rites romantic—that he'd see them as a link with the past and that they might even help with those English roots he wants to strike. So I said: "All right—that'll be lovely," and began to unpack the basket.

He watched with much interest: "Rose never told me about the packet of cooking herbs. What are they for?"

"We burn them—they're a charm against witchcraft. Of course they oughtn't to be shop herbs—they should have been gathered by moonlight. But I don't know where to find any that smell nice."

He said I must get them from the Scoatney herb-garden in future: "It'll be grateful to be used, after being a dead failure in salads. What's the white stuff?"

"That's salt—it wards off bad luck. And turns the flames a lovely blue."

"And the cake?"

"Well, we show that to the fire before we eat it. Then we drink wine and throw a few drops into the flames."

"And then you dance round the fire?"

I told him I was much too old for that.

"Not on your life, you're not," said Simon. "I'll dance with you."

I didn't tell him about the verses I usually say, because I made them up when I was nine and they are too foolish for words.

The high flames were dying down; I could see we should need more kindling if we were to keep the fire spectacular. I had noticed some old wood in the tower—a relic of the days when we often had picnics on the mound. I asked Simon to help me get it.

As we came to the tower he stood still for a moment, looking up at its height against the sky. "How tall is it?" he asked. "It must be seventy or eighty feet, surely."

"Sixty," I told him. "It looks taller because it's so solitary."

"It reminds me of a picture I once saw called 'The Sorcerer's Tower.' Can you get to the top?"

"Thomas did, a few years ago, but it was very dangerous; and the upper part of the staircase has crumbled a lot more since then. Anyway, there's no place to get out on, if you do get to the top—the roof went hundreds of years ago. Come in and see."

We went up the long outside flight of stone steps that leads to the entrance and climbed down the ladder inside. When we looked up at the circle of sky far above us it was still pale blue, yet filled with stars—it seemed strange to see them there when scarcely any had been visible outside.

Enough light came down through the open door for Simon to look around. I showed him the beginning of the spiral staircase, which is stowed away in a sort of bulge. (It is up there that I hide this journal.) He asked what was through the archway that leads to the opposite bulge.

"Nothing, now," I told him. "It's where the garderobes used to be." They should really be called privy chambers or latrines, but garderobes are more mentionable.

"How many floors were there originally?"

"Three—you can see the staircase outlets to them. There was an entrance floor, a chamber above it and a dungeon below—here, where we are."

"I bet they enjoyed sitting feasting while the prisoners clanked in chains below."

I told him they probably feasted somewhere else—there must have been much more of Belmotte Castle once, though no other traces remain: "Most likely this was mainly a watch tower. Mind you don't bump into the bedstead."

The bedstead was there when we first came—a double one, rather fancy, now a mass of rusty iron. Father meant to have it moved but when he saw it with the cow-parsley growing through it, stretching up to the light, he took a fancy to it. Rose and I found it useful to sit on—mother was always complaining because our white knickers got marked with rust rings from its spirals.

"It's pure Surrealist," said Simon, laughing. "I can never understand why there are so many derelict iron bedsteads lying about in the country."

I said it was probably because they last so long, while other rubbish just moulders away.

"What a logical girl you are—I could never have worked that out." He was silent for a moment, staring up into the dim heights of the tower. A late bird flew across the circle of stars and fluttered down to its nest in a high arrow-slit.

"Can you get it—the feeling of people actually having lived here?" he said at last.

I knew just what he meant. "I used to try to, but they always seemed like figures in tapestry, not human men and women. It's so far back. But it must mean something to you that one of your ancestors built the tower. It's a pity the de Godys name died out."

"I'd call my eldest son 'Etienne de Godys Cotton,' if I thought he could get by with it in England—would you say he could? It'd certainly slay any American child."

I said I feared it would slay any child in any country. Then Heloïse appeared above us in the doorway, which reminded us to go on with our job of getting wood.

I dragged it out from under the rustic table and handed each branch to Simon, who stood half-way up the ladder—the technique Rose and I always used came back to me. When I climbed the ladder at last, Simon helped me out and said: "Look—there's magic for you."

The mist from the moat was rolling right up Belmotte; already the lower slopes were veiled.

I said: "It's like the night when we saw the Shape."

"The what?"

I told him about it as we carried the branches to the fire: "It happened the third year we held the rites, after a very hot, windless day like to-day. As the mist came towards us, it suddenly formed into a giant shape as high as—oh, higher than—the tower. It hung there between us and the castle; it seemed to be falling forward over us—I never felt such terror in my life. And the queer thing was that neither of us tried to run away; we screamed and flung ourselves face downwards before it. It was an elemental, of course—I'd been saying a spell to raise one."

He laughed and said it must have been some freak of the mist: "You poor kids! What happened then?"

"I prayed to God to take it away and He very obligingly did—Rose was brave enough to look up after a minute or two and it had vanished. I felt rather sorry for it afterwards; I dare say no one had summoned it since the Ancient Britons."

Simon laughed again, then looked at me curiously: "You don't, by any chance, *still* believe it was an elemental?"

Do I? I only know that just then I happened to look down towards the oncoming mist—its first rolling rush was over and it was creeping thinly—and suddenly the memory of that colossal shape came back so terrifyingly that I very nearly screamed. I managed a feeble laugh instead and began to throw wood on the fire so that I could let the subject drop.

Rose believed it was an elemental, too—and she was nearly fourteen then and far from fanciful.

When the fire was blazing high again I felt we had better get the rites over. My self-consciousness about them had come back a little so I was as matter-of-fact as possible; I must say leaving out the verses made things rather dull. We burnt the salt and the herbs (in America it is correct to drop the *h* in

herbs—it does sound odd) and shared the cake with Heloïse;
Simon only had a very small piece because he was full of
dinner. Then we drank the Vicar's port—there was only one
wineglass so Simon had his out of the medicine bottle, which
he said added very interesting overtones; and then we made our
libations, with an extra one for Rose. I hoped we could leave
things at that, but Simon firmly reminded me about dancing
round the fire. In the end, we just ran round seven times, with
Heloïse after us, barking madly. It was the smallest bit as if
Simon was playing with the children, but I know he didn't
mean it, and he was so very kind that I felt I had to pretend I
was enjoying myself—I even managed a few wild leaps. Topaz
is the girl for leaping; last year she nearly shook the mound.

"What now?" asked Simon when we flopped down at last.
"Don't we sacrifice Heloïse?" At the moment, she was trying to
give us tremendous washings, delighted to have caught us
after her long chase. I said:

"If we drove her across the embers it would cure her of
murrain, but she doesn't happen to have it. There's nothing
more, except that I usually sit still while the flames die down
and try to think myself back into the past."

Of course that was very much in Simon's line, but we didn't
get very far into the past because we kept talking. One thing
he said was that he would never get used to the miracle of the
long English twilight. It had never before struck me that we
have long twilights—Americans do seem to say things which
make the English notice England.

A carpet of mist had crept to within a few feet of us, then
crept no further—Simon said I must be putting a spell on it.
Down by the moat it had mounted so high that only the castle
towers rose clear of it. The fire died quickly, soon there was
nothing but grey smoke drifting in the grey dusk. I asked
Simon if we were seeing by the last of the daylight or the first
of the moonlight—and really it was hard to tell. Then
gradually the moonlight won and the mist shrouding the
castle turned silver.

"Could anyone paint that?" said Simon. "Debussy could
have done it in music. Are you fond of him?"

I had to admit that I'd never heard a note of Debussy.

"Oh, surely you must have. Not on records or the radio?"

When I told him we had neither a gramophone nor a wireless he looked staggered—I suppose Americans find it hard to believe there is anyone in the world without such things.

He told me they had a new machine at Scoatney that changed its own records—I thought he was joking till he began to explain how it worked. He finished by saying: "But why don't I drive you over to hear it now? We'll have some supper."

"But you said you were full of dinner," I reminded him.

"Well, I'll talk to you while you eat. And Heloïse can have a bone in the kitchen. Look at her trying to rub the dew off her nose with her paws! Come on, this grass is getting very damp." He pulled me to my feet.

I was glad to accept because I was fabulously hungry. Simon stamped out the dying embers while I went up to close the door of the tower. I stood at the top of the steps for a moment, trying to capture the feelings I usually have on Midsummer Eve—for I had been too occupied in entertaining Simon to think about them before. And suddenly I knew that I had been right in fearing this might be my last year for the rites—that if I ever held them again *I* should be "playing with the children." I only felt the smallest pang of sadness, because the glory of supper at Scoatney was stretching ahead of me; but I said to myself that, Simon or no Simon, I was going to give the farewell call—a farewell for ever this time, not just for a year. The call is a queer wordless cry made up of all the vowel sounds—it was thrilling when Rose and I used to make it together, but I do it fairly well by myself. "Ayieou!" I called—and it echoed back from the castle walls as I knew it would. Then Heloïse raised her head and howled—and that echoed, too. Simon was fascinated; he said it was the best moment of the rites.

Walking down Belmotte was the oddest sensation—every step took us deeper into the mist until at last it closed over our heads. It was like being drowned in the ghost of water.

"You'd better get a coat," said Simon as we crossed the

bridge to the courtyard, "because the car's open. I'll wait for you in it."

I ran upstairs to wash my hands; they were dirty from handling the wood. And I put some of the "Midsummer Eve" scent on my dress and handkerchief—it seemed just right for a supper party. My garland was still fresh so I wore it outside my coat, but as I hurried downstairs I decided it might look affected and it would certainly be longing for a drink; so I dropped it into the moat as I crossed the drawbridge.

It wasn't the usual Scoatney car but a new one, very long and low—so low that one feels one is going to bump one's behind on the road. "I think it's a bit too spectacular," said Simon, "but Rose lost her heart to it."

The night was beautifully clear once we were well away from the castle—we looked back at it from the high part of the Godsend road and could only see a little hill of mist rising from the moonlit wheat fields. "If you ask me, it's bewitched," said Simon. "Maybe when I bring you back we shall find it's gone for keeps." The new car was fascinating to drive in. Our eyes were on a level with the steep banks below the hedges and every spear of grass stood out brilliantly green in the headlights, seeming more alive than even in the brightest sunshine. We had to go very slowly because of rabbits—Heloïse kept trying to go head first through the windscreen after them. One poor creature ran in front of us for such a long time that Simon finally stopped the car and turned the headlights off, so that it could summon up the strength of mind to dive into a ditch. While we waited he lit a cigarette, and then we leaned back looking up at the stars and talking about astronomy, and space going on for ever and ever and how very worrying that is.

"And of course there's eternity," I began—then Godsend church struck ten and Simon said we must make up for lost time.

There were very few lights on at Scoatney—I suddenly wondered if all the servants would be in bed; but the butler came out to meet us. How extraordinary it must be to be able to tell a large, imposing man "Just bring a tray of supper for

Miss Mortmain to the pavilion, will you?"—without even apologizing for giving trouble so late at night! I apologized myself, and the butler said: "Not at all, miss," but rather distantly. As he stalked away after Heloïse (she knows her way to the kitchen now) it struck me that he would soon be Rose's butler. I wondered if she would ever get used to him.

We crossed the dim hall and went out at the back of the house.

"Here are your *h*erbs by moonlight," said Simon, "and did you notice how carefully I put my aitch in?" He led the way through the rather dull little herb-garden—the idea of herbs is so much more exciting than the look of them—into the water-garden, and turned on the fountains in the middle of the big oval pool. We sat on a stone bench watching them for a few minutes, then went into the pavilion. Simon only lit one candle—"I'll put it out when I start the phonograph," he said. "Then you can still see the fountains while you listen to Debussy—they go well together."

I sat down by one of the three tall, arched windows and peered around; I hadn't been in the pavilion since it had been turned into a music room. A large grand piano had arrived as well as the wonderful gramophone, and dozens of albums of records were arranged on the shelves of two painted cupboards. Simon walked along with the candle, looking for the Debussy albums.

"I suppose we ought to start you right at the beginning," he said, "but I don't believe we have anything from 'The Children's Corner.' I'll try *Clair de Lune* on you—and I bet you'll find you know it."

He was right—as soon as it began I remembered; a girl once played it at a school concert. It is beautiful—and the gramophone was amazing, it might have been someone really playing the piano, only much better than I ever heard a piano played. Then the record changed all by itself—Simon called me away from the window to watch it, and told me about the next piece, *La Cathédrale Engloutie*. You hear the drowned cathedral rise with its bells ringing, then sink into the sea again.

"Now you know why I said Debussy could have composed the castle in the mist," Simon told me.

The third record was *La Terrasse des Audiences au Clair de Lune*. It was wonderful to watch the fountains while I listened to it—there were fountains in the music, too.

"Well, Debussy's certainly made a hit with you," said Simon, "though I'm not sure you wouldn't outgrow him. You're the kind of child who might develop a passion for Bach."

I told him I hadn't at school. The one Bach piece I learnt made me feel I was being repeatedly hit on the head with a teaspoon. But I never got very far with my music—the money for lessons ran out when I was twelve.

"I'll find you some Bach that you'll like," said Simon. He lit the candle again and began to hunt through a big album. The gramophone had stopped playing. I went over to the cupboards and looked at the backs of the albums—even to read the names of the composers was exciting.

"You shall hear them all in time," Simon told me. "I'd like to try some really modern stuff on you. What a pity Rose doesn't like music."

I turned to him in astonishment. "But she does! She plays much better than I do—she sings, too."

"All the same, she doesn't really like it," he said firmly. "I took her to a concert and she looked quite wretched with boredom. Ah, here's your supper."

It came on a silver tray, and the butler spread a lace cloth on a little table for it. There was jellied soup, cold chicken (all breast), fruit and wine—and lemonade in case I didn't like the wine, but I did. Simon told the butler to light all the candles and he went round to the crystal wall-brackets with a taper in a long holder—it made me feel I was back in the eighteenth century. "I'm determined not to have electricity in here," said Simon.

When the butler had poured out wine for us both, Simon told him he needn't wait—I was glad because he would have made me feel I ought to bolt my supper. His name, by the way, is Graves, but I have never yet brought myself to call him by it in the nonchalant way one should.

Simon had found the record he wanted. "But it must wait until afterwards—I'm not going to let you eat your way through Bach." He put on some dance records and turned the gramophone very low; then came back and sat at the table with me.

"Tell me about Rose," I said—for it suddenly came to me that I had asked very little about her. I *had* been self-centred.

He talked about the trousseau and how much admired Rose is everywhere. "Topaz is, too, of course—and my mother's a pretty good-looker. When the three of them go out together, well, it's something."

I said they needed me to bring the average down—and instantly wished that I hadn't. That kind of a remark simply asks for a compliment.

Simon laughed and told me not to fish. "You're far prettier than any girl who's so intelligent has a right to be. As a matter of fact"—he sounded faintly surprised—"you're very pretty indeed."

I said: "I think I'm a bit better-looking when Rose isn't around."

He laughed again. "Well, you're certainly very pretty to-night." Then he raised his glass to me, as I once saw him raise it to Rose. I felt myself blushing and hastily changed the conversation. "Have you been doing any writing lately?" I asked.

He said he had begun a critical essay on father, but couldn't bring himself to finish it—"There seems no way of not drawing attention to his inactivity. If only one could give the faintest hint that he had something in hand . . . !"

For a moment I thought of telling him of my hopes, but it would have meant describing father's recent behaviour; and the idea of putting into words things like his reading *Little Folks* and studying willow-pattern plates made me realize how very peculiar they are. So I let Simon go on talking about his essay, which sounded very much over my head. He must be terribly clever.

When I finished my magnificent chicken, he peeled a peach

for me—I was glad, because it is a job I make a mess of; Simon did it beautifully. I noticed what very fine hands he has, and then I suddenly saw what Topaz meant when she once said that all his lines were good. He was wearing a white silk shirt—he had taken his coat off—and the line of his shoulders seemed exactly right with the line of his jaw (how wise Rose was to get rid of that beard!). I had the oddest feeling that I was drawing him—I knew exactly how I would do the little twist of his eyebrows, the curve where his lips pressed together as he concentrated on the peach. And as I drew each stroke in imagination, I felt it delicately traced on my own face, shoulders, arms and hands—even the folds of the shirt when I drew them seemed to touch me. But the drawn lines made no picture before my eyes—I still saw him as he was, in the flickering candlelight.

I had eaten the peach and was drinking the last of my wine when the gramophone began a most fascinating tune. I asked what it was called.

"This? 'Lover', I believe," said Simon. "Do you want to dance once? Then I must take you home."

He went to turn the gramophone up a little, then came back for me. I had never danced with him before and was rather nervous—I found it quite difficult that time I danced with Neil. To my surprise, it was far easier with Simon; he holds one more loosely, it seems more casual, I had a feeling of ease and lightness. After the first few seconds, I stopped worrying about following his steps—my feet took care of it on their own. The odd thing is that Neil helps one to follow far more, almost forces one to. Never did I feel any pressure from Simon's hold.

The "Lover" record was the last of the stack, so the gramophone stopped at the end. We were close enough for Simon to re-start it without taking his arm from my waist; then we danced the tune through again without saying one word—indeed, we never spoke all the time we were dancing. I can't remember that I even thought. I seemed to move with a pleasure that was mindless.

When the gramophone stopped again, Simon said: "Thank

you, Cassandra," still holding me in his arms, and smiling down at me.

I smiled back and said: "Thank you, too—it was lovely."

And then he bent his head and kissed me.

I have tried and tried to remember what I felt. Surely I must have felt surprised, but no sense of it comes back to me. All I can recall is happiness, happiness in my mind and in my heart and flowing through my whole body, happiness like the warm cloak of sunlight that fell round me on the tower. It was a darkness, too—and the darkness comes again when I try to recapture the moment . . . and then I find myself coldly separate—not only from Simon, but from myself as I was then. The figures I see in the candlelit pavilion are strangers to me.

The next thing I remember quite normally is the sound of Simon laughing. It was the kindest, most gentle laugh but it startled me.

"You astonishing child," he said.

I asked what he meant.

"Only that you kiss very nicely." Then he added teasingly: "You must have had quite a lot of practice."

"I never kissed any man in my life before——" Instantly I wished I hadn't said it—for I saw that once he knew I wasn't used to kissing, yet had returned his kiss, he might guess how much it had meant to me. I pulled away from him and ran to the door, only knowing that I wanted to hide my feelings.

"Cassandra—stop!" He caught me by the arm just as I got the door open. "Oh, my dear, I'm so sorry! I ought to have known that you'd mind."

He hadn't guessed. I could see he just thought I was angry. I managed to pull myself together.

"What nonsense, Simon! Of course I didn't mind."

"You certainly didn't seem to——" He looked worried and puzzled. "But why did you run away from me like that? Good heavens, surely you weren't frightened of me?"

"Of course I wasn't!"

"Then why——?"

I thought of something that might sound reasonable: "Simon, I wasn't frightened and I didn't mind—how could I

221

mind being kissed by anyone I'm as fond of as I am of you? But afterwards—well, just for a second, I was angry that you'd taken it for granted that you could kiss me."

He looked quite stricken. "But I didn't—not in the way you mean. Can you understand that it was a sudden impulse—because you've been so sweet all evening and because I'd enjoyed the dance, and because I like you very much?"

"And because you were missing Rose, perhaps," I put in helpfully.

He flushed and said: "I'm damned if I'll pass that—that'd be an insult to both of you. No, it was a kiss in your own right, my child."

"Anyway, we're making too much of it," I told him. "Let's forget it—and please forgive me for being so silly. Now may I hear the Bach record before I go home?" I felt that would set him at his ease a bit.

He still stood looking at me worriedly—I think he was trying to find words to explain more clearly. Then he gave it up.

"Very well—we'll play it while I put the candles out. You sit outside, then my moving round won't disturb you. I'll turn the fountains off so that you'll be able to hear."

I sat on the stone bench watching the dimpled water grow smooth. Then the music began in the pavilion—the most gentle, peaceful music I ever heard. Through the three tall windows I could see Simon going slowly round putting out each candle flame with a small metal hood. Each time, I saw the light on his upturned face and each time, the golden windows grew a little dimmer until at last they were black. Then the record ended and it was so quiet that I heard the tiny plop of a fish jumping, far across the pool.

"Well, did I get a customer for Bach?" Simon called, as he shut the door of the pavilion behind him.

"Yes, indeed! I could have listened to that for ever," I said, and asked the name of the piece. It was "Sheep May Safely Graze." We went on talking about music while we collected Heloïse from the kitchen, and all during the drive home I found it quite easy to carry on a casual conversation; it was as if my real feelings were down fathoms deep in my mind and what we said was just a feathery surface spray.

Godsend church was striking twelve as we drew up in front of the gatehouse. "Well, I've managed to get Cinderella home by midnight," said Simon, as he helped me out of the car. He saw me into the kitchen and lit the candle for me, laughing at the unctuous bee-line Heloïse made for her basket. I thanked him for my lovely evening and he thanked me for letting him share in my Midsummer rites—he said that was something he would always remember. Then, as he shook hands, he asked:

"Am I really forgiven?"

I told him of course he was. "I made a fuss about nothing. Heavens, what a prig you'll think me!"

He said earnestly: "I promise you I won't. I think you're everything that's nice, and thank you again." Then he gave my hand a brisk little squeeze—and the next second the door had closed behind him.

I stood absolutely still for a minute or so—then dashed upstairs, up through the bathroom tower and out on to the walls. The mist had cleared away, so I could watch the lights of the car travel slowly along the lane and turn on to the Godsend road. Even after they vanished on the outskirts of the village I still watched on, and caught one last glimpse of them on the road to Scoatney.

All the time I stood on the walls I was in a kind of daze, barely conscious of anything but the moving car; and when I pulled myself together enough to go in and undress, I deliberately held my thoughts away from me. Only when I lay down in darkness did I at last let them flow into my mind. And with them came nothing but happiness—like the happiness I felt when Simon kissed me, but more serene. Oh, I told myself that he belonged to Rose, that I could never win him from her even if I were wicked enough to try, which I never would be. It made no difference. Just to be in love seemed the most blissful luxury I had ever known. The thought came to me that perhaps it is the loving that counts, not the being loved in return—that perhaps true loving can never know anything but happiness. For a moment I felt that I had discovered a great truth.

And then I happened to catch sight of Miss Blossom's silhouette and heard her say: "Well, you just hang on to that comforting bit of high-thinking, duckie, because you're going to need it." And in some strange, far-off way I knew that was true—yet it still made no difference. I fell asleep happier than I had ever been in my life.

Chapter XIII

OH, HOW BITTER IT IS TO READ THAT LAST LINE I WROTE LITTLE
over three weeks ago—now when I cannot even remember
what happiness felt like!

I didn't read back any further. I was too afraid of losing
the dead, flat, watching-myself feeling which has come this
morning for the first time. It is utterly dreary but better than
acute wretchedness, and has given me a faint desire to empty
my mind into this journal, which will pass a few hours. But shall
I be able to write about the wicked thing I did on my birthday?
Can I bring myself to describe it fully? Perhaps I can work up
to it.

Heavens, how miserable the weather has been—floods of
rain, cold winds; my birthday was the only sunny day. To-
day is warm, but very dull and depressing. I am up on the
mound, sitting on the stone steps leading to Belmotte Tower.
Heloïse is with me—it is one of those times when she has to
retire from society, and she gets so bored if I leave her shut up
by herself. Her leash is safely tied to my belt, in case she takes
a sudden fancy to go visiting. Cheer up, Heloïse darling, only a
few more days now before you're free.

The rain began just after I finished my last entry that
Sunday in the attic—when I looked out I saw great storm
clouds blowing up in the evening sky. I hurried down to close
any open windows. I still seemed perfectly happy then; I
remember telling myself so.

As I leaned out to pull the bedroom window in I noticed
how motionless and expectant the wheat seemed; I hoped it was
young enough not to mind being battered. Then I looked down
and saw that my forgotten garland had drifted round and was

225

lying just below on the grey glass of the moat. The next second, down came the rain—thousands of new shillings seemed to bounce off the water. I had thoughts of rushing out and trying to rescue the garland, but even as I watched it was driven under.

Heloïse was whimpering at the back door—and though I ran down at once to let her in, she was soaking wet. I dried her, then re-lit the kitchen fire, which had gone out while I was writing in the attic. I had just got it going when Stephen arrived, back from London. I sent him off to change his wet clothes; then we had tea together, sitting on the fender. I told him about my evening with Simon—but hugging all the secret bits to myself, of course—and then he talked quite a lot about his trip; he seemed much less self-conscious over being photographed, though I gathered he had been embarrassed by the Greek tunic Leda Fox-Cotton had persuaded him to wear. He said he'd had all his meals with the Fox-Cottons and slept in a room with gold curtains and gold cupids over the bed. And Aubrey Fox-Cotton had given him a dressing-gown, almost as good as new. I admired it and agreed that they were very kind people—all my resentment of Leda Fox-Cotton seemed to have vanished.

"Did she show you the photographs she took last time?" I asked.

"Oh, yes. I saw them." He didn't sound enthusiastic.

"Well, when am *I* going to see them? Didn't she give you any?"

"She told me I could take some, but I didn't like to. They're so large and—well, flattering. I'll ask for some next time if you really want to see them."

"You're going again, then?"

"Yes, but for something different." He went very red. "Oh, it's too silly to talk about."

I remembered Rose's letter. "Does she want you to go on the pictures?"

He said it was nonsense, really—"But there was a man came to dinner last night who has to do with them and he thought I'd be all right. They got me to read a piece aloud. I'm supposed to go and be tested—that's what they call it. Only I don't know that I'll do it."

"But of course you must, Stephen," I said encouragingly.

He looked at me quickly and asked if I'd like it if he acted—and I suddenly saw that I had been wrong in thinking he had lost interest in me. (Though little did I then know *how* wrong.) I had only been asking him questions out of politeness—nothing but Simon mattered to me in the least—but I tried to sound enthusiastic: "Why, Stephen, it would be splendid—of course I'd like it."

"Then I'll try. They said they could teach me."

I thought they probably could—he has such a nice speaking-voice, though it gets a bit muffled and husky when he feels shy.

"Well, it's most exciting," I said brightly. "Perhaps you'll go to Hollywood."

He grinned and said he didn't think he'd count on that.

After we finished tea he helped me with the washing-up and then went over to Four Stones Farm; the Stebbinses were having a party. I bet Ivy was thrilled about his going on the pictures. (Not that anything more has happened about it yet.) I went to bed early, still feeling happy. Even the sound of the rain beating on the roof gave me pleasure, because it reminded me that Simon had had all the leaks mended for us. Everything in the least connected with him has value for me; if someone even mentions his name it is like a little present to me—and I long to mention it myself, I start subjects leading up to it, and then feel myself going red. I keep swearing to myself not to speak of him again—and then an opportunity occurs and I jump at it.

Father came home the next morning with a London telephone directory sticking out of the carpet-bag.

"Goodness, are we going to have a telephone?" I asked.

"Great heavens, no!" He plonked the bag on one of the kitchen chairs—from which it instantly fell to the floor, throwing out the directory and various other books. Father shoved them back into the bag as fast as he could, but I had time to notice a very fancy little *Language of Flowers, Elementary Chinese* and a paper called *The Homing Pigeon*.

"Where's the willow-pattern plate?" I asked, trying to make my voice sound casual.

"I dropped it on Liverpool Street Station—but it had served its purpose." He turned to go to the gatehouse, then said he'd like a glass of milk first. While I got it for him, I asked if he had stayed at the Cottons' flat.

He said: "Oh yes, I had Simon's room—by the way, he particularly asked to be remembered to you; he said you entertained him very nicely."

"Where did you go when he came home yesterday?"

"I just stayed on in his room. He went to Neil's hotel; very obliging of him. Simon has a charming nature—unfortunately."

"Why 'unfortunately'?" I asked, as I gave him his milk.

"Because Rose takes advantage of it," said father. "But then no man ought to be as much in love as Simon is—it makes one resent the whole female sex."

I took the milk jug back to the larder and called over my shoulder: "Well, I don't see why it should—considering Rose is in love with him."

"Is she?" said father—and when I stayed in the larder hoping he would let the subject drop, he called me back. "Are you sure she's in love with him, Cassandra? I'd be interested to know."

I said: "Well, she told me she was—and you know how truthful she is."

He thought for a minute, then said: "You're right. I can't remember her ever telling a lie. Truthfulness so often goes with ruthlessness. Yes, yes, if she says she's in love, she is—and her manner last night was quite compatible with it, given Rose's nature."

He put down his empty glass so I was able to take it to the sink and keep my back to him. "What was her manner like?" I asked.

"So damned unresponsive—and so obviously sure of her power over him. Oh, I dare say she can't help it—she's one of the women who oughtn't to be loved too kindly; when they are, some primitive desire for brutality makes them try to provoke it. But if she's really in love, it'll work out all right. Simon's so intelligent that he'll adjust the balance, eventually—because he isn't weak, I'm sure; it's simply that being so much in love puts a man at a disadvantage."

I managed to say: "Oh, I'm sure things will turn out right," and then concentrated on the glass—I never dried a glass so thoroughly in my life. Father started off to the gatehouse again, to my great relief. As he passed me, he said: "Glad we've had this talk. It's eased my mind considerably."

It hadn't eased mine. I suppose I ought to have been pleased at hearing him talking so rationally, but I was much too submerged in my own troubles—for that was when misery engulfed me, and guilt too. Everything he said about Simon's feelings for Rose was such agony that I suddenly knew it wasn't only the wonderful luxury of being in love that had been buoying me up: deep down, in some vague, mixed way I had been letting myself hope that he didn't really care for her, that it was me he loved and that kissing me would have made him realize it. "You're a fool and worse——" I told myself, "you're a would-be thief." Then I began to cry and when I got out my handkerchief it smelt of Rose's scent and reminded me I hadn't written to thank her for it. "Before you do, you've got to get your conscience clear," I said to myself sternly, "and you know the way to do it. Things you let yourself imagine happening, never do happen; so go ahead, have a wonderful day-dream about Simon loving you, marrying you instead of Rose—and then he never will. You'll have given up any hope of winning him from her."

That made me wonder if I could have put up any opposition to Rose in the early days, when it would have been quite fair. I thought of the chance I missed on May Day when Simon and I walked to the village together. If only I could have been more fascinating! But I decided my fascination would have been embarrassing—I know Simon didn't care much for Rose's until he had fallen in love with her beauty; after that, of course, he found the fascination fascinating.

Then I remembered Miss Marcy once saying "Dear Rose will lead men a dance," and it struck me that father meant much the same thing when he spoke of Rose showing her power over Simon. Suddenly I had a great desire to batter her, and as I was going to imagine away any chance of getting Simon, I decided to have a run for my money and batter Rose into the bargain. So I stoked up the kitchen fire and put the stew on for lunch, then drew the arm-chair close and gave my imagination its head—I was longing to, anyhow, apart from its being a noble gesture.

I visualized everything happening at Mrs. Cotton's flat—I gave it a balcony overlooking Hyde Park. We began there, then moved indoors. Rose came in while Simon was kissing me and was absolutely livid—or was that in a later imagining? There have been so many that they have gradually merged into each other. I don't think I could bring myself to describe any of them in detail because, though they are wonderful at the time, they give me a flat, sick, ashamed feeling to look back on. And they are like a drug, one needs them oftener and oftener and has to make them more and more exciting—until at last one's imagination won't work at all. It comes back after a few days, though. Goodness knows how I can ever look Rose in the face after the things I have imagined saying and doing to her—I got as far as kicking her once. Of course I always pretend that she isn't in love with Simon, merely after his money. Poor Rose! It is extraordinary how fond I can feel of her really, not to mention guilty towards her—and yet hate her like poison in my imaginings.

Coming back to earth after that first one was particularly awful, because it was the one which gave Simon up irrevocably —the others didn't have the same tampering-with-fate feeling (but it is always dreadful when the pictures in front of one's eyes become meaningless, and the real world is there instead and seems meaningless, too). I certainly wasn't in any mood for writing to Rose, but in the afternoon I forced myself to— it was like making up a letter for a character in a book to write. I told her how pleased I was with the bottle of scent, and put in bits about Hel and Ab and the miserable weather—the rain was useful as a lead into: "How lucky it was fine on Midsummer Eve. It was so nice that Simon was here for it—tell

him I enjoyed every minute——" It was glorious writing that
—almost like telling him I was glad he had kissed me. But
after I posted the letter I was worried in case he guessed what
I meant. And as I walked back from the post-office I had the
most agonizing thought; supposing he had told Rose about
kissing me and they had laughed about it?

It hurt me so much that I moaned out loud. I wanted to
fling myself down in the mud and beat my way into the
ground. I had just enough sense to know what I should look
like after trying, so I stayed upright; but I couldn't go on
walking. I went and sat on a stile and tried to turn the
thought out of my head—and then worse thoughts rushed in
on me. I asked myself if it wasn't wrong of Simon to kiss me
when he is in love with Rose—if he was the sort of man who
thinks any girl will do to kiss? Of all the agonies, the worst
is when I think badly of Simon; not that I ever do for very
long.

After I had been sitting there in the rain for a while, I saw
that there was nothing dreadful in his having kissed me. In
spite of his saying it wasn't due to his missing Rose, it probably
was. Anyway, I think Americans kiss rather easily and
frequently—Miss Marcy had some American magazines once
and there were pictures of people kissing on almost every page,
including the advertisements. I expect Americans are affectionate, as a nation. I should certainly never have been surprised
if Neil had kissed me and I shouldn't have thought it meant
he was seriously in love. Somehow it seemed unlike Simon
but . . . Then I wondered if he had thought I expected it,
if I had somehow invited a kiss. That made me want to die of
shame and yet was comforting because it put Simon in the
right if he had done it out of kindness.

Suddenly I said aloud into the rain : "He won't tell Rose and
laugh. And he didn't do anything wrong—whatever his
reasons were, they weren't wrong. If you love people, you take
them on trust."

Then I got off the stile and walked home. And in spite of
the drenching rain, I felt quite warm.

That little glow of comfort lasted me right through the

evening but was gone when I woke up next morning. Wakings are the worst times—almost before my eyes are open a great weight seems to roll on to my heart. I can usually roll it off a bit during the day—for one thing, food helps quite a lot, unromantic as that sounds. I have grown more and more ravenous as I have grown more and more miserable. Sleep is wonderful, too—I never thought of it as a pleasure before, but now I long for it. The best time of all is before I fall asleep at night, when I can hold the thought of Simon close to me and feel the misery slip away. I often sleep in the daytime, too. Surely it isn't normal for anyone so miserably in love to eat and sleep so well? Am I a freak? I only know that I *am* miserable, I *am* in love, but I raven food and sleep.

Another great luxury is letting myself cry—I always feel marvellously peaceful after that. But it is difficult to arrange times for it, as my face takes so long to recover; it isn't safe in the mornings if I am to look normal when I meet father at lunch, and the afternoons are no better, as Thomas is home by five. It would be all right in bed at night but such a waste, as that is my happiest time. Days when father goes over to read in the Scoatney library are good crying-days.

On the Wednesday of that first week of mud and misery I went to see the Vicar; he has a lot of old music and I hoped I might find "Sheep May Safely Graze." The rain stopped for a few hours that morning but it was very cold and damp, and the battered countryside looked rather as I felt. As I sloshed along the Godsend road, planning to be careful not to give myself away to the Vicar, I found myself wondering if it would be a relief to confess to someone, as Lucy Snowe did in *Villette*. The Vicar isn't High Church enough for confessions, and certainly most of me would have loathed to tell him or anybody else one word; but I did have a feeling that a person as wretched as I was ought to be able to get some sort of help from the Church. Then I told myself that as I never gave the Church a thought when I was feeling happy, I could hardly expect it to do anything for me when I wasn't. You can't get insurance money without paying in premiums.

I found the Vicar starting to plan a sermon, wrapped in the

collie dog carriage-rug. I do love his study; it has old green panelling except for the wall that is bookshelves from floor to ceiling. His housekeeper keeps everything very shining and clean.

"Now this is splendid," he said. "An excuse to stop working —and to light a fire."

He lit it; even to watch it crackling up was cheering. He said he didn't think he had "Sheep May Safely Graze," but I could look through his music. Most of it is in old calf-bound volumes he bought at a country-house sale. They have a musty smell, and the printing looks different from modern music; there is an elaborately engraved page in front of each piece. As one turns the pages, one thinks of all the people who have turned them in the past and it seems to take one back closer to the com- posers—I like to think of the Beethoven pieces being played not very many years after he died.

I soon came across "Air from Handel's Water Music"— which was no longer specially valuable to me—but I never found "Sheep May Safely Graze." Still, looking through the old volumes was soothing, because thinking of the past made the present seem a little less real. And while I was searching, the Vicar got out biscuits and madeira. I never had madeira before and it was lovely—the idea almost more than the taste, because it made me feel I was paying a morning call in an old novel. For a moment I drew away from myself and thought: "Poor Cassandra! No, it never comes right for her. She goes into a decline."

We talked of the Cottons and Scoatney and how wonderful everything was for everybody and how happy we were for Rose. He was most interested to hear Simon had spent Midsummer Eve with me and asked lots of questions about it. After that, we got started on religion, which surprised me rather, as the Vicar so seldom mentions it—I mean, to our family; naturally it must come up in his daily life.

"You ought to try it, one of these days," he said. "I believe you'd like it."

I said: "But I have tried it, haven't I? I've been to church. It never seems to take."

He laughed and said he knew I'd exposed myself to infection occasionally. "But catching things depends so much on one's state of health. You should look in on the church if ever you're mentally run down."

I remembered my thoughts on the way to the village. "Oh, it wouldn't be fair to rush to church because one was miserable," I said—taking care to look particularly cheerful.

"It'd be most unfair not to—you'd be doing religion out of its very best chance."

"You mean 'Man's extremity is God's opportunity'?"

"Exactly. Of course, there are extremities at either end; extreme happiness invites religion almost as much as extreme misery."

I told him I'd never thought of that. He helped me to some more madeira, then said:

"In addition, I think religion has a chance of a look-in whenever the mind craves solace in music or poetry—in any form of art at all. Personally, I think it *is* an art, the greatest one; an extension of the communion all the other arts attempt."

"I suppose you mean communion with God."

He gave such a snort of laughter that his madeira went the wrong way.

"What on earth did I say that was funny?" I asked, while he was mopping his eyes.

"It was the utter blankness of your tone. God might have been a long, wet week—which He's certainly treating us to." He glanced at the window. The rain had started again, so heavily that the garden beyond the streaming panes was just a blur of green. "How the intelligent young do fight shy of the mention of God! It makes them feel both bored and superior."

I tried to explain: "Well, once you stop believing in an old gentleman with a beard . . . It's only the *word* God, you know—it makes such a conventional noise."

"It's merely shorthand for where we come from, where we're going, and what it's all about."

"And do religious people find out what it's all about? Do they really get the answer to the riddle?"

"They get just a whiff of an answer sometimes." He smiled

234

at me and I smiled back and we both drank our madeira. Then he went on: "I suppose church services make a conventional noise to you, too—and I rather understand it. Oh, they're all right for the old hands and they make for sociability, but I sometimes think their main use is to help weather churches—like smoking pipes to colour them, you know. If any—well, unreligious person, needed consolation from religion, I'd advise him or her to sit in an empty church. Sit, not kneel. And listen, not pray. Prayer's a very tricky business."

"Goodness, is it?"

"Well, for inexperienced pray-ers it sometimes is. You see, they're apt to think of God as a slot-machine. If nothing comes out they say 'I knew dashed well it was empty'—when the whole secret of prayer is knowing the machine's full."

"But how can one know?"

"By filling it oneself."

"With faith?"

"With faith. I expect you find that another boring word. And I warn you this slot-machine metaphor is going to break down at any moment. But if ever you're feeling very unhappy —which you obviously aren't at present, after all the good fortune that's come to your family recently—well, try sitting in an empty church."

"And listening for a whiff?"

We both laughed and then he said that it was just as reasonable to talk of smelling or tasting God as of seeing or hearing Him. "If one ever has any luck, one will know with all one's senses—and none of them. Probably as good a way as any of describing it is that we shall 'come over all queer'."

"But haven't you already?"

He sighed and said the whiffs were few and far between. "But the memory of them everlasting," he added softly. Then we fell silent, both of us staring at the fire. Rain kept falling down the chimney, making little hissing noises. I thought what a good man he is, yet never annoyingly holy. And it struck me for the first time that if such a clever, highly educated man can believe in religion, it is almost impudent of an ignorant person like me to feel bored and superior about it—for I realized that it wasn't only the word "God" that made me feel like that.

I wondered if I was an atheist. I have never thought of myself as one, and sometimes on very lovely days I have felt almost sure there is *something* somewhere. And I pray every night, though I think my prayers are only like wishing on the new moon—not quite, though: I pray just *in case* there is a God. (I haven't prayed about my misery over Simon because I mustn't ask that he shall love me, and I won't ask that I shall stop loving him—I'd rather die.) Certainly I never felt any sense of communion with God while praying—the only flicker of that I ever had was during those few minutes I wandered round King's Crypt cathedral at sunset, and it went off when I heard our headmistress's voice droning on about the Saxon remains. Sitting there with the Vicar, I tried to recapture my feelings in the cathedral, but they merged into the memory of the cathedral-like avenue I saw when I was describing Midsummer Eve—and then the cathedral, the avenue, my love for Simon and myself writing about all these in the attic were in my mind together, each enclosed in its own light and yet each one part of the other. And all the time, I was staring into the Vicar's fire.

I didn't come to earth until the church clock struck the half-hour. Then I jumped up to go—and got invited to stay and lunch; but I felt I ought to get back to cook father his meal.

While the Vicar was helping me on with my raincoat, he asked me to look in at the church in case he had left the vestry window open and the rain was driving in. Actually, we found the rain had stopped, but he still wanted the window shut; he said it was sure to start pouring again, probably just as he was beginning his after-luncheon nap. He stood watching me as I ran across the churchyard—I gave him one last wave before I went into the church by the little side door. As I closed it behind me, it struck me as almost funny that he had sent me into a church, even advised me how to get consolation from religion, without having the faintest idea I was in need of it.

The window wasn't open, after all. As I came from the vestry, I thought: "Well, here you are in an empty church— you'd better give it a chance." I was close to the altar so I had a good look at it. The brasses and the altar-cloth seemed quite extraordinarily meaningless to me. The white roses were fresh but rain-battered; they had the utterly still look that altar flowers always have—everything about the altar seemed unnaturally still . . . austere, withdrawn.

I thought: "I don't feel helped or comforted at all." Then I remembered the Vicar's nice, fat voice saying: "Sit— listen." He had told me not to pray, and as looking at an altar always seems to turn my thoughts to prayers, I sat on the steps and looked towards the main body of the church. I listened hard.

I could hear rain still pouring from the gutters and a thin branch scraping against one of the windows; but the church seemed completely cut off from the restless day outside—just as I felt cut off from the church. I thought: "I am a restless- ness inside a stillness inside a restlessness."

After a minute or so, the enclosed silence began to press on my ears—I thought at first that this was a good sign, but nothing interesting happened. Then I remembered what the Vicar had said about knowing God with all one's senses, so I gave my ears a rest and tried my nose. There was a smell of old wood, old carpet hassocks, old hymn books—a composite musty, dusty smell; no scent from the cold altar roses and yet there was a faint, stuffy sweetness around the altar—I found it came from the heavily embroidered cloth. I tried my sense of taste next, but naturally it only offered a lingering of madeira and biscuits. Touch: just the cold stone of the steps. As for sight—well of course there was plenty to see: the carved rood- screen, the great de Godys tomb, the high pulpit—which managed to look both particularly empty and slightly rebuk- ing. Oh, I noticed dozens of things, many of them beautiful, but nothing beyond sight came in by the eyes. So I closed them—the Vicar had said: "All senses—and none of them" and I thought that perhaps if I made my mind a blank——

I have often tried—I once had an idea it was the way to

237

foresee the future, but I never got any further than imagining blackness. Sitting on the altar steps, I saw a blacker blackness than ever before, and I felt it as well as saw it—tons of darkness seemed to be pressing on me. Suddenly I remembered a line in a poem by Vaughan: "There is in God (some say) a deep but dazzling darkness"—and the next second, the darkness exploded into light. "Was that God—did it really happen?" I asked myself. But the honest part of my mind answered: "No. You imagined it." Then the clock up above boomed the three-quarters, filling the air with sound. I opened my eyes and was back in a beautiful, chilly, stuffy church that didn't seem to care whether I lived or died.

The clock made me realize that I was going to be late with father's lunch, so I ran most of the way home—only to find that he had helped himself to food (the cold meat looked as if he had carved it with a trowel) and gone out. As his bicycle was missing, I guessed he had ridden over to Scoatney. I took a chance on getting my face right in time for tea and had a very good cry, with cake and milk afterwards; and felt so much better than I usually do, even after crying, that I wondered if I really had come by some little whiff of God while I was in the church.

But the next morning, the weight on my heart was the worst I had ever known. It didn't move at all while I got our breakfasts, and by the time Stephen and Thomas had gone and father had shut himself in the gatehouse, it was so bad that I found myself going round leaning against walls—I can't think why misery makes me lean against walls, but it does. For once, I didn't feel like crying; I wanted to shriek. So I ran out in the rain to an empty field a long way from anywhere and screamed blue murder; and then felt quite extraordinarily silly—and so very wet. I had a sudden desire to be sitting with the kind Vicar by his fire, drinking madeira again, and as I was almost half-way to Godsend as the crow flies, I went on, scrambling through hedges and ditches. I kept trying to think of a good excuse for this second visit—the best I could manage was that I had been caught out without my raincoat and was frightened of taking a chill—but I was really past minding what the Vicar or anyone else thought of me, if only I could get to the warm fire and the madeira.

And then, when I arrived at the vicarage, there was no one in.

I stood there ringing the bell and banging on the door, feeling I could somehow *make* someone be there, yet knowing all the time that I couldn't.

"Shall I crawl into the church and wait?" I wondered, coming down the streaming garden path. But just then, Mrs. Jakes called across from "The Keys" that the Vicar and his housekeeper were shopping in King's Crypt and wouldn't be home until the evening.

I ran over and asked if she would trust me for the price of a glass of port. She laughed, and said she couldn't legally sell me a drink before twelve o'clock, but she would give me one as a present.

"And, my goodness, you need it," she said, as I followed her into the bar. "You're wet through. Take that dress off and I'll dry it by the kitchen fire."

There was a man mending the sink in the kitchen so I couldn't sit in there without my dress; but she bolted the door of the bar and said she would see that no one came through from the kitchen. I handed my gym-dress over and sat up at the bar in my vest and black school knickers, drinking my port.

The port was nice and warming, but I don't think old country bars are very cheerful places; there is something peculiarly depressing about the smell of stale beer. If I had been in a good mood, I might have liked the thought of villagers drinking there for three hundred years; but as it was, I kept thinking of how dreary their lives must have been, and that most of them were dead. There was a looking-glass at the back of the bar, facing the window, and reflected in it I could see the wet tombstones in the churchyard. I thought of the rain going down, down to the sodden coffins. And all the time my wet hair kept dripping down my back inside my vest.

However, by the time I finished the port I was less violently miserable. I just felt lumpish and my eyes kept getting fixed on things. I found myself staring at the bottles of crème de menthe and cherry brandy that Rose and I had our drinks out of on May Day. And suddenly I felt the most bitter hatred for Rose's green crème de menthe and a deep affection for my ruby cherry brandy.

I went to the kitchen door and put my head round.

"Please, Mrs. Jakes," I called, "can I have a cherry brandy? It's striking twelve now, so I can owe you for it without breaking the law."

She came and got it for me, and after she put the bottle back I could gloat over there being more gone out of it than out of the crème de menthe bottle. "Now everyone will think the cherry brandy's the popular one," I thought. Then two old men came knocking at the door, wanting their beer, and Mrs. Jakes whisked me and my drink out of the bar.

"You can wait in Miss Marcy's room," she said. "Your dress won't be dry for quite a while yet."

Miss Marcy has an upstairs room at the inn, well away from the noise of the bar. Ever since she came to Godsend she has talked of having her own cottage, but year after year she stays on at "The Keys" and I don't think she will ever move now. Mrs. Jakes makes her very comfortable and the inn is so handy for the school.

As I climbed the stairs I was surprised to find how wobbly my legs were. I said to myself: "Poor child, I'm more exhausted than I realized." It was a relief to sit down in Miss Marcy's wicker arm-chair—except that it was much lower than I expected; I spilt a valuable amount of cherry brandy. I finished the rest of it with deep satisfaction—each time I took a sip I thought: "That's one in the eye for the crème de menthe." And then the very confusing thought struck me that generally green is my colour and pink is Rose's, so the liqueurs were all mixed up and silly. And then I wondered if I was a little bit drunk. I had a look at myself in Miss Marcy's dressing-table glass and I looked awful—my hair was in rats'-tails, my face was dirty and my expression simply maudlin. For no reason at all, I grinned at myself. Then I began to think: "Who am I? Who am I?" Whenever I do that, I feel one good push would shove me over the edge of lunacy; so I turned away from the glass and tried to get my mind off myself—I did it by taking an interest in Miss Marcy's room.

It really is fascinating—all her personal possessions are so very small. The pictures are postcard reproductions of Old Masters. She has lots of metal animals about an inch long, little wooden shoes, painted boxes only big enough to hold stamps. And what makes things look even tinier than they are is that the room is large, with great oak beams, and all Mrs. Jakes's furniture is so huge.

While I was examining the miniature Devon pitchers on the mantelpiece (five of them, with one wild flower in each), the glow from the cherry brandy wore off—probably because the wind down the chimney was blowing right through my knickers. So I wrapped myself in the quilt and lay on the bed. I was on the fringe of sleep when Miss Marcy arrived home for her lunch.

"You poor, poor child," she cried, coming over to put her hand on my forehead. "I wonder if I ought to take your temperature?"

I told her there was nothing wrong with me but strong drink. She giggled and blinked and said "Well, reely!" and I suddenly felt very world-worn and elderly in comparison with her. Then she handed me my gym-dress and got me some hot water. After I had washed I felt quite normal, except that the whole morning lay on my conscience in a dreary, shaming sort of way.

"I must dash home," I said. "I'm half an hour late with father's lunch already."

"Oh, your father's at Scoatney again," said Miss Marcy. "They're giving him a nice, thick steak." She had heard from Mrs. Jakes, who had heard from the butcher, who had heard from the Scoatney cook. "So you can stay and have your lunch with me. Mrs. Jakes is going to send up enough for two."

She has her meals on trays, from the inn kitchen, but she keeps things she calls "extra treats" in the big mahogany corner-cupboard.

"I like to nibble these at night," she said as she was getting some biscuits out. "I always wake up around two o'clock and fancy something to eat."

I had a flash of her lying in the wide, sagging bed, watching the moonlit square of the lattice window while she crunched her biscuits.

"Do you lie awake long?" I asked.

"Oh, I generally hear the church clock strike the quarter. Then I tell myself to be a good girl and go back to sleep. I usually make up some nice little story until I drop off."

"What sort of story?"

"Oh, not real stories, of course. Sometimes I try to imagine what happens to characters in books—after the books finish, I mean. Or I think about the interesting people I know—dear Rose shopping in London, or Stephen being photographed by that kind Mrs. Fox-Cotton. I love making up stories about people."

"Don't you ever make them up about yourself?"

She looked quite puzzled. "Do you know, I don't believe I ever do? I suppose I don't find myself very interesting."

There was a thump on the door and she went to take the tray in. Mrs. Jakes had sent up stew and apple pie.

"Oh, good," said Miss Marcy. "Stew's so comforting on a rainy day."

As we settled down to eat, I said how extraordinary it must be not to find oneself interesting. "Didn't you ever, Miss Marcy?"

She thought, while she finished an enormous mouthful. "I think I did when I was a girl. My dear mother always said I was very self-centred. And so discontented!"

I said: "You aren't now. What changed you?"

"God sent me a *real* grief, dear." Then she told me that her parents had died within a month of each other, when she was seventeen, and how dreadfully she had felt it. "Oh, dear, I couldn't believe the sun would ever shine again. Then our local clergyman asked me to help with some children he was taking into the country—and, do you know, it worked a miracle for me? I suppose that was the beginning of finding others more interesting than myself."

"It wouldn't work a miracle for me," I said, "—I mean, if I were ever unhappy."

She said she thought it would in the end; then asked me if I was missing Rose much. I noticed she was looking at me rather searchingly, so I said "Oh, yes" very casually and talked brightly about Rose's trousseau and how happy I was for her, until we heard children's voices under the window as they trooped back to school. Then Miss Marcy jumped up and powdered her nose very white with a tiny powder-puff out of a cardboard box.

"It's singing this afternoon," she said. "We always look forward to that."

I thought of the singing on May Day, and of Simon, so embarrassed and so kind, making his speech to the children. Oh, lovely day—before he had proposed to Rose!

We went downstairs and I thanked Mrs. Jakes for every-thing, including the loan of the cherry brandy. (A shilling—and that was a reduced price. Drink is ruinous.) The rain had stopped, but it was still very grey and chilly.

"I hope it cheers up by Saturday," said Miss Marcy, as we dodged the drips from the chestnut tree, "because I'm giving the children a picnic. I suppose, dear, you couldn't find time to help me? You'd think of such splendid games."

"I'm afraid I'm a bit busy at the castle," I said quickly—the children were screaming over some game in the playground and I didn't feel I could stand an afternoon of that.

"How thoughtless of me! Of course you have your hands full at the week-ends—with the boys home to be looked after as well as your father. Perhaps you have some free time in these long, light evenings—some of the old folks do love to be read to, you know."

I stared at her in astonishment. Neither Rose nor I have ever gone in for that sort of thing; incidentally, I don't believe the villagers really like good works being done to them. Miss Marcy must have noticed my expression because she went on hurriedly: "Oh, it was just an idea. I thought it might take you out of yourself a bit—if you're finding life dull without Rose."

"Not really," I said, brightly—and heaven knows, one can't

call misery dull, exactly. Dear Miss Marcy, little did she know I had more than missing Rose on my mind. Just then, some children came up with a frog in a cardboard box, so she said good-bye and went off with them to the pond to watch it swim.

When I got home, the castle was completely deserted, even Ab and Hel were out. I felt guilty, because they had had no dinner, and called and called them but they didn't come. My voice sounded despairing and I suddenly felt lonelier than I ever remember feeling, and more deeply sad. Everything I looked at was grey—grey water in the moat, great grey towering walls, remote grey sky; even the wheat, which was between green and gold, seemed colourless.

I sat on the bedroom window-seat, staring woodenly at Miss Blossom. Suddenly her voice spoke, in my head: "You go to that picnic, dearie."

I heard myself ask her why.

"Because little Miss Blinkeyes is right—it would take you out of yourself. And doing things for others gives you a lovely glow."

"So does port," I said cynically.

"That's no way to talk, not at your age," said Miss Blossom. "Though I must say you'd have made a cat laugh, walking about in your drawers with that cherry brandy. Fancy you having a taste for drink!"

"Well, I can't drown my sorrows in it often," I told her, "it's too expensive. Good works are cheaper."

"So's religion," said Miss Blossom. "And some say that's best of all. You could get it all right if you went on trying, you know—you being so fond of poetry."

Now it is very odd, but I have often told myself things through Miss Blossom that I didn't know I knew. When she said that about my "getting" religion, I instantly realized that she was right—and it came as such a surprise to me that I thought: "Heavens, have I been converted?" I soon decided that it wasn't quite so drastic as that; all that had come to me, really, was—well, the *feasibility* of conversion. I suddenly knew that religion, God—something beyond everyday life— was there to be found, provided one is really willing. And I saw that though what I felt in the church was only imagination,

244

it was a step on the way; because imagination itself can be a kind of willingness—a pretence that things are real, due to one's longing for them. It struck me that this was somehow tied up with what the Vicar said about religion being an extension of art—and then I had a glimpse of how religion really can cure you of sorrow; somehow make use of it, turn it to beauty, just as art can make sad things beautiful.

I found myself saying: "Sacrifice is the secret—you have to sacrifice things for art and it's the same with religion; and then the sacrifice turns out to be a gain." Then I got confused and I couldn't hold on to what I meant—until Miss Blossom remarked: "Nonsense, duckie—it's perfectly simple. You lose yourself in something beyond yourself and it's a lovely rest."

I saw that, all right. Then I thought: "But that's how Miss Marcy cured her sorrow, too—only she lost herself in other people instead of in religion." Which way of life was best— hers or the Vicar's? I decided that he loves God and merely likes the villagers, whereas she loves the villagers and merely likes God—and then I suddenly wondered if I could combine both ways, love God and my neighbour equally. Was I really willing to?

And I was! Oh, for a moment I truly was! I saw myself going to church regularly, getting myself confirmed, making a little chapel with flowers and candles—and being so wonderful to everyone at home and in the village, telling stories to the children, reading to the old people (I daresay tact could disguise that one was doing good works to them). Would I be sincere or just pretending? Even if it began as pretence, surely it would grow real before very long? Perhaps it was real already—for the very thought of it rolled the weight of misery off my heart, drove it so far away that, though I saw it still, I no longer felt it.

And then a most peculiar thing happened: I found myself seeing the new road that skirts King's Crypt—wide, straight, with plenty of room for through-traffic. And then I saw the busy part of the town, with its tangle of narrow old streets that are so awful for motorists on market days, but so very, very beautiful. Of course, what my mind's eye was trying to tell me was that the Vicar and Miss Marcy had managed to by-pass the suffering that comes to most people—he by his religion, she by her kindness to others. And it came to me that if one does that, one is liable to miss too much along with the suffering—perhaps, in a way, life itself. Is that why Miss Marcy seems so young for her age—why the Vicar, in spite of all his cleverness, has that look of an elderly baby?

I said aloud: "I don't want to miss *anything*." And then misery came rushing back like a river that has been dammed up. I tried to open my heart to it, to welcome it as a part of my life's experience, and at first that made it easier to bear. Then it got worse than ever before—it was physical as well as mental, my heart and ribs and shoulders and chest, even my arms ached. I longed so desperately for someone to comfort me that I went and laid my head on Miss Blossom's bust—I thought of it as soft and motherly, under a royal-blue satin blouse, and imagined her saying: "That's right—go through it, not round it, duckie. It's the best way for most of us in the end."

And then a different voice spoke in my head, a bitter, sarcastic voice—my own at its very nastiest. It said: "You've sunk pretty low, my girl, clasping a dressmaker's dummy. And aren't you a bit old for this Miss Blossom nonsense?" Then, for the first time in my life, I began to wonder how I "did" Miss Blossom. Was she like Stephen's mother, but not so humble—or nearer to a charwoman of Aunt Millicent's? Or had I taken her from some character in a book? Suddenly I saw her more vividly than ever before, standing behind the bar of an old-fashioned London pub. She looked at me most reproachfully, then put a sealskin jacket over her blue blouse, turned off all the lights, and went out into the night closing the door behind her. The next second, her bust was as hard as a board and smelt of dust and old glue. And I knew she was gone for ever.

Luckily, Heloïse came in then or I should have cried myself into a state beyond recovery before tea-time. You can't cry on Heloïse; she thumps her tail sympathetically, but looks embarrassed and moves away. Anyhow, I had to get her long-overdue dinner.

I haven't been able to bear looking at Miss Blossom since then. It isn't only that she is now nothing more than a dressmaker's dummy—she makes me think of the corpse of a dressmaker's dummy.

Religion, good works, strong drink—oh, but there is another way of escape, a wicked one, far worse than drink. I tried it on my birthday a week ago.

When I woke up that morning the sun was shining—the first time for over a fortnight. I had barely taken this in when I heard music just outside my bedroom door. I sprang up and dashed out to the landing, and there on the floor was a small portable wireless, with a card on it saying: "Many happy returns from Stephen." That was what he had been saving up for! That was why he had posed for Leda Fox-Cotton!

I yelled out: "Stephen, Stephen!"

Thomas shouted from the hall. "He's gone off to work early —I think he felt embarrassed about being thanked. It's quite a good little wireless. Get dressed quickly and we'll play it over breakfast."

He came bounding upstairs and had carried the wireless off before I had so much as turned the dials. I was just going to tell him to bring it back when I thought: "Heavens, what does it matter?" The early-morning weight had descended on my heart. While I dressed, I worked it out that only two weeks and two days before, owning a wireless would have made me deliriously happy; and now it didn't mean a thing. Then it struck me that I could at least do my suffering to music.

When I got down, I found that Stephen had set the breakfast table for me and put flowers on it.

"And there's *my* present," said Thomas. "I haven't wrapped it up because I'm just in the middle of it." It was a book on astronomy, which he is very much interested in; I was glad he had chosen something he wanted himself, because though he gets a little pocket-money now, it will take a long time to make up for all the years he didn't have any.

Father came down then; of course *he* hadn't remembered my birthday. "But Topaz will," he said, cheerfully. "She'll send you something from me." He was horrified to see the wireless

—he has always said that being without one is one of the few pleasures of poverty; but he got interested during breakfast. Only he couldn't bear the music or voices—what he liked were the atmospherics.

"I suppose you wouldn't care to lend it to me for an hour or so?" he said, after Thomas had gone off to school. "Those noises are splendid."

I let him take it. All that really mattered to me was whether or not Simon would send me a present.

The parcel-post came at eleven. There was a dressing-gown from Topaz, a Shakespeare from father (so tactful of Topaz to remember how he hates lending me his), a nightgown—real silk—from Rose, six pairs of silk stockings from Mrs. Cotton, and a big box of chocolates from Neil. Nothing from Simon.

Nothing from Simon, indeed! I was still sitting numbed with disappointment when a motor horn hooted in the lane. The next minute a van drew up and the driver plonked a crate down on the drawbridge. I yelled up asking father to come down and between us we prised the lid off. Inside was a wireless and a gramophone combined—oh, the most wonderful thing! When shut, it is like a fat suitcase, with a handle to carry it by. The outside is a lovely blue, like linen but shiny. There was a record case to match. Nobody ever had such a glorious present.

Simon had enclosed a note saying:

Dear Cassandra,

I wanted to send you an electric one, but remembered you've no electricity. The radio works from batteries that can be recharged at the garage in Scoatney, but the phonograph is only the old-fashioned type that has to be wound up—still, it's better than nothing. I am sending you the Debussy you liked, but couldn't get the Bach record I played to you. Borrow anything you want from Scoatney until you find out what your musical tastes really are and then I'll buy you lots more records.

They swear the thing will get to you on the right day and I do hope it does. Many, many happy returns. I'll be seeing you soon. Love from

SIMON

It was in pencil, written at the shop, so I couldn't expect it to be long or personal. And it did say "Love"—he might have put just "Yours" or "In haste" or something. Of course, I knew it didn't mean my kind of love, but it was valuable.

I read the note again and again, while father got the most agonizing noises out of the wireless.

"Oh, stop!" I cried at last. "It can't be good for it to shriek like that."

"Sounds like the lost souls of seagulls, doesn't it?" he shouted above the din.

I pushed past him and turned it off. In the sudden quietness, we could just hear Stephen's wireless playing away by itself up in the gatehouse room. Father said:

"Has it occurred to you what this thing is going to do to your swain?"

All that I felt was resentment against Stephen because his being hurt was going to interfere with my pleasure in Simon's present; not very much though—nothing could do that.

Luckily father didn't wait for an answer. "This is a much stronger wireless," he went on. "I'll borrow it awhile."

I shouted "No!" so loudly that he stared in astonishment. "I'm longing to try the gramophone," I added, trying to sound calm and reasonable. He suddenly smiled and said: "Well, well"—in an almost fatherly voice; then actually carried the machine indoors for me and left me alone with it. I got the records out of their corrugated paper and played them and played them. There were some Bach Preludes and Fugues as well as the Debussy album.

Simon hadn't sent the "Lover" record.

By the time Stephen got home, my better nature had asserted itself and I was terribly worried about his feelings. I had his wireless in the kitchen (father had lost interest in it) and was careful to have it on full blast when he came in. I nearly burst myself thanking him for it and I don't think I have ever seen him look so pleased. I had asked father during lunch if it would be a good idea to hide Simon's present for a day or two, but he thought that would be harder for Stephen in the end.

"Just tell him how glad you are to have a really lightweight wireless you can carry around—and that you'll probably only use Simon's for the gramophone," he suggested, and I thought it was very sensible of him; but the next minute I saw him turning a record round and round as if he were reading the grooves, and surely a man who tries to read a gramophone record cannot be normal?

I did my best to break the news to Stephen tactfully—I said all father had advised and a lot more besides. "Yours has a real wooden case," I told him, "with such a beautiful high polish." But the light went out of his eyes. He asked if he could see Simon's present—I had carried it up to my bedroom. After staring at it a few seconds, he said: "Yes, that's very handsome"—and turned to go.

"The wireless part isn't very good," I called after him, untruthfully.

He went on downstairs.

Oh, I was so sorry for him! After all the months he had been saving up! I ran after him and, from the top of the kitchen stairs, I could see him staring at his little brown wireless. He turned it off, then went out into the garden with a most bitter expression on his face.

I caught up with him as he was crossing the drawbridge.

"Let's go for a little walk," I said.

"All right, if you want to." He said it without looking at me.

We trudged down the lane. I felt as I did once when Rose had very bad toothache—that it was callous of me to be so separate from the pain, that just being sorry for suffering people isn't enough. Yet when I asked myself if on Stephen's account I would be willing not to have had Simon's present, I knew that I wouldn't.

I tried to talk naturally about the two machines, enlarging on how I could carry his little one from room to room and even take it out of doors (although I knew that unless Stephen was around I should lug Simon's everywhere, even if it broke my back). I suppose I overdid it because he interrupted and said:

"It's all right, you know."

I looked at him quickly. He tried to smile reassuringly, but didn't quite let his eyes meet mine.

"Oh, Stephen!" I cried. "It was a much bigger present from you. Simon didn't have to save—or work for it."

"No, that was my privilege," he said quietly.

That seemed to me a most beautiful way for him to have put it. It made me sorrier for him than ever—so sorry that I found myself almost wishing I had fallen in love with him instead of with Simon. Just then he added, very softly, "My dear." And that second, a wild idea flashed into my mind. Oh, why did it? Was it something in his voice awoke that feeling in me? Or was it because we were passing the larch wood and I remembered how I once imagined going into it with him?

I stopped walking and stared at him. His face was golden from the sunset. He asked me if I wanted to turn back.

I said: "No. Let's see if there are any late bluebells in the wood."

He looked at me quickly, right into the eyes at last.

"Come on," I said.

As we pushed aside the first green trails of larch I thought: "Well, this will disprove my theory that things I've imagined happening never really do happen." But it didn't—because everything was so different from my imagining. The wood had been thinned out, so it wasn't cool and dark as I expected; the air was still warm and the rays of the sinking sun shone in from behind us. The tree-trunks glowed redly. There was a hot, resinous smell instead of the scent of bluebells—the only ones left were shrivelled and going to seed. And instead of a still, waiting feeling there was a choking excitement. Stephen didn't say any of the things I once invented for him; neither of us spoke a word. I led the way all the time and reached the little grassy clearing in the middle of the wood before he did. There I turned and waited for him. He came closer and closer to me, then stood still, staring at me questioningly. I nodded my head and then he took me in his arms and kissed me, very gently. It didn't mean a thing to me—I know I didn't kiss him in return. But suddenly he changed, and kissed me more and more, not gently at all—and I changed, too, and wanted him to go on and on. I didn't even stop him when he pulled my dress down over my shoulder. It was he who stopped in the end.

"Don't let me, don't let me!" he gasped, and pushed me away so violently that I nearly fell over. As I staggered backwards I had a wild feeling of terror and the minute I regained my balance I plunged blindly back through the wood. He called after me: "Mind your eyes—it's all right, I'm not coming after you." But I went on thrusting my way through the larches, shielding my face with my arm. I ran all the way to the castle and dashed up the kitchen stairs meaning to lock myself in my room but I slipped when I was half-way up, banging my knee badly, and then I burst into tears and just lay there, sobbing. The awful thing is that something in me hoped that if I stayed there long enough he would come in and see how wretched I was—though I still can't make out why I wanted him to.

After a little while, I heard him at the kitchen door. "Cassandra, please stop crying," he called. "I wasn't coming in, but when I heard you—— Please, please stop."

I still went on. He came to the foot of the stairs. I began to pull myself up by the banisters, still crying. He said:

"But it's all right—really it is. There's nothing wrong in it if we love each other."

I turned on him fiercely: "I don't love you. I hate you."

And then I saw the look in his eyes and realized how dreadful it all was for him—until then I had only been thinking of my own misery. I gasped out: "No, no—I don't mean that but—— Oh, I'll never be able to explain." And then I dashed through to my room and locked both doors. I was just going to fling myself on the bed when I caught sight of Simon's present, on the window-seat. I went over, closed the gramophone part and lay with my head and arms on it. And for the first time in my life I wished I were dead.

When it was quite dark I pulled myself together enough to light a candle and begin to go wretchedly to bed. A few minutes later, there was a knock on the door to the landing

252

and Stephen called out: "I don't want to come in, but please read the note I'm pushing through to you." I called back "All right," and saw the note coming under the door. As I picked it up I heard his footsteps going downstairs, and then the noise of the front door shutting.

He had written:

DEAREST CASSANDRA,

Please do not be unhappy. It will come right. It is just that you are so young. I forget that sometimes, because you are so clever. I cannot explain because I think it would make you feel worse and anyway I do not know how. But there was nothing wrong happened. It was all my fault. If you forgive me for shocking you so, please write YES on a piece of paper and put it under my door. I am going out now and will not come back until your light is out so you need not be frightened of meeting me. And I will go to work before you are up in the morning. We won't talk about it—anyway, not for a long time. You say when. Truly it is all right.

With love from
STEPHEN

XXXXXX but not until you want them.

On a separate sheet he had written: "Perhaps this will help you to understand. Of course it is only for when we are married"—and then he had copied out four lines from "Love's Philosophy."

> Nothing in the world is single,
> All things by a law divine
> In one another's being mingle—
> Why not I with thine?

By Percy Bysshe Shelley. (Born 1792, died 1822.)

I guessed he had put Shelley's name and dates so that I wouldn't think he was stealing poetry again. Oh, Stephen—I know so well why you used to steal it! I long and long to express my love for Simon and nothing of my own is worthy.

I wrote YES and put it under his door. I couldn't bear not to

—and, of course, it was true in a way; I did forgive him. But it let him believe a lie—that I was upset just because he had shocked me. Since then, we haven't been alone once. We talk fairly naturally in front of the others, but I never look straight at him. I suppose he just thinks I am shy.

Of course the honest thing would be to tell him it will never be any good but, even if I could bear to hurt him so, I doubt if I could convince him without owning that I care for someone else—because I certainly showed every sign of its being some good while he was making love to me. Oh, why did I let him? Let him? You encouraged him, my girl! But why, why? When my whole heart was longing for Simon! Perhaps I could understand myself better if I didn't so loathe remembering it— even now I haven't quite put down everything that happened.

I know this: asking him to go into the wood was a wicked thing, wicked to him and wicked to myself. Truly, being so sorry for him had something to do with it, but it was mostly sheer wickedness. And it was only due to Stephen that it didn't turn out much wickeder.

I have really sinned. I am going to pause now, and sit here on the mound repenting in deepest shame. . . .

Oh dear, that was a great mistake! My mind wandered from repenting to thinking it wouldn't have been sin if Stephen had been Simon. And changing them over has made me realize more and more how I have spoilt the memory of Simon's kiss. Oh, how can I face my wretched future? I shall have to be Rose's bridesmaid, see her living with Simon at Scoatney year after year, watch him worshipping her. And how am I going to hide my feelings, when I see them together?

If only I could go away! But the one thing I live for is to see Simon again.

I have just remembered I once wrote that I didn't envy Rose, that I thought a happy marriage might be dull. Heavens, what a fool I was! . . .

Father is cycling along the lane, after spending the day at Scoatney again, and the boys will be home any minute now. I suppose I must go down and get tea; tinned salmon would cheer me up most, I think. It is most strange and wretched coming back to the present after being in this journal so long—I have been writing all day with only one break when I took Heloïse indoors for her dinner and gave myself a very few cold sausages.

One of my worst longings to cry has come over me. I am going to run down the mound grinning and singing to fight it off.

Nine o'clock—written in bed.

Something has happened. Oh, I know I mustn't build on it —but I know I *am* building.

While we were at tea, a telegram came for Stephen from Leda Fox-Cotton; she wants him to go up to London next week-end. So he went back to the farm to ask if they could spare him on Saturday morning. As soon as he had gone out, I turned off his wireless and went upstairs to play Simon's—I never play it when Stephen is in the house. Thomas came too, and asked me to put the Bach Preludes and Fugues on the gramophone—he particularly likes them. We lay on the beds listening companionably. It seems to me that Thomas has been getting much more grown-up and intelligent lately. He was always bright about his school work, but I never found him interesting to talk to. Now he often astonishes me. Perhaps all the good food he has had lately has flown to his brain.

After we had played the Bach records he suddenly said:

"Do you remember Rose wishing on the stone head?"

I asked what on earth had made him think of that.

"Oh, listening to Simon's gramophone, I suppose—it's part of the difference the Cottons have made to our lives. It never struck me before that Rose wanted to sell herself to the Devil, wished—and then in they walked."

I stared at him. "But Rose isn't selling herself—she's in love with Simon. She told me so and you know she never lies."

"That's true," said Thomas. "Then perhaps she managed to kid herself—because I know she isn't in love. And she's all wrong for Simon."

255

"But how can you possibly know that she isn't in love?"

"Well, for one thing, she hardly ever mentions Simon. Harry's sister's in love and she never stops talking about her fiancé. Harry and I make bets about it. That last week-end I stayed there she mentioned him fifty-one times."

"That's nonsense," I said. "Rose happens to be more reticent."

"Reticent? Rose? Why, she always talks her head off about anything she's keen on. Do you know that in the letter I had from her there isn't one word about Simon?"

"When did you have a letter?" I asked. "Couldn't I see it?"

He said he had happened to meet the postman in the lane a few days ago. "And I didn't show you the letter because she asked me not to—but for a very silly reason, so I don't see why I shouldn't. I'll get it now."

It was a most peculiar letter. There was certainly nothing about Simon in it—but there was nothing about anyone else, not even Rose herself, really. It was just one enormous list of things that had been bought for her and how much everything cost. At the end, she wrote: "I would rather you didn't show this to Cassandra, because it seems awful that I have so many lovely things when she has so few. You won't be envious as you are not a girl. And it is nice to be able to tell someone."

"And I bet I know why she made that list," said Thomas. "It was to convince herself that marrying for money is worth it. Oh, I wouldn't worry about it too much; women are always marrying for money, you know. Anyway, it's a godsend for us, all right, even if it's a bit of a devilsend for Rose."

"And what about Simon?" I demanded.

"Simon? Oh, he's past help. Do you remember our last visit to Scoatney—before they all went up to London? He mentioned Rose's name forty-two times while we were walking round the stables—I counted. The horses must have been sick of the sound of her."

I told him he hadn't any real evidence about Rose's feelings; but a wild hope was rising in my heart—for surely it *is* strange that there is nothing about Simon in her letter, surely one wants to write about the person one is in love with? Why, I even write Simon's name on scraps of paper! (And then get fits of nerves that I haven't really torn them up.)

After Thomas had gone off to do his homework, I got out the only letter Rose has written to me. At first it sent my hopes down to zero—for what could be more definite than: "It's so wonderful that I can be in love with Simon as well as everything else"? But suppose she really is "kidding herself," as Thomas suggested? There is so little *about* Simon. And part of the letter seems so sad—she writes of loneliness, of having to sit in the bathroom until she cheers up. Heavens, if I had Simon I could never be lonely!

I have been lying in bed trying to imagine the kind of letter I would have written had I been Rose. I don't think I would have said much about my deepest feelings—I can quite understand Rose keeping those to herself. But I know I would have said which dresses Simon liked, what he thought about theatres——

I know he would have been the most important thing in the letter.

Am I making it all up—believing what I want to believe? And even if she doesn't love him, I know he loves *her*. But perhaps if she gave him up. . .

Oh, it is so hot in this room! I daren't open the window wide in case Heloïse takes a flying leap out of it—one of her suitors, the sheep-dog from Four Stones, is prowling round the castle. Heloïse, darling, he would be a most unsuitable match. I wonder if he has gone. . . . No, he hasn't. There are two dogs now, just the other side of the moat; I can see four eyes glowing in the darkness. I feel terribly sorry for love-lorn dogs. I can't say Heloïse is minding much, though—she is looking rather smug. . . .

I have just decided what to do. Somehow I have got to find out the truth. If Rose really loves him I will never try to take him from her, even in my thoughts. I will go away—perhaps to college, as she suggested. But I must know the truth. I must see her.

I will go to London with Stephen on Saturday.

Chapter XIV

I AM BACK. IT WASN'T ANY GOOD.

Nothing will ever be the same again between Rose and me.

All the time that Stephen and I were cycling to Scoatney Station very early yesterday, I kept remembering the start of my last trip to London, when she was with me. I found myself talking to her as she was then; even asking her advice about what I should say to the new Rose. The Rose with the thousand-pound trousseau seemed an utterly different person from the Rose in the skimpy white suit who set out with me that bright April morning. How fresh the countryside was then! It was green yesterday, after the rain, but there was no hopeful, beginning feeling. The sun was hot, and though I was glad the bad weather was over, I found it rather glaring. High summer can be pitiless to the low-spirited.

Being alone with Stephen was far less difficult than I had expected. We talked very little and only about the most ordinary things. I felt guilty towards him and, most unfairly, slightly annoyed with him because I did. I resented being worried about him on top of everything else.

While we were waiting at the station, Heloïse arrived, exhausted—having eluded Thomas and raced after our bicycles. She is out of purdah now, and we didn't like to leave her on the platform, because once when we did that she stowed away on the next train and ended up at King's Crypt police station. So Stephen got her a dog-ticket and the station-master gave her a long drink and found some string to make a leash. She behaved beautifully on the journey, except that after we changed into the London train she took a little boy's cake away from him. I quickly thanked him for giving it to her and he took my word for it that he had meant to.

Stephen insisted on escorting me all the way to Park Lane. We arranged to telephone each other about what train we would go home by, and then he dashed off to St. John's Wood.

I walked Heloïse round the block of flats, then went in. It was a most palatial place with bouncy carpets and glittering porters and a lift you work yourself. There is a queer, irrevocable feeling when you have pressed the button and start to go up. Heloïse got claustrophobia and tried to climb the padded leather walls. It didn't do them any good.

I have never seen any place look so determinedly quiet as the passage leading to the flat; it was hard to believe anyone lived behind the shining front doors. When Mrs. Cotton's was opened to me it came as quite a shock.

I asked for Rose and told the maid who I was.

"They're all out," she said.

I suddenly realized I ought to have let them know I was coming.

"When will they be back, please?" I asked.

"Madam said six-thirty—in time to dress for dinner. Won't you come in, miss?"

She offered to get water for Heloïse, who was panting histrionically, and asked if I would like anything. I said perhaps some milk and might I tidy up? She showed me into Rose's bedroom. It was superb—the carpet was actually white; it seemed awful to walk on it. Everything was white or cream, except a great bunch of red roses in a marble vase on the bedside table. By it was a card sticking out of an envelope with "Good morning, darling," on it, in Simon's writing. While I was staring at the roses the maid came back with my milk, and water for Heloïse; then left us alone.

Rose's bathroom looked as if it had never been used—even her toothbrush was hidden away. She had said in her letter that there were clean towels every day, but I hadn't visualized there being so many—three sizes, and the most fetching monogrammed face-cloths.

When I had washed, I went back to the bedroom—and found Heloïse blissfully relaxed on the white quilted bed-spread; she did look nice. I took off my shoes and lay down beside her, trying to think out what I had better do. The scent of the roses was most beautiful.

I saw that it would be hopeless to talk to Rose if she didn't get back until so late; I needed to go slow and be tactful, and there would be no time for that either before or after dinner, even if I waited until the nine-thirty train. I wondered if I could find her—surely she would come back if she knew I was at the flat?

I rang for the maid, but when she came she had no idea where they had all gone.

"Wouldn't anyone know?" I said desperately.

"Well, we could try Mr. Neil—though we haven't seen much of him lately." She rang up his hotel; but Neil was out. Then I wondered if the Fox-Cottons could help, and we got their number.

Leda Fox-Cotton didn't sound at all pleased to talk to me.

"You silly child, why didn't you warn them?" she said. "No, of course I don't know where they are. Wait a minute, I'll ask Aubrey. Topaz might have mentioned something to him."

She was back in a minute. "He only knows that Topaz will be home this evening—because he's calling for her. I suppose you'd better lunch with us—you'll have to wait till two, though, because I'm having a long morning with Stephen. I've got to take him to some film people this afternoon. You can amuse yourself for an hour or so, can't you? Get a taxi at half-past one."

I thought of refusing, but I did want to see her house and studio—and have another look at her and her husband; it sounded as if Topaz was very thick with him. So I thanked her and accepted. After I stopped hearing her bleating voice, I told myself that it was really very kind of her to ask me and that I ought to get over my prejudice against her.

"That'll be nice for you," said the maid, "though Cook would have given you some lunch, of course. Let's see, you've got an hour and a half to put in—I expect you'd like to look at some shops."

But I didn't fancy lugging Heloïse round crowded streets, so I said I would just walk in Hyde Park.

"Your frock's quite a bit creased, miss," she told me. "I could press it, if you like."

I had a look at myself in Rose's long glass. It is strange what surroundings can do to clothes—I had washed and ironed my green dress the day before and thought it very nice, but in Rose's room it seemed cheap and ordinary. And lying on the bed in it hadn't helped matters. But I didn't like to take it off to be pressed, because my underclothes were so old and darned, so I thanked the maid and told her I wouldn't bother.

It was hot walking in the Park so I sat down on the grass under some trees. Heloïse rolled and then enticed me with waving paws to tickle her; but I was too lazy to make a good job of it so she turned over and went to sleep. I leaned back against a tree-trunk and gazed around me.

It struck me that this was the first time I had ever been on my own in London. Normally, I should have enjoyed getting the "feel" of it—you never quite do until you have been alone in a place—and even in my anxious state of mind it was pleasant sitting there quietly, looking at the distant scarlet 'buses, the old cream-painted houses in Park Lane and the great new blocks of flats with their striped sun-blinds. And the feel of the Park itself was most strange and interesting—what I noticed most was its separateness; it seemed to be smiling and amiable, but somehow aloof from the miles and miles of London all around. At first I thought this was because it belonged to an older London—Victorian, eighteenth century, earlier than that. And then, as I watched the sheep peacefully nibbling the grass, it came to me that Hyde Park has never belonged to any London—that it has always been, in spirit, a stretch of the countryside; and that it thus links the Londons of all periods together most magically—by remaining forever unchanged at the heart of the ever-changing town.

After I heard a clock strike quarter-past one, I went out to Oxford Street and found a nice open taxi. It was Heloïse's first drive through London and she barked almost continuously— the driver said it saved blowing his horn.

I had never been to St. John's Wood before; it is a fascinating place with quiet, tree-lined roads and secret-looking houses, most of them old—so that the Fox-Cottons' scarlet front door seemed startling.

Aubrey Fox-Cotton came out into the hall to meet me.

"Leda's still busy," he said, in his beautiful, affected voice. By daylight his narrow face looked even greyer than it did that night at Scoatney. He is a most shadowy person and yet there is something unforgettable about his dim elegance. Heloïse took rather a fancy to him, but he just said, "Comic creature," and waved a vague hand at her.

He gave me some sherry and talked politely, but without really noticing me, until it was well after two. At last he said we would "drift over" and rout the others out.

We went through the back garden to a building that looked as if it had originally been a stable. Once inside, we were faced with a black velvet curtain stretching right across. There was a little spiral staircase in one corner.

"Go on up," he whispered, "and keep quiet in case it's a psychological moment."

At the top of the staircase was a gallery from which we could look down into the studio. It was brilliantly lit, with all the lights focused on a platform at the far end. Stephen was standing there, in a Greek tunic, against a painted background of a ruined temple. He looked quite wonderful. I couldn't see Leda Fox-Cotton anywhere but I could hear her.

"Your mouth's too rigid," she called out. "Moisten your lips, then don't quite close them. And look up a fraction."

Stephen did as she said, and then his head jerked and he went bright scarlet.

"What the hell——" began Leda Fox-Cotton—then she realized he had seen someone in the gallery, and went and stood where she could see us herself. "Well, that's that," she remarked. "I shan't get anything more out of him now. He's been self-conscious all morning—I suppose it's that tunic. Go and change, Stephen."

She was all in black—black trousers, black shirt—and very hot and greasy, but there was a hard-working look about her which made the greasiness less unpleasant than it had seemed at Scoatney. While we were waiting for Stephen, I asked if I could see some of her work and she took me through into what must have been the stable of the next-door house. It was furnished as a sitting-room, with great divans piled with cushions. Everything was black or white. On the walls were enlargements of photographs she had taken, including one of a magnificent, quite naked Negro, much larger than life. It reached from the floor up to the high ceiling and was terrifying.

There was a huge framed head of Stephen waiting to be put up. I admired it and said how beautifully he photographed.

"He's the only boy I ever had the chance to do who was beautiful without looking effeminate," she said. "And his physique's as good as his head. I wish the silly child would strip for me—I'd like to put him up beside my Negro."

Then she handed me a whole sheaf of Stephen's photographs, all wonderful. The queer thing was that they were exactly like him and yet he seemed quite a different person in them—much more definite, forceful, intelligent. Not one of them had that look of his that I used to call "daft." While we were lunching (on a mirror-topped table) I wondered if it hadn't perhaps gone in real life. He was certainly much more grown-up, and surprisingly at ease with the Fox-Cottons. But he still wasn't —well, so much of a person as in the photographs.

The food was lovely—so was everything in the place, for that matter, in an ultra-modern way.

"All wrong for this old house," said Aubrey (they told me to call them by their Christian names), after I had been admiring the furniture. "But I prefer modern furniture in London and Leda won't leave her studios and take a flat. Modernity in London, antiquity in the country—that's what I like. *How* I wish Simon would let me rent Scoatney!"

"Perhaps Rose will fall in love with New York when they go there for their honeymoon," said Leda.

"*Are* they going?" I asked, as casually as I could.

"Oh, Rose was talking about it," said Leda vaguely. "It would be a nice time to go, if they get married in September. New York's lovely in the autumn."

The most awful wave of depression hit me. I suddenly knew that nothing would stop the wedding, that I had come up to

London on a wild-goose chase; I think I had begun to know it when I saw Simon's roses in the flat. I longed to be back at the castle so that I could crawl into the four-poster and cry.

Leda was talking to Stephen about posing for her again the next morning.

"But we've got to go home to-night," I said quickly.

"Oh, nonsense—you can sleep at the flat," said Leda.

"There isn't room," I said. "And, anyway, I must get back."

"But Stephen needn't, surely? You can go by yourself."

"No, she can't—not late at night," said Stephen. "Of course I'll take you if you want to go, Cassandra."

Leda gave him the swiftest, shrewdest look—it was as if she had suddenly sized up how he felt about me, wasn't pleased about it, but wasn't going to argue with him.

"Well, that's a bore," she said, then turned to me again. "I'm sure they can fix you up at the flat somehow or other. *Why* can't you stay?"

I longed to tell her to mind her own business. But as she was my hostess, I just said politely that father and Thomas needed me.

"But, good lord," she began—then took in my determined expression, shrugged her shoulders and said: "Well, if you change your mind, ring up."

Luncheon was over then. As we walked across the hall, Heloïse was lying on the black marble floor, very full of food. Leda stopped and looked at her.

"Nice—her reflection in the marble," she said. "I wonder if I'll photograph her? No—there isn't time to rig up the lights in here."

She didn't give a flicker of a smile when Heloïse thumped her tail. It struck me that I never had seen her smile.

While she was dressing to take Stephen to the film studios, I felt it would be polite to talk to Aubrey about his work and ask to see pictures of it. Of course I don't know anything about modern architecture, but it looked very good to me. It is odd that such a desiccated man should be so clever—and odd that anyone who sounds as silly as Leda does can take such magnificent photographs. When she came downstairs she was wearing a beautiful black dress and hat, with dark red gloves and an antique ruby necklace; but she still looked quite a bit greasy.

I had decided to go back to the flat in case Rose came home earlier than the maid expected, so Leda dropped me there on their way to the film studios. Stephen arranged to call for me at half-past eight.

Leda had one last nag at me. "You are a trying child, making him take you home to-night. He'll have to come straight back to London if he lands this job."

"He doesn't have to go with me unless he wants to." I don't *think* I said it rudely. "Anyway, good luck with the job, Stephen."

As they drove off I started to walk Heloïse round the block of flats, but I hadn't got far before the car stopped and Stephen came running back to me.

"Are you sure you want me to take this job if I can get it?" he asked.

I said of course I was, and that we should all be very proud of him.

"All right—if you're sure——"

As I watched him racing back to the car I had a wrongful feeling of pride—not so much because he was devoted to me as at the thought of Leda having to realize it.

I spent the afternoon in the drawing-room of the flat. I read a little—there were some very serious American magazines, not a bit like the ones Miss Marcy had. But most of the time, I just thought. And what I thought about most was luxury. I had never realized before that it is more than just having things; it makes the very air feel different. And *I* felt different, breathing that air: relaxed, lazy, still sad but with the edge taken off the sadness. Perhaps the effect wears off in time, or perhaps you don't notice it if you are born to it, but it does seem to me that the climate of richness must always be a little dulling to the senses. Perhaps it takes the edge off joy as well as off sorrow.

And though I cannot honestly say I would ever turn my back on any luxury I could come by, I do feel there is something a bit wrong in it. Perhaps that makes it all the more enjoyable.

At five o'clock the kind maid brought iced tea and cucumber sandwiches—and biscuits for Heloïse, but she much preferred the sandwiches. After that, I fell asleep on the sofa.

And suddenly they were all back—the room was full of them, laughing and talking. All three of them were in black—apparently most smart London women wear black in hot weather; it does seem unsuitable, but they looked very nice in it. And they were so pleased to see me—Rose simply hugged me. Everyone was determined that I should stay for the week-end. Rose insisted her bed was big enough for two and when I said we should kick each other she said:

"All right—I'll sleep on the floor but stay you must."

"Yes, do, dear," said Mrs. Cotton. "And then we can see about your bridesmaid's dress on Monday morning."

"If only I'd known you were here, I'd have rushed home," cried Rose. "We've been to the dullest matinée."

She was fanning herself with the programme. Three months ago no matinée in the world would have been dull to her.

Topaz urged me to stay, but in the same breath asked if father would be all right without me. I told her exactly what food I had left for him and Thomas.

"We'll call up Scoatney and have a cold roast of beef sent over," said Mrs. Cotton. "They can eat their way through that."

Then Simon came in and just to see him again was so wonderful that I suddenly felt quite happy.

"Yes, of course she must stay," he said, "and come out with us to-night."

Rose said she could lend me a dress. "And you telephone Neil, Simon, and say he's to come and dance with her. You shall have a bath in my bathroom, Cassandra."

She put her arm round me and walked me along to her bedroom. The quiet flat had come to life. Doors and windows were open, the maid was drawing up the sun-blinds, a cool breeze was blowing in from the Park, smelling of dry grass and petrol —a most exciting, Londony smell which mixed with a glorious smell of the dinner cooking.

"The kitchen door must have been left open," said Mrs. Cotton to the maid, quite crossly. As if anyone could mind the smell of a really good dinner!

While I was in the bath, Rose telephoned the Fox-Cottons' house for me—I was afraid Leda would answer and I didn't fancy telling her myself that I had changed my mind. Then I felt it would be most unkind not to ask Stephen how his interview had gone, so I yelled to Rose that I would like to talk to him.

"He's in the studio with Leda," Rose called back. "Aubrey says he'll ask him to telephone you later."

After she had hung up she told me that Stephen had got the film job. "Aubrey says Leda's terribly excited about it— Stephen's to have ten pounds a day for at least five days. He doesn't have to say anything—just keep wandering about with some goats. It's symbolic or something."

"Gracious, fancy Stephen earning fifty pounds!"

"He'll earn more than that before Leda's finished with him," said Rose. "She's crazy about him."

When I came back from the bath there was an evening dress laid out for me—again, the fashionable black! Though it turned out that Rose had only chosen that dress for me because it was her shortest. It fitted me very well, just clearing the ground, and was utterly luxurious—though Rose said: "Oh, it's only one of the ready-made ones, bought to tide me over."

As I finished dressing, I heard Neil's voice in the hall.

"You're complimented," said Rose, "he hasn't been near us for weeks. Dear me, I hope he won't put poison in my soup."

I said it was a pity they didn't get on with each other.

"Well, it's not my fault," said Rose. "I'm perfectly willing to be friends with him—for Simon's sake. I've tried again and again, and I'll try to-night, just to show you. But it won't be any good."

When she said "for Simon's sake" I thought: "Of course she loves him. I was an idiot to believe Thomas." Yet I went on feeling happy. I kept saying to myself: "I've seen him—in a minute I shall see him again. That's almost enough."

Neil knocked on the bedroom door and called: "Where's my friend Cassandra?"

Rose wasn't quite ready so I went out to him alone. I had forgotten how very nice he is. We went into the drawing-room and Simon said: "Why, she's grown up!"

"And grown up very prettily," said Mrs. Cotton. "We must go shopping next week, my dear."

I think I did look reasonably nice in Rose's dress.

Everyone was wonderfully kind to me—perhaps they felt that I had been a bit neglected. When Rose came in she put her arm through mine and said: "She must stay a long, long time, mustn't she? Father will just have to look after himself."

Topaz would never have passed that, but she had gone out with Aubrey Fox-Cotton.

After dinner (four courses; the jellied soup was marvellous), they decided where we should dance. Mrs. Cotton wouldn't come—she said she was going to stay at home and re-read Proust.

"I started last night," she told Simon, "and I'm longing to get back to him. This time I'm making notes—trying to keep track of my favourite paragraphs, as you did."

Then they began a conversation about Proust that I longed to listen to, but Rose swept me out to her bedroom to get ready.

"The way those two talk about books!" she said. "And without ever mentioning an author I've read a line of."

It was fascinating strolling along Park Lane to the hotel where the dance was, with the sky deep blue beyond the street lamps. But after the first steps I realized that I was in for trouble with Rose's satin shoes—they had seemed to fit quite well when I put them on, but I found that they slipped off when I walked unless I held my feet stiffly. Dancing proved to be worse than walking—after one turn around the room I knew it was hopeless.

"I shall just have to watch," I told Neil.

He said, "Not on your life," and then led me to a deserted corridor just off the ballroom. It must have been intended as a sitting-out place—there were little alcoves let into the pink brocaded walls—but Neil said people hardly ever came there.

"Now take those darn shoes off," he told me, "and I'll take mine off, too, in case I step on you."

It was the queerest feeling, dancing on the thick carpet, but I quite enjoyed it. When the music stopped, we sat in one of the alcoves and talked.

"I'm glad you came to London," he said. "If you hadn't, I might not have seen you again. I'm going back home a week to-day."

I was most astonished. "You mean California? Aren't you going to stay for the wedding? I thought you were to be best man."

"Simon will have to get someone else. I can't miss this chance. I've been offered a partnership in a ranch—got the cable to-day. They need me at once."

Just then we saw Rose and Simon coming out of the ball-room, obviously looking for us. "Don't mention it, will you?" said Neil, quickly. "I want to break it to mother before I tell the others. She isn't going to be pleased."

The music started again soon after Rose and Simon joined us. She turned to Neil and said in a really nice voice: "Will you dance this with me?"

I saw then that she had been right in thinking it was hopeless to be friends with him—for a moment I thought he would actually refuse to dance. But in the end he just said: "Sure, if you want me to," quite politely but without the flicker of a smile, and they went off together, leaving me alone with Simon.

We talked first about Rose; he was worried in case so much shopping had tired her.

"I wish we could be married at once and get out of London," he said. "But both she and mother insist on waiting for the trousseau."

I had thought myself that Rose seemed a little less alive than usual, but nothing like so tired as he, himself, did. He was paler than usual and his manner was so quiet. It made me care for him more than ever—I wanted so terribly to be good to him.

After we had taken a great interest in Rose for a very long time, he asked about father and we discussed the possibility that he was doing some work and keeping it quiet.

269

"He was most odd when he stayed in the flat a few weeks ago," said Simon. "Mother told me he went into the kitchen and borrowed all the cookery books."

I began to have a desperate feeling that time was rushing by and we weren't talking about anything I could treasure for the future—he was being charming and kind, as he always is, but he hardly seemed to notice me as a person. I longed to say something amusing but couldn't think of anything, so I tried to be intelligent.

"Do you think I ought to read Proust?" I asked.

Apparently that was more amusing than it was intelligent, because it made him laugh. "Well, I wouldn't say it was a *duty*," he said, "but you could have a shot at it. I'll send you *Swann's Way*."

Then I talked about his birthday present to me, and he said what a nice letter I had written to thank him.

"I hope you're borrowing all the records you want from Scoatney," he told me.

When he said that, I suddenly saw the pavilion, lit by moonlight and candlelight—and then, by the most cruel coincidence, the band, which had been playing a medley of tunes, began "Lover." I felt myself blushing violently—never have I known such embarrassment. I sprang up and ran towards a mirror, some way along the corridor.

"What's the matter?" Simon called after me.

"An eyelash in my eye," I called back.

He asked if he could help but I said I could manage, and fidgeted with my handkerchief until the blush died down—I don't believe he ever noticed it. As I walked back to him he said:

"It's odd how that dress changes you. I don't know that I approve of your growing up. Oh, I shall get used to it." He smiled at me. "But you were perfect as you were."

It was the funny little girl he had liked—the comic child playing at Midsummer rites; she was the one he kissed. Though I don't think I shall ever quite know why he did it.

After that I talked easily enough, making him laugh quite a bit—I could see he was liking me again. But it wasn't my present self talking at all; I was giving an imitation of myself as I used to be. I was very "consciously naïve." Never, never was I that with him before; however I may have sounded, I always felt perfectly natural. But I knew, as I sat there amusing him while the band played "Lover," that many things which had felt natural to me before I first heard it would never feel natural again. It wasn't only the black dress that had made me grow up.

Rose and Neil came back when the music stopped; then Neil went off to order us some drinks.

"That was a good tune that last one," she remarked. "What's it called?"

"I'm afraid I didn't notice," said Simon.

"Nor I," I said.

Rose sat down in the opposite alcove and put her feet up.

"Tired?" Simon asked, going over to her.

She said: "Yes, very," and didn't offer to make room for him; so he sat on the floor beside her. "Would you like me to take you home as soon as we've had our drinks?" he asked, and she said she would.

Neil would have stayed on with me, but I said we couldn't keep dancing without shoes in that corridor.

"It does begin to feel like a padded cell," he admitted.

I shall never forget it—the thick carpet, the brocade-covered walls, the bright lights staring back from the gilt mirrors; everything was so luxurious—and so meaningless, so lifeless.

When we reached the entrance to the flats Neil said he wouldn't come up, but he walked along to the lift with us and managed so that he and I were well behind the others.

"This looks like being good-bye for us," he said.

I felt a sadness quite separate from my personal ton of misery. "But we'll meet again some day, won't we?"

"Why, surely. You must come to America."

"Won't you ever come back here?"

He said he doubted it—then laughed and added: "Well, maybe I will, when I'm a rich old man."

"Why do you dislike us so, Neil?"

"I don't dislike *you*," he said quickly. "Oh, I don't dislike anything. But I'm just all wrong over here."

Then the others called that the lift was waiting for me, so we shook hands quickly. I hated to think it might be years and years before I saw him again.

There was a message from Stephen for me at the flat—I had quite forgotten that he was going to telephone me. Rose read aloud: "For Miss C. Mortmain from Mr. S. Colly. The gentleman asked to say that he was completely at your service if required."

"I do call that a nice message," said Simon. "Hadn't you better call him back?"

"Oh, leave it till the morning," said Rose, "and let's go to bed. I've hardly had a chance to talk to you yet."

Just then Topaz came out of her bedroom and said she wanted to speak to me.

"Can't you wait until to-morrow?" asked Rose.

Topaz said she didn't see why she should. "It's only half-past ten and I came back early on purpose."

"Well, hurry up, anyway," said Rose.

Topaz took me up to the roof-garden. "You never know if you're going to be overheard in that flat," she said. It was nice on the roof, there were lots of little trees in tubs, and some pretty garden furniture. No one but us was about. We sat down on a large swinging seat and I waited for her to say something important; but, as I might have guessed, she only wanted to talk about father.

"I hardly had a minute with him when he stayed here," she said. "My room's too small to share. And Mrs. Cotton kept him up talking very late both nights."

I asked if she was still worried about them.

"Oh, not in the way I was. Anyway, there's certainly nothing on *her* side. I see now it's not the man she's interested in, but the famous man—if he'll oblige her by being one again. She hopes he will and she wants to have a hand in it. So does Simon."

"Well, what's wrong with that?" I said. "You know they mean it kindly."

"Simon does; he's interested in Mortmain's work for its own sake—and for Mortmain's sake. But I think Mrs. Cotton's just a celebrity collector—she even values me now that she's seen some of the paintings of me."

"She asked you to stay with her *before* she saw them," I said. I like Mrs. Cotton; and her kindness to our family has been little short of fabulous.

"Go on—tell me I'm unjust." Topaz heaved one of her groaning sighs, then added: "I know I am, really. But she gets on my nerves until I could scream. Why doesn't she get on Mortmain's? It's a mystery to me. Talk, talk, talk—and never did I see such vitality. I don't believe it's normal for a woman of her age to be so healthy. If you ask me, it's glandular."

I began to laugh, then saw she was perfectly serious; "glandular" has always been a popular word with Topaz. "Well, come back to the castle and take a rest," I suggested.

"That's what I wanted to ask you about. Has Mortmain shown the slightest sign of needing me?"

I tried to think of a tactful way to say "No." Fortunately, she went straight on: "I've got to be needed, Cassandra—I always have been. Men have either painted me, or been in love with me, or just plain ill-treated me—some men have to do a lot of ill-treating, you know, it's good for their work; but one way or another, I've always been *needed*. I've got to inspire people, Cassandra—it's my job in life."

I told her then that I had a faint hope that father was working.

"Do you mean I've inspired him just by keeping away from him?"

We both roared with laughter. Topaz's sense of humour is intermittent, but good when it turns up. When we had calmed down, she said:

"What do you think of Aubrey Fox-Cotton?"

"Not much," I said. "Does *he* need inspiring? He seems to be doing pretty well as it is."

"He could do greater work. He feels he could."

"You mean, if you both got divorces and married each other?"

"Well, not *exactly*," said Topaz.

I suddenly felt it was an important moment and wondered what on earth I could say to influence her. It was no use pretending that father needed her, because I knew she would find out he didn't before she had been home half an hour. At last I said:

"I suppose it wouldn't be enough that Thomas and I need you?"

She looked pleased—then came out with a dreadful Topazism: "Oh, darling! But can't you see that art comes before the individual?"

Inspiration came to me.

"Then you can't leave father," I said. "Oh, Topaz—don't you see that whether he misses you or not, a shock like that might wreck him completely? Just imagine his biographer writing: 'Mortmain was about to start on the second phase of his career, when the faithlessness of his artist-model wife shattered the fabric of his life. We shall never know what was lost to the world through this worthless young woman——' and you never *would* know, Topaz, because if father never wrote another line after you left him, you'd always feel it might be your fault."

She was staring at me—I could see I was making a magnificent impression. Luckily it hadn't struck her that no one will write father's biography unless he does do some more work.

"Can't you see how posterity would misjudge you?" I piled it on. "While if you stick to him, you may be 'this girl, beautiful as a Blake angel, who sacrificed her own varied talents to ensure Mortmain's renaissance.'" I stopped, fearing I had overdone it, but she swallowed it all.

"Oh, darling—you ought to write the biography yourself," she gasped.

"I will, I will," I assured her, and wondered if she would consider staying on to inspire *me*; but I think she only sees herself as an inspirer of men. Anyway, I didn't need to worry, because she said in her most double-bass tones:

"Cassandra, you have saved me from a dreadful mistake. Thank you, thank you."

Then she collapsed on my shoulders with such force that I shot off the swinging seat.

Oh, darling Topaz! She calls Mrs. Cotton's interest in father celebrity collecting, and never sees that her own desire to inspire men is just another form of it—and a far less sincere one. For Mrs. Cotton's main interests really are intellectual—well, social-intellectual—while my dear beautiful step-mother's intellectualism is very, very bogus. The real Topaz is the one who cooks and scrubs and sews for us all. How mixed people are—how mixed and nice!

As we went down from the roof she said she would come home in ten days or a fortnight—just as soon as Macmorris finished his new portrait of her. I said how very glad I was, though it suddenly struck me how hard it would be to hide my troubles from her. Talking to her had taken my mind off them, but as we went into the flat it was just as if they were waiting for me there.

Everyone had gone to bed. There was a line of light under Simon's door. I thought how close to me he would be sleeping and, for some reason, that made me more unhappy than ever. And the prospect of seeing him again in the morning held no comfort for me; I had found out in that glittering corridor off the ballroom that being with him could be more painful than being away from him.

Rose was sitting up in bed waiting for me. I remember noticing how pretty her bright hair looked against the white velvet headboard.

She said: "I've put out one of my trousseau nightgowns for you."

I thanked her and hoped I wouldn't tear it—it seemed very fragile. She said there were plenty more, anyway.

"Well, now we can talk," I said, brightly—meaning "*you* can." I no longer had any intention of questioning her about her feelings for Simon—of course she loved him, of course nothing would stop the marriage, my coming to London had been an idiotic mistake.

"I don't think I want to to-night," she said.

This surprised me—she had seemed so keen on talking—but I just said: "Well, there'll be plenty of time to-morrow."

She said she supposed so, hardly sounding enthusiastic; then asked me to put the roses in the bathroom for the night. As I went to get them, she looked down at Simon's card on the bedside table and said: "Chuck that in the wastepaper-basket, will you?"

She didn't say it casually, but with a sort of scornful resentment. My resolution not to speak just faded away and I said:

"Rose, you don't love him."

She gave me a little ironic smile and said: "No. Isn't it a pity?"

There it was—the thing I had hoped for! But instead of feeling glad, instead of feeling any flicker of hope, I felt angry—so angry that I didn't dare to let myself speak. I just stood staring at her until she said:

"Well? Say something."

I managed to speak quite calmly. "Why did you lie to me that night you got engaged?"

"I didn't. I really thought I was in love. When he kissed me—— Oh, you wouldn't understand—you're too young."

I understood, all right. If Stephen had kissed me before I knew that I loved Simon, I might have made the same mistake —particularly if I had *wanted* to make it, as Rose did. But I went on feeling angry.

"How long have you known?" I demanded.

"Weeks and weeks, now—I found out soon after we came to London; Simon's with me so much more here. Oh, if only he wasn't so in love with me! Can you understand what I mean? It isn't only that he wants to make love to me—every minute we're together I can feel him *asking* for love. He somehow links it with everything—if it's a particularly lovely day, if we see anything beautiful or listen to music together. It makes me want to scream. Oh, God!—I didn't mean to tell you. I longed to—I knew it would be a relief; but I made up my mind not to, only a few minutes ago, because I knew it would be selfish.

I'm sorry you got it out of me. I can see it's upset you dreadfully."

"That's all right," I said. "Would you like me to tell him for you?"

"Tell him?" She stared at me. "Oh, no wonder you're upset! Don't worry, darling—I'm still going to marry him."

"No, you're not," I told her. "You're not going to do anything so wicked."

"Why is it suddenly wicked? You always knew I'd marry him whether I loved him or not—and you helped me all you could, without ever being sure I was in love with him."

"I didn't understand—it was just fun, like something in a book. It wasn't real." But I knew in my heart that my conscience had always felt uneasy and I hadn't listened to it. All my unhappiness had been a judgement on me.

"Well, it's real enough now," said Rose grimly.

My own guilt made me feel less angry with her. I went and sat on the bed and tried to speak reasonably. "You can't do it, you know, Rose—just for clothes and jewellery, and bathrooms——"

"You talk as if I were doing it all for myself," she broke in on me. "Do you know what my last thoughts have been, lying here night after night? 'Well, at least they've had enough to eat at the castle to-day'—why, even Heloïse is putting on weight! And I've thought of you more than anyone—of all the things I can do for you when I'm married——"

"Then you can stop thinking, because I won't take anything from you——" Suddenly my anger came rushing back and words started to pour out of me. "And you can stop pretending that you're doing it for us all—it's simply to please yourself, because you can't face poverty. You're going to wreck Simon's life because you're greedy and cowardly——" I went on and on, in a sort of screaming whisper—all the time I was conscious that I might be overheard and managed to stop myself shouting, but I lost all control of what I said; I can't even remember most of it. Rose never once tried to interrupt—she just sat there staring at me. Suddenly a light of understanding dawned in her eyes. I stopped dead.

"You're in love with him yourself," she said. "It only needed that." And then she burst into choking sobs and buried her head in a pillow to stifle the noise.

"Oh, shut up," I said.

After a minute or two, she stopped roaring into the pillow and began to fish round for her handkerchief. You can't see a person do that without helping, however angry you are, so I gave it to her—it had fallen on the floor. She mopped up a bit, then said:

"Cassandra, I swear by everything I hold sacred that I'd give him up if I thought he'd marry you instead. Why, I'd jump at it—we'd still have money in the family, and I wouldn't have to have him as a husband. I don't want Scoatney—I don't want a lot of luxury. All I ask is, not to go back to quite such hideous poverty—I won't do that, I won't, I won't! And I'd have to, if I gave him up, because I know he wouldn't fall in love with you. He just thinks of you as a little girl."

"What he thinks of me has nothing to do with it," I said. "It's him I'm thinking of now, not me. You're not going to marry him without loving him."

She said: "Don't you know he'd rather have me that way than not at all?"

I had never thought of that; but when she said it I saw that it was true. It made me hate her more than ever. I started to tear the black dress off.

"That's right—come to bed," she said. "Let's put the light out and talk things over quietly. Perhaps you only fancy you're in love with him—couldn't it be what's called 'calf love,' darling? You can't really know if you're in love until you've been made love to. Anyway, you'll get over it when you meet other men—and I'll see that you do. Let's talk—let's try to help each other. Come to bed."

"I'm not coming to bed," I said, kicking the dress away. "I'm going home."

"But you can't—not to-night! There are no trains."

"Then I'll sit in the station waiting-room till the morning."

"But why——"

"I'm not going to lie down beside you."

278

I was struggling into my green dress. She sprang out of bed and tried to stop me.

"Cassandra, please listen——"

I told her to shut up or she would rouse the flat. "And I warn you that if you try to stop me going, *I'll* rouse it—and tell them everything. Then you'll *have* to break your engagement."

"Oh, no, I won't——" It was the first time she had sounded angry. "I'll tell them you're lying because you're in love with Simon."

"One way and another, we'd better not rouse the flat."

I was hunting everywhere for my shoes which the maid had put away. Rose followed me round, half angry, half pleading.

"But what am I to tell them, if you leave to-night?" she asked.

"Don't tell them anything until the morning—then say I had a sudden fit of conscience about leaving father alone and went by the early train." I found my shoes at last and put them on. "Oh, tell them what you damn well like. Anyway, I'm going."

"You're failing me—and just when I need you most desperately."

"Yes, to listen to your woes sympathetically and pat you on the back—sorry, nothing doing!" By then I was pulling all the drawers open, searching for my handbag. When I had unearthed it, I pushed past her.

She had one more try at getting round me: "Cassandra, I beg you to stay. If you knew how wretched I am——"

"Oh, go and sit in your bathroom and count your peach-coloured towels," I sneered at her. "*They'll* cheer you up—you lying, grasping, little cheat."

Then out I went, controlling myself enough to shut the door quietly. For a second I thought she would come after me but she didn't—I suppose she believed I really would scream out the truth; and I think I might have, I was in such a blind rage.

The only light in the hall was a glimmer round the edges of the front door, from the outside passage. I tiptoed towards it. Just as I got there, I heard a faint whimper. Heloïse! I had completely forgotten her. The next moment she was there in the dark with me, thumping her tail. I dragged her through the front door and raced to the lift—by a bit of luck it was there, waiting. Once we were going down, I sat on the floor and let her put her paws round my neck and get her ecstasy over.

She had her collar on and I used my belt as a leash—there was still too much traffic about to let her run loose, even when we turned off Park Lane into a quieter street. I was thankful to be out in the cool air, but after the first few minutes of relief my mind began to go over and over the scene with Rose—I kept thinking of worse things I might have said and imagining saying them. My eyes were still so full of the white bedroom that I scarcely noticed where I went; I just have a vague memory of going on and on past well-to-do houses. There was a dance taking place in one of them and people were strolling out on to a balcony—I dimly remember feeling sorry I was too absorbed in myself to be interested (a few months ago, it would have been splendid to imagine about). At the back of my mind I had an idea that sooner or later I should see 'buses or an entrance to the Underground, and then I could get back to the railway station and sit in the waiting-room. The first time I really came to earth was when I struck Regent Street.

I decided I must pull myself together—I remembered hearing things about Regent Street late at night. But I think I must have mixed it up with some other street, for nothing was in the least as I expected. I had imagined a stream of brightly dressed, painted women going along winking—and the only women I saw seemed most respectable, very smartly dressed in black and merely taking a last stroll: some of them had brought their little dogs out, which interested Heloïse. But I did notice that most of the ladies were in couples, which made me realize that I oughtn't to be out on my own so late at night. Just after I had thought that, a man came up to me and said:

"Excuse me, but haven't I met your dog before?"

I took no notice, of course—but, unfortunately, Heloïse started wagging her tail. I dragged her on but he came with us, saying idiotic things like: "Of course she knows me—old friends, we are—met her at the Hammersmith Palais de Danse." Heloïse got more and more friendly. Her tail was doing an almost circular wag and I was very much afraid that at any moment she would climb up the man and kiss him. So I said sharply: "Hel, who's *that*?"—which is what we say if a suspicious-looking tramp comes prowling round the castle. She let off such a volley of barks that the man jumped backwards into two ladies. He didn't try to follow us any more, but I couldn't stop Heloïse barking—she kept it up right through Piccadilly Circus, making us terribly conspicuous.

I was thankful to see an entrance to the Underground at last —but not for long, because I found they don't let dogs on the trains. You can take them on the tops of 'buses, but there seemed to be very few still running; by then it was long after midnight. I was beginning to think I had better take a taxi when I remembered that there is a Corner House restaurant close to Piccadilly and that Topaz had once told me it keeps open all night. I had a great longing for tea, and I felt Heloïse could do with a drink—she had stopped barking at last and was looking rather exhausted. So along we went.

It was such a grand place that I was afraid they might not let Heloïse in, but we chose a moment when the man on the door was interested in something else. And I got a table against the wall so that she could be fairly unnoticeable under it—the waitress did spot her but only said: "Well, if you got her past the door—— But she'll have to keep quiet"—which, by a miracle, she did. After I had unobtrusively slipped her three saucers-full of water she went solidly to sleep on my feet; which was very hot for them, but I didn't dare risk waking her by moving.

The tea was a comfort—and by that time I more than needed comfort. Most of me ached with tiredness and my eyes felt as if they had been open for years; but worse than that— worse even than my misery over Simon, which I was more or less used to—was the gradual realization that I had been utterly in the wrong with Rose. I saw that the main reason for my outburst hadn't been noble anxiety about Simon's happiness but sheer, blazing jealousy. And what could be more unjust than to help her to get engaged and then turn on her for it? How right she had been in accusing me of failing her! The least I could have done would have been to talk things over quietly. What made me feel worst of all was that I knew in my heart that she was fonder of me than of anyone in the world; just as I was of her, until I fell in love with Simon.

But she shouldn't have said that about calf-love. "How dare she!" I thought. "Who's she to decide that what I feel is calf-love, which is funny—instead of first love, which is beautiful? Why, she's never been in love at all, herself!"

I went over and over it all, while I drank cup after cup of tea—the last one was so weak that I could see the lump of sugar sitting at the bottom of it. Then the waitress came and asked if I wanted anything more. I didn't feel like leaving so I studied the menu carefully and ordered a lamb cutlet—they take a nice long time to cook and only cost sevenpence each.

While I waited, I tried to ease my misery about Rose by thinking of my misery about Simon, but I found myself thinking of both miseries together. "It's hopeless," I thought. "All three of us are going to be unhappy for the rest of our lives." Then the lamb cutlet arrived surrounded by a sea of white plate and looking smaller than I had believed any cutlet could. I ate it as slowly as possible; I even ate the sprig of parsley they throw in for the sevenpence. Then the waitress put the bill down on the table and cleared away my plate in a very final way, so after a long drink of free water I felt I had better go. I opened my bag to get out a tip for the waitress and then——

All my life I shall remember it. My purse wasn't in my bag.

I hunted frantically, but without any hope. Because I knew that purse was still in the evening bag Rose had lent me. All I found through my search was a gritty farthing in the comb pocket.

I felt icy cold and sick. The lights seemed to be much more glaring, the people all around seemed suddenly noisier and yet quite unreal. A voice in my head said: "Keep calm, keep calm now—you can explain to the manager. Give him your name and address and offer to leave something of value." But

I didn't have anything of value; no watch or jewellery, my bag was almost worn out, I hadn't even a coat or hat—for a wild minute I wondered if I could leave my shoes. "But he'll see you're a respectable person—he'll trust you," I tried to re-assure myself—and then I began to wonder if I looked a respectable person. My hair was untidy, my green dress was bright and cheap compared with London clothes, and Heloïse needing its belt didn't improve matters. "But they *can't* send for the police just for a pot of tea and one cutlet," I told myself. And then it dawned on me that it wasn't only for my bill that I needed money—how was I to get to the station without a taxi? I couldn't walk Heloïse all those miles, even if I could manage them myself. And my railway ticket——

That was in the purse, too.

"I've got to get help," I thought, desperately.

But how? There were call-boxes in the front part of the restaurant, but apart from feeling I would rather die than telephone the flat, I knew it would involve Rose in impossible explanations. Then I suddenly remembered Stephen's message that he was always at my service—but could I bring myself to wake the Fox-Cottons up at nearly two in the morning? I was still arguing with myself when the waitress came back and looked at me very pointedly, so I felt I had to do something.

I got up, leaving my bill lying on the table. "I'm waiting for someone who's late—I'll have to telephone," I said. "Will you please keep this place for me?"

Heloïse hated being wakened, but I didn't dare leave her under the table; mercifully, she was too sleepy to do any barking. I explained at the pay-desk that I was going to telephone—I noticed the girl watching to see that I did go into a call-box. It was dreadfully hot inside, particularly with Heloïse slumped against me like a fur-covered furnace. I opened the book to find the Fox-Cottons' number——

And then I remembered. You need pennies to telephone from a public call-box.

"You'll laugh at this one day," I told myself, "you'll laugh like anything." And then I leaned against the call-box wall and began to cry—but I soon stopped when I remembered

283

that my handkerchief was in Rose's evening bag. I stared at the box you put the pennies in and thought how willingly I would rob it, if I knew how. "Oh, please, God—*do* something!" I said in my heart.

Then a person who didn't seem to be me put my hand up very quickly and pressed Button B. When the pennies came out, my inner voice said: "I knew they would."

And then, in memory, I heard the Vicar talking of prayer, faith and the slot machine.

Can faith work backwards? Could the fact that I was *going* to pray have made someone forget to take their pennies back? And if it was really prayer that did it, couldn't Button B have saved me from troubling Stephen by giving me a pound? "Though, of course, it would have had to be in pennies," I thought. I prayed again, then pressed the button, wondering how I could cope with a shower of two hundred and forty pennies—but I needn't have worried. So I got on with telephoning the Fox-Cottons.

Leda answered—sooner than I had expected. She sounded furious. I told her I was dreadfully sorry to disturb her but that I simply couldn't help it. Then I asked her to get Stephen.

She said: "Certainly not. You can't talk to him now."

"But I've got to," I told her. "And I know he won't mind if you wake him—he'd want you to, if he knew I was in difficulties."

"You can stay in difficulties until to-morrow morning," she said. "I won't let you bother Stephen now. It's disgusting the way——"

She broke off, and for an awful second I thought she had hung up the receiver. Then I heard voices, though I couldn't distinguish any words—until she suddenly yelled out: "Don't you dare do that!" Then she gave a shrill little squawk—and the next second, Stephen was speaking to me.

"What's happened, what's wrong?" he cried.

I told him as quickly as I could—leaving out the quarrel with Rose, of course. I said I had meant to go home by a late train.

"But there isn't any late train——"

"Yes, there is," I said quickly, "there's one you didn't know about. Oh, I'll explain it all later. All that matters now is that I'm stranded here and if you don't come along quickly I shall get arrested."

"I'll start at once——" He sounded terribly upset. "Don't be frightened. Go back to your table and order something else —that will stop them suspecting you. And don't let any men talk to you—or any women either, especially hospital nurses."

"All right—but do be as quick as you can."

Afterwards, I wished I hadn't said that about being arrested, because I knew he would believe it—as I never *quite* had done myself. But being stranded like that in a London restaurant can be very panic-striking, particularly in the middle of the night, and I did want to make sure he would come. I was wringing wet when I hung the receiver up. I had to roll Heloïse off my feet and simply drag her back to my table. Her eyes were just two pink slits. She was practically sleep-walking.

I told the waitress my friend would arrive very soon, and ordered a chocolate ice-cream soda. Then I sat back and just wallowed in relief—it was so great that I forgot how unhappy I was and began to take an interest in my surroundings. There were some people at a near-by table who were connected with a new play—one of them was the author—and they were waiting for the morning papers with the notices of it to come out. It was funny how nice and interesting almost everyone looked once my panic was over—before, there had been just a sea of noisy faces. While I was having my ice-cream soda (it was glorious), a hospital nurse came in and sat at the very next table. I almost choked through my straw—because I knew what poor Stephen had been driving at. Miss Marcy had a story that fake nurses rush about drugging girls and shipping them to the Argentine to be what she calls: "Well—daughters of joy, dear." But as I picture the Argentine, it has plenty of its own joyful daughters.

Stephen didn't arrive until after three o'clock—he said he'd had to walk nearly a mile before finding a taxi. He had an odd, strained look, which I put down to his having been so frightened about me. I made him have a long, cold lemonade.

"Did you snatch the telephone from Leda?" I asked. "It

sounded like that. What luck for me that you overheard her talking! Is their telephone on the upstairs landing or something?"

"There's one in the studio—we were in there," he said.

"Do you mean she was still photographing you?"

He said no, it was the other studio—"The one where the big photographs are. We were just sitting talking."

"What, till two in the morning?" Then I saw that he was avoiding my eyes, and went on quickly: "Well, tell me about your interview with the film people."

He told me, but hardly a word of it sank in—I was too busy picturing him in the studio with Leda. I was sure she had been making love to him. I imagined them sitting on the divan with only one dim light burning, and the great naked Negro looking down. The thought was horrible, yet fascinating.

I came back to earth as Stephen was saying: "I'll take you home and pack up my clothes—though Leda says I shall have to buy some better ones. And I'll see Mr. Stebbins. He said he wouldn't stand in the way of my career."

"Career" sounded a funny word for Stephen.

"What will Ivy say?" I asked.

"Oh, Ivy——" He seemed to be remembering her from a long way back. "She's a good girl, is Ivy."

Somebody brought the morning papers to the people who were waiting for them. All the notices seemed to be very bad. The poor little author kept saying again and again: "It isn't that I mind for myself, of course——" And his friends were all very indignant with the critics and said notices didn't mean a thing, never had and never would.

"I suppose *you'll* be getting notices soon," I said to Stephen.

"Well, not notices exactly, but my name's going to be in print. There's to be a piece about me under the photograph Leda's getting into the papers—saying how I'm a young actor of great promise. After this one picture where I keep coming on with goats, I'm to go on a contract and be taught to act. But not too much, they say, because they don't want to spoil me."

There was actually a note of conceit in his voice. It was so unlike him that I stared in astonishment—and he must have guessed why I did, because he flushed and added: "Well, that's what they said. And you wanted me to do it. Oh, let's get out of this place."

I was glad to go. My relief at being rescued had worn off; and there seemed to me a stale, weary, unnatural feeling about the restaurant—the thought that it never closed made me feel exhausted for it. Most of the people now seemed tired and worried—the poor little author was just leaving, looking utterly downcast. The hospital nurse looked pretty cheerful, though; she was having her second go of poached eggs.

We sat on a bench in Leicester Square for a while, with Heloïse lying across both our laps. Her elbows dug into me most painfully; and I didn't like the feel of the Square at all—it isn't a bit like most London squares—so I said: "Let's go and have a look at the Thames, now that it's getting light."

We asked a policeman the way. He said: "You don't want to use it for jumping in, do you, miss?" which made me laugh.

It was quite a walk—and Heloïse loathed it; but she perked up after we bought her a sausage roll from a coffee stall. We got to Westminster Bridge just as the sky was red with dawn. I thought of Wordsworth's sonnet but it didn't fit—the city certainly wasn't "All bright and glittering in the smokeless air"; there was a lurid haze over everything. And I couldn't get the feeling of "Dear God! the very houses seem asleep" because half my mind was still in the Corner House, which never gets a sleep at all.

We stood leaning against the bridge, looking along the river. It was beautiful, even though I didn't get any feeling of peace. A gentle little breeze blew against my face—it was like someone pitying me. Tears rolled out of my eyes.

Stephen said: "What is it, Cassandra? Is it—something to do with me?"

For a second I thought he was harking back to his having kissed me in the larch wood. Then I saw the ashamed expression in his eyes. I said: "No, of course not."

"I might have known that," he said bitterly. "I might have guessed that nothing I've done to-night could matter to you. Who are you in love with, Cassandra? Is it Neil?"

I ought to have told him he was talking nonsense, that I wasn't in love with anyone, but I was too tired and wretched to pretend. I just said: "No. It isn't Neil."

"Then it's Simon. That's bad, that is—because Rose will never let him go."

"But she doesn't love him, Stephen. She admitted it——" I found myself telling him about our dreadful quarrel in her bedroom, describing how I had crept out of the flat.

"You and your late trains!" he put in. "I knew right well there wasn't one."

I went on pouring it all out. When I told him I had realized how wrongly I had behaved to Rose, he said:

"Don't you worry about that. Rose is bad."

"Not really bad," I said, and began to make excuses for her, telling him she had wanted to help the family as well as herself. He cut me short by saying:

"But she's bad, really. Lots of women are."

I said: "Sometimes we're bad without meaning to be." And then I asked him if he could ever forgive me for letting him kiss me, when I knew I was in love with someone else. "Oh, Stephen, *that* was bad! And I let you go on thinking I might get to love you."

"I only did for a day, or two—I soon saw I was making a fool of myself. But I couldn't make it out—why you ever let me, I mean. I understand now. Things like that happen when you're in love with the wrong person. Worse things. Things you never forgive yourself for."

He was staring straight ahead of him, looking utterly wretched. I said:

"Are you miserable because you made love to Leda Fox-Cotton? It was her fault, wasn't it? You don't need to blame yourself."

"I'll blame myself as long as I live," he said, then suddenly turned to me. "It's you I love and always will. Oh, Cassandra, are you sure you couldn't ever get to care for me? You liked it when I kissed you—well, you seemed to. If we could get married——"

The glow from the sunrise was on his face, the breeze was blowing his thick fair hair. He looked desperate and magnificent, more wonderful even than in any of Leda's photographs of him. The vague expression was gone from his eyes—I had a feeling it had gone for ever——

"I'd work for you, Cassandra. If I'm any good at acting perhaps we could live in London, a long way from—the others. Couldn't I help you through, somehow—when Simon's married to Rose?"

When he said Simon's name, I saw Simon's face. I saw it as it had looked in the corridor off the ballroom, tired and rather pale. I saw the black hair growing in a peak on his forehead, the eyebrows going up at the corners, the little lines at the sides of his mouth. When first he shaved his beard I thought he was quite handsome, but that was only because he looked so much younger and so much less odd; I know now that he isn't handsome—compared with Stephen's, his looks aren't anything at all.

And yet as my eyes turned to Stephen facing the sunrise, from Simon in the darkness of my mind, it was as if Simon's had been the living face and Stephen's the one I was imagining —or a photograph, a painting, something beautiful but not really alive for me. My whole heart was so full of Simon that even my pity for Stephen wasn't quite real—it was only something I felt I ought to feel, more from my head than my heart. And I knew I ought to pity him all the more because I could pity him so little.

I cried out: "Oh, please, please stop! I'm so fond of you— and so deeply grateful. But I could never marry you. Oh, Stephen, dear—I'm so very sorry."

"That's all right," he said, staring in front of him again.

"Well, at least we're companions in misfortune," I said.

Then Heloïse stood up and put her front paws on the parapet, between us, and my tears dropped down and made grey spots on her gleaming white head.

Chapter XV

I AM WRITING THIS AT FATHER'S DESK IN THE GATEHOUSE. If it were the King's desk in Buckingham Palace I could not be more surprised.

It is now half-past nine in the evening. (This time last week I was talking to Simon in that corridor off the ballroom—it feels like years and years ago.) I mean to work at this journal until I wake Thomas at two o'clock. Last night he kept this watch and I took the second one. And very dreadful I felt during most of it. I am less upset to-night, but still get nervous sinkings in my stomach every now and then. Oh, have we accomplished a miracle—or done something so terrible that I daren't face thinking about it?

I never finished my last entry—the memory of my tears falling on Heloïse so flooded me with self-pity that I couldn't go on. But there wasn't much more to say about the trip to London. We came back on the first train. I slept most of the way, and slept again when we got home.

It was the middle of the afternoon when I woke up—to find myself alone in the castle; Stephen had gone over to Four Stones, father was at Scoatney and Thomas was spending the week-end with his friend Harry. Stephen came home around nine o'clock and went to bed without disturbing me—I was up in the attic writing this journal. As I heard him crossing the courtyard I wondered if I ought to go down and talk to him, but I felt there was nothing helpful I could say. Later on, I thought I would at least make him some cocoa and chat about his film job, but by the time I got to the kitchen the light in his room was out.

He went back to London early on Monday morning, with his clothes in a little iron-bound sea-chest that old Mrs. Stebbins lent him: it had belonged to her brother who ran away to be a cabin boy. I didn't go to the station because Stephen told me Mr. Stebbins was driving him there and I guessed Ivy would go, too. I felt Stephen ought to have every chance to find consolation—and I would rather he found it with Ivy than with Leda, because Ivy is a really nice girl. I went out to talk to her and Mr. Stebbins when they drove up, as Stephen wasn't quite ready. Ivy had on a pale grey suit, tight white gloves, and the brightest blue hat I ever saw, which accentuated the red in her cheeks. She *is* a good-looking girl. Enormous feet, though.

Stephen was so long coming that I went to find out what he was doing. I saw him through the open door of his bedroom, just staring around him. The window is so overgrown now that he seemed to be in a green cavern.

"Perhaps you'll be famous when you see this room again," I said. "Though don't wait too long before you come and stay with us, will you?"

"I won't be coming back," he said, quietly, "even if I'm no good as an actor. No, I won't come back."

I said of course he would, but he shook his head. Then he gave one last look round the room. The photographs of me and his mother were gone. The bed was stripped and the one blanket neatly folded.

"I've swept the room out so that you won't have anything extra to do," he said. "You can shut this place up and forget it. I gave Mr. Mortmain his books back before he went off to Scoatney. I'll miss having books."

"But you can buy them for yourself now," I told him.

He said he hadn't thought of that—"I don't seem able to take in the money part, somehow."

"Mind you save—just in case," I warned him.

He nodded and said he'd probably soon be feeding pigs again. Then we heard Mr. Stebbins hooting his horn.

I said: "I'll see you off but let's say a private good-bye here." I held out my hand, but added: "Please kiss me if you'd like to—I'd like it if you would."

For a second I thought he was going to; then he shook his head and barely clasped my hand. I tried to help him carry the little sea-chest but he hoisted it up on his shoulder. We went out to the car. Heloïse was there, investigating the wheels, and after Stephen had strapped the chest on to the luggage-carrier he stooped and kissed her on the head. He never looked back once as they drove along the lane.

While I was washing up the breakfast things, I realized that I had no idea where he would be staying. Would he go back to the Fox-Cottons? I suppose Rose will know. (I wrote to her that morning, saying I had been in the wrong and asking her to forgive me. I must say she took her time about answering; but this afternoon I had a telegram from her which said she would write when she could and would I please try to understand. She didn't put in anything about forgiving me but as it was signed "your ever loving Rose" I suppose she has.)

I worked on my journal most of Monday, finishing in floods of tears too late to get my face right before Thomas came home. He said: "You've been howling, haven't you? I suppose the castle's depressing after being in London"—which made things nice and easy for me. I said yes, that was it, and that it had been sad seeing Stephen go and wondering what would happen to him.

"I wouldn't worry about Stephen," said Thomas. "He's sure to be a riot on the pictures. All the girls in the village are in love with him—they used to hang about on the Godsend road trying to waylay him. One of these days you're going to find out what you've missed."

I started to get tea; Thomas had brought a haddock.

"Father'll get tea at Scoatney, so we needn't wait," I said.

"The servants must be tired of feeding him," said Thomas. "What does he do there, day after day? Does he just read for the fun of it, or is he up to something?"

"Ah, if we only knew that," I said.

"Harry says he ought to be psycho-analysed."

I turned in astonishment. "Does Harry know about psycho-analysis?"

"His father talks about it sometimes—he's a doctor, you know."

"Does he believe in it?"

"No, he's always very sneery. But Harry rather fancies it."

I had to concentrate on cooking the haddock then; but while we were eating it I brought up the subject of psycho-analysis again, and told Thomas of the conversation Simon and I had about it that first time we talked on the mound—though I couldn't remember it very clearly.

"I wish I'd got Simon to tell me more," I said. "Would Harry's father have any helpful books, do you think?"

Thomas said he would find out, though now that Rose was going to marry Simon, it didn't matter so much whether father wrote or not.

"Oh, Thomas, it does!" I cried. "It matters most terribly to father. And to us, too—because if all the eccentric things he's been doing, on and off for months now, aren't leading somewhere, well, then he *is* going crazy. And a crazy father's not a good idea, quite apart from our tender feelings towards him."

"Have you tender feelings towards him? I don't know that I have—not that I dislike him."

Just then, father came in. He barely said "Hello" in answer to mine and started up the kitchen stairs to his bedroom. Half-way up, he stopped and looked down at us; then came back quickly.

"Can you spare me this?" he asked, picking up the back-bone of the haddock between his forefinger and thumb.

I thought he was being sarcastic—that he meant we had left him no fish. I explained that we hadn't expected him, and offered to cook some eggs at once.

He said: "Oh, I've had tea," and then carried the haddock-bone, dripping milk, out through the back door and across to the gatehouse. Ab followed him hopefully. By the time he got back—a very disappointed cat—Thomas and I were lurching about, laughing in a way that hurts.

"Oh, poor Ab!" I gasped, as I gave him some scraps from my plate. "Stop laughing, Thomas. We shall be ashamed of our callousness if father really is going off his head."

"He isn't—he's putting it on or something," said Thomas. Then a scared look came into his eyes and he added: "Try to keep knives away from him. I'm going to talk to Harry's father to-morrow."

But Harry's father wasn't in the least helpful.

"He says he's not a psycho-analyst or a psychiatrist or a psycho-anything, thank God," Thomas told me, when he got back in the evening. "And he couldn't think why we wanted to make father write again, because he once had a look at *Jacob Wrestling* and didn't understand a word of it. Harry was quite embarrassed."

"Does Harry understand it, then?"

"Yes, of course he does—it's the first I've heard about its being hard to understand. Anyway, what's double-Dutch to one generation's just 'The cat sat on the mat' to the next."

"Even the ladder chapter?"

"Oh, that!" Thomas smiled tolerantly. "That's just father's fun. And who says you always have to understand things? You can like them without understanding them—like 'em better sometimes. I ought to have known Harry's father would be no help to us—he's the kind of man who says he enjoys a good yarn."

I certainly have been under-estimating Thomas—only a few weeks ago I should have expected him to enjoy a good yarn himself. And now I find he has read quite a lot of difficult modern poetry (some master at his school lent it to him) and taken it in his stride. I wish he had let me read it—though I know very well *I* can't like things without understanding them. I am astonished to discover how high-brow his tastes are—far more so than mine; and it is most peculiar how he can be so appreciative of all forms of art, but so matter-of-fact and unemotional about it. But then, he is like that over most things—he has been so calm and assured this last week that I often felt he was older than I was. Yet he can get the giggles and plunge back into being the most ordinary schoolboy. Really, the puzzlingness of people!

After we talked about Harry's father, Thomas settled down to his homework and I wandered out into the lane. There was a vast red sunset full of strangely shaped, prophetic-looking clouds, and a hot due-south wind was blowing—an exciting sort of wind, I always think; we don't often get it. But I was too depressed to take much interest in the evening. All day long I had been hopeful about psycho-analysis; I had expected Thomas to bring home some books we could get our teeth into. And I hadn't only been thinking of father's welfare. Early that morning it had struck me that if he started writing again, Rose might believe there would be enough money coming in to make life bearable, and still might break her engagement off. I wasn't banking on winning Simon even if she gave him up. But I knew, and shall always know, that he ought not to marry a girl who feels towards him as Rose does.

I went to the end of the lane and turned on to the Godsend road, trying all the time to think of some way of helping both father and myself. When I came to the high part of the road I looked back and saw his lamp alight in the gatehouse. I thought how often I had seen it shining across the fields on my summer evening walks, and how it always conjured up an image of him—remote, withdrawn, unapproachable. I said to myself: "Surely one ought to know a little more of one's father than we do?" And as I began walking back to the castle I wondered if the fault could be ours, as well as his. Had I myself really tried to make friends with him? I was sure I had in the past—but had I lately? No. I excused myself by thinking: "Oh, it's hopeless to make friends with people who never talk about themselves." And then it came to me that one of the few things I do know about psycho-analysis is that people have to be *made* to talk about themselves. Had I tried hard enough with father—hadn't I always been rebuffed too easily? "Are you frightened of him?" I asked myself. I knew in my heart that I was. But why? "Has he ever in his life struck any of you?" Never. His only weapon has been silence—and sometimes a little sarcasm. "Then what is this insurmountable barrier round him? What's it made of? Where did it come from?"

It had become as if someone outside myself were asking the questions, attacking me with them. I tried to find answers. I wondered if mother's training that we must never worry or disturb him had gone on operating—and Topaz had perpetuated it by her habit of protecting him. I wondered if I had some undetected fear left from the day when I saw him brandishing the cake-knife—if I believed, without ever having admitted it, that he really did mean to stab mother. "Heavens," I thought, "I'm psycho-analysing myself, now! If only I could do this to father!"

I had come round the last bend of the lane and could see him through the lamp-lit window of the gatehouse. What was he doing? The fact that he was at his desk didn't necessarily mean he was writing—he always sits there when reading the *Encyclopædia*, because it is so heavy to hold. Was he reading now? His head was bent, but I couldn't see what over. Just then he raised his hand to push his hair back. He was holding a pencil! And that instant, the voice that had been attacking me as I walked home said: "Suppose he's really working all the time? Supposing he's writing some wonderful, money-earning book—but you don't find out until it's too late to help you and Rose?"

I began walking towards the castle again. I don't remember planning anything, even making a definite decision—it was as if my mind could not go ahead of my steps. I went into the dimness of the gatehouse passage, then into the blackness of the tower staircase. I groped my way up to father's door. I knocked on it.

"Go away," came the instant reply.

The key was in the outside keyhole so I knew he hadn't locked himself in. I opened the door.

As I went in, he swung round from his desk looking furious. But almost before I had time to notice his expression it was as if a curtain came down over it, and the fury was hidden.

"Something important?" he asked, in a perfectly controlled voice.

"Yes. Very," I said, and shut the door behind me.

He got up, looking at me closely. "What's the matter, Cassandra? You're unusually pale. Are you ill? You'd better sit down."

But I didn't sit. I stood there staring at the room. Something had happened to it. Facing me, instead of the long rows of bookshelves stretching between the north and south windows, was an expanse of brightly coloured paper.

"Heavens, what have you been doing in here?" I gasped.

He saw what I was staring at. "Oh, those are just American comic strips—commonly called 'the funnies.' Now what is it, Cassandra?"

I went closer and saw that what I had taken for wallpaper was sheets and sheets from newspapers, the top edges of which were tacked to the edges of the bookshelves. In the dim light from the lamp I couldn't see the pictures clearly, but they seemed to be small coloured illustrations joined together.

"Where did they come from?" I asked.

"I brought them back from Scoatney yesterday. They're from the American Sunday papers—I gather Neil can't live without them. Good heavens, don't start reading them."

"Are they to do with your work?"

He opened his mouth to reply, and then a nervous, secretive look came into his eyes.

"What have you come here for?" he said sharply. "Never you mind about my work."

I said: "But it's that I've come about. Father, you've got to let me know what you're doing."

For a second he stared at me in silence. Then he said icily: "And is that the sole reason for this visitation—to cross-examine me?"

"No, no," I began, and then pulled myself up. "Yes, it is—it's exactly that. And I'm not giving up until I get an answer."

"Out you go," said father.

He took me by the arm and marched me to the door—I was so astonished that I put up hardly any resistance. But at the last second, I jerked away from him and dashed across to his desk. I had a wild hope that I might see some of his work there. He was after me instantly, but I just had time to catch a glimpse of pages and pages with long lists on them in his writing. Then he grabbed me by the wrist and pulled me round —never have I seen such fury as was in his eyes. He flung me away from the desk with such force that I went right across the room and crashed into the door. It hurt so badly that I let out a yell and burst into tears.

"Oh, God, is it your elbow?" said father. "That can be agony."

He came over and tried to feel if there were any broken bones—even through the pain I noticed how astonishingly his anger had vanished. I went on choking with tears—it really was agony, right down to my wrist and hand. After a minute or so, father began to walk me up and down, with his arm round me.

"It's going off," I told him as soon as I could. "Let me sit down for a bit."

We sat on the sofa together and he lent me his handkerchief to mop up on. Soon I was able to say:

"It's almost better now—look!" I moved my hand and arm to show him. "It was nothing serious."

"It might have been," he said in a queer, strained voice. "I haven't lost my temper like that since——" He stopped dead, then got up and went back to his desk.

I said: "Not since you went for mother with the cake-knife?"—and was astounded to hear the words coming out of my mouth. I added hastily: "Of course I know you didn't really go for her, it was all a mistake, but—well, you were very angry with her. Oh, father—do you think that's what has been the matter with you—that you stopped getting violent? Has repressing your temper somehow repressed your talent?"

He gave a sarcastic snort and didn't even bother to look round. "Who put that brilliant idea into your head? Was it Topaz?"

"No, I thought of it myself—just this minute."

"Very ingenious of you. But it happens to be nonsense."

"Well, it's no sillier than believing you dried up because you went to prison," I said—astonishing myself again. "Some people do think that, you know."

"Idiots!" said father. "Good God, how could a few months in prison do me any harm? I've often thought I'd like to be back there; at least the warders never sat round holding post-mortems on me. Oh, for the peace of that little cell!"

His tone was very sarcastic but nothing like so angry as I had expected, so I plucked up my courage to go on. "Have you any idea yourself what stopped you working?"—I kept my voice calm and conversational. "Simon thinks, of course——"

He swung round instantly, interrupting me. "Simon? Were you and he discussing me?"

"Well, we were being interested in you——"

"And what theories did Simon put forward?"

I had meant to say that Simon had suggested psycho-analysis, but father looked so angry again that I funked it and racked my brains for something more tactful. At last I brought out: "Well, he once thought you might have been held back because you were such an original writer that you couldn't just develop like ordinary writers—that you'd have to find some quite new way——" I was floundering, so I finished up quickly. "He said something like it that first evening they ever came here—don't you remember?"

"Yes, perfectly," said father, relaxing. "I was very much impressed. I've since come to the conclusion that it was merely a bit of supremely tactful nonsense on Simon's part, God bless him; but at the time it certainly fooled me. I'm not at all sure that wasn't what started me on——" He broke off. "Well, well, run along to bed, my child."

I cried out: "Oh, father—do you mean you *have* found a new way to work? Do all these crazy things—the crosswords and *Little Folks* and *The Homing Pigeon* and what not—do they really mean something?"

"Great heavens, what do you take me for? Of course they mean something."

"Even the willow-pattern plate—and trying to read gramophone records? How exciting! Though I simply can't imagine——"

"You don't have to," said father, firmly. "You just have to mind your own business."

"But couldn't I help you? I'm reasonably intelligent, you know. Don't you ever feel you want to talk to anyone?"

"I do not," said father. "Talk, talk—you're as bad as Topaz. As if either of you would have the remotest idea what

299

I was driving at! And if I'd talked to her, she'd have told every painter in London—and you'd tell Simon and he'd write a well-turned article about it. Good Lord, how long does an innovation remain one if it's talked about? And, anyway, with me secrecy's the very essence of creation. Now go away!"

I said: "I will if you'll answer me just one question. How long will it be before the book's finished?"

"Finished? It isn't even begun! I'm still collecting material —though that'll go on indefinitely, of course." He began to walk about, talking more to himself than to me. "I believe I could make a start now if I could get a scaffolding that really satisfied me. I need a backbone——"

"Was that why you took the haddock's?" I said involuntarily.

He turned on me at once. "Don't be facetious!" Then I think he saw from my face that I hadn't meant to be, because he gave a snort of laughter and went on: "No, the haddock may be said to have turned into a red herring across the trail— lots of things do. I don't know, though—the ladderlike pattern was interesting. I must study the fishes of the world—and whales—and the forerunners of whales——" He was talking to himself again, moving about the room. I kept dead quiet. He went on: "Primeval, antediluvian—the ark? No, not the Bible again. Prehistoric—from the smallest bone of the mammoth? Is there a way there?" He hurried to his desk and made a note; then sat there, still talking to himself. I could only make out broken phrases and disjointed words—things like: "Design, deduction, reconstruction—symbol—pattern and problem—search forever unfolding—enigma eternal . . ." His voice got quieter and quieter until at last he was silent.

I sat there staring at the back of his head framed in the heavy stone mullions of the window beyond it. The lamp on his desk made the twilight seem a deep, deep blue. The tick of the little travelling clock that used to be mother's sounded unbelievably loud in the quietness. I wondered if the idea he was searching for was coming to him. I prayed it might—for his own happiness; by then I had no hope it could be in time to help Rose and me.

After a few minutes I began to think I had better creep out, but I was afraid that opening the door would make a noise. "And if his idea *has* come," I thought, "disturbing him now might wreck everything." Then it struck me that if he once got used to having me in the room, I might be a real help—it came back to me that he had liked mother to sit with him while he wrote, provided she kept quite still; he wouldn't even let her sew. I remembered her telling me how hard she had found it in the beginning, how she had told herself she would manage just five more minutes, then another five—until the minutes grew into hours. I said to myself: "In ten minutes her little clock will chime nine. I'll sit still until then." But after a couple of minutes, bits of me began to tickle maddeningly. I stared at the lamplit face of the clock almost praying to it to hurry—its ticking seemed to get louder and louder, until it was right inside my ears. I had just got to a stage when I felt I couldn't bear it a second longer when the wind burst one of the south windows open, the American newspapers tacked to the bookshelves blew up with a great flap, and father swung round.

His eyes seemed to have sunk deeper into his head; he blinked—I could see he was coming back from very far away. I expected him to be angry at my still being there, but he just said "Hello" with a sort of dazed pleasantness.

"Was the idea any good?" I ventured.

For a second, he didn't seem to know what I was talking about. Then he said: "No, no—another marsh light. Were you holding your fingers crossed for me, poor mouselike child? Your mother used to sit like that."

"I know. I was thinking of her a minute ago."

"Were you? So was I. Probably telepathy."

The newspapers flapped again and he went to close the window; then stood looking down into the courtyard. I thought he was going to forget me again, so I said, quickly:

"Mother helped you quite a lot, didn't she?"

"Yes, in an odd, oblique way." He sat down on the window-seat apparently quite prepared for a little chat. "God knows she never had an idea in her head, dear woman, but she'd the most extraordinary habit of saying useful things by accident—

301

like mentioning the name 'Jacob' when I was searching for a central idea for *Jacob Wrestling*. Actually, she was talking about the milkman. And having her in the room seemed to give me confidence—the atmosphere used to become quite thick with her prayers. Well, good night, my child——" He got up and came towards me. "Is the elbow better?"

I said: "Quite, thank you."

"Good. Next time you come I'll try to give you a better welcome—put the red carpet down. But you must wait until you're invited. I must say I'm curious to know what keyed you up to this attack to-night. Mrs. Cotton wasn't doing a little prodding by proxy, was she?"

"Gracious, no!" Of course I had no intention of telling him my real reason for coming; it would have worried him quite uselessly, besides being unfair to Rose. "It was only that I was anxious."

"Good Lord, do you mean about my state of mind?" He chuckled, then looked concerned. "You poor girl, did you really think my brain was going? Well, I daresay I seemed pretty eccentric, and plenty of people will think that's an understatement when this book gets out. If it ever does. Why can't I take the plunge? It's just the initial idea that eludes me. I've lost confidence, you know—it isn't laziness, I swear"—there was a humble, almost pleading note in his voice—"it never has been—I hope you believe that, my dear. It—well, it just hasn't been possible."

I said: "Of course I believe it. And I believe you're going to start very soon now."

"I hope so." He laughed a little, in an odd, nervous kind of way. "Because if I don't get going soon, the whole impetus may die—and if that happens, well, I really shall consider a long, restful plunge into insanity. Sometimes the abyss yawns very attractively. There, there—don't take me seriously."

"Of course not," I said briskly. "Now, look, father. Why not let me sit here as mother used to? I'll pray, as she did; I'm really quite good at it. And you go to your desk and start this very night."

"No, no, I couldn't yet"—he looked positively frightened.

302

"I know you mean well, my dear, but you're making me nervous. Now run along to bed. I'm going, myself."

He lifted up the American papers and dived under to the shelf holding his old detective novels, grabbing one quite at random. Then he put the lamp out. Just as we went out of the room, mother's little clock began to strike nine. Even after father had locked the door and we were groping our way down the pitch-black stairs, I could hear the tiny, tinkling chimes.

"I must remember to carry matches," he said, "now there's no Stephen to leave a lamp outside my door."

I said I would see to it in future. There was no lantern in the gatehouse passage, either—another of Stephen's jobs; all the time I find out more and more things he did without my ever realizing it.

"Let me make you some cocoa, father," I suggested as we went into the kitchen, but he said he didn't need anything— "Except a biscuit, perhaps—and find me a candle with at least three hours' reading in it." I gave him a whole plate of biscuits and a new candle. "The richness of our life these days never ceases to astonish me," he said as he went up to bed.

Thomas was deep in his homework, at the kitchen table. I waited until I heard father go through to Windsor Castle, then said quietly: "Come on out, I've got to talk to you. Bring a lantern so that we can go into the lane—I don't want father to hear our voices through some open window."

We went as far as the stile, and sat on it with the lantern balanced between us. Then I told him everything—except my true reason for bearding father; I said it was due to a sudden impulse.

"Well, how does it sound to you?" I finished up.

"Perfectly awful," said Thomas. "I'm afraid he really is going crazy."

I was taken aback. "Then I've made him sound worse than he seemed—through telling it too quickly. It was only at the very end that his manner was odd—and a bit, perhaps, when he was talking to himself, about whales and mammoths."

"But all those changes of manner—being furious with you one minute and then really pleasant. And when you add up all the silly things he's been interested in lately—oh, lord, when I think of him taking that haddock bone——" He began to laugh.

I said: "Don't, Thomas—it's like people in the eighteenth century laughing at the lunatics in Bedlam."

"Well, I bet I'd have laughed at them myself—things can be funny even when they're awful, you know. But, I wonder" —he was suddenly serious—"are we like Harry's father jeering at *Jacob Wrestling*? Perhaps he really has something up his sleeve. Though I don't like the sound of all those lists he's making—it's like taking too many notes at school; you feel you've achieved something when you haven't."

"You mean he may never get going on the book itself." I was quiet for a minute, staring into the lantern, though what I saw all the time was father's face when he was looking humble and nervous. "Oh, Thomas, if he doesn't, I think he *will* go out of his mind. He said he wasn't serious about plunging into insanity, but I believe I felt he was. He may be a border-line case—madness and genius are very close to each other, aren't they? If only we could push him the right way!"

"Well, you haven't made much of a start to-night," said Thomas, "you've just driven him to bed with a detective novel. Anyway, I'm going in. Whether father's sane or off his rocker, I've still got to do my algebra."

"You can make him *x*, the unknown quantity," I said. "I think I shall stay here for a while. Can you manage without the lantern?"

He said he could—there was quite a bit of starlight. "Though it won't do you any good to sit here brooding," he added.

But I didn't plan to brood. I had decided to look up the record of my talk with Simon about psycho-analysis, on the off-chance of finding something helpful; and I had no intention of letting Thomas know where my journal was hidden. I waited until I felt sure he would be back in the castle, then cut across the meadow and climbed the mound. A little cloud of white moths came all the way with me, hovering round the lantern.

It felt strange going from the warm, blowy night into the cool stillness of Belmotte Tower. As I climbed down the ladder

inside I thought of being there with Simon on Midsummer Eve
—as I do every time I go into the tower. Then I pulled myself
together. "This may be your last hope of keeping your father
out of a padded cell," I told myself severely. And by then a
faint flicker of hope on my own account had re-awakened. I
felt that if I once got him even started on an important book,
Rose just might be persuaded to *postpone* her marriage—and
then anything might happen.

I crawled up the crumbling staircase and brought down my
bread-tin—I have used that for some time now, because ants
kept getting into the attaché case. I spread my three journals
out on the old iron bedstead and sat there looking through
them; I could read quite well by the light from the lantern. It
didn't take me long to find the entry for May Day, with the bit
about psycho-analysis.

First came the speech in which Simon said he didn't believe
father stopped writing just because he had been in prison—
that the trouble probably lay much further back. But prison
might have brought it to the surface. Anyway, a psycho-
analyst would certainly ask father questions about the time he
spent there—in a way, try to put him mentally back in prison.
And then there was the bit about it being possible that another
period of physical imprisonment might resolve the trouble.
But Simon said that was unworkable as a treatment, because it
couldn't be done without father's consent—and if he gave it,
of course he wouldn't *feel* imprisoned.

There didn't seem to be anything I could do along those
lines. I glanced through another page in case I had missed
something, and came to the description of Simon's face as he
lay on the grass with his eyes closed. It gave me a stab in
which happiness and misery were somehow a part of each other.
I closed the journal and sat staring up into the dark shaft of
the tower.

And then——! Suddenly the whole plan was complete in
my mind almost to the last detail. But surely I meant it as a
joke then? I remember thinking how it would make Thomas
laugh. It was still a joke while I put my journals away and
began to climb out of the tower—I had to mount the ladder

very slowly because I needed one hand for the lantern. I was half-way up when the extraordinary thing happened. Godsend church clock had begun to strike ten—and suddenly, as well as the far-off booming bell, I heard in memory the tinkling chime of mother's little travelling clock. And then my mind's eye saw her face—not the photograph of it, which is what I always see when I think of her, but her face as it was. I saw her light brown hair and freckled skin—I had forgotten until then that she had freckles. And that same instant, I heard her voice in my head—after all these years of not being able to hear it. A quiet, clipped little voice it was, completely matter-of-fact. It said: "Do you know, dear, I believe that scheme of yours might work quite well?" I heard my own voice answer: "But, mother—surely we couldn't? It's fantastic——" "Well, your father's quite a fantastic man," said mother's voice.

That second, a gust of wind slammed the tower door just above me, startling me so that I nearly lost my footing on the ladder. I steadied myself, then listened again for mother's voice, asked her questions—— All I heard was the last stroke of the church clock. But my mind was made up.

I hurried back to the castle and got Thomas to come out again. To my surprise, he didn't think my plan was as wild as I did myself—he was dead keen from the beginning, and most businesslike.

"You give me the housekeeping money and to-morrow I'll buy everything we need," he said. "And then we'll do it the very next day. We've got to act quickly, because Topaz may be home next week."

I didn't mention my strange experience of being advised by mother; I might have if he had put up any opposition to the scheme, but he never did. Do I really believe I was in touch with mother—or was it something deep in myself choosing that way to advise me? I don't know. I only know that it happened.

Father went to Scoatney the next morning, so there was no danger of his seeing what I was up to. By the time Thomas came home I had everything in readiness except for the few things that were too heavy for me to carry alone. He helped me with those and then we made our final plans. "And we must do it the first thing after breakfast," said Thomas, "or he may go off to Scoatney again."

The minute I woke up on Thursday morning I thought: "I can't go through with it. It's dangerous—something dreadful might happen." And then I remembered father saying that if he didn't start work soon the impetus might die. All the time I was dressing I kept thinking: "Oh, if only I could be sure it's the right thing to do!" I tried to get more advice from mother. Nothing happened. I tried praying to God. Nothing happened. I prayed to "Anyone who is listening, please"—to the morning sun—to Nature, via the wheat field . . . At last I decided to toss for it. And just then Thomas came rushing in to say that father wasn't waiting until after breakfast, would be off to Scoatney at any minute—and instantly I knew that I did want to carry through our scheme, that I couldn't bear not to.

The squeak of bicycle tyres being pumped up came in through the open window.

"It's too late. We're sunk for to-day," said Thomas.

"Not yet," I said. "Get out of the house without letting him see you—go along the walls and down the gatehouse stairs. Then dash up the mound and hide behind the tower. Be ready to help. Go on—quick!"

He bolted off and I hurried down to the courtyard, pretending to be very worried that father was leaving without his breakfast. "Oh, they'll give me some at Scoatney," he said airily. Then I talked about his bicycle, offering to clean it for him, telling him it needed new tyres. "Let me pump that back one a bit harder for you," I said, and kept at it until I felt Thomas would have had enough time. Then, just as I was handing the bicycle over, I remarked casually: "Oh, can you spare a minute to come up to Belmotte Tower? I think you may want to let someone at Scoatney know what's been happening in there."

"Oh, lord, did that last heavy rain do a lot of damage?" said father.

"Well, I think you'll see quite a few changes," I said, with the utmost truthfulness.

We crossed the bridge and started to climb the mound.

"One doesn't often see an English sky as blue as this," he said. "I wonder if Simon's agent has authority to do repairs to the tower?"

He went on chatting most pleasantly and normally. All my misgivings were rushing back; but I felt the die was cast.

"Really, I ought to spend more time in here," he said as he followed me up the steps outside the tower. I opened the heavy oak door and stood back for him to pass me. He climbed down the ladder inside and stood blinking his eyes.

"Can't see much yet, after the sunlight," he called up, peering around. "Hello, have you been camping-out down here?"

"One of us is going to," I said—then added quickly: "Go up the staircase a little way, will you?"

"The crumbling's worse, is it?" He went through the archway and began to make his way up the stairs.

Thomas had already crept from behind the tower. I beckoned and he was beside me in a flash. Together we dragged the ladder up and flung it down outside.

Father shouted: "Come and show me what you mean, Cassandra."

"Don't say anything until he comes back," whispered Thomas.

Father called again and I still didn't answer. After a few seconds he returned through the archway.

"Couldn't you hear me calling?" he said, looking up at us. "Hello, Thomas, why haven't you gone to school?"

We stared down at him. Now that the ladder had gone he seemed much further away from us; the circle of stone walls rose round him dungeonlike. He was so foreshortened that he seemed only to have a face, shoulders and feet.

"What's the matter? Why don't you answer?" he shouted. I racked my brains to think of the most tactful way of telling him what had happened to him. At last I managed: "Will you please look round you, father? It's a sort of surprise."

We had put the mattress from the four-poster on the old iron bedstead, with blankets and pillows. The most inviting new stationery was spread on the rustic table, with stones to use as paper-weights. We had given him the kitchen arm-chair.

"There are washing arrangements and drinking water in the garderobe," I called down—my enamel jug and basin had come in handy again. "We think you'll have enough light to work by, now we've cleared the ivy from all the lowest arrow-slits— we'll give you a lantern at night, of course. Very good meals will be coming down in a basket—we bought a Thermos . . ." I couldn't go on—the expression on his face was too much for me. He had just taken in that the ladder wasn't there any more.

"Great God in heaven!" he began—and then sat down on the bed and let out a roar of laughter. He laughed and laughed until I began to fear he would suffocate.

"Oh, Thomas!" I whispered. "Have we pushed him over to the wrong side of the border-line?"

Father mopped his eyes. "My dear, dear children!" he said at last. "Cassandra, are you—what is it, seventeen, eighteen? Or are you eight? Bring that ladder back at once."

"*You* say something, Thomas," I whispered.

He cleared his throat and said very slowly and loudly: "We think you ought to start work, father—for your own sake far more than for ours. And we think being shut up here may help you to concentrate—and be good for you in other ways. I assure you we've given the matter a lot of thought and are in line with psycho-analysis——"

"Bring back that ladder!" roared father. I could see that Thomas's weighty manner had infuriated him.

"There's no point in arguing," said Thomas, calmly. "We'll leave you to get settled. You can tell us at lunch-time if there are any books or papers you need for your work."

"Don't you dare go away!" Father's voice cracked so pitifully that I said quickly:

"Please don't exhaust yourself by shouting for help, because there's no one but us within miles. Oh, father, it's an ex- periment—give it a chance."

"But, you little lunatic——" father began, furiously.

Thomas whispered to me: "I warn you this will only develop into a brawl. Let me get the door shut."

It was a brawl already on father's side. I stood back and Thomas closed the door.

"Luncheon at one, father," I called encouragingly.

We locked and bolted the door. There wasn't the faintest chance that father could climb up to it, but we felt the psychological effect would be good. As we went down the mound, father's yelling sounded surprisingly weak; by the time we reached the bridge we couldn't hear it at all.

I said: "Do you think he's fainted?"

Thomas went a little way up the mound. "No, I can still hear him. It's just that the tower's a sound-trap."

I stared back at it. "Oh, Thomas, have we done something insane?"

"Not a bit," said Thomas, cheerfully. "You know, even the change of atmosphere may be enough to help him."

"But to lock him in—and it used to be a dungeon! To imprison one's father!"

"Well, that's the whole idea, isn't it? Not that I set quite as much store on the psycho stuff as you do. Personally, I think knowing he won't be let out until he's done some work is almost more important."

"That's nonsense," I said. "If it doesn't come right psychologically—from the depths of father—it won't come right at all. You can't trammel the creative mind."

"Why not?" said Thomas. "His creative mind's been untrammelled for years without doing a hand's-turn. Let's see what trammelling does for it."

We went indoors and had breakfast—it seemed awful that father was starting his adventure on an empty stomach, but I knew we should be making that up to him soon. Then I wrote to Thomas's school to say he would be indisposed for a few days, and went up to make the beds. Thomas kindly undertook the dusting.

"Hello!" he said suddenly. "Look at this!"

The key to the gatehouse room was lying on father's dressing-table.

"Let's go in and have a look at those lists you told me about," said Thomas.

As we climbed the gatehouse stairs I said: "Oh, Thomas, is it like spying?"

"Yes, of course it is," said Thomas, unlocking the door.

I suddenly felt frightened as well as guilty—it was as if part of father's mind was still in the room and furious with us for intruding. Sunlight was streaming through the south window, the "comic strips" were still tacked to the bookshelves, mother's little clock was ticking away on the desk. But the lists weren't there any longer—and the desk was locked.

I was glad we couldn't find anything. I felt worse about snooping round his room than about locking him up in the tower.

Thomas stayed to read the comic strips while I began preparations for father's lunch. At one o'clock we took it out in a basket—soup in a Thermos, chicken salad, strawberries and cream, and a cigar (ninepence).

"I wonder if we're right to pamper him with this rich food," said Thomas as we started up the mound. "Bread and water would create the prison atmosphere better."

Everything was quiet when we got up to the tower. We unlocked the door and looked down. Father was lying on the bed, staring upwards.

"Hello," he said, in a perfectly pleasant voice.

I was astounded—and still more so when he smiled at us. Of course I smiled back, and said I hoped he had a good appetite.

Thomas began to lower the basket on a length of clothes-line.

"It's only a light luncheon, so that it won't make you sleepy," I explained. "There'll be a bigger meal to-night—with wine." I noticed he had already got himself a drink of water, which looked as if he were settling down a bit.

He thanked Thomas most politely for the basket and spread the contents out on the table; then smiled up at us.

"This is superb," he said, in his most genial voice. "Now, listen, you comics: I've had a long, quiet morning to think in—it's really been most pleasant, lying here watching the sky. I'm perfectly sincere when I say that I'm *touched* at your doing this to try to help me. And I'm not at all sure you haven't succeeded. It's been stimulating; I've had one or two splendid ideas. It's been a *success*—do you understand? But the novelty has worn off now—if you keep me here any longer, you'll undo your good work. Now I'm going to eat this delightful luncheon, and then you're going to bring back the ladder—aren't you?" His voice quavered on the "aren't you?" "And I swear there'll be no reprisals," he finished.

I looked at Thomas to see what he made of this. He just said, woodenly: "Any books or papers you want, father?"

"No, there aren't!" shouted father, his *bonhomie* suddenly departing. "All I want is to get out."

Thomas slammed the door.

"Dinner at seven," I called—but I doubt if father heard me as he was yelling louder than when we first locked him in. I hoped it wouldn't ruin his appetite.

I spent the early part of the afternoon reading the comic strips—you start by thinking they are silly, but they grow on you. Then I got everything ready for father's meal—it was to be full dinner, not just glorified tea: melon, cold salmon (we put it down the well to get it really cold), tinned peaches, cheese and biscuits, a bottle of white wine (three shillings), coffee and another ninepenny cigar. And about an egg-cup full of port which I still had in the medicine bottle.

We carried it all out on trays just as Godsend church clock struck seven. It was a glorious, peaceful evening. Soon after we crossed the bridge we could hear father yelling.

"Have you been wearing yourself out by shouting all afternoon?" I said, when Thomas had opened the door.

"Pretty nearly," said father—his voice sounded very hoarse. "Someone's bound to pass through the fields sooner or later."

"I doubt it," said Thomas. "The hay's all in and Mr. Stebbins isn't cutting his wheat for some weeks yet. Anyway, your voice doesn't carry beyond the mound. If you'll re-pack the lunch basket, I'll haul it up and send your dinner down."

I expected father to rave but he didn't even reply; and he at once began to do what Thomas had suggested. His movements were very awkward and jerky. He had taken off his coat and undone his collar, which gave him a pathetic look—rather as if he were ready to be led out to execution.

312

"We must bring him pyjamas and a dressing-gown for to-night," I whispered to Thomas.

Father heard me and jerked his head upwards. "If you leave me here all night I shall go out of my mind—I mean it, Cassandra. This—this sense of imprisonment, I'd forgotten how shocking it can be. Don't you know what it does to people—being shut up in small spaces? Haven't you heard of claustrophobia?"

"There's plenty of space upwards," I said, as firmly as I could. "And you never suffer from claustrophobia when you lock yourself in the gatehouse."

"But it's different when someone else locks you in." His voice cracked. "Oh, you damned little idiots—let me out! Let me out!"

I felt dreadful, but Thomas seemed quite unconcerned. He hauled up the basket father had filled, took out the plates and dishes, and put the dinner in. I think he knew I was weakening, because he whispered: "We've got to go through with it now. You leave it to me." Then he lowered the basket and called down, firmly:

"We'll let you out as soon as you've written something— say fifty pages."

"I never wrote fifty pages in less than three months even when I *could* write," said father, his voice cracking worse than ever. Then he flopped into the arm-chair and gripped his head with his hands.

"Just unpack your dinner, will you?" said Thomas. "You'd better take the coffee-pot out first."

Father looked up and his whole face went suddenly scarlet. Then he made a dive at the dinner basket, and the next second a plate flew past my head. A fork whizzed through the door just before we got it closed. Then we heard crockery breaking against it.

I sat down on the steps and burst into tears. Father croaked: "My God, are you hurt, Cassandra?" I put my face close to the crack under the door and called: "No, I'm perfectly all right. But please, please don't throw all your dinner dishes until you've eaten what's on them. Oh, won't you just *try* to write, father? Write anything—write 'The cat sat on the mat' if you like. Anything, as long as you write!"

Then I cried harder than ever. Thomas pulled me to my feet and steered me down the steps.

"We ought never to have done it," I sobbed as we went down the mound. "I shall let him out to-night even if he kills us."

"No, you won't—remember your oath." We had sworn not to give in until both of us agreed to it. "I'm not weakening yet. We'll see how he is after dinner."

As soon as the daylight began to fade, Thomas got the pyjamas and dressing-gown, and lit a lantern. There wasn't a sound as we approached the tower.

"Oh, Thomas—suppose he's dashed his head against the wall!" I whispered. And then a faint, reassuring smell of cigar smoke was wafted to us.

When we opened the door, father was sitting at the table with his back towards us. He turned round with the cigar in one hand and a pencil in the other.

"Your brilliant idea's done the trick!" he cried, hoarsely but happily. "The miracle's happened! I've begun!"

"Oh, how wonderful!" I gasped.

Thomas said in a level, most unexuberant voice: "That's splendid, father. May we see what you've written?"

"Certainly not—you wouldn't understand a word of it. But I assure you I've made a start. Now let me out."

"It's a ruse," Thomas whispered.

I said: "How many pages have you written, father?"

"Well, not many—the light's been very bad down here for the last hour——"

"You'll be all right with the lantern," said Thomas, beginning to lower it.

Father took it, and then said in a perfectly reasonable tone: "Thomas, I give you my word I have begun work—look, you can see for yourself." He held a sheet of paper close to the lantern, then whisked it away. "Cassandra, you write yourself, so you'll understand that one's first draft can be—well, not always convincing. Damn it, I've only started since dinner!

314

An excellent dinner, by the way; thank you very much. Now hurry up with that ladder—I want to get back to the gate-house and work all night."

"But you're in an ideal place to work all night," said Thomas. "Moving to the gatehouse would only disrupt you. Here are your pyjamas and dressing-gown. I'll come along early in the morning. Good night, father." He threw the clothes down, shut the door, and took me firmly by the elbow. "Come on, Cassandra."

I went without argument. I didn't believe father was bluffing, I believed our cure really had begun to work; but I thought it ought to have time to "take." And with father in that sane, controlled mood, I was quite willing to leave him there for the night.

"But we've got to keep guard," I said, "in case he sets fire to his bedding, or something."

We divided the night into watches. I slept—not very well—until two; then took over from Thomas. I went up the mound every hour, but the only thing I heard was a faint snore round about five o'clock.

I woke Thomas at seven this morning, intending to go up with him for the first visit of the day; but he slipped off on his own while I was in Windsor Castle. I met him coming back across the bridge. He said all was well and father had been pleased with the bucket of nice hot water he had taken up. "And I'm beginning to believe he really is working—he was certainly writing when I opened the door. He's calm, and he's getting much more co-operative—he had all his dinner things packed in the basket ready for me. And he says he'd like his breakfast now."

Each time we have gone up with meals to-day, he has been writing like mad. He still asks to be let out, but without wasting much breath on it. And when we took the lantern this evening, he said: "Come on, come on—I've been held up for that." Surely, surely he wouldn't carry on a bluff for so long? I would have let him out to-night, but Thomas says he must show us some of his work first.

It is now nearly four o'clock in the morning. I didn't wake

Thomas at two because I wanted to bring this entry up to date; and the poor boy is sleeping so exhaustedly—he is on the sofa here. He didn't think there was any need for us to keep watch to-night, but I insisted—apart from the fear of anything happening to father, the barometer is falling. Could we remain adamant if it rained heavily?

Thomas is firmer than I am. He sent an umbrella down with the lantern.

I have looked out of the south window every hour—our main reason for choosing the gatehouse to spend the night in is that we can see Belmotte Tower through one window and keep a watch on the lane through the other. Though who would come to the castle in the middle of the night? No one, no one. And yet I feel like a sentinel on guard.

Men must have kept guard in this gatehouse six hundred years ago. . . .

I have just had another look at the tower. The moon is shining full on it now. I had a queer feeling that it was more than inanimate stones. Does it know that it is playing a part in life again—that its dungeon once more encircles a sleeping prisoner?

Four o'clock now. Mother's little clock is beginning to seem alive in its own right—a small, squat, busy person a few inches from my hand.

How heavily Thomas is sleeping! Watching sleeping people makes one feel more separate than ever from them.

Heloïse is chasing rabbits through her dreams—she gives little nose-whimpers, her paws keep twitching. Ab honoured us with his company till midnight; now he is out hunting under the moon.

Surely we must let father out to-morrow—even if he still won't show us his work? His upturned face looked so strange as he took the lantern from us last night—almost saintlike, as if he had been seeing visions.

Perhaps it was only because he needed a shave.

Shall I wake Thomas now this journal is up to date? I don't feel at all sleepy. I am going to put the lamp out and sit in the moonlight. . . .

I can still see well enough to write. I remember writing by moonlight the night I started my journal. What a lot has happened since then!

I shall think of Simon now. Now? As if I didn't think of him all the time! Even while I have been so worried about father, a voice in my heart has kept saying: "But nothing *really* matters to you but Simon." Oh, if only Rose will break her engagement off, surely he will turn to me some day?

There is actually a car on the Godsend road! It is strange to watch the headlights and wonder who is driving through the night.

Oh, heavens! The car has turned into our lane! Oh, what am I to do?

Keep calm, keep calm—it has only taken the wrong turning. It will back out, or at worst turn round when it gets to the castle. But people who get as far as the castle usually stop to stare at it—and if father has heard the car, could his voice possibly carry? It just might, in the still night air. Oh, go back, go back!

It is coming on and on. I feel like someone keeping a journal to the last second of an approaching catastrophe——

The catastrophe has happened. Simon and Topaz are getting out of the car.

Chapter XVI

WE RAN INTO THE KITCHEN JUST AS TOPAZ WAS STRIKING A match to light the lamp. I heard Simon's voice before I saw his face.

"Is Rose here?"

"Rose?" I must have sounded utterly blank.

"Oh, my God!" said Simon.

The lamp shone out and I caught his look of utter misery.

"She's disappeared," said Topaz. "Now don't be frightened —it's not an accident or anything; she left a note for Simon. But——" She looked at him quickly, then went on: "It didn't really explain anything. Apparently she went off this morning. Simon was away driving his mother to stay with some friends— Rose hadn't felt like going with them. He stayed there for dinner so didn't get back to the flat until late. I was out all day sitting for Macmorris and went to a theatre with him—I only got home as Simon was reading Rose's note. We thought she might have come here to be with you—so we drove straight down."

"Well, she's safe, anyway," I said to Simon. "I had a telegram from her—though it only said she'd write when she could and would I please try to understand." It had just dawned on me that the bit about understanding didn't refer to our quarrel at all, but to her running away.

"Where was the telegram handed in?" said Topaz.

"I didn't notice. I'll get it and see."

It was in my bedroom. As I dashed off to the front stairs I heard Topaz say: "Fancy Mortmain sleeping through all this!" I was afraid she would go up to wake him before I got back, but she didn't.

I spread the telegram out under the lamp.

"Why, it's from that little seaside place where we went for the picnic!" I said to Simon.

"Why on earth would she go there?" said Thomas. "And why couldn't the silly ass explain in her note?"

"She explained all right," said Simon. "Thanks for trying to spare my feelings, Topaz, but it's really rather pointless." He took the note from his pocket and put it down by the telegram. "You may as well see what she says."

It was just a pencilled scribble:

DEAR SIMON,

I want you to know that I wasn't lying in the beginning. I really thought I loved you. Now there is nothing I can do but beg your forgiveness.

ROSE

"Well, that's that," said Thomas, shooting me a private "I told you so" look.

"But it's not final," said Topaz, quickly. "I've been telling Simon it's just a fit of engagement nerves—she'll feel differently in a day or two. She's obviously gone to this place to think things out."

Simon looked at his watch. "Would you be too tired to start right away?" he said to Topaz.

"You mean, go after her? Oh, Simon, are you sure that's wise? If she wants to be on her own for a bit——"

"I won't worry her. I won't even see her, if she doesn't want me to. You can talk to her first. But I must know a little more than I do now."

"Of course I'll come, then. Let me just have a word with Mortmain first——"

She moved towards the kitchen stairs, but I got in front of her.

"It's no use going up," I said.

"What, is he in London again?"

"No——" I shot a look at Thomas, hoping he would help me out. "You see, Topaz——"

"What is it? What are you hiding from me?" She was so scared that she forgot to be a contralto.

319

I said hastily: "He's perfectly all right, but he's not up-stairs. It's good news, really, Topaz—you'll be terribly pleased."

Then Thomas took over and said calmly: "Father's been in Belmotte Tower for two days. We locked him up to make him work—and if we're to believe him, we've done the trick."

I thought he had put it with admirable clearness, but Topaz asked a great many frantic questions before she took it in. When she finally did, her rage was terrific.

"You've killed him!" she screamed.

"Well, he was alive and kicking last night," I said. "Wasn't he, Thomas?"

"Not kicking," said Thomas. "He'd quite settled down. If you've any sense, Topaz, you'll leave him there for a few more days."

She was already at the dresser, where the key to the tower usually hangs. "Where is it? Give it me at once! If I don't get that key in two minutes I'll hack through the door with an axe!"

And wouldn't she have enjoyed that! I could tell she had stopped being really frightened because her voice was most tragically sepulchral.

"We shall have to let him out now," I said to Thomas. "I would have to-morrow, in any case."

"*I* wouldn't," said Thomas. "It's going to wreck the whole experiment." But he went to get the lantern.

The moon was down, but the stars were still bright when we went out into the courtyard.

"Wait, I'll get my flashlight from the car," said Simon.

"I do apologize," I told him, as we followed the others across Belmotte bridge. "We've no right to drag you into our family troubles when you're so worried."

He said: "Worried or not, I wouldn't miss this."

No sound came from the tower as we climbed the mound.

"Now don't go yelling that you're coming to rescue him," I said to Topaz. "You know what it's like being wakened up suddenly."

"If he ever does wake!"

320

I could have slapped her—partly for being at her most bogus and partly because I was nervous myself. I certainly didn't think that father would be dead, but I did have a slight fear that we might have unhinged him—the state of his hinges being a bit in doubt even before we started.

Still no sound when we got to the foot of the steps.

"Give me the key," Topaz whispered to Thomas. "I want to face it alone."

"If you're not careful, you'll face it headfirst down fifteen feet," he told her. "Let Cassandra and me get the door open and the ladder fixed, and then you can descend like a ministering angel."

The ministering angel idea fetched her. "All right, but let me be the first one he sees."

"Be as quiet as you can," I whispered to Thomas as we got the ladder. "I'd like to have one look at him before he wakes up. I've borrowed Simon's torch."

We got the door open almost noiselessly, then I shone the torch down into the blackness.

Father was lying on the bed—so utterly still that for a moment I was terrified. Then a little curling snore relieved my mind. It did look peculiar down there. In the light from the torch the tall, sun-starved weeds were white as skeleton leaves. The legs of the old iron bedstead were sticking out oddly—evidently it was only just standing up to father's weight. Beside it lay the umbrella, opened; I felt his brain must be all right to be capable of such forethought. And my spirits rose still more when I shone the torch on the rustic table. As well as the big pile of unused paper there were four small ones, carefully weighted down with stones.

Thomas and I lowered the ladder quietly—Topaz was behind us simply panting to descend. She had to go down backwards, of course, which was most unlike a ministering angel, but she made up for that when she got to the bottom. Holding the lantern as high as she could, she cried: "Mortmain, I've come to rescue you! It's Topaz, Mortmain! You're safe!" Father shot up into a sitting position, gasping: "Great God! What's happened?" Then she swooped on to him and the bed went down wallop, its head and foot very nearly meeting over them.

Choking with laughter, Thomas and I dodged out of sight and down the steps. From there we could hear a perfect hullabaloo—father was managing to curse, make waking-up noises, and laugh all at the same time, while Topaz did a sort of double-bass cooing.

"Hadn't you better leave them together for a while?" said Simon.

"Yes, let her work off her worst histrionics," I said to Thomas.

We waited in the courtyard until we saw the lantern coming down the mound. Then Simon tactfully decided not to be seen and went to wait in his car.

"Shall we vanish, too?" said Thomas.

"No, we'd better get the meeting over."

We ran towards them as they crossed the bridge. Topaz was hanging on to father's arm—I heard her say: "Lean on me, Mortmain, lean on me"—like little Lord Fauntleroy to his grandfather.

"Are you all right, father?" I called brightly.

"My dear young jailers," said father, rather exhaustedly. "Yes, I think I shall survive—if Topaz will stop treating me as if I were *both* the little princes in the Tower."

As he went into the kitchen Topaz hung back, grabbed my arm and did one of her most endearing quick changes into hard-headedness.

"Cut back and see what he's written," she whispered.

We dashed up the mound; luckily I still had Simon's torch.

"Heavens, this is a thrilling moment," I said as we stood in front of the rustic table. "Perhaps one day I shall be describing it in father's biography."

Thomas took the stone off the first pile of paper. "Look, this is the beginning," he said as the torch lit up a large "Section A". He snatched the top sheet off, then let out a gasp of astonishment.

The whole of the page underneath was covered with large block capitals—badly formed ones, such as a child makes when learning to write. As I moved the torch along the lines, we read: THE CAT SAT ON THE MAT. THE CAT SAT ON THE MAT. THE CAT SAT ON THE MAT . . . on and on to the end of the page.

"Oh, Thomas!" I moaned. "We've turned his brain."

"Rubbish. You heard how sanely he was talking——"

"Well, perhaps he's recovering but—don't you see what's happened?" Suddenly it had come back to me. "Don't you remember what I shouted under the door when I was so upset? 'Write anything you like as long as you write,' I told him. 'Write "The cat sat on the mat."' And he's written it!"

Thomas was turning over more pages. We read: THE CAT BIT THE FAT RAT, and so on, still in block capitals. "It's just second childhood," I wailed. "We've brought it on prematurely."

"Look, this is better," said Thomas. "He's growing up." At last we saw father's normal handwriting, at its neatest and most exquisite. "But what on earth—good Lord, he's been making up puzzles!"

There was an easy acrostic, a rebus, some verses with the names of animals buried in them—every kind of childish puzzle that is in our old bound volume of *Little Folks*. Then came a page of simple riddles. On the last page of all, father had written:

"Investigate:
>Old Copy-books
>Samplers
>*Child's Guide to Knowledge*
>Jig-saw Puzzles
>Toys in the London Museum"

"That's sane enough," said Thomas. "I tell you this stuff means something."

But I didn't believe him. Oh, I had got over my first fear that father had gone insane; but I thought all the childish nonsense was a way of passing the time—something like the game he plays with the *Encyclopædia*.

Thomas had taken the stone off Section B. "Well, there's

nothing childish about this," he said after a few seconds. "Not that I can make head or tail of it."

There were a lot of numbered sentences, each about two or three lines long. At first I thought they were poetry; there were beautiful combinations of words, and though they were mysterious I felt there was a meaning behind them. Then my new-born hope died suddenly.

"They're the clues to a crossword puzzle," I said disgustedly. "He's just been amusing himself—I'm not going to read any more." It had just struck me that if I didn't hurry back to the castle, I might not see Simon again before he went.

"Here, come back with that torch," shouted Thomas, as I started up the ladder. "I'm not leaving until I've looked at everything he's written." I didn't stop, so he snatched the torch from me. By the time I reached the top of the ladder he was calling after me: "You should see Section C—it's all diagrams showing the distances between places. And he's drawn a bird, with words coming out of its mouth."

"It's a homing pigeon," I called back derisively. "You'll probably come to the carpet-bag and the willow-pattern plate before long."

He shouted that I was just being Harry's father, jeering at *Jacob Wrestling*—— "There's something in all this, I'm positive."

But I still didn't believe him. And for the moment, I didn't much care one way or the other. My whole mind had swung back to Simon.

Topaz came running downstairs from the bedroom as I went into the kitchen. "It's all right to talk—Mortmain's gone to have a bath," she said. "Oh, isn't it wonderful that he's begun work? What did you find?"

I so hated having to disappoint her that I told her Thomas might be right and I might be wrong. But the minute I mentioned the crossword puzzle her spirits sank.

"Though I'm sure he *thinks* he's been working," she said, worriedly. "His mind must be confused—it's all he's been through. I've a few things to say to you, my girl—— But there's no time for that now; we must do something about

Simon. Cassandra, will you go with him instead of me? Then I can stay with Mortmain. I don't want him to know about Rose until he's recovered a bit—he doesn't even know that Simon's here."

My heart gave a leap. "Yes, of course I'll go."

"And for goodness' sake try to make Rose see sense. I've told Simon I'd rather you went and he thinks it's a good idea—that you may have more influence with her. He's waiting in his car."

I ran upstairs and got ready. It was the wickedest moment of my life, because in spite of believing we had failed with father, in spite of the wretchedness I had seen on Simon's face, I was wildly happy. Rose had given him up and I was going to drive with him into the dawn.

It was still dark when I ran out to the car, but there was a vague, woolly look about the sky and the stars were dimming. As I crossed the drawbridge I heard Heloïse howling in the gatehouse room where we had left her shut in. She was up on father's desk with her long face pressed close to the dark window. Seeing her reminded me that my journal was still on the desk, but luckily Topaz came after me with some sandwiches and promised to put it away without trying to read the speed-writing.

"And give my love to father and tell him we meant it for the best," I said—I was so happy that I wanted to be kind to everyone in the world. Then off we went—past the barn where I once overheard Simon, past the cross-roads where we started quoting poetry on May Day, past the village green where we stood counting scents and sounds. As we drove under the chestnut tree in front of the inn I felt a pang for Simon—would he remember Rose's hair against its leaves? "Oh, I'll make it up to him," I told myself. "I swear I can, now that I'm free to try."

We had talked a little about father soon after we started off. Simon wouldn't believe that what Thomas and I had found really was nonsense; he said he would have to see for himself. "Though I must admit it sounds very peculiar," he added. After that, he fell silent. We were some miles beyond Godsend before he said:

"Did you know how Rose felt about me?"

I was so long thinking out what to say that he went on:

"Forget it. It's not fair to ask you."

I began: "Simon——"

He stopped me. "I believe I'd rather not talk about it at all —not until I'm sure she really means it."

Then he asked if I was warm enough or if he should close the car; it had been hot when they left London and Topaz had wanted it open. I said I did, too. The air was fresh and cool, but not really cold.

It was a queer feeling, driving through the sleeping villages —each time, the car suddenly seemed noisier, the headlights more brilliant. I noticed that Simon always slowed down; I bet most men feeling as he did would have driven through like fury. In one cottage there was candlelight beyond the diamond panes of an upstairs window and a car at the door.

"Perhaps a doctor's there," I said.

"Somebody dying or getting born, maybe," said Simon.

Gradually the dark sky paled until it looked like faraway smoke. There was no colour anywhere; the cottages were chalk drawings on grey paper. It felt more like dusk than dawn, but not really like any time of day or night. When I said that to Simon, he told me that he always thought of the strange light before dawn as limbo-light.

A little while after that, he stopped to look at a map. All around us, beyond the hedgeless ditches, were misty water-meadows dotted with pollarded willow trees. Very far away, a cock was crowing.

"Pity there isn't a good sunrise for you," said Simon.

But no sunrise I ever saw was more beautiful than when the thick grey mist gradually changed to a golden haze.

"That really is remarkable," Simon said, watching it. "And one can't actually see any sun at all."

I told myself it was symbolic—that he couldn't yet see how happy I would make him one day.

"Could you fancy a sandwich?" I asked.

I think he only took one to keep me company, but he talked quite naturally while we ate—about the difficulty of finding

326

words to describe the luminous mist, and why one has the desire to describe beauty.

"Perhaps it's an attempt to possess it," I said.

"Or be possessed by it; perhaps that's the same thing, really. I suppose it's the complete identification with beauty one's seeking."

The mist grew brighter and brighter. I could have looked at it for ever, but Simon hid the sandwich paper neatly in the ditch and we drove on.

Before long, there was the feel of the sea in the air. The mist over the salt marshes was too thick for the sunrise to penetrate, but the whiteness was dazzling. It was like travelling through a tunnel in the clouds.

"Are you sure this is where we came for the picnic?" Simon asked as we drove along the main street. "It looks different, somehow."

I said that was due to the summer-holiday atmosphere. In May, the village had seemed just like an inland village; now, children's buckets and spades and shrimping nets were standing outside doors, bathing-suits were hanging over window ledges. I had a sudden fancy to be a child waking up in a strange bedroom, with a day on the sands ahead of me—though, goodness knows, I wouldn't have changed places with anyone in the world just then.

We didn't see a soul in the main street, but we found the front door of the one hotel open and a charwoman scrubbing the hall. She let us look at the hotel register.

There was no sign of Rose's name.

"We'd better wait until people are awake and then try every house in the village," I said.

"I suppose she wouldn't be at 'The Swan'?" said the char-woman. "It's not rightly a hotel but they do take one or two."

I remembered it from the day of the picnic, a tiny inn right down by the sea, about a mile away; but I couldn't believe Rose would ever stay there.

"Still, it's somewhere to try until the village wakes up," said Simon.

We drove along the lonely coast road. There was no mist

over the sea; it was all pale, shimmering gold, so calm that the waves seemed only just able to crawl on to the shore and spread a lacy film over the sands.

"Look! That's where we had the barbecue," I cried. Simon only nodded and I wished I hadn't spoken. It wasn't a moment to remind him of a very happy day.

We could see "The Swan" from far off, it was the only building ahead of us: an old, old inn, rather like "The Keys" at Godsend but even smaller and simpler. The windows glittered, reflecting the early sun.

Simon drew up just outside the door.

"Someone's awake," he said, looking upwards.

A window was open in the gable—a window extraordinarily like the gable window at "The Keys," even to the jug and basin standing there. Floating out to us came the sound of a girl's voice singing "Early One Morning."

"It's Rose!" I whispered.

Simon looked astonished. "Are you sure?"

"Certain."

"I'd no idea she could sing like that."

He sat listening, his eyes suddenly alight. After a few seconds, she stopped singing the words and just hummed the tune. I heard her moving about, a drawer being opened and closed.

"Surely she couldn't sing like that if she wasn't happy?" said Simon.

I forced myself to say: "Perhaps it's all right—perhaps it was just nerves, as Topaz said. Shall I call up to her?"

Before he could answer, there was a knock on a door inside the inn. Then a man's voice said: "Good morning! Are you ready to come out and bathe?"

I heard Simon gasp. The next instant he had re-started the car and we shot forward.

"But what does it mean?" I cried. "That was *Neil*!"

Simon nodded. "Don't talk for a bit."

After a few minutes, he stopped the car and lit a cigarette.

"It's all right—don't look so agonized," he said. "I feel now as if I'd always known it."

328

"But, Simon, they hate each other!"

"Looks like it, doesn't it?" said Simon, grimly.

We drove on until we found a different road to go back by, to avoid re-passing the inn. Simon didn't talk much, but he did tell me that he had known Neil was attracted by Rose in the beginning. "Then he decided she was affected and mercenary—at least, that's what he said. I kidded myself he was piqued because she preferred me—just as I kidded myself she really cared for me; that is, I did at first. For weeks now, I've had my doubts, but I hoped things would come right after we were married. God knows I never had the remotest idea she was in love with Neil, or Neil with her. They might have told me honestly. This isn't like Neil."

"I shouldn't have thought it was like Rose," I said miserably.

We went home through the full brightness of the morning. All the villages were waking up and a great many cheerful dogs were barking in them. There were still a few scarves of mist floating in the water-meadows where we had watched the veiled sunrise. As we drove past I remembered how I had told myself I would make Simon happy. I didn't feel the same person. For I now knew that I had been stuffing myself up with a silly fairy tale, that I could never mean to him what Rose had meant. I think I knew it first as I watched his face while he listened to her singing, and then more and more, as he talked about the whole wretched business—not angrily or bitterly, but quietly and without ever saying a word against Rose. But most of all I knew it because of a change in myself. Perhaps watching someone you love suffer can teach you even more than suffering yourself can.

Long before we got back to the castle, with all my heart and for my own heart's ease as well as his, I would have given her back to him if I could.

Now it's October.

I am up on the mound, close to the circle of stones. There are still some bits of charred wood left from my Midsummer fire.

329

It is a wonderful afternoon, golden, windless—quite a bit chilly, though, but I am wearing Aunt Millicent's little seal-skin jacket, which is gloriously warm, and I have father's old travelling rug to sit on. He now uses the big bearskin coat. One way or another all Aunt Millicent's furs have at last fulfilled themselves.

Now the wheat fields are all string-coloured stubble. The only bright colour I can see anywhere is the spindle-berry bush down in the lane. Over towards Four Stones, Mr. Stebbins and his horses are ploughing. Soon we shall be surrounded by what Rose used to call a sea of mud.

I had a letter from her this morning.

She and Neil have driven across America and are now in the Californian desert, which sounds less and less like my idea of a desert; Rose says there are no camels and the ranch has three bathrooms. She is perfectly happy—except about her trous-seau which has turned into fairy gold. She only needs slacks and shorts now, she says, which it didn't happen to contain. But Neil is going to take her to stay in Beverly Hills so that she can dance in her evening dresses.

I wish I didn't still feel so angry with her; it is wrong of me when I have officially forgiven her. And she and Neil didn't really run away without explaining to Simon. Neil wrote the explanation and left it with Rose's note on the hall table, but it got under the letters that came by the afternoon post. Simon never thought of opening anything else after reading Rose's message.

I only saw her alone once before she went to America. It was on the awful day when we all went to the flat and every-thing was patched up. First Mrs. Cotton had an interview with Rose and Neil to forgive them, and then Simon had an interview with each of them separately, to go on with the forgiving. Then Mrs. Cotton asked father if he would like to see Rose alone and he said: "Great God, no! I can't think why Simon endures all this horror." Mrs. Cotton said: "One must be civilized"—at which father gave such an angry snort that Topaz grabbed his arm warningly. After that we all had a hollow champagne lunch.

Stephen came, in a very well-cut suit, looking quite stagger-ingly handsome. When Rose shook hands with him she said: "I'll thank you as long as I live."

I didn't know what she meant until I was alone with her afterwards, helping her to pack. Then she told me that Stephen had gone to Neil's hotel and told him plainly that she wasn't in love with Simon. I think Neil must have believed me when I wrote and told him she was; anyway, he had hardly let himself see her while she was in London. But after talking to Stephen, he went to the flat and asked her straight out.

"And do you know what it was like?" she said. "Can you remember me coming home after I had scarlet fever—how we hugged and hugged each other without saying a word? It was like that only a million times more so. I thought we never would stop holding on to each other. I'd have married him if he hadn't had a penny—and I would weeks ago if only he'd given me the chance. You see, I didn't know that he cared for me."

"But, Rose, how did Stephen know he did?" I asked.

"Well, he had a little clue that Neil was, well, *interested* in me," she said, then went off into one of her nicest giggles. "Do you remember that night they mistook me for a bear, when I slapped Neil's face? After he carried me across the railway line to the field behind the station, he set me down and said: 'This is for slapping me,'—and then he kissed me. And Stephen saw."

So that was what she had up her sleeve when we talked in bed that night! I *felt* she was hiding something—and then I forgot all about it.

I said: "But just because he saw Neil kiss you once——"

"It was more than once, it was quite a lot of times. And it was wonderful. But I thought he needed punishing for the things you heard him say about me in the lane—and for daring to kiss me like that, even though I'd liked it. Besides, he wasn't the rich one. Though—truly, Cassandra, I don't believe I'd have let that stand in the way if he'd ever shown he really cared for me. But he never did—he wasn't ever nice to me again, always rude and horrid; because he thought I was

331

chasing Simon—which I certainly was. And when Simon kissed me, that was a bit wonderful, too—you can't really judge by kisses—so I got mixed. But not for long."

Oh, so many things came back to me! I could see how she had tried to work herself up into hating Neil—her dislike for him had always seemed exaggerated. I remembered how quick she had been to tell Simon to make him come to the flat that night I was there, how she had asked him to dance with her, how depressed she had seemed when they came back to the glittering corridor. And, of course, so much of Neil's anger on the night of the engagement had been due to jealousy!

They had walked out of the flat that morning hoping to get married at once—"You can do that in America, Neil says; but we soon found you can't here. So we went down to the inn to wait until we could. We chose that place because Neil said the picnic was the last time he'd seen me human. And of course, darling, it's really you I have to thank for everything, because I'm sure Stephen only went to Neil on your account. He told Neil *you* were the right one for Simon—I suppose he'd guessed you were in love and was trying to help you."

Oh, my dear, dear Stephen, how can I ever repay you for such unselfishness? But the happiness you hoped to win for me will never be mine.

"And of course everything will come right now," Rose chattered on. "Just as soon as Simon's got over me a bit, you'll be able to get him."

"I should have thought you'd have grown out of talking about 'getting' men," I said coldly.

She flushed. "I didn't mean it that way—you know I didn't. I'm hoping he'll really fall in love with you. He likes you so much already—he said so only to-day."

A dreadful thought struck me. "Rose—oh, Rose!" I cried. "You didn't tell him I'm in love with him?"

She swore she hadn't.

But I fear she had. He has been so kind ever since then—he was always that, but now his kindness seems deliberate. Or do I imagine it? I know it has made me feel I can hardly bear to see him; but it takes so much strength of mind not to, when he comes to talk to father nearly every day. They are in the gatehouse together, now.

Apparently I was all wrong about father. Apparently it is very clever to start a book by writing THE CAT SAT ON THE MAT nineteen times.

Now stop it, Cassandra Mortmain. You are still piqued because Thomas was the one to guess that what we found in the tower wasn't just nonsense. You are trying to justify your stupidity—and it *was* stupidity, considering father had told you plainly that all his eccentricities meant something. And it isn't true that the book starts with nineteen cats on mats; in the revised version there are only seven of them. And there is a perfectly logical explanation of them, according to that bright boy Thomas. They are supposed to be in the mind of a child learning to read and write.

Am I unusually stupid? Am I old-fashioned? Am I really Harry's father jeering at *Jacob Wrestling*? Oh, I can see that father's puzzles and problems are clever in themselves, that the language in which he sets them out conjures up beautiful images; but why are they supposed to be *more* than puzzles and problems?

Thomas and I were used as guinea-pigs for the first four sections when father had fully revised them; there is a lot more in them now than when we found them two months ago. I really did try. I worked out the children's puzzles quite easily. I managed to do the crossword—and I can't say I enjoyed it, as the clues are all to do with nightmares and terror. I treated that homing pigeon with the greatest respect (it is the hero of a kind of comic strip called "Pigeon's Progress"). I even fought my way through most of Section D, which is a new kind of puzzle invented by father, partly words, partly patterns, with every clue taking you further and further back into the past. But none of it *meant* anything to me—and it did to Thomas, though he admitted he couldn't get his feelings into words.

Father said: "If you could, my boy, I'd go out and drown myself." Then he roared with laughter because Topaz said Section A had "overtones of eternity."

As far as I am concerned, it all has overtones of lunacy——

333

NO. I am jeering again. I am DENSE. If Simon says father's Enigmatism is wonderful, then it is. (It was Simon who christened it "Enigmatism"—and a very good name for it.) And publishers both in England and America have paid father an advance, even though the whole book may not be finished for years. And the first four sections are going to be printed in an American magazine very soon. So now will I stop jeering?

If only father would answer a few questions! If Thomas would throw out some more of his bright ideas! (After telling me Section A was a child learning to read and write, he decided he was not "prepared" to say any more.) Topaz, of course, is always delighted to air her views, but I hardly find them helpful. Her latest contributions are "cosmic significance" and "spherical profundity."

The one person who could help me, of course, is Simon; but I don't like to ask him to have a private talk in case he thinks I am running after him. I try to avoid meeting him unless someone else is there. Often I keep out of the way until I know he has gone back to Scoatney.

Shall I let myself see him to-day? Shall I run down from the mound when he comes out of the gatehouse, then say I want to ask him about father's work? I do indeed, but more than anything I just want to be with him. If only I could be sure that Rose didn't tell him about me!

I will wait until to-morrow. I *promise* myself to-morrow——

It is out of my hands. I looked down and saw him standing in the courtyard—he waved to me—started towards the bridge—he is coming up! Oh, I won't let myself be self-conscious! It will help if I talk hard about father——

How much one can learn in an hour!

All I really want to write about is what happened just before he left. But if I let myself start with that I might forget some of the things which came first. And every word he said is of deepest value to me.

We sat side by side on the rug. He had come to say good-bye; in a few days he is going to America—partly because Mrs. Cotton wants to be in New York for the winter and partly so that he can be there when father's work first comes out in the magazine. He is going to write some articles on it.

"Your father says I'm like an alert terrier shaking a rat," he told me. "But I think he's rather glad to be shaken. And it's important that he should be dropped at the feet of the right people."

I said: "Simon, as a parting present, could you tell me anything that would help me to understand what he's driving at?"

To my surprise, he said he'd already made up his mind to try. "You see, when I'm gone you'll be the one person in close touch with him who's capable of understanding it. Oh, Thomas is a clever lad, but there's an oddly casual quality about his interest—in a way, it's still the interest of a child. Anyhow, I'm sure it's *your* understanding that your father hankers for."

I was astonished and flattered. "Well, I'm only too willing. But if he won't explain—— Why won't he, Simon?"

"Because it's the essence of an enigma that one must solve it for oneself."

"But at least one is allowed to know—well, the *rules* for solving puzzles."

He said he rather agreed with me there and that was why he had persuaded father to let him talk to me. "Do you want to ask me questions?"

"I certainly do. The first one is: Why does his work have to be an enigma at all?"

Simon laughed. "You've started off with a honey. No one will ever know why a creator creates the way he does. Anyway, your father had a very distinguished forerunner. God made the universe an enigma."

I said: "And very confusing it's been for everybody. I don't see why father had to copy Him."

Simon said he thought every creative artist did, and that perhaps every human being was potentially creative. "I think one of the things your father's after is to stimulate that potential creativeness—to make those who study his work share in its actual creation. Of course, he sees creation as

335

discovery. I mean, everything *is* already created, by the first cause—call it God, if you like; everything is already there to be *found*."

I think he must have seen me looking a little bewildered because he stopped himself and said: "I'm not putting this clearly—wait—give me a minute——"

He thought with his eyes closed, as he did once on May Day; but this time I only dared take one quick glance at his face. I was trying to hold my deepest feelings back—I hadn't even let myself realize he was going away. There would be a long time for realizing it after he had gone.

At last he said: "I think your father believes that the interest so many people take in puzzles and problems—which often starts in earliest childhood—represents more than a mere desire for recreation; that it may even derive from man's eternal curiosity about his origin. Anyway, it makes use of certain faculties for progressive, cumulative *search* which no other mental exercise does. Your father wants to communicate his ideas through those faculties."

I asked him to repeat it, slowly. And suddenly I saw—oh, I saw absolutely! "But how does it *work*?" I cried.

He told me to think of a crossword puzzle—of the hundreds of images that pass through the mind while solving one. "In your father's puzzles, the sum-total of the images adds up to the meaning he wants to convey. And the sum-total of all the sections of his book, all the puzzles, problems, patterns, progressions—I believe there's even going to be a detective section—will add up to his philosophy of search-creation."

"And where do those cats on mats come in?" I enquired, a bit satirically.

He said they were probably there to induce a mood. "Imagine yourself a child faced with the first enigmatic symbols of your life-time—the letters of the alphabet. Think of letters before you understood them, then of the letters becoming words, then of the words becoming pictures in the mind—— Why are you looking so worried? Am I confusing you?"

"Not in the least," I said. "I understand everything you've

said. But—oh, Simon, I feel so resentful! Why should father make things so difficult? Why can't he say what he means plainly?"

"Because there's so much that just can't be said plainly. Try describing what beauty is—plainly—and you'll see what I mean." Then he said that art could *state* very little—that its whole business was to evoke responses. And that without innovations and experiments—such as father's—all art would stagnate. "That's why one ought not to let oneself resent them—though I believe it's a normal instinct, probably due to subconscious fear of what we don't understand."

Then he spoke of some of the great innovations that had been resented at first—Beethoven's last quartets, and lots of modern music, and the work of many great painters that almost everyone now admires. There aren't as many innovations in literature as in the other arts, Simon said, and that is all the more reason why father ought to be encouraged.

"Well, I'll encourage him for all I'm worth," I said. "Even if I still do resent him a bit, I'll try to hide it."

"You won't be able to," said Simon. "And resentment will paralyse your powers of perception. Oh, lord, how am I to get you on his side? Look—can you always express just what you want to express, in your journal? Does everything go into nice tidy words? Aren't you constantly driven to metaphor? The first man to use a metaphor was a whale of an innovator— and now we use them almost without realizing it. In a sense your father's whole work is only an extension of metaphor."

When he said that, I had a sudden memory of how difficult it was to describe the feelings I had on Midsummer Eve, and of how I wrote of the day as a cathedral-like avenue. The images that came into my mind then have been linked with that day and with Simon ever since. Yet I could never explain how the image and the reality merge, and how they somehow extend and beautify each other. Was father trying to express things as inexpressible as that . . . ?

"Something's clicked in your mind," said Simon. "Can you put it into words?"

"Certainly not into nice tidy ones——" I tried to speak lightly; remembering Midsummer Eve had made me so very conscious of loving him. "But I've stopped feeling resentful. It'll be all right now. I'm on his side."

After that we talked about what started father writing again. I suppose we shall never know if locking him in the tower really did any good.

Simon thought it was more likely that everything worked together—"Our coming here; mother's very stimulating, you know. And his reading at Scoatney may have helped—I strewed the place with stuff that I thought might interest him. I believe he does feel that being shut in the tower caused some kind of emotional release; and he certainly hands you full credit for telling him to write, 'The cat sat on the mat.' That started him off—gave him the whole idea of the child learning to read."

Personally, I think what helped father most was losing his temper. I feel more and more sure that the cake-knife incident taught him too much of a lesson, somehow tied him up mentally. Simon thought that was quite a good theory.

"What's his temper like nowadays?" he asked.

"Well, most of the time he's nicer than I ever remember him. But in spasms, it's terrific. Topaz is adoring life."

"Dear Topaz!" said Simon, smiling. "She's the perfect wife for him now that he's working—and he knows it. But I don't see how life at the castle can be much fun for *you* this winter. There'll be a maid at the flat, if you feel like staying there sometimes. Are you sure you don't want to go to college?"

"Quite sure. I only want to write. And there's no college for that except life."

He laughed and said I was a complete joy to him—sometimes so old for my age and sometimes so young.

"I'd rather like to learn typing and real shorthand," I told him. "Then I could be an author's secretary while I'm waiting to be an author."

He said Topaz would arrange it for me. I know he is leaving money with her for all of us—he made her feel that she ought to take it to shield father from anxiety. Oh, he is indeed a most gracious and generous "patron"!

"And you must write to me for anything you want," he added. "Anyway, I shall be back soon."

"I wonder."

He looked at me quickly and asked what I meant. I wished I hadn't said it. For weeks now I have feared that having been hurt so much by Rose may have put him off living in England.

"I just wondered if America might claim you," I said.

He didn't answer for so long that I visualized him gone for ever and the Fox-Cottons installed at Scoatney as they so much want to be. "Perhaps I shall never see him again," I thought, and suddenly felt so cold that I gave a little shiver. Simon noticed it and moved closer, pulling the rug up around us both. Then he said:

"I shall come back all right. I could never desert Scoatney."

I said I knew he loved it dearly.

"Dearly and sadly. In a way, it's like loving a beautiful, dying woman. One knows the spirit of such houses can't survive very much longer."

Then we spoke of the autumn—he hoped he would be in time to catch a glimpse of it in New England.

"Is it more beautiful than this?" I asked.

"No. But it's less melancholy. So many of the loveliest things in England are melancholy." He stared across the fields, then added quickly—"Not that I'm melancholy this afternoon. I never am, when I'm with you. Do you know this is our third conversation on Belmotte mound?"

I knew it very well. "Yes, I suppose it is," I said, trying to sound casual. I don't think I managed it, because he suddenly slipped his arm round me. The still afternoon seemed stiller, the late sunlight was like a blessing. As long as I live I shall remember that silent minute.

At last he said: "I wish I could take you to America with me. Would you like to come?"

For a second, I thought it was just a joking remark, but he

339

asked me again—"Would you—Cassandra?" Then something about the way he spoke my name made me sure that if I said yes, he would ask me to marry him. And I couldn't do it—though I don't think I fully knew why until now.

I said, in as normal a voice as I could manage: "If only I were trained already, I could come as your secretary. Though I don't know that I'd care to be away from father too long this year."

I thought that if I put it that way he wouldn't know I had guessed what was in his mind. But I think he did, because he said very quietly: "Oh, wise young judge."

Then we talked quite ordinarily about a car he is lending to father and about our all going over to Scoatney whenever we feel like it. I didn't say very much myself—most of my mind was wondering if I had made a dreadful mistake.

When he got up to go he wrapped the rug tightly round me, then told me to slip out my hand. "It's not a little green hand this time," he said as he took it in his.

I said: "Simon, you know I'd love to see America if ever the circumstances were—well, favourable."

He turned my hand over and kissed the palm, then said: "I'll report on them when I come back."

And then he went quickly down the mound. As his car drove along the lane, a sudden gust of wind sprang up and blew brown leaves from the hedges and trees, so that a cloud of them seemed to be following him.

I didn't make any mistake. I know that when he nearly asked me to marry him it was only an impulse—just as it was when he kissed me on Midsummer Eve; a mixture of liking me very much and longing for Rose. It is part of a follow-my-leader game of second-best we have all been playing—Rose with Simon, Simon with me, me with Stephen, and Stephen, I suppose, with that detestable Leda Fox-Cotton. It isn't a very good game; the people you play it with are apt to get hurt. Perhaps even Leda has, though I can't say the thought of that harrows me much.

But why, oh why, must Simon still love Rose? When she has so little in common with him and I have so much? Part of me longs to run after him to Scoatney and cry "Yes, yes, yes!" A few hours ago, when I wrote that I could never mean anything to him, such a chance would have seemed heaven on earth. And surely I could give him—a sort of contentment?

That isn't enough to give. Not for the giver.

The daylight is going. I can hardly see what I am writing and my fingers are cold. There is only one more page left in my beautiful blue leather manuscript book; but that is as much as I shall need. I don't intend to go on with this journal; I have grown out of wanting to write about myself. I only began to-day out of a sense of duty—I felt I ought to finish Rose's story off tidily. I seem to have finished my own off, too, which I didn't quite bargain for. . . .

What a preposterous, self-pitying remark—with Simon still in the world, and a car being lent to us and a flat in London! Stephen has a flat there, too, now; just a little one. He wandered about with the goats so satisfactorily that he is to speak lines in his next picture. If I stay at the Cottons' flat I can go out with him sometimes and be very, very kind to him, though in a determinedly sisterly way. Now I come to think of it, the winter ought to be very exciting, particularly with father so wonderfully cheerful or else so refreshingly violent. And there are thousands of people to write about who aren't me. . . .

It isn't a bit of use my pretending I'm not crying, because I am. . . . Pause to mop up. Better now.

Perhaps it would really be rather dull to be married and settled for life. Liar! It would be heaven.

Only half a page left now. Shall I fill it with "I love you, I love you"—like father's page of cats on the mat? No. Even a broken heart doesn't warrant a waste of good paper.

There is a light down in the castle kitchen. To-night I shall have my bath in front of the fire, with Simon's gramophone playing. Topaz has it on now, much too loud—to bring father back to earth in time for tea—but it sounds beautiful from this distance. She is playing the Berceuse from Stravinsky's "The Firebird." It seems to say: "What shall I do? Where shall I go?"

You will go in to tea, my girl—and a much better tea than you would have come by this time last year.

A mist is rolling over the fields. Why is summer mist romantic and autumn mist just sad?

There was mist on Midsummer Eve, mist when we drove into the dawn.

He said he would come back.

Only the margin left to write on now. I love you, I love you, I love you.

VIRAGO MODERN CLASSICS
&
CLASSIC NON-FICTION

The first Virago Modern Classic, *Frost in May* by Antonia White, was published in 1978. It launched a list dedicated to the celebration of women writers and to the rediscovery and reprinting of their works. Its aim was, and is, to demonstrate the existence of a female tradition in fiction, and to broaden the sometimes narrow definition of a 'classic' which has often led to the neglect of interesting novels and short stories. Published with new introductions by some of today's best writers, the books are chosen for many reasons: they may be great works of fiction; they may be wonderful period pieces; they may reveal particular aspects of women's lives; they may be classics of comedy or storytelling.

The companion series, Virago Classic Non-Fiction, includes diaries, letters, literary criticism, and biographies – often by and about authors published in the Virago Modern Classics.

'A continuingly magnificent imprint' – *Joanna Trollope*

'The Virago Modern Classics have reshaped literary history and enriched the reading of us all. No library is complete without them' – *Margaret Drabble*

'The writers are formidable, the production handsome. The whole enterprise is thoroughly grand' – *Louise Erdrich*

'The Virago Modern Classics are one of the best things in Britain today' – *Alison Lurie*

'Good news for everyone writing and reading today' – *Hilary Mantel*

'Masterful works' – *Vogue*

VIRAGO MODERN CLASSICS
&
CLASSIC NON-FICTION

Some of the authors included in these two series –

Lisa Alther, Elizabeth von Arnim, Dorothy Baker, Pat Barker,
Nina Bawden, Nicola Beauman, Isabel Bolton, Kay Boyle,
Vera Brittain, Leonora Carrington, Angela Carter, Willa Cather,
Colette, Ivy Compton-Burnett, Barbara Comyns, E.M. Delafield,
Maureen Duffy, Elaine Dundy, Nell Dunn, Emily Eden, George Eliot,
Miles Franklin, Mrs Gaskell, Charlotte Perkins Gilman,
Victoria Glendinning, Elizabeth Forsythe Hailey, Radclyffe Hall,
Shirley Hazzard, Dorothy Hewett, Mary Hocking, Alice Hoffman,
Winifred Holtby, Janette Turner Hospital, Zora Neale Hurston,
Elizabeth Jenkins, F. Tennyson Jesse, Molly Keane,
Margaret Laurence, Maura Laverty, Rosamond Lehmann,
Rose Macaulay, Shena Mackay, Olivia Manning, Paule Marshall,
F.M. Mayor, Anaïs Nin, Mary Norton, Kate O'Brien, Olivia,
Grace Paley, Mollie Panter-Downes, Dawn Powell,
Dorothy Richardson, E. Arnot Robertson, Jacqueline Rose,
Vita Sackville-West, Elaine Showalter, May Sinclair,
Agnes Smedley, Dodie Smith, Stevie Smith, Christina Stead,
Carolyn Steedman, Gertrude Stein, Jan Struther, Han Suyin,
Elizabeth Taylor, Sylvia Townsend Warner, Mary Webb,
Eudora Welty, Mae West, Rebecca West, Edith Wharton,
Antonia White, Christa Wolf, Virginia Woolf, E.H. Young

'Found on all the best bookshelves' – *Penny Vincenzi*

'Their huge success is solid proof of the fact that literary fashion is
a snare and a delusion – people like a good old-fashioned read' –
Good Housekeeping

Now you can order superb titles directly from Virago

☐	Playing the Harlot	Patricia Avis	£6.99
☐	The Way of an Eagle	Ethel M. Dell	£6.99
☐	A Suppressed Cry	Victoria Glendinning	£7.99
☐	Three Weeks	Elinor Glyn	£6.99
☐	The Transit of Venus	Shirley Hazzard	£6.99
☐	The Land of Spices	Kate O'Brien	£7.99
☐	Devastating Boys	Elizabeth Taylor	£6.99

Please allow for postage and packing: **Free UK delivery**.
Europe; add 25% of retail price; Rest of World; 45% of retail price.

To order any of the above or any other Virago titles, please call our credit card orderline or fill in this coupon and send/fax it to:

Virago, P.O. Box 121, Kettering, Northants NN14 4ZQ
Tel: 01832 737526   Fax: 01832 733076
Email: aspenhouse@FSBDial.co.uk

☐ I enclose a UK bank cheque made payable to Virago for £ ....

☐ Please charge £.............. to my Access, Visa, Delta, Switch Card No.

☐☐☐☐☐☐☐☐☐☐☐☐☐☐☐☐☐☐☐

Expiry Date ☐☐☐☐   Switch Issue No. ☐☐

NAME (Block letters please) ....

ADDRESS ....

....

....

Postcode ....Telephone ....

Signature ....

Please allow 28 days for delivery within the UK. Offer subject to price and availability.

Please do not send any further mailings from companies carefully selected by Virago ☐